A Casino for Gods

The Allies of Theo, Book 3

David E Dresner

Clink Street

Published by Clink Street Publishing 2021

Copyright © 2021

First edition.

ISBN:
978-1-913340-98-8 - paperback
978-1-913340-99-5 - ebook

With the greatest appreciation to my reviewing team.

*Thank you, Morgan and Nancy, your comments
and suggestions made the story much stronger. Your
encouragement and praise kept the many rewrites
flowing without undue pain for the author.*

Please join me again for book 4!

With the greatest appreciation to my reviewing team.

Thank you, Morgan and Nancy, your comments and suggestions made the story much stronger. Your encouragement and praise kept the many rewrites flowing without undue pain for the author.

Please join me again for book 4!

Prologue

Everyone imagines, from time to time, what they would do with special powers. As children we often dream of flying. Sometimes that dream results in harsh scrapes, or worse, busted limbs when we jumped off a porch or low roof wearing a makeshift cape. Of course those nasty landings never happen to Batman or Spiderman.

Residing in a magical sanctuary in Chicago, Glenda and Traveler are teens who are actually developing those imagined powers. Their powers are real and hard-earned. They are the result of daily, exhausting study demanded by their sentient books. The books are expanding and reshaping their minds and bodies as containers to accept these powers.

The teens naturally enjoy using their newfound powers, they are exhilarating! While the teens cannot fly, they can jump quite high. They control gravity enough to ensure soft landings. Beyond jumping they have learned an invisibility skill called "stealth." They can blend into any surrounding. Traveler, a frequent prankster, unwisely uses stealth to surprise Glenda. A big mistake.

To continue developing their powers there is a high cost. Book learning alone is not enough. They must face life-threatening real-world challenges.

The ongoing development of their powers is essential for them to evolve into protective allies of a benevolent god named Theo. Theo has been an observer of our world since its birth. He predates the Big Bang with knowledge that is far beyond mankind's understandings.

While observing our world Theo is suddenly threatened by a host of powerful demigod fire creatures called jinn. The jinn host has pursued Theo for eons, intent on absorbing him to gain his knowledge. Theo needs allies.

The teens faced their initial "beyond the books" challenge when they were charged by Theo to confront a single jinn. The creature had time-shifted choosing remote fifth-century Transylvania.

The fifth century was a darkening time in Europe. Rome was rapidly collapsing. Asiatic invaders, led by Attila the Hun, were rampaging across Europe. Large, carnivorous animals ruled the dense forests of the Carpathian Mountains stalking humans as acceptable prey.

With much hesitancy, the two accepted the daunting mission. Aided by a giant named Olaff, they survived the confrontation. Believing they had succeeded they returned to their Chicago sanctuary.

Subsequent events proved their mission had come up short. The threat to Theo has actually increased. They must return once more to the Dark Ages and the Carpathian Mountains.

Chapter 1

How Does It Start?

Existence! What is it? How does it happen? Why does it happen?

These most basic of questions have baffled mankind since the earliest of times. From ancient cave paintings, to Greek philosophers speculating about atoms, to the mind-boggling math of string theory, to the particles generated by the Hadron Collider, mankind has sought answers. Efforts to present and explain our universe have resulted in many insights and clues but sadly no all-encompassing final answers.

Answers exist but not for humans. "They" were the creators. Their presence defined all of existence. There was nothing before them. "Nothing" itself did not exist.

Within their existence they contained all knowledge, all awareness, all understanding, and all power. Dimensionally intertwined they were a single collective, yet they could become separate beings when desired.

All creation flowed from their collective self. As they created, their thoughts generated a vast field of dark energies. These energies defined and filled an endless void. Their creations were made within this dark, energy-filled void. The void was their laboratory.

They observed each creation in the void from its inception to its ending. Each of their creations was unique. As they observed and studied, they advanced their knowledge and understandings. They were entertained and they were pleased.

They thought of themselves as the "dark gods." This name was not a description of any dark intention; it was simply a recognition of the dark matters and dark energies they used to construct their universes.

Time had no meaning in their existence, it was simply another controllable dimension. There were no limitations on their creations. They constructed dimensions, energies, and base elements of their choosing, then combined them to produce new realities, called universes. There was an immeasurably large set of possible construct groupings. Each creation held great interest for the dark god observers.

After observing countless creations, an unsettling awareness crept into their collective consciousness. While each creation had offered interesting observations, all events throughout each universe's life cycle were predictable to the dark gods. The gods foresaw all outcomes the moment they sparked a new universe. *Where*, they asked, *is the value in creativity if it does not offer unforeseen experiences with unexpected outcomes?*

The dark gods concluded that they needed to create outcomes that were unpredictable even to themselves. Despite changing the input mix of dimensions, energies, and elements, they found that they were looking into a mirror that always reflected their own existence. Unlike many humans, they became bored by the fascinating but predictable reflections of themselves and their constructs.

They first attacked the problem by attempting to create unpredictability within themselves. They attempted to solve the problem by combining ever-greater combinations of obscure dimensions, elements, and energies. All efforts failed. No outcome ever surprised them.

They had never encountered failure. Failure was outside of their experience, and they were all of existence. For the first time, in existence without time or measure, they felt an emotion that humans would call "frustration."

They understood that what they needed was not simply more combinations of their input constructs, but a tool that would generate randomness independent of their construct inputs. They called this tool for generating unpredictability their "randomness tool."

The randomness tool was not present within their all-knowing existence. Their challenge was how to create such a tool. They attacked the tool creation problem with great purpose. As they did with all challenges, they succeeded.

With the tool created, they proceeded to test its effect. They inserted the tool within previously tested sets of dimensions, energies, and matters. They studied the resulting outcomes against previous creations. They compared the "before" and "after" observations. To their great surprise and disappointment, the inclusion of the tool resulted in creations that behaved exactly the same as was previously experienced.

Undaunted, they expanded the set of attempts. The "before" and "after" results were always the same. They concluded that the starting set of construct inputs overpowered the randomness tool's effect. Creative inertia among the constructs seemed determined to follow a predetermined path.

They came to accept that their randomness tool would not operate within their own existence. Their very existence always predetermined outcomes. Since they could not eliminate their own existence, they appeared to face an unsolvable dilemma.

They pondered the dilemma until a solution was found. They saw that what they needed was to place their randomness tool and the construct sets outside of their own existence. They called their "outside of existence vessel" an "ex-singularity."

The dark gods proceeded to put selected construct sets along with the randomness tool into this newly created ex-singularity vessel. Much to their frustration these initial results were also failures. Before and after outcomes were unchanged. The new ex-singularity always collapsed back into the creator gods' own existence.

The dark gods understood that they were the mother singularity. Like many earthly offspring, their ex-singularity offspring, regardless of separation and intent, seemed destined to return home.

Undaunted by failures, they continued to construct universes within the ex-singularity. There were no limits on their experimentations. They created countless groupings of dimension sets, energies, and elements, always including the randomness tool. They never stopped their efforts regardless of countless, frustrating failures. They never doubted themselves.

In the far distant human future, an inventor named Thomas Edison, blessed with a strong mind and self-confidence, used the same trial and error process. In building the first practical electric light bulb he experimented with over seventeen hundred types of filaments, including a hair from a friend's beard, before success. When asked by a reporter what it was like to fail over a thousand times he answered, "I have not failed. I just found a thousand ways that won't work."

Predating Edison by billions of years, the dark god's countless attempts suddenly exploded in success. Their ex-singularity filament lit up! Rather than returning to the mother singularity, this offspring chose to embrace its own destiny. The new universe began to actively self-define in unpredictable ways. Unexpected outcome followed unexpected outcome!

In observing their success, the dark gods saw that the randomness tool had interacted not only with the construct inputs but within the containment ex-singularity itself. Randomness was infused in both container and content. A single thought resonated in their collective mind. *We have succeeded!* **Their creation was a casino for gods!**

Chapter 2

The Creators Explore Their Casino

At the instant of its birth, the creators saw this was the sought-after, unpredictable universe. To best acquire the knowledge being generated by this newborn universe, the dark gods decided they would embed themselves directly into the expansion. Rather than taking a single observation position, they chose countless viewing sites.

For the first time in their endless existence, they separated into their individual selves. They had no concern regarding the separation. Each god knew that when this universe ended its life cycle and blinked out, they would be re-joined. Once re-joined they would share their separate experiences.

As they studied the universe's outward rushing expansion, it resembled a chaotic train station. There was an infinite number of trains racing out of the station. The trains' cars were carrying the earliest passengers of dimensions, mass, and energy to unknown distant destinations.

Each dark god chose to ride in its own private observation car. Once on board each creator found that its chosen car was soon morphing into a carnival midway. One instant they were on the rapidly twisting Tilt-A-Whirl, the next moment they were inside jerking bumper cars. Then they were on a screaming rollercoaster or aboard an incredibly fast-moving Ferris wheel.

Each god experienced the universe's expansion ride with a teenager's thrill and joy. It was fresh and unpredictable. Each god was awash in new experiences and new knowledge. They sat back as passive observers exerting no authorship. They let the new universe continue as a self-directing creation with random outcomes.

The casino was a kaleidoscope of everchanging events. There was an endless creation and reorganization of matter, energy, and dimensions. The universe's ongoing restructuring at every level of its existence provided an ever-fresh set of observations for the dark gods.

The dark gods observed how the starting mix of dimensions, energy, and elements interacted with each other. They saw how initial dimensions, present at the moment of birth, were being reshaped to expand or collapse. They observed that as certain dimensions became dominant, other dimensions curled up on themselves. These curled up dimensions retreated into infinitesimally small spaces.

Countless particles were attracted to each other, resulting in new elemental constructs. While some constructs shrunk, others gained strength. Certain energies, such as gravity, began to influence and dominate the elemental haze of birth.

They watched over eons of time as newly-formed base elements of matter accumulated into increasingly large spheres. The buildup in a sphere's size and density could be visualized as a sticky snowball moving through space collecting additions to itself.

The increasingly powerful force of gravity packed the elemental snowball ever tighter. When the density of a packed sphere reached a critical point, internal nuclear explosions resulted and stars were born. These earliest stars were the first children birthed by the young universe.

As the infant universe grew, individual stars were drawn toward each other by the force of gravity. Gravity acted as a cosmic housemaid sweeping piles of stars together into shared sectors of dark space. These star sharing regions were called galaxies. Young and adventuresome the galaxies moved at high speeds through the dark void.

The universe continued to create unique existences. No two galactic regions arose with identical content and shape. Randomness was operating on a scale that spared nothing. No object was too big or too small to escape its effects.

Within the infant universe, the dark gods were already widely scattered throughout the proliferating galaxies. Each god had its own galactic casino to occupy and observe the various events being played out. No two casinos were the same.

Contrary to what Einstein believed, each god watched their galactic casino roll its own dice of creation.

Chapter 3

An Isolated Creator

The gods knew that they could better observe the evolving creations within their galaxy by pulling matter and energy closer to their own observation positions. To enhance the efficiency of their observation site, each creator entered a massive star within its own galaxy. Once inside the selected star, the resident creator caused the star to collapse into a highly concentrated mass.

This collapsing star produced a powerful gravitational field that drew nearby matter and energy toward the observing dark god. The resulting star's gravitational strength was such that even light was a captive. Distant observers looking toward the dense star would only see a black hole. Resting inside, gods watched light and matter as they were set upon by fierce gravity.

Over time a vast gravitational collection net was formed around the dark star. This collection net took on the shape of a funnel that channeled mass and energy down the collapsed star's throat toward the resident god. The dark god resting in its observation laboratory was similar to a spider centered in its web.

Not every creator chose to observe from inside a black hole. One creator, we know it as Theo, decided to study formations at the microlevel of a single star system and a single planet. This micro-study would complement its brethren's macro observations. It would add in-depth knowledge about the evolution of a single star system and a single planet.

Theo selected a yet unformed region for his study. Entering, he found himself within a massive cloud of elemental particles. He was immediately fascinated by the earliest creations it was producing. Suns were born within his cloud. He watched as his own elemental cloud slowly developed a geometric shape.

The shape evolved as a rotating disk. The disk contained millions of stars packed into a central hub. Extending from the hub were twisting, spiraling arms of stars. These spiraling arms extended far out into the dark void.

To Theo the arms appeared as if the hub was grasping at fresh stars to add to its galactic empire. Theo concluded that even in this infant universe a rule was emerging, "Eat or be eaten." His hub was hungry.

Theo pondered whether the eating rule would exist at the microlevel. Much later his observations confirmed the rule dominated. The rule evidenced itself when the earliest form of life arose on his planet. Life was always hungry, driven to consume.

His next decision was which emerging star system should be selected. After appraising the multitude of choices, he made his selection. He chose a newly birthed star of average size toward the outer rim of one spiral arm. This star would provide insights into the life of a star system that had masses orbiting around the star at varying distances. The god would observe the fate of each of these masses.

He picked one of the orbiting masses as his observation site. The selected mass was close enough to the star to receive heat and light energy but far enough away to avoid becoming a charred cinder. Theo settled in to watch this volatile, volcanic mass evolve. *What will its eventual fate be?* he wondered. *Will it stabilize or ultimately explode from internal heat pressures?*

As the mass matured Theo was pleased with his choice. The mass stabilized into a solid spheroid called a planet. As the planet's internal temperature fell, the atmosphere surrounding it cooled and began releasing suspended water down to the surface. Slowly the planet's surface developed large bodies of water. Over eons the water offered a favorable birthing environment for life.

When the earliest life form developed Theo was beyond pleased. He watched the evolution of life as it proliferated in multiple directions. Randomness was at work again. He saw that many directions for early life were dead ends. Other directions produced the most amazing creatures. Life was increasingly complex and evolving.

He felt the best was yet to come. What new life would emerge? What fascinating creatures would appear?

Chapter 4

Chicago: A Winter Wonderland

While people are not observing gods, they often find themselves fascinated by their natural surroundings as well as their own creations. The Christmas season in Chicago is such a magical observation time for all people. The environment presents a blend of nature and human creations. Together they result in a bright, glowing, festive season.

Casting shadows over this bright winter season, however, are many dark days. Known as the "City of Big Shoulders," Chicago's tall skyscrapers add to the street level dimness by blocking out many of the sun's pale downward rays. Increasing the daytime shadows are the shorter days of winter.

Further infringing on the seasonal festivities is the never-ending snow and wind coming off Lake Michigan. This uninvited guest arrives as a swirling, misty, white fog. The whiteness often floats on strong winds high above the streets before landing. This unwelcome guest frequently obscures many of the office window displays that shine down from the big shoulders of the skyscrapers.

Settling snow brings visual beauty but also danger. The city managers care for their citizens year-round; however, in the darker winter season, the managers know that shoppers of all ages must be protected from nasty falls, broken presents, and possible broken bones.

Beyond concern for personal injury, the city's management knows full well that Christmas shoppers are the lifeblood of commerce and tax revenue. Keeping streets and sidewalks safe is a critical duty that extends from the mayor down to the street cleaners.

City workers willingly accept this responsibility and do their best to keep the major shopping streets clear using ice scrapers and snow removal machines. Their clearing efforts are often followed by trucks and workers scattering salt.

Freshly scattered sidewalk salt glistens in a rainbow of colors reflecting the lamplights and blazing store windows. Shimmering rainbows proclaim to hurrying shoppers that Chicago is a magical winter wonderland.

Despite the city's best efforts to protect its citizens, experienced Christmas shoppers know they still need to watch their footing. Even with the best of street cleaning efforts, foot traffic is a "walker beware" activity. Black ice can quickly be obscured by softly falling flakes. This treacherous ice lies hidden, waiting to ambush the too hastily-placed foot.

As shoppers move along crowded streets, their faces appear like images on old television screens. Eyes and heads flicker downward to view sidewalk surfaces, then upward to view oncoming pedestrians and department store windows. As the flickering cycle is repeated, bobblehead movement would be a fitting description.

Decorated streetlamps add to the sense of traveling through a fairyland. Their lights not only illuminate sidewalks but also lift shoppers' eyes upward to gaze on overhead decorations. Elevated, smiling Frosty Snowmen wink at street corner policemen. Grinning elves, peeking through colorful wreaths, foretell of coming Christmas presents.

Playful, but purposeful, red-nosed Rudolphs match the determined look of shoppers carrying their presents. Many young children holding a parent's hand would later tell friends they were sure these decorations appeared to be watching them. Some were positive a Rudolph winked at them.

Adding to the street decorations are a multitude of red-faced, sidewalk Santas. These Santas are dedicated to their charitable fundraising as they enthusiastically swing their clanging bells. With ringing bells in hand, many Santas seek out the glow from overhead lamplights for a little heat. Beyond heat, they use the light to direct charitable hands toward their tripod-suspended red buckets.

Despite Mother Nature's chilling intrusions, it is a time of magic and excitement for children of all ages. The profusion of festive sights and sounds help traveling shoppers ignore the biting Chicago winter and embrace the season's magic. Even the most cynical citizens enjoy positive attitudes and smiles radiating from passing strangers.

Chapter 5

Seasonal Memories

Standing comfortably beside the large picture window in her hotel room, Virginia looked down at the street. While there were still lingering rays of sunlight, streetlamps lit the sidewalks. They stood as tall, silent, snow-covered soldiers assuring safe passage for shoppers.

Watching the shoppers Virginia felt a wave of sweet nostalgia pass through her. The sidewalk decorations had enchanted her from her earliest downtown visits with her mother. As a young girl she followed her mother into many festively decorated department stores. Once inside a store she felt the joy of the Christmas songs lifting her spirits. Her body quickly forgot the lingering outside chills and rejoiced in the glow of a song's words and melody.

Christmas shopping naturally added greatly to the downtown excitement. The department stores were a decorated bazaar offering so many choices. As the two of them did their shopping, Virginia's mom taught her how to spot quality and bargain prices. "Always go for quality first, then check prices. You never make a mistake with quality."

Smiling down at her daughter, Virginia's mother added, "Quality first in friends and later in boyfriends is your measuring stick." Laughing, she added, "You'll understand about boyfriends in the future, there's no rush to shop for them for many years."

Virginia knew she had just been given a life lesson but didn't really understand it. *Who cares about stupid boys?* Wanting to feel like she was nearly a grownup at age seven, she looked back up at her mom and smiled. "I'll always comparative shop, Mom. I understand it's the smart thing to do. I'm lucky to have you as my teacher." Her mom gave a glowing smile back to her young daughter.

With her mom's childhood advice still lingering in her mind, Virginia heard a knock at the door. Opening it she was greeted by a very pungent odor of workout sweat. The two health-clubbers were back. Pressing his way past her, a tall, dark-haired boy pleaded, "Shower please, Mom. I need to get away from myself."

Virginia laughed. "Please do! You know the way to your bathroom. Glenda, you can use my bathroom, it's all set up for you. There are plenty of fresh towels for both of you. Eddie, please throw your stuff in the hamper and lock it down so nothing can crawl out." Glenda grinned while a disappearing Traveler chose to ignore his mom's wit.

"Both of you will find tonight's evening wear on your beds. Glenda, you were such a help in shopping, I have a surprise laid out for you. I think I know what you like, let me know what you think."

An appreciative smile swept across the tall girl's face. Everybody, young or old, loves a surprise gift. "Thank you so much, Virginia! I already know I'll love it. You have such great taste! Thank you again. Now I better get to that shower before our neighbors call the front desk asking about wet cows in the hotel."

As they disappeared Virginia chuckled to herself. *Shower quickly, my wet cows, please!* Her mind shifted from wet cows to the coming adventure. *We're going to explore the mysterious world of M tonight, and I'm excited.*

Chapter 6

Party Prep Time

As the two teens entered their showers, they each anticipated the best part of the day was yet to come. With health club workouts over, the fun night was starting. They knew M would surprise them and they were eager to see what he had in store.

Falling waters in the form of hot showers chased the smelly cows away. The two accepted the shower's transformative magic as they relaxed tired workout muscles.

Finished in the bathroom, Traveler came out to inspect the evening's attire laid out on the bed. He saw a charcoal suit with a formal white shirt and a soft yellow tie. Beside the shirt was an open box presenting a pair of heavy gold cufflinks shaped like miniature shields. *Really cool Mom, you've still got it!*

Dressing quickly, he looked in the full-length mirror and felt pleased with the guy looking back. Entering the living room he said, "So why the fancy dress-up, Mom? The prom's not until spring."

Virginia smiled back and started to answer, then paused. She found herself staring at her son. She had a sense of déjà vu. Just yesterday evening she had looked at her son and thought he seemed different. Looking at him this evening, just a day later, she thought exactly the same thing, but more so. Had he somehow aged a year in a single day? He projected the confidence of a college athlete while his eyes seemed to be those of a thoughtful businessman.

As Virginia studied his face, she thought for a moment that he seemed closer in age and carriage to his father Daniel than to the high school boy who got on the train with her. *Don't grow up too fast my son, you have a lot of carefree years still in front of you. Don't age yourself trying to impress the young lady. After this week you will never see her again.*

Taking a quick breath, she answered, "Tonight is another big surprise from M, our friendly train magician. He asked that the three of us dress in formal attire and be prepared to explore a magical side of Chicago. He would not give me any details except that his limo will pick us up shortly. I'm excited to see what this evening brings.

"By the way, I emailed your dad about the invite and he said to let M knock himself out hosting us. He also asked about your Norwegian friend, so be prepared to be pumped about her. I told him she is a terrific young lady but will be moving out of your life when we return." Virginia paused before adding, "I think he was a little relieved."

Traveler was amused as he instantly caught his mom's real purpose with the casual remark. *Mom, you and Dad have no idea how much she's in my life. She's sometimes fun and sometimes a big pain but she is literally always around. She couldn't leave if she wanted to, but neither can I. Theo runs the show for both of us.*

Virginia saw a strange look slip over her Eddie's face. *I think he is annoyed that his remaining time with the Nordic Princess will get cut short by his mother and M. He's aware of how limited his time is with her and resents losing a chunk of it to the grown-ups. Too bad Eddie, I'm all in favor of M and I acting as chaperones over you two.*

Traveler saw the wheels spinning in his mom's head and her lips pursing to ask a question. Whatever her question was going to be, she suddenly changed gears. Turning away from him she said, "Glenda my dear, you look so grown up! The boys at your school should see you. Your prom dance card won't be big enough."

Traveler's head rotated from his mom to an approaching Glenda. He discovered his friendly old frog was back in his throat. He stifled a chug-a-rum croak then said, "Nice dress choice, Mom. She'll be the belle of the ball back in school."

Glenda gave Traveler a quick look that said, *Your mom knows the prom queen when she sees her. By that frog in your throat, so do you.*

Glenda gave Virginia her warmest smile followed by a curtsy. "I feel like Cinderella! You picked the perfect outfit for a night on the town." With that, Glenda twirled around presenting a green cloud floating under a mass of misty red hair.

Completing the twirl, she said, "I just love your classic black dress, Virginia, and your Cleopatra hairstyle fits the Egyptian necklace. You look like Cleopatra might have looked as she joined Caesar for a night at the amphitheater."

Traveler was aware of the flush on his mom's face with Glenda's compliments. *Score one for the princess*, he thought, *her stock just soared with Mom.*

"Well, I have another surprise for you, try this on," said Virginia, as she handed Glenda a silver case. "It's a loaner gift from M for the evening." Accepting the box Glenda moved the heavy gold slide to open it. Inside, resting on a deep blue taffeta liner, was a string of perfect pearls. Glenda just stared at them.

"Eddie, be a gentleman and help put them on please."

Fortunately, Traveler didn't need to speak, Mr. Frog would have embarrassed him if he tried. He took the pearls out, stepped behind the green dress then carefully passed them around Glenda's neck. He became slightly embarrassed when he found the clasp did not want to close.

"Need help back there?" came a joking voice through a haze of reddish hair. The clasp suddenly closed with a definitive snap. Embarrassed hands work even when frog throats fail.

Glenda did another pirouette then stood motionless for inspection. "Perfect," said Virginia. "Don't you agree, Eddie?" She enjoyed watching the pink slowly climb up both teens' necks.

Traveler's mind searched for a casual, but witty reply. *I got nothin'* was all that came to his mind. His lack of a snappy answer was saved by the bell, in this case, the phone. As Virginia answered Glenda and Traveler heard her say, "We're ready, we'll be right down."

Glancing at the two teens Virginia said, "It's showtime. Put on your winter coats and let's see what excitement M has in store for us tonight. Head down and I'll catch up in a minute."

Pausing a moment, she added, "Eddie be sure to bring your earmuffs." Traveler winced twice. First at being called Eddie, then at being treated like a five-year-old being dressed by his mother to go outside. He ignored a smiling Glenda.

Grunting he said, "Sure thing, Mom. Let's go explore this great place M is taking us to. I can't wait."

Chapter 7

The Casino Adds a Dangerous Wild Card

Too often when life's events are all going our way people will humorously ask, "What can go wrong?" Sadly, as the scales of life balance out, certain unwanted answers frequently appear. These answers often begin with an unnoticed event. Such an unnoticed event happened in the infant universe. The event gave rise to a life form that would grow over time to threaten a dark god Theo's very life.

The exploding universe was a cosmic supermarket, begging to be explored by the creators. There were endless new aisles appearing as galaxies, each offering rich shelves of knowledge for study. Despite their near-limitless ability to absorb new experiences, the creators were close to being overwhelmed by this evolving unpredictable universe.

With the avalanche of new offerings for study, the creators missed the earliest form of emerging life. Within this exploding random universe, the statistically impossible could, and did, happen. An unforeseen threat to the creators themselves was born. It would grow into a dangerous wild card. It was a nasty joker unexpectedly added to the universe's playing deck.

This early wild card began as a routinely developing compacted sphere of primary elements. As the sphere was approaching its metamorphosis into a young star, its component elements were altered by the randomness tool. A jolting hit from a small meteor altered the sphere's development. The hit diverted the sphere's packed elements away from nuclear reactions; shaken, the elements morphed into a loosely linked network.

Over time the linked network continued to grow, resembling a three-dimensional spider's web of random connections between clusters of elements. These clusters slowly thickened and became nodes. As the nodes evolved and their connections increased, they resembled a primitive network.

The network continued to evolve in complexity as it carried random electrical messages between the nodes. As increasing numbers of data packets flowed, the network responded with a greater density of connections. With denser connections came greater speed.

The network was evolving into a small, asteroid-sized platform that offered the potential for cognitive development. It was not, however, conscious. It was unaware of itself. It had no self-identity; it was simply a very large, very dumb computer.

Externally, the sphere appeared to be a small, failed sun. Under a cosmic microscope it would appear as a reddish ember resting in space.

While the sphere had no self-directing cognitive abilities, it did sense and react to certain stimuli. Its unconscious instinct was to survive. It recognized, on some rudimentary level, that morphing into a flaring sun would destroy its network. Without conscious intention the network stopped further development toward becoming a star.

For eons the ever-developing network was passive. Messages randomly flowed as data packets between nodes; however, there were no understood directions within the received messages. Over time the message content became increasingly complex but remained without consequence.

Once again, the randomness tool interceded. A nearby passing comet flared into a burnout. The escaping energy altered the chemical construct of the nodes. Messages that were previously gibberish became understood. Once understood, messages had purpose. The randomness tool via the comet's demise had inadvertently activated the dumb computer's "on" switch. It was suddenly far from dumb.

The network burst into awareness of its own existence in an instant. It recognized itself as a being. It knew it was unique from all other entities in the surrounding space. As the French philosopher Descartes famously said, "I think, therefore I am." The being thought, and these thoughts drove future actions.

Fully sentient at the moment of its awakening, it immediately understood its limitless potential for cognitive development and power. It knew it had the potential to develop abilities to shape environments to its will. It was born a demigod. Over time it aspired to be much more.

Alive, it was famished for knowledge. It was a born predator lurking in the dense birthing cloud. It studied the energy and matter that surrounded it. No substance was a threat to it. It was a wolf ready to dine on a herd of elemental sheep. It pondered which nearby substance would be its first meal.

Fortunately for its survival, it became aware of a powerful dark presence. It intuitively understood this being was far superior to itself. This dark god could easily place a choker chain around its wolf's throat. It would become a meal to this vastly greater alpha. It stopped its movement toward the nearby elements. The time for ingesting would come later.

With a strong instinct for self-preservation, the sphere behaved accordingly. It understood the need for camouflage. It sent low-level pulsating energies outward to project a dark reddish hue onto its exterior. This camouflage maintained its appearance as a dying red ember. "I'm just another failed star. You will learn nothing from me," was the sphere's message to the surrounding cosmos and any dark god observer.

The dark god had indeed noticed the sphere's outward appearance and dismissed it. The god believed that as this ember cooled it would become inert matter. It was destined to float in the void until it was destroyed or absorbed by a larger mass. The camouflage had worked, the sphere warranted no further study by the god.

While by choice it was not a blazing sun, the sphere thought of itself as a sun's cousin. It named itself a "fire being." Much later others would call it a "fire beast." In Norse mythology this fire beast would be named Surtr, the great fire god that could destroy all Asgardian gods.

Chapter 8

As the Creature Grows, So Does Frustration

The fire being remained stationary in the dark void for eons as it observed the ever-changing, evolving universe. As it observed the unfolding universe it also focused inward. It had rich resources within itself, and it began to direct these resources.

Its first priority was to strengthen the power of its neural network. All resources were committed to expanding its cognitive abilities. There were occasional setbacks as a network underperformed. Like early Spartan babies, a weakling was not offered aid or comfort. Failure was not acceptable.

To survive, successful networks quickly adjusted to the expected Spartan standard of performance. The strong networks grew and prospered. Weak networks were dismantled and converted into building materials for the stronger networks. Perform or be eaten. The law of the universe held, even within a demigod.

After it had greatly increased its cognitive abilities the sphere proceeded to develop stealth capabilities. Without drawing attention to itself, it explored nearby regions of space rich with floating elements.

It was pleased to discover that it could absorb elements then modify them. It experimented with available matters and energies present in its nearby space neighborhood. It found it could transmute resources into desired hybrids. It became an accomplished space alchemist. It was the first designer chemist in this young universe.

As eons passed it was frequently bumped into by random traveling objects such as meteors. These objects often contained newly formed, advanced chemical elements. The creature found it could absorb these new matters, study their inner workings, and add to its knowledge base.

While pleased with its alchemy efforts, the creature eventually became frustrated. There were major constraints on its research. The constraints came from its inability to move freely. To explore it knew it needed to distance itself from the dark god; movement, however, was an unacceptable risk.

If this dark god detected the fire creature as a life form, it would immediately bring the creature under its control for study. The creature did not want to dwell on its fate if captured. All chemists know what happens to used laboratory specimens and equipment once the study is completed. It would be washed clean or trashed.

Unexpectedly, life changed again for the creature. The opportunity to move suddenly arose. The opportunity presented itself when the dark god disappeared. It briefly reappeared next to a distant massive star in the center of the galaxy, then it entered the star. At first the fire creature thought the dark god may have been destroyed by the glowing star, then it saw the true power of the god on display.

Once merged with the star the dark god began to re-engineer it. The embedded god contorted, twisted, then shrank the giant into a compressed mass. Unimaginable energies poured out from the giant star's contraction. The dark god continued the restructuring until the massive star was collapsed into a small, enormously dense glob.

Curiosity, fear, and respect held the fire creature spellbound as it watched the dark god compress the massive star. As the star was being squeezed down, the fire creature could detect the increased force of gravity even from an enormous distance. The powerful mass held energy emanations, such as light, prisoner. The creature knew it could never escape if discovered. It continued to bide its time, watching for any movement from the distant god.

Chapter 9

The Creature Moves

After eons of a forced stationary existence the creature rejoiced, the god never reappeared. Given its great distance from the black hole, the creature realized that cautious stealth movement was possible. A distant portion of the galaxy was an inviting domain to explore as long as it maintained a sufficient distance from the black hole.

Movement over the vast distances was indeed possible. The creature had reached a state of knowledge that permitted it to manipulate the forces that controlled this universe. Using this knowledge, it experimented with bridges to move between distant points. Eons later these bridges would be called "wormholes" by human physicists.

The creature's bridge would connect suns as the entry and exit points. By using suns as the entry and exit doors, the creature's travel would be hidden from the scrutiny of a dark god. The creature had designed interstellar stealth travel.

The choice of the entry point was easy, it was a sun at the center of its current system. The creature would enter this star by presenting itself as a blazing comet. Comets were common and often crashed into stars and disappeared. The comet's travel should not generate any interest for the distant observing god.

The critical decision was picking an exit point. That point needed to be far from the god's black hole. The exit also needed to place the creature in a region that was rich in star systems with orbiting masses.

The creature began an intense study of candidate star systems with orbiting masses. It observed that for many orbiting planets, life was often short-lived. Some planets were smashed by larger objects moving through their solar system; some became floating cinders due to their proximity to the system's sun. Some never achieved a stable gravitational orbit and became traveling space tramps.

After a careful review of possible destinations, the creature made its choice. This galaxy had star collections that moved away from the center hub like spiraling arms. The creature chose an arm that was rich in planet-bearing star systems. Within the selected region it chose a normal-sized star as its exit point.

The creature had its plan and the bridging ability to execute it. As the Romans would say many eons later, "carpe diem," or "seize the day." The creature turned up its exterior glow and presented itself as a traveling comet heading into the furnace of the nearby sun. Without hesitation the fire creature rode into its entry star.

Ironically, in this vast casino for gods, both Theo and the creature had selected the same star region. What are the odds? Only the randomness tool would venture a guess.

Chapter 10

Star Bridges and Star Portals

The star bridge worked perfectly; the creature emerged from the wormhole directly inside the interior of the large exit sun. The creature was unfazed by the intense heat of the star's internal nuclear explosions. The creature embraced the sun's energy much as old friends will embrace upon meeting each other.

It remained inside the sun, gathering resources while waiting to see if there was any pursuit from the distant dark god. There was none. Feeling secure, it emerged as a comet and moved away from the exit star. Its first impression was relief at how distant it was from the gravity grasp of the black hole. It had achieved the necessary separation to begin freely exploring.

The challenges of searching the enormous number of star systems for life forms dawned on it. It realized it could not visit the multitude of candidate star systems one at a time. It needed to throw out a much larger net for an efficient search.

The challenge of such a search was resolved by using its own internal resources. It was capable of breaking itself into many fully capable, smaller entities. With the increased resources gained from immersion in the exit star, it could create a vast number of scouting entities.

These scouts were its pseudo-children. While the children were small compared to the parent host, they each had enormous powers. Their powers were similar to those of the host creature, diminished only by the scout's reduced size. Even size limitations could be partially overcome by individual scouts combining with each other. Once combined, a single, more powerful being resulted. Individually or combined, the scouts would be the alpha to any life form they encountered.

The next step was for the scouts to establish portals on targeted planets. The portals functioned as communication networks and as travel corridors between planets. They were imbued with a high level of AI, or artificial intelligence. This AI capability gave portals the ability to monitor their surrounding environment. If life was detected, the portal transmitted this finding to each of the other portals as well as to the host parent.

The creature had observed the various natural threats to a planet that the random universe could produce. Such threats included volcanic activity, earthquakes, and floods. If a portal found that it was being damaged, it was programmed to send a signal calling for scouts to visit and repair. The creature had constructed an interactive intelligent portal system similar to its own internal structure. It had learned from observing its own efficiencies.

The host was now ready to launch an armada of scouting legions. It studied the candidate systems and prioritized the richest star regions. After a careful review it selected a nearby region that offered a plethora of planet-rich star systems. Given the vast number of stars and orbiting planets, the host was optimistic. It expected to find many forms of developing life.

As eons passed the host became frustrated as scouts failed to identify any significant intelligent life. With continuing failure, the host creature concluded: *These dark gods have seriously erred. They are powerful but incompetent. They are not gods suited to building a life-rich universe.*

An intriguing thought came to the host. At some point it might become powerful enough to absorb a god. Once absorbed, all of the god's knowledge would belong to the fire creature. The creature could then change the construct of this universe to satisfy its own wishes.

How to absorb an all-powerful opponent was the issue. With continuing reflections, the creature determined its approach. The strategy was risky but doable. An unexpected, full host attack on a lone god, residing outside of a protective black hole, was the answer. It only needed to find such an isolated, unprotected god. It began the god-search using its highly energized scouts and portals.

Chapter 11

Chicago Bridges

When Virginia got off the elevator, she saw the check-in counter was fully staffed and hyper-busy. It was the beginning of the Christmas season and the Drake was a major hotel destination for people staying in downtown Chicago. Searching for the teens she quickly spotted them next to the lobby's giant, decorated Christmas tree.

The teens were watching in childlike fascination as a miniature train was weaving its way under and around the large tree. They stared as it sped past villages then over a bridge on top of a miniature lake. The lake was a festively decorated mirror with miniature skaters moving randomly about on the lake's surface. Captivated by the sights the teens visualized themselves riding on the train. *Trains are magic*, they thought at the same time.

Adding to the display's realism, movement appeared everywhere. Activated by the train's passing, flagmen waved lanterns, crossing gates lowered, and flashing signal lights announced the train's presence. The two teens were spellbound as the train crossed over the bridge, whistled, then ascended a long incline to disappear into a tunnel. Horn calls echoed from inside the tunnel.

Captivated by the display, the two were oblivious to Virginia as she moved past them to the exit. As she approached the door the heavily suited doorman nodded at her, "It's a brisk one tonight, take care." Stepping forward, he opened the heavy door.

Virginia saw the waiting limo and tentatively stepped outside. The piercing Lake Michigan wind cut into her and she felt a shiver despite her heavy coat. She made eye contact with the driver and sent a hand wave that was immediately acknowledged by a gloved wave back. Smiling, Virginia pointed inside to indicate she would be back shortly.

Returning to the Christmas tree, she slipped an arm around both Eddie and Glenda. "I love the train setup, it's mesmerizing. It must have taken weeks to create this work of Christmas art. I can imagine myself on board a magic train as it winds its way along."

Her face brightened as she added, "Eddie, I think we were just on a magic train getting here. Mr. M is a wonderful magician and he certainly entertained us in the dining car. I have no idea how he did those tricks." Traveler responded with an understanding nod. *Truer than you know, Mom.*

"I hate to take you away right now children, but time and limos wait for nobody, so we better get to our ride. Hold your breath outside, trust me it's like the Arctic." Pausing, she added, "Oh, Eddie, you forgot your earmuffs, but I picked them up."

"Thanks, Mom. I can probably make it to the limo without them but always good to have." He slipped them into a deep pocket.

Again, the tall doorman went outside and did his duty. As they stepped out Traveler winced. "You're right Mom, this is a killer night. I can imagine polar bears skating down Michigan Avenue."

Taking Virginia's arm, Traveler helped her down the wide steps to the limo. Glenda noted his chivalry thinking, *Kudos Traveler, great way to kick off the evening.*

The driver was standing outside holding one of the doors open and offered Virginia a hand as she bent to enter. "Thank you, sir. This lady always appreciates good manners and definitely on a night like tonight."

The driver next offered a gloved hand to Glenda who accepted it with a simple "Thank you." Traveler looked the driver in the eye and shook his head. The driver smiled back, he understood the message. *Young men don't need or accept help from other men, too embarrassing.*

Shutting the passenger door, the driver was quickly inside. Virginia smiled at her fellow riders. "Is this a limo, or is this a carriage for a queen? I rode in it last night, and it's a Cinderella dream coach. Everything is genuine leather and the seats are heated." Looking at Traveler sitting across from her she rhetorically exclaimed, "Eddie, does M know how to travel in style or what?"

Traveler had to agree on the luxury of the limo coach that was now carrying them through the snow and wind-whipped Chicago streets. As they moved along, he noticed how although other cars would frequently lose traction and slide sideways, the limo was steady as a rock. "Yeah Mom, this is a special limo. It's really stable on these slick streets, must be German-built."

Glenda had been sitting quietly watching the flow of freezing people move along with turtle-like heads tucked into thick coat collars. *I'm lucky to be inside, it's brutal out there.* Her mind then left the outside to rejoin her companions.

"You're so right Virginia about trains. Didn't you say that this Mr. M fascinated you with magic on the train?" Laughing, she added, "I bet he is a real-live sorcerer living right here with us in Chicago. What do you think, Eddie?"

Traveler grunted. "For sure, he's the magic man all right. Let's see what magic he's come up with for tonight."

Virginia smiled at her son, "I think he's going to make tonight an evening to remember."

Glenda knew Traveler thought the world of M, but at the same time she also knew he wanted his mom to be missing his dad as much as he did. Glenda saw a less positive comment about M forming on Traveler's face. She wanted Virginia to enjoy a magical evening without her son detracting from her upbeat mood. She headed it off with, "Wow Eddie, look at that Santa! He is shaking the biggest bell I've ever seen."

Traveler visibly grimaced at the "Eddie" but immediately searched the street and noted the bell ringer. He gave an involuntary grin, "You're right! And look at his padding, I think it's the real deal. That Santa has enjoyed more than his share of holiday cookies and fruit cake."

Virginia had noticed that her son had a frowning reaction to being called "Eddie" by the girl. She had clearly annoyed him, and nobody wants a pouty Eddie starting the evening. Virginia the mother knew what to do. "So, my learned history son, assuming I bear some resemblance to Cleopatra tonight, can you tell us how Caesar met her?"

With the question still hanging in the air, Traveler became a fish leaping out of the water to capture a too close, silly fly. "I'm glad you asked, Mom. It's a great story of love and war. I'll give the short version.

"Caesar met Cleo when he arrived in Alexandria, Egypt chasing his archenemy Pompey. Both were competing to rule Rome. They had just faced off with a decisive battle in Greece which, against all odds, Caesar won. Pompey fled to Alexandria with Caesar hot on his trail.

"When Caesar reached Alexandria a few days behind Pompey he was met by the young pharaoh Ptolemy and Ptolemy's senior advisor. The advisor was actually ruling Egypt in the pharaoh's name and loved the power. The advisor was full of himself and he and Caesar disliked each other immediately.

"The advisor presented Caesar with a covered vase and suggested that he look at its contents. A curious Caesar did so, only to find Pompey's head inside. This was a very ill-conceived offering. Offended that the arrogant advisor had killed Pompey, a Roman consul, Caesar was soon drawn into a brewing civil war between Ptolemy and his advisor and Ptolemy's sister Cleopatra. Cleo was powerful and a threat to the advisor's power.

"As a side note, Cleopatra was not only Ptolemy's sister she was his wife. The Egyptians believed both siblings had gods residing in their human bodies making them in fact gods. As gods they should necessarily marry each other to maintain the purity of their godly offspring.

"To control Cleo the advisor kept her isolated from the royal court. Frustrated and eager to regain her position as co-ruler she needed an ally. How she escaped confinement to seek Caesar's help is a great story. She had herself rolled into a beautiful rug that was carried by her slave as a gift to Caesar. When the rug was unrolled Caesar and his generals came face to face with a rising Cleopatra.

"Immediately upon standing, a confident Cleo took charge. She was a commanding presence even to powerful Caesar and his generals. Cleo could spot a winner with a glance. Her glances swept Caesar to her side in many ways and he quickly became her ally.

"Naturally there was a big battle. It's famous and called the Battle of the Nile. The Romans were outnumbered but they were the cream of Caesar's army, they were battle-hardened killers. The opposing Egyptians were brave and fought fiercely for their pharaoh. It was a pitched battle in which the young pharaoh and the advisor were killed. With her brother's death Cleo emerged from the palace to face the Egyptian army.

"She addressed them as their now rightful leader. With her appearance they all knelt, she was, after all, a goddess to them.

"One tragic result of this pitched battle was an accidental fire that burned the most famous library in the ancient world. Caesar had ships burned in the harbor to prevent Egyptian reinforcements from coming in. Sparks from a burning ship reached the library of Alexandria and fire broke out. Scrolls containing the original writings of the finest minds in mathematics, science, and philosophy were lost. Many were irreplaceable.

"After his successes in Egypt he returned to Rome a conqueror. When a triumphant Caesar met with the senate, he described his victory with a short and still famous phrase: 'Veni, vidi, vici,' meaning, 'I came, I saw, I conquered.' Many in the senate felt his message could be interpreted to mean his intention was to now rule Rome.

"Caesar remained enthralled with Cleo. She was not only mesmerizing but was also a ruler of Egypt. She joined him in Rome bearing his young son. Caesar visualized an Egyptian and Roman dynasty beginning. His many opponents in the Senate also saw his intention but with far less enthusiasm. They acted decisively against him, but that's another story. Hail Caesar! End of history lesson!"

Virginia smiled at her son then gave a soft, enthusiastic clapping with her gloved hands. Glenda joined her, adding, "Great story! Well told!" Traveler was beaming, his mood was all positive now.

Suddenly the limo slowed and a shadow passed over it. Then it came to a complete stop as the driver announced, "We have arrived!" The driver slid out and quickly opened the passenger door. He offered a hand first to Virginia, then to Glenda. Traveler, of course, ignored the hand.

Once all three passengers were outside, they simultaneously looked skyward. "Up" was the instinctive direction to look, the miserable weather had seemed to clear.

They immediately saw that above them was a protective umbrella of steel girders supporting a wide overhead street. They heard the quiet vibration of the overhead traffic as it moved slowly on the snowy street. Chicago provided many respites from weather, including elevated bridges. Native Chicagoans knew how to use the overhead protection as they moved below toward their destinations.

"Mr. M is waiting for you," announced the driver. "Please follow me." The driver moved across the parking area toward a building resting a short distance from the overhead street. Snow was continuing to drift down past the protection of the bridge, and the driver advised, "Watch your step please, this could be slippery."

As they approached their destination each of them noted that the building was slowly swaying. *Now this is weird even for M* both teens thought. Virginia was unfazed by the moving building and walked confidently toward it.

Chapter 12

Rollin' on the River

As the group neared their destination, they confirmed the building was indeed gently swaying. A closer examination presented a majestic houseboat. The front of the boat was an elevated, illuminated curved bow. Christmas lights ran along the rooftop and side rails. Subdued light came through large tinted windows. The effect was a floating jewel.

The driver stopped in front of the entry ramp and did a small salute by tipping his hat toward a waiting M. "Your guests are here, sir. A word of caution: this snow looks like it's getting thicker. I'd advise a careful lookout to avoid possible collisions with other party boats." Exchanging a knowing look with M he added, "I suspect some of the other boaters may overindulge in their spiked eggnog."

"Good advice, James, thank you. These are my special guests and I'll be sure to bring them back nice and dry. None of us want a swim in this freezing Michigan water. Now please get yourself a hot dinner, take an evening nap, and we'll see you back here around midnight."

Standing beside the entry ramp to greet them was a tall M, resplendent in formal attire. He welcomed his guests with a broad smile, a short bow, and a wide sweep of his left hand. Extending his right hand to Virginia he said, "Welcome aboard your yacht, Virginia. Are you prepared to see Chicago from a unique travel perspective? Prepare yourself for a special evening."

Glancing down at the trailing Glenda and Traveler, he gave a warm greeting. "Welcome young people!" Smiling back Glenda thought, *Based on your age M, everyone born in the last five thousand years is a young person.*

Once they were on board, Glenda and Traveler quickly found themselves alone as they saw M leading Virginia toward the beckoning stateroom. Upbeat classical music was coming from hidden speakers inside and out. Both young people were surprised to find that they were enjoying the music from a distant generation.

Standing outside they immediately noticed the surrounding air was warm, and the falling snow did not land on their heads or shoulders. "How cool is this?" said Glenda. "It's like being inside, yet we're still in the wild elements of a Chicago winter. I can see the snow coming down over my head, then it just disappears."

Traveler nodded, "No need to worry, princess, about your hair getting disturbed. M is using a little modern science to heat this area. He uses overhead blowers to move the snow away; not everything M does runs on magic."

Looking about, Traveler walked to the end of the boat. Reaching the stern, he motioned to Glenda to join him. "It's OK, I'm still in a protected zone all the way back here. M's equipment is amazing. Join me and enjoy the view."

Glenda moved toward him while keeping a watchful eye on the falling snow. *Boys have no idea about the work that goes into making our hair look great. All they do is brush theirs back with fingers and let the mirror congratulate them on how great they look.*

Comfortable within the protective science cocoon, Glenda stood beside Traveler. Both looked down the wide expanse of the dark river. They tracked the dark water for many blocks until it made a gentle twist to the right, disappearing between two skyscrapers. *M was right, this is a totally different view of Chicago.*

Shifting her gaze and body stance, Glenda leaned over the railing and looked into the surrounding dark water. "Hate to fall in, that water looks like it could be holding icebergs. Hope our ship isn't named Titanic."

Grinning, Traveler responded, "For sure! I'm in no mood to play Leonardo DiCaprio tonight with my nose pointing into that Lake Michigan wind." Grinning he added, "Nose frostbite, a scary thought. What I am in the mood for is food. Let's find out what M has prepared for us."

"Lead on Leo, I'm famished. My guess is that whatever our dining feast is, it's prepared for your mom. She's the real guest, we're just two tagalongs."

Upon entering the boat's large stateroom Glenda and Traveler paused to take in the grand interior, it was stunning. They first noticed the room's size. It offered a variety of areas for functional activities including a dancefloor. They saw the conversation area was easily identified with thick leather seats positioned to look out of wide windows onto the city.

Floor-to-ceiling glass windows presented a moving diorama of Chicago buildings peeking through the snowy mist. Giant skyscrapers far above the river canal illuminated the dark sky. Many had their windows decorated with holiday images projecting wreaths, elf heads, or a giant Santa. At ground level, streetlamps lit the sidewalks for pedestrians. The effect was a glistening North Pole wonderland Walt Disney would have approved of.

Looking at the view, Glenda said, "This is magical, I feel like I'm back in Norway. The skyscrapers are like our mountains coming right down to our fields and cities. You can imagine the old gods living among us on dark nights."

Smiling back, Traveler added, "I believe you have a lot of dark days as well as dark nights in winter. I bet the old gods keep it dark so they can play outside without humans bothering them."

"Well, you're mostly right. During winter we have limited sunlight, maybe six hours if we're lucky. Our constant snowfalls dim the sunlight even further."

"Sounds like Chicago, but more so." Grinning he continued, "Must be easy to walk into things. I see Norway as a land of skinned knees." Laughing at the image, Glenda nodded back. She had accumulated her share of falls, bumps, and bruises as an active youngster outside.

Shifting his gaze from the frigid outside to the inside, Traveler spotted an elegantly covered table with silver chafing dishes. "I see my future: it's warm and delicious, and telling me to start hunting for my dinner."

Giving him a negative headshake, Glenda said, "Slow down mighty hunter, we'll all eat together."

"Ah, my faithful gun bearer. Always present and always quick to give advice. So where are Mom and M?"

"Well, they were not at the back, and are not here either. I think you can conclude they're likely in the front. What do you think, mighty hunter?"

"Was that question veiled sarcasm? I certainly hope not, you are looking so Christmassy."

Glenda gave a sheepish smile back. "Sorry Traveler, nobody likes a Grinch. Let's go hunt them down together."

"Good plan. Let's see what else is on this yacht while tracking them down." Passing through the stateroom, they entered a wood-paneled hallway softly illuminated by bronze wall sconces. On both sides were heavy unmarked doors.

They stood in front of the first door on the left then dropped the heavy iron cat's head knocker down to strike the catch plate. A grinning Traveler said, "Does that head remind you of anyone?" An echoing reply sounding suspiciously like "It should" came from inside. They waited for a polite moment then entered.

They were stunned. The room was a combination of an elegant bedroom fit for a prince and a serious study. A working fireplace was flickering beside an elegant wooden desk. Opposite the desk was an antique four-poster Elizabethan bed. The bed's overhead canopy was solid oak, with carved scenes for upward-facing heads to enjoy. The canopy was supported by two carved support pillars at the foot, and a carved headboard at the top.

The center of the headboard presented a shield with inlaid hieroglyphs above it. As Glenda studied the detailed artwork she asked, "Does M have a coat of arms? I noticed that the center of the shield is a finely detailed sphinx. Maybe that references his early life."

"Good catch, I bet you're right. With his extraordinarily long life, I bet M's earned a coat of arms more than once."

They paused beside the desk and took in the smooth writing surface and nearby sunken cup holders offering an assortment of writing instruments. To the right of the desk was a bookcase that could have come from the library of Alexandria. Thick leather books of obvious great age seemed to call out to them. Staring at the books Glenda wondered, "Siblings to our own books?"

With the room inspection completed the two retreated into the corridor.

They quickly passed a second door on the opposite side and peeked inside. This door opened to a lavatory with a throne, a marble sink, and a many-headed shower. Dimly lit sconces on each side of an antique mirror softened and flattered the face of anybody looking at themselves.

"Nothing interesting here," said Traveler as he quickly glanced around. Glenda paused longer to check herself out. Pleased with the reflection, she nodded back at the smiling image. Closing the door gently she rejoined Traveler.

At the end of the hallway was a heavy wooden door. Traveler the gentleman pushed it open as he gave a beckoning sweep of his hand. A smiling Glenda stepped past him. Once outside they looked at the oncoming dark waterway. They immediately noticed that the warmth from the overhead air ducts protected them from the gusting, freezing Lake Michigan wind.

Without the distraction of nasty weather, the two stood taking in the passing scenes. Buildings were slowly coming toward them out of the drifting mist on each side of the wide river.

Watching the buildings as they emerged from the snowy mist Traveler quipped, "Remember the Doors' song from the sixties,

'People Are Strange'? I'm feeling it right now. These blurred buildings are strange but fascinating." Glenda recalled the old song, one of her favorites, and immediately nodded back.

The everchanging viewing angles created by the moving yacht presented a scene of wide and narrow, short and tall buildings packed together. Many were ultramodern glass caves. Others were built from aged red bricks affording a glimpse into Old Chicago before the city was rebuilt following the devastating fire of 1871. Old and new standing together declared how the past was married to the present.

Their eyes shifted from the buildings to the front of the boat. Standing comfortably at the bow, M and Virginia were also captivated by the view. Virginia, the native Chicagoan, was the enthusiastic tour guide pointing out various buildings coming toward them for the nodding M.

"I like to think of Chicago as the Venice of the Midwest. We built canals and brought the waters of Lake Michigan right into the heart of our city. Our city streets pass over these water canals on beautiful bridges, many of them raise and lower." M's nods and smiles assured her she had a captivated audience.

"Hi, Mom."

Virginia turned and smiled at Traveler and Glenda. "Welcome children, please join us. Isn't this view spellbinding? Notice how protected we are from the freezing wind; I think M is an engineer as well as a magician."

Traveler nodded, "You're right Mom, I love the views. Forgive me please if I'm breaking the tour mood, but I really loved the view of the dining table. I'm a hungry guy right now."

Virginia accepted the change in priorities with a smile. "I understand dear, I bet you're both starving. So am I. I've been talking M's ear off about Chicago's history, and I think he now knows more than he wants to about my beautiful city." M shook his head indicating a "not so" response.

Before reentering the access hallway Virginia paused. "Have you noticed there is no steering wheel and no captain? Isn't that amazing? M employs state-of-the-art self-driving gear using lasers." Pausing, Virginia added, "I understand why robots continue to take over our jobs. That's scary. I mean, what replacement job can a boat captain find?"

As he opened the door, Traveler said, "Relax, Mom. Captains are smart, they'll figure it out. Maybe the younger ones will become doctors like Dad. Robots can do a lot but don't bet against us wily humans, we're very adaptive."

Virginia smiled. "Well, that's reassuring coming from my 'science is everything' son. There is one thing that hasn't changed on a boat, and that's having a mascot: a cat in this case." Outside the captain's door, she pointed. "M, may we show them Theo?"

M smiled. "Of course."

Stepping inside, Virginia motioned for them to join her. She pointed down toward the fireplace's red embers. "There he is. His name is Theo and he's sleeping beside the fireplace. It's so dark in here that it's easy to miss him. M tells me he is the real captain on board.

"With M's permission I petted him. Isn't he magnificent with his size, thick coat, and exotic look? Be careful looking into those eyes, you may fall in. M says he's one of a kind, an ancient breed, and I believe it. He's a wonder."

Glenda and Traveler focused on the resting mascot who looked back at them. M motioned for the relaxed feline to join them. Rising gracefully, as only a cat can, Theo padded forward to stand beside Virginia. She immediately rubbed the head that was at her waist, and low vibrations of pleasure came out. "He is very friendly, so feel free to rub his head, he loves it."

Glenda smiled at Traveler and the two of them joined Virginia in the rubbing and stroking. "I'd hate to be a bad pantry mouse or bilge rat with this guy," said Virginia.

"I'd hate to be a bad anything," said Traveler.

As the four of them left, the giant cat returned to the pile of blankets and curled back into being a dark pile of fur. M was correct of course, it was indeed the captain in charge, the humans were the mascots.

Chapter 13

Dine like Royalty

Nodding toward the serving table M said, "I suggest we begin with our starting course and retire to the picture window for views and conversation."

The meal began with a thick, steaming soup. When the cover was lifted a soft cloud rose to spread across the table. Traveler's mouth was an embarrassing Niagara Falls. He swallowed fast, filled an elegant soup bowl, and moved to a seat by the window.

When the four were seated M began, "Starting with soup is always dangerous for our formal wear. Please note that the chair's side tables slide up and can be raised to your desired height to avoid spillage."

Smiling at Traveler, he added, "Of course, leaving a little empty space on the spoon also provides a margin of safety." A slight pink stole across Traveler's face to the delight of Virginia and Glenda. M's nod gave the green light to begin.

Before the meal progressed from the soup course to the entrée, M placed a magnum-sized bottle of wine into a metal mechanism. Looking at Traveler, he said, "This bottle of wine needs to be decanted before being poured." M knew Traveler was hesitating to ask the meaning of "decanted," and continued.

"You have noted that I previously uncorked the bottle to let the wine breathe. Aerating wine can improve its taste. Since some wines collect sediment at the bottom of the bottle you need to pour carefully, without including the sediment. That pouring process is called decanting. We will decant using this mechanism, please observe."

With the arms of the decanting machine securely holding the bottle in place, M proceeded to slowly turn a side wheel. As the bottle moved from the vertical toward the horizontal the wine flowed from the bottle into the receiving crystal container. As it was filled the container's crystal facets sparkled. There was an immediate excitement among the viewers to sample the glowing contents.

With the transfer concluded, M proceeded to pour a starting sample into crystal wine glasses. Four hands immediately lifted glasses, then three heads nodded toward M. "Cheers," M offered, and four sets of lips kissed the glass edges.

The third stage of the feast began with the entrée offerings. There were three choices, uncovered and on display on the serving table. Each competed for the diners' attention. Traveler solved the choosing-dilemma by heaping his plate with some of everything. As Glenda passed by him, she looked down at his plate. "Don't be embarrassed, you can ask M for a bigger plate."

"Men plan ahead. This is just efficient planning. I'll enjoy watching you act like a jack-in-the-box every time you pop up to get more."

"Your food, your choice. Personally, I like my food to stay hot, but to each his own."

Looking down, Traveler felt a twinge of regret. *Maybe the princess was right. I guess I'll just eat faster.*

With the group again seated, M filled each diner's glass from the crystal container. Lifting his glass, M gave a short, welcoming toast that was echoed by the three guests. The best toasts are short ones, and the four diners quickly made their opening forays into their initial choices.

After several minutes of early tasting, Virginia paused. "M, this rabbit is wonderful. The brown sauce must be a French recipe." M smiled back at the compliment.

What M did not say was that his rabbit creation started many thousands of years ago when he was a young boy hiding from the jinn on a deserted island. Trapped rabbit was a frequent fare, and the sauce recipe gradually developed as he experimented with the dish. Giving a clever pun reply, best understood by himself, he answered, "Trust me Virginia, it's definitely a time-tested recipe. Thank you."

Looking over at Traveler, M noted, "Edward, I see from your plate that you are the designated sampler. Would you please share your unbiased opinion regarding your favorite?"

Traveler looked up to see the three were waiting for his answer. He saw the grin on Glenda's face and winced. Of course, fast eating has a drawback, called a "full mouth." Unable to respond, his now-reddening face recorded his embarrassment.

Virginia saw her son struggling to answer. She knew his eating habits too well. "Honey, take your time. I know M is pleased with your enthusiasm for his wonderful meal."

Glenda offered her unwanted advice. "Your mom is so right, Eddie. I find chewing slowly is a good thing to avoid choking, and also leaves more room for dessert." Traveler's eyes narrowed as they shot his unspoken retort back at her.

With a final swallow he was able to come up for air. "Mom's right, M. I guess I just got carried away by the wonderfulness of all this goodness. I can't pick a winner yet, I need a second sampling." With that he stood and headed back to the serving table.

Watching Traveler rise, a smiling M said, "That's the greatest compliment any chef can receive."

Glenda looked down at her empty plate and shrugged. *Big boy's right every so often.* She rose and followed Traveler to make her own sampler selections.

Virginia and M soon followed the two youths. As Virginia led M back to the selection table she quipped, "I'll try my best to keep a model's smooth walk and not waddle now like a stuffed duck." M simply shook his head at this duck-walk comment. Virginia was born with a model's natural stride.

As Traveler passed Glenda with his second plate, she gave him a sweet smile. "Try not to quack when you walk, Donald."

Despite himself, Traveler started to laugh. He responded with a Donald Duck headshake and a sharply toned, "Quack, quack!" Glenda laughed, answering with a Daisy Duck echoing quack.

The second round went at a slower pace and was accompanied by animated conversation. Virginia found herself telling her companions about her early days as a college student attending Northwestern University and living near downtown Chicago. She regaled them with her flashback account of unexpectedly meeting her future husband, Daniel, in the university library.

"This could have been a story that started with, 'It was a dark and stormy night, and all the student-gremlins were gathered in the library.' In truth it was a beautiful spring day, everyone wanted to be outside. Unfortunately, final exams were around the corner, so the library was crammed.

"I had gotten to the library early to secure an isolated, quiet study place. I was deep into my studies when a tall, geeky, longhaired guy slammed a ton of books down on my table. It sounded like the crack of doom.

"I know I jumped and had a surge of anger, but I controlled myself. I had to reorganize my carefully spread-out papers to accommodate this late arrival. I knew he was another party boy arriving late after a fun night with beer, buddies, and likely babes."

She then changed the story's direction and described how she and Daniel had bonded over pizza and cokes in the late afternoon. "I think the moral of my tale is to remember how easy it is to miss a positive opportunity when there is a lot of starting bias. Remaining objective, even in the face of annoying circumstances, is how we sometimes find gold. I found my gold with Daniel." Pausing, she pointed at Traveler. "Later on we found more gold."

Traveler had a strong pink blush rising from his neck and spreading across his face. He wasn't quite a cooked lobster but was working on a definite sunburn. Glenda was twitching with gold-quips regarding "fool's gold" on her tongue but bit them off. This was a mother's sincere, sweet comment, and must be respected.

With all plates clean and all bellies happy, M stood up. "The best way to enjoy a continued night of dining is to get in motion between servings. I suggest we move our bodies to the dancefloor. This is the time in a meal when some movement will add back incentive, as well as room, for the desserts."

Chapter 14

I Can Dance!

M stood behind Virginia's chair, offered his hand as she rose, then led her to the dance area. Traveler and Glenda sat there, staring at each other. "Can you dance better than you waddle Donald?" a grinning Glenda asked.

"Bring it on Daisy," answered Traveler as he quickly rose and offered his hand. Standing, Glenda gave a smile and a short curtsy then led him to the floor.

The music was a rousing waltz. Virginia and M moved effortlessly around the perimeter of the floor as Traveler and Glenda watched them. "They're pretty good," said a subdued Traveler.

"Of course they are," said Glenda. "Your mom had to dance as a drama major. And M was probably there when this waltz was created by Strauss in nineteenth-century Vienna."

Formal dancing has humbled many a young man. Traveler's normal confidence and male bravado were rapidly fading. He was regretting his presence on this dancefloor. His schoolmates generally just stood in place, waving their arms around while thumping loud music blared, no skill was required.

Glenda waited until Virginia and M glided past them, then took Traveler's hand. "Relax big boy, I'm not a fire beast. Step back one full step, extend your other hand to my waist, and move to the music."

An intimidated, skeptical Traveler started trying to remember the basic foot placements for the box step movement. Amazingly, he found himself taking a confident lead. His feet and body moved without his planning, and he found that leading his partner was easy and natural. They were quickly caught up in their own swirling dance with coordinated, smooth foot and body movements.

Traveler's mind pulled up a fun YouTube video from the 1970s: Leo Sayer's "Long Tall Glasses (I Can Dance)." He could see Sayer initially protesting dancing for his dinner, then doing his dance moves while shouting, "I can dance!"

Staring at a smiling Glenda all he could say was, "How?"

Through a soft red haze drifting around her face, Glenda gave the simple answer. "Our books. Dance and enjoy."

The waltz then flowed into a formal French minuet. Once again, Traveler found that his body knew what to do, and he was relaxed as he moved rapidly around the floor. As they moved, Virginia watched them, "Now when did my little boy learn to waltz and minuet? I'm not surprised that Glenda has all the moves, but I always thought Eddie's feet were made for running, not dancing."

"Well, we don't always know as much about our children as we think we do. They have lives away from home, and they don't always share those lives."

With a slightly perplexed look Virginia said, "I guess you're right M, still I've seen his dance moves at high school parties. Anyway, I can't wait to tell Daniel about his son's dancing talents. I'll use that to goad my dear husband into lessons. We're going on a Queen Mary transatlantic crossing in the spring, and ship dancing is a big event. I'll drag poor Daniel kicking and screaming into lessons."

M laughed, "Oh, with you as his partner Virginia, I think the kicks will be small and the screams soft."

Chapter 15

Unexpected Threats

Boats on the Chicago River were not excluded from the casino's random throws of the dice. Dangers arose in unexpected places and unexpected ways, as the dancers soon discovered.

The music had returned to another Strauss waltz, and the dancers focused for a moment on changing their minuet body moves. When they were back in the waltz groove, a new sound came in, interrupting the elegant music. They shifted their eyes to the source of loud clapping.

Standing at the entrance were four "hoodie" figures wearing dark ponchos. *Ninjas*, went through Traveler's mind, *or pirates. Pirates on the Chicago River, you must be kidding*.

As the four dancers became immediately motionless, a hooded man in the center stepped forward. He lowered his hood and the dancers looked at a trimmed black beard below a smirking mouth. Next, he opened his poncho, leading the dancers' gazes down to a long gladius on his left hip.

"We were cruising along behind you when we heard the music. Music always announces a party, and parties always have food and drink. Since we've been out for hours in this harsh weather, in an open boat no less, we need to refresh our bodies. In my experience boaters always share, so I'll thank you in advance for your hospitality."

M forced a thin smile back at the leader. "Indeed, we sympathize with your needs. Life at sea, or on choppy Chicago

58

canals, can be demanding, particularly in nasty weather. We are celebrating the Christmas season and will be pleased to offer you gifts of warmth and food."

M extended an open hand inviting a shake and moved forward. The three hoodies quickly joined their leader, creating a four-man fence that contained the dancers. As the other three intruders moved forward, they kept their hoods on but opened their ponchos. They placed hands on the hilts of their hanging gladius swords. The intruders signaled they were interested in far more than warmth and food.

With gladius weapons now making a threatening display, M immediately stepped back to stand protectively beside Virginia.

Traveler found his battle blood rising, his heart rate increasing, muscles tensing, and his reflexes going into overdrive. He noticed that Glenda was staring at him, making subtle headshakes. Her whispered message was clear, "Stay calm and say nothing. This is a tipping point for sending these pirates into action, your mom would be at risk." Traveler quickly backed down from his attack stance.

The leader noted that the dancers were all displaying the expected subservient body language. He knew this would happen. People have an instinctive fear of weapons with sharp cutting edges and pointy ends.

In 1863, during the American Civil War, a Northern officer named Chamberlain was greatly outnumbered and out of ammunition. Rather than surrender, he ordered his men to fix bayonets and charge. The charge of screaming men extending six-foot knives routed the advancing southern army. Chamberlain's charge is credited with changing the course of the three-day battle of Gettysburg and altering the course of the entire war.

With his captives now in subdued acceptance mode, the leader approached the grouped dancers. Pointing at M he said, "Move away from the lady." M immediately took two long steps back and never made eye contact; any eye contact would be viewed as a challenge. He remained the whipped dog obeying a master's harsh command.

Standing in front of Virginia, the leader studied Virginia's face. *Well isn't she the beauty and looking me straight in the eye. I like a woman with guts.* His eyes then dropped to her heavy gold necklace. He reached forward, put his palm under the necklace, and admired the workmanship.

Traveler stared at the leader as he felt his battle-rage rushing back. Glenda placed a calming hand on his arm.

"Gentlemen, we have hit a literal gold mine. This necklace is pure gold. Even better, I'm thinking it's a historic antique. I bet this comes from an Egyptian princess and got purchased at a black-market auction. This necklace will soon have us living in a warm climate away from this freezing canal."

Motioning to the captives he added, "Don't judge us too harshly, even pirates need shelter and food…and not on this wretched, freezing canal."

Feeling his dominance, he leaned forward while continuing to look Virginia in the eyes. They were nearly nose-to-nose. "Stay calm, my dear, I'm going to lighten your load and open the clasp. We don't want to ruin the clasp with any sudden movement. Even this clasp is an antique and worth a fortune itself."

Virginia was internally torn. A barely controlled fear was trying to dominate her. She remained frozen in place focusing hard to maintain control. Somehow the presence of her three companions sent a reassuring vibe. Bracing herself, she looked back into the leader's eyes as he undid the clasp. She never blinked.

Holding the freed necklace, the leader acknowledged Virginia to his crew. "Well done my dear, you never jerked away. Brave girl."

Holding his treasure for a closer examination he concluded, "This necklace is priceless; it belongs in a world-famous museum. I'm thinking the Louvre in Paris. I don't know how it came to the lady, but I bet your Arab friend there," and he motioned toward M, "is as much of a pirate as I am.

"I bet his ancestors were tomb raiders for many generations. They sailed on camels across the hot seas of the Sahara sand while we sail on frigid Chicago waters. Both of us have the same goal.... treasure!"

The leader then motioned to his crew, "Companions, I see more treasure all around us, go pick it up." Adding a few words of caution, he said, "Don't upset the girl, she looks very emotional. Watch the two men, they may start to regain their lost courage. The Arab is already mourning the loss of the necklace as well as his self-respect."

Heeding the leader's words, each of the crew picked out a victim. The man in front of Traveler studied him hard without noticing any item worth taking. Yes, he had a nice suit coat and expensive shoes but that was not real plunder. Traveler had craftily pulled his shirtsleeves up into the suit coat to hide the gold cufflinks.

The man was ready to move on when he paused, "Extend your arms, pretty boy." The cufflinks immediately came out of hiding. The inset jewels gleamed and the man grinned.

"Well, well, something up the old sleeve. Trying to hide the goods, are we? I should give you a gladius jab to the stomach. Nothing takes longer to heal than a blade to the stomach. Doesn't need to kill, but the trouble it creates will be with you forever."

With a big grin the thug added, "Relax, you're in luck. I'm in a generous mood so no pointy pokes, I'll just relieve you of those links." Traveler was reaching his own tipping point for action as he looked at the smirking face in front of him. Every muscle in his body screamed to hurl this thug across the floor. Then he noticed that the leader was still beside his mother, and his anger lost its edge.

The links were quickly gone, then presented to the leader. The leader studied them, feeling their weight, then declared, "These are more works of antiquity. They could have been made for the English king, Richard the Lionheart. The gold shields are sculpted to hold the inset rubies in the lion's eyes.

Those red eyes alone must be worth a small fortune. Well done Clyde, you have an eye for discovering hidden treasure."

The youngest thug was standing in front of the tall redhead. Sizing her up, he suddenly removed his hood. He was in his early twenties, thugly handsome with a dark blond mullet cut. A diamond sparkled in his left ear.

Looking at him, Glenda knew the guy; not the actual individual, but the type. She had humbled a few in her Norwegian skiing days. *He thinks he is the stuff girls dream of, that's why he took off the hood. Bet he drives a Harley to fill out the bad boy impression he wants to make. Pity the girl who climbs behind him to become his "BOB," the "Babe On Back." It will be a rough ride for her.*

The mullet guy semi-whispered, "I'm Hans. Please relax, I'm the good guy here. I'm the one you want to be friends with."

Glenda gave an accepting nod and subdued smile. "Thank you, Hans, I knew you were better than the others." *Sure you are. I can see you have many redeeming qualities.*

Standing close Hans carefully removed the pearl necklace while projecting his best winning bar-smile. The smile's message was, "I'm really a charming, great guy once you know me."

He paused for a moment before taking the necklace to the crew chief. His mind was racing to offer a parting, memorable phrase to the beautiful young woman but all he could think of was, *Tonto must return to Lone Ranger with treasure.* Somehow that didn't seem to register on the coolness meter. In the neighborhood bars, with a few drinks in him, he knew his one-liners were all classics. *Why can't I think of one now?*

Shrugging, Tonto returned to the Lone Ranger with his treasure. The leader held the offered pearls up to the light and inspected them. "These are the real deal and worth a small fortune. Well done, Hans."

The leader placed the collected jewelry on the table. Walking toward M he gave his crew a nod and smile. "Guard our treasure, men, while I take the measure and treasure of the man of the house…or houseboat as the case may be." His crew dutifully chuckled at their leader's humor. "I think our ship owner here has a lot to donate to our early retirement fund."

Standing in front of M, the leader paused to study the tall, dark-haired man more closely. The thug knew from past encounters that it was best to quickly size up every opponent. Occasionally even a nerd showed a flash of fight. The leader did not anticipate any resistance, but sometimes the presence of women gives a shot of manliness to even the mildest of guys.

At first glance the man was not threatening. His age seemed hard to judge, he had a youthful persona and face but must be older to have earned this boat. *Maybe he inherited it* was a flash answer. He was tall, with a solid body, but his attitude was placid. He looked even more docile than the other three victims. There was no fight in this guy, he was a sheep heading for the shearing barn.

Satisfied, the thug paused for a final moment and looked into M's eyes. He knew that a hard stare would further intimidate. For a moment time froze, and then something strange happened. The thug had a sudden bout of vertigo. The floor seemed to shift under him as he stared into eyes that were tunnels into a deep abyss. The thug instinctively placed his hand on the nearby table to steady himself.

M's eyes were looking back at him and through him. The eyes conveyed an ancient time and place, they did not convey modern Chicago or being on this boat at this time. They spoke of a world of ancient mysteries and terrors.

The man's eyes reminded the thug of Egyptian statues he had seen in museums as a young boy on field trips. While carved into stone, the pharaohs and their gods appeared to be looking directly at the passing visitors. Those powerful impressions returned to him as unsettling memories.

Museum visitors who stopped to study the staring faces found that an overlong look led to an uncomfortable shiver running through their body. "Move on mortal" was the message. The thug remembered himself and his classmates staying close to his teacher.

Shaking his head, the leader steadied himself. *All this Egyptian jewelry has me a little spooked, and this guy does look like he's carrying some old Middle Eastern DNA in him.*

If I believed in the mummy curse stuff from movies, I would guess that he's a reincarnated high priest. The name Imhotep comes to mind. But I don't buy into that whole superstitious nonsense. It's fun in movies but don't ever let yourself start to believe it.

The leader snapped out of his mood; he had an audience watching him. He pressed the blade against M's back hard enough to move the man forward. "OK Daddy Warbucks, show me the treasure room. Make my day and I'll permit your evening to turn out just fine."

"As you wish sir," M said, as he proceeded to the entry hallway.

Following closely, the leader stepped inside the hallway then turned to his crew. "Keep an eye on our friends while I bring more treasure to our booty board. I'm guessing we may need two tables. Watch that young guy, I think he has the beginnings of a hero inside him. Remind him that heroes never grow old, they only become remembered heroes after they mess up while showing off their bravery."

Traveler nodded to show that he understood the message and did his best to appear scared and humbled. Glenda kept her "poor me" face on. Virginia's face said that she accepted their fate and hoped this would all be over shortly.

Virginia, the college actress, had already thought about how she would improvise and change the final act to this creep-show. She knew the closing scene would be bad news for all of them. She knew a thug when she saw one, and she was looking at four. *Don't expect a happy outcome* went through her mind.

Virginia's mind and motherly emotions were focused on protecting her son, and of course, M and Glenda. She had devised a rescue plan. When the leader returned with the treasure, and everyone was staring at it, she would break and run through the open door.

Once outside she would dive over the side into the freezing canal waters. Braving the frigid waters she would find a ladder up to the street. There was no chance that any of the thugs would chase her once she was overboard. They were really cowards. With her exit they would panic, grab their loot, and motor away, leaving Traveler, Glenda, and M safe. Her plan was set.

Chapter 16

The Treasure Is All Yours

Following closely behind M, gladius in hand, the leader pushed open the door into the study. Following the tall Middle Eastern man inside, his first impression was that the ceiling seemed to be even higher than it was in the elegant dining room with its dancefloor. *Never noticed this superstructure from the water. I'd think the height would make the boat top-heavy, I guess modern materials can work miracles.*

Next, he noticed a lazy fire of glowing embers casting a warm radiance out of an elegant fireplace. The marble mantel and surround presented inlaid scenes of mythical characters. The flickering fire seemed to animate the figures; he shook his head to clear the impossible movements.

Taking in the room's surroundings he found himself reluctantly impressed. *Walt Disney would love this room. I already saw a red-haired Cinderella dancing in the ballroom, all that's needed is a king sitting here in front of his yule log sipping his mulled wine with a big guard mastiff beside him.* The leader was on the right trail in his fantasy; however, the imagined giant guard mastiff was a pup compared to what would soon appear.

At ease, the leader permitted the gladius blade to point down toward the floor. This was the time to send a conciliatory message. *Work with me and I'll work with you.*

Giving M his most sincere smile he said, "So Captain, it's just the two of us now. Let's act like men and we can quickly put this affair behind us. I'm a fair man and not a greedy man. Well, not too greedy. I'll take a reasonable portion, just our fair share, and you will recover the loss with your insurance. You can continue onward with your holiday party, and brag to your guests about how you bested me in hard negotiations."

Tightening his face and tone he continued, "It's time to show me the rest of the treasure. I'd advise doing it quickly; my men have limited patience when I'm not around."

While the leader had been making his pitch, M had slowly moved a short distance away from the hanging blade. He had projected the blade's strike zone if it involuntarily jerked upward. He knew that the leader would never make a controlled forward thrust. The leader's control of the blade would shortly be lost.

He returned the leader's smile with a deliberately weak look. "Are you quite sure you want to meet the treasure? I must tell you that trying to divide it will be impossible. It will all be yours, but I strongly recommend you choose to leave this treasure alone. It will seem cursed to you."

The leader felt an involuntary wince. *He's trying to spook me with that ancient Egyptian curse nonsense.* He continued to stare hard at M.

Continuing in a tentative voice M said, "Like you, I am a generous man. If you forget the treasure, I will offer a compensating gift that will carry you and your crew nicely through the holidays and beyond. I think a gift in cash, tax-free of course, of $80,000 would add a great deal of Christmas cheer to your holiday. That's $20,000 for each of you."

Giving a sly smile, M continued. "I will add to that a hidden bonus of $20,000 just for you. Let's call it an even $100,000. Accept and leave now without hard feelings on either side."

The leader listened to M's offer and gave a crocodile smile back. The bargaining phase had officially started, the leader understood this exercise. Bargaining, like chess, has an opening move but that is far from the endgame. The other person always offers an opening bid that appears generous, but the experienced bargainer knows it is no more than an opening move.

The leader immediately shook his head, he had decided to close the bargaining phase. The man had nothing to bargain with. "I'm afraid that won't do at all. The night is getting drawn-out and my men are restless by now. Rather than lengthen the evening further with pointless negotiations, let's examine the treasure. I suggest this is a good time for show, tell, and take."

To make his point, the leader swung the point of the blade in small circles while keeping the point aimed at the floor. M shrugged indicating his acceptance of the inevitable. "Well, treasure time it is then. The treasure is behind you beside the fire. Please remember that I made a generous offer in good faith."

The leader spun on his heels toward the fire. If there was a treasure, he had not seen it. Possibly the fire had distracted his eyes. *Hidden wall safe* flashed through his mind.

Staring at the fireplace and its surroundings he failed to see what the man was talking about. *Is this guy dumb enough to stall for time?* A mental jolt went through him. *Maybe this boat has a hidden mayday button and a police rescue boat is on its way.*

His reasonable-guy demeanor was discarded like an old coat. Staring into M's face his lips made a downward snarl, his demanding bully voice followed. "Tell me quickly where this hidden treasure is, my patience is exhausted."

"It is directly in front of you. If you turn slightly and lift your eyes, you will see it."

The leader paused for a moment, confused at the suddenly relaxed tone in the tall man's voice. He turned slightly to look again. Was that where the wall safe was located? As he looked up two impressions hit him.

First, the black wall beside the fire shimmered slightly then moved toward him. While his mind was struggling to understand the moving wall, his eyes lifted further up, widened, and a cry froze in his voice.

His second impression was clear, it was his approaching death. His stomach churned, his lower region wanted to collapse, his hand strength disappeared, and the gladius fell onto the carpeted floor.

A steam-shovel-sized mouth was opening and descending over him. Above the cavernous mouth, huge eyes looked down. The eyes told him his immediate future would be a living terror. Every mouse knows that look and accepts its fate; they only hope the cat's playtime will be short.

The mouth lowered and long incisor teeth lifted the man. He was held on each side of his shoulders in their grip. His head was pointed down and his view was limited. The view disappeared as his eyes squeezed shut.

His mind and breath were frozen, his heart was a triphammer. An ER doctor would conclude he was passing away from his racing heart and his record-breaking blood pressure.

Theo stood patiently in place while M opened the door leading to the bow deck. "I believe our friend could use a breath of fresh air. In fact, it appears he would benefit from any breath right now."

Theo padded through the door and proceeded to the elevated bow and extended the man beyond the blowers' comfort zone. The man felt the freezing wind off Lake Michigan hitting his face. He instinctively squinted out at the dark green waters.

Passing Christmas lights blinked from bordering towers and storefronts, but their beauty was lost on him. The hanging man was only aware of the gripping mouth, hot breath on his neck, and the approaching water.

Theo now lowered the hanging man further down into the frigid river spray that the ship's bow was churning up. The spray forced the man's mind out of his mental closet to an awareness of his plight. He could not stay wrapped in his mental cocoon; he was being forced to live in this moment. The moment would live with him for a lifetime, however long that would be.

"That's probably enough fresh air, the bow spray seems to have given him a nice wake-up call. I think we need to offer his crew a similar experience to teach them proper manners.

They have taken advantage of the Christmas season's goodwill in a most inappropriate manner."

Back inside the warm stateroom Theo set the leader down beside the fire. The man's body instinctively curled into a tight protective ball, as did his mind. Looking down at him M said, "Let's share the treasure with the rest of your crew."

Walking to the door M, opened it and observed the crew as they stood, impatiently waiting for their leader to come out with treasure-filled arms. M noted that while Glenda and Traveler were relaxed, sitting on a soft couch, Virginia had taken a chair near the door.

Seeing the door was opened to the stern deck M instantly concluded, *I believe our smart, brave Virginia is preparing to distract this miserable bunch of rogues with an icy plunge. I wonder if Traveler appreciates the many sides to his mother.*

With his appearance at the door, the crew was instantly on full alert and focused on him. "Where's the boss?" demanded the oldest of the three.

"He is struggling with the treasure and requests your help. The treasure surprised him, it was far more than even he had expected." The crew eagerly moved toward the hallway.

Before M stepped back inside, he looked at Virginia. He saw she was preparing herself for the icy water plunge. "Virginia, I suggest you relax. Please make yourself more comfortable. Join Edward and Glenda on that soft couch. This bitter evening is in its final stage, sweet dessert will be served shortly."

Virginia stared at M, knowing his words contained a hidden message for her. Just as she was trying to decipher the message Traveler stood up. "Mom that seat is way too hard, please join Glenda and me. I think M has the situation in hand."

Virginia stood and suddenly felt herself relax. She couldn't quite put her finger on why, but her instincts told her to accept that M was in charge. He would manage these thugs using some of his magician skills.

Satisfied that Virginia would stay on board, M remained beside the open passageway door. "Please enter gentlemen, join your leader and behold your share of the treasure. You will be stunned at what he has discovered."

The three thugs quickly passed by M. Part of their incentive for speed was their awareness that their boss would try to select and hide the most valuable pieces for himself. They all had the same thought as they entered: *There is no honor among us thieves, don't pretend otherwise.*

Now in the luxurious stateroom all three immediately looked at the comforting fire. "This is sure some boat!" A wide-eyed Hans blurted out. "It's even got a fire in the captain's stateroom, that's class."

In another moment as all three sets of eyes adjusted to the dim surroundings, they saw their leader curled up on the carpet. "What did you do to him?" the three shouted in unison.

The oldest man sprung in front of M. "Did you poison him?" With his face inches away, he snarled, "If you poisoned him that's the end for all of you. I told him not to trust you, you are one sneaky rich guy. You rich people think we're all just stupid street peasants but there're more smarts in us than you could ever imagine."

M stood still and looked the accuser back in the face. "Trust me, I never poisoned your friend. He has been slowly poisoning himself with rude, crude hostile acts from a young age. His own internal poison, call it the greed of a bully, has simply caught up with him."

This matter-of-fact, truthful insult was a slap in the man's face. As the thug was balling his fists for a strike, he heard a soft groan behind him. Staying in place, he turned his head and shoulders to identify the sound's source.

The source came from his two friends, both were standing like statues. Their faces were pictures of frozen fright with open mouths and bulging eyes, neither appeared to be breathing.

Could his comrades have been poisoned in this short a time? He quickly glanced around to see if there was an open bottle that they could have imbibed while he was confronting the man.

Then his eyes landed on the answer and he understood what was happening. The answer was something out of an adult's horror story, it could have come from an HP Lovecraft novel.

The answer appeared as an ancient monster. The black being filled the wall space from floor to ceiling. Saucer size eyes held all three intruders with their gaze. A bottomless mouth opened to show them where they were going.

To look into those eyes was to understand the ancient saying across the gates of Hell, "Abandon all hope…" When they had boarded the ship the four intruders had unknowingly passed through gates guarded by a dark god. Hope was lost. Their lives and their fates were no longer in their control. Control rested with the tall man and this being.

M reached his judgement quickly. "Theo, it is the Christmas season and we are, metaphorically speaking, the ghosts of Christmas present. I believed we have changed these wretched lives in the last few minutes.

"So far, they have just been street thugs. They are the grownup versions of cafeteria bullies, taking what they want and mixing in some adult nastiness. Left alone, however, they will become much worse in the coming years. We will not leave them alone.

"I choose to believe they are still young enough to turn their lives around. My guess is that each of them will make a sharp turn in their downhill road after tonight. This is a season for gentleness and grace. I think they can be released to their boat. How find you?"

Theo vibrated his agreement with M's judgement. Theo understood the benefit of softened punishment following a person's insights into their past actions and the resulting consequences. How many people wish they could have a do-over because of some selfish or nasty thing they had done? That honest, harsh self-reflection has never been better expressed than in Dickens' classic about Scrooge the miser in *A Christmas Carol*.

With judgement passed, M reached down and lifted the leader to his feet. He lifted the large man easily from the floor using a single arm. He paused a moment holding him straight out with the one arm. Twitching feet danced above the floor. Then he slowly lowered the feet to the surface.

The four were beyond stunned at the strength in his single arm. He was a Samson or Hercules. They realized he could have easily bested all of them at the same time. His final demonstration of power was to remove each gladius and bend it back into a tightly closed iron loop.

While they stared at M's power, Theo had faded back down to become a large cat resting in front of the fire. Their eyes darted from M to the resting cat and back again. Theo's look sent each of them a message from Shakespeare's *Hamlet*, "There are more things in heaven and Earth, Chicago pirates, than are dreamt of in your philosophy."

M broke the silence. "Gentlemen, I believe each of you has received a most beneficial experience this evening. Consider it a life-altering Christmas present, far better than any bike or pony. Now we part company. I suggest you move quickly to your boat, avoid eye contact." With a bright smile he added, "Needless to say, leave the jewelry on the table."

Four heads vigorously nodded in agreement, then the leader sank down to take a knee in front of M. "Whoever or whatever you two are, you have assuredly changed my life. Something just happened that's beyond my understanding. Maybe there is a Santa Claus or a Christmas spirit of sorts. If there is, I think it's you. Please expect to see me on your 'good boy' list next year...and all the coming years."

Each of the three standing men immediately followed their leader in taking a knee, bowing a head, and crossing themselves. With heads bowed each of the four glanced at the resting fireplace cat. Each later claimed they had received a nod from the dark feline and had felt a warmth spread throughout their body.

Each knew with certainty there was magic in this world. Each knew how fortunate they were to have experienced it and survived. Their exit came as fast as they could hustle out to board their boat.

Watching them leave, Virginia was stunned. *How was this threatening trauma turned around? What magic did M use?* Traveler and Glenda simply thought, *Well done, M.*

Chapter 17

Earlier Times

Once the crew had departed M became the affable, relaxed host. "Well, that bit of excitement has me ready for the double D's: dessert and discussion."

Each of the three guests returned to the serving table to find M standing beside it with a large cutting knife. "While it is a brisk night outside, the special dessert this evening is Baked Alaska. Fear not, the chill of ice-cream is balanced by the flaming sauce. You may warm your hands in the flame if the ice cream gives you a little shiver."

Cutting thick slices of the rich dessert, M placed a piece for each into deep china bowls. Clapped his hands the sauce burst into multicolored flames. Virginia jumped at the appearance of the flames and a smiling M responded, "Forgive my occasional desire to act on the center stage. The magician in me can't help the urge to show off with a bit of table magic. Now let the dessert magic begin. Bon appétit!"

As the first serving disappeared all four companions took deep breaths, leaned back into the soft leather chairs, and were ready to discuss the evening's events.

Virginia started the discussion with the obvious question. "M, how did you manage that? They owned me from the minute they showed up."

M gave an understanding look back, "Yes, they were intimidating as only bullies can be. The shoe dropped when the leader joined me in my stateroom. I was simply waiting to separate him from his crew.

"I keep a semi-automatic handgun in my desk drawer. He assumed I was scared witless and retrieving valuables, then out came the gun. It is a frightening piece. Like Wyatt Earp, I am quite adept with it. He saw my confidence and his own wilted.

"All I had to say was, 'Never bring a knife to a gunfight.' Like all bullies facing a stronger force, he caved in. His crew immediately knew that the tables had turned when they joined him."

Virginia nodded. "Well, of course. I should have guessed you had something up your sleeve. You are a lifesaver, Mr. Magic."

Traveler was past M's faux explanation and focused on his own desires. "Mom, is it OK if I return to Alaska?" Virginia laughed and nodded. With the nod he stood and moved to the dessert serving table.

As he was returning with a heaping bowl, Glenda gave him a sweet smile. "Looks like you're bringing half of Alaska back with you, be careful you don't sprain your wrist."

Virginia was amused. *I guess she can poke fun at him, he certainly seems to like the attention. Of course, Mom's comments would just annoy him.*

M saw it was time to change the pirate subject. "So Virginia, you were a drama major in college. Where did your career go?" Glenda sat straighter; she was eager to hear the answer. She had similar questions about Virginia's life choices, and maybe her own future ones.

"After graduating I had to make a decision regarding my professional career. Emotionally I loved acting, but practically speaking I needed to be gainfully employed, bills must be paid. So I made the sensible choice. I used my computer degree to land an interesting job as a consultant for a national technology firm.

"My job required that I learn their computerized sales system. Then I got to travel nationally to present the system to various clients. The travel part was a lot of fun, plus I racked up a lot of freebies from my air mileage."

Glenda nodded enthusiastically at this. She could visualize herself flying on important missions, always going first class of course. "I can sure see the fun and excitement in that life. Why leave it?"

Virginia smiled at Glenda's reaction, of course flying around to big cities sounded like a Hollywood movie to the young girl. "Deciding to leave the travel world of business was easy. I quickly tired of airport and hotel life. You spend a lot of time waiting to board planes, then breathe the bad circulated air. Hotels offer two things at night, unhealthy rich foods and drink, followed by slamming doors at one in the morning.

"Trust me, the novelty of constant travel wears thin quickly. Most importantly though, you lose contact with people that matter. Bar acquaintances are just that, sad ships passing in the night. A year was enough for me. I chose Daniel and a family over the life of planes and hotels."

Seeing a questioning look crossing Glenda's face, she continued. "No, I did not become a house vegetable, I stayed as busy as I was in business. When Eddie arrived, I began homeschooling him at an early age. Before he headed off to first grade, I had already taught him basic math and how to read using phonics. Eddie and I continued to be a study team through middle school, we worked at learning and it was lots of fun for both of us."

M was listening with a keen interest in Virginia's story. "Well, my strongest compliments to your choices and efforts. You have indeed created quite an amazing young man. Now a final question, given that Edward is basically of age to move on, what is the next step in your own life?"

Virginia gave a relaxed laugh. "I know what you're really asking. Don't worry, I'm still young in body and mind and have no intention of being a successful doctor's idle country club wife.

"I've been thinking about this for a while and know what's next. I am going to take a shot at writing fantasy fiction for young people. I've always been intrigued by the idea of magic.

There is a lot more to this world than modern technology gives us." She looked M directly in the eye, saying, "As an amazing magician you know this, of course."

As Virginia talked all three of her table companions became silent. She was describing their world living with Theo.

Is Mom prescient? wondered Traveler.

Did Traveler inherit his magic aptitude from his mom? speculated Glenda.

Did Theo and I miss an ally in Virginia? wondered M.

Traveler broke the table's quiet mood. In a soft voice he said, "Mom, I'm tired. This night has been nothing short of amazing, but I'm ready for bed. What do you think?"

Virginia immediately nodded and M responded, "I anticipated this was closure time for the night's festivities. While we were enjoying our dessert and conversation our ship has been returning to our dock. Your carriage will be waiting… as well as a great night's sleep."

Just as M finished, the boat made a subtle bumping motion. They had docked. Traveler stood first, came to his seated mother, gave her a slight bow, and offered his hand. Virginia accepted the offer, rising with the smoothness she had displayed many times on the dancefloor.

Glenda inwardly smiled at Traveler's courtesy. *I guess he knows that he is forever indebted to her. Good for him in so many ways.*

As the three came down the exit ramp M stayed behind waving a vigorous farewell. "The driver will be careful in this weather. I'm staying on board to wrap a few things up."

Virginia turned to face M and gave a returning dramatic wave and her best smile. "Take care, M. This is a night that will be retold many nights in future holiday times! Daniel will love it. So many thanks!" With that Virginia entered the limo as the driver held the door for her. Traveler and Glenda gave smaller waves then slipped inside.

As the driver began the return trip Glenda said, "Driver, please go to the Drake first, then drop me off after."

"As you wish," answered the driver.

Once at the Drake, the driver stepped outside to assist Virginia. Traveler followed. The driver quickly re-entered the warm vehicle, then looked in the mirror for instructions.

"Driver, would you please just drive around for about thirty minutes, then come back here?"

"Of course." *Well, I think a little nighttime hijinks are going on between these two once Mom's in bed.*

When the driver returned to the hotel, he knew he was proven right. The young man was waiting outside with his coat collar turned up. "Young master looks like he's freezing. I'll get the door open quickly."

"Relax, stay seated. Young master can live with a little Chicago winter weather, let's not baby him."

The driver laughed. "As you wish Miss, and here he comes."

Traveler opened the door, then shook the snow from his head and coat before sliding inside. For a second he considered sharing the snow with the seated Glenda, then wisely decided not to. "Home, Jeeves," he said with a smile in his voice.

"Home would be at the corner of...?" asked the driver. Leaning forward, Glenda give the cross streets.

When they approached the intersection, the driver slowed. "Is this where you want to be? I don't think anything is going on around here. Are you sure you have the correct address?"

"Absolutely, we're right where we need to be. Our holiday party time never ends. We'll hop out here, and thank you for your service," said Traveler.

When the limo stopped, the two slid out the sidewalk-side door into a gusting Chicago midnight wind. "Wow!" they said in unison. They put their heads down and began to walk cautiously. Owners are responsible for clearing their own snow-covered front walks, but it's an honor system. Freezing wind and snow often bury the honor.

As they cautiously proceeded, Traveler suddenly felt an arm wrap around his arm. *Balance or companionship?* he wondered. Either way he was quite pleased with the closeness. His mother would not have been surprised at all.

Chapter 18

Shared Driver Tales

The limo driver watched the two in his headlights as they began to fade into the falling snow. He continued to track them up the narrow, snow-covered street until his windshield wipers suddenly got stuck. The last thing he saw was red hair fluttering below a festive holiday cap.

I need new wipers, he thought as he looked down at the control panel to increase the wiper speed. The wipers responded by slinging heavy snow off the glass. Satisfied with the cleared windshield he looked out. The two passengers were no longer in sight. He hit his bright lights to cast a long glimmer through the downward-drifting flakes. The two were simply gone. Impossible. Where were they?

He recalled a conversation he had the prior night at Saint Monica's church. He and his cab driver friend routinely met there after their workday was finished. A little pew meditation was followed by coffee and small talk. Last night his friend told an unbelievable tale.

According to his cabbie friend, he had picked up two young people, coincidently at the Drake. He said he had dropped them off on a semi-deserted street late in the evening. "I was concerned for their welfare. I knew there was no place open on the street. I stayed in my cab to be sure they knew where they were going.

"One minute they were walking up the street and the next they were gone. I got out of my cab and went to their footprints. Believe it or not, they simply ended in the middle of a solid wall on the street."

The limo driver recalled the tale now, but without chuckling like he had done the prior evening. He remembered saying to his friend, "Describe them, please."

The cabbie friend did so in detail. "Both were tall, and the girl's long red hair was distinctive. The boy seemed mature in his eyes, well beyond his apparent age."

After his cabbie friend had concluded the tale both chuckled, quipping back and forth. "Never drink eggnog and drive, you can lose your license."

"Or worse, hit an angel."

The limo driver was suddenly anxious to tell his own tale to his friend. He parked in the nearby empty church lot and found his friend in their normal pew. He greeted him then motioned that they should retire to their coffee shop.

Once inside the shop the limo driver quickly began his tale, he had to get it off his chest. "I would tell no one this experience except you, my friend. I only share this story because of your tale last night.

"I believe I drove them this evening. I had the same experience. One minute they were walking up the street, the next they were gone. They were my fare from a wealthy man of Middle Eastern descent. I have always felt he comes from a different place than our world.

"I believe there is a place neither you nor I have ever imagined. I know you are as sane as am I. We have shared similar experiences that are not explainable. I think we may be well-served to go back to Saint Monica's for a final prayer… or two."

The two left their still-full coffee cups and were quickly back in the quiet church.

Chapter 19

Ambush Stories

Sleep was great for the teens. Their sanctuary beds welcomed them. While sleeping, their books were fascinated by their recent river pirate adventure.

They emerged from deep, long sleeps with high energy and headed for breakfast. They were eager to eat then immerse themselves in their studies. Overnight the books had hinted at powerful new powers coming if they kept themselves fully committed to meeting the demands of their instructors. *Nothing worth doing is ever easy* was the books' constant mantra.

Settling at the breakfast table beside the cascading fountain, Traveler started the morning with, "OK M, spill the goods. Exactly why did those street toughs suddenly decide to leave? I've never seen you with a gun, that sounded like an answer for Mom."

Glenda was ready to indulge herself with a piece of the thick bacon when she paused. "Yes M, tell us what really happened, we're dying to know. I thought I would need to make a 'man overboard' move on the young guy who kept staring at me."

M paused to enjoy a thick slice of yellow Crenshaw melon. "Well, there is a saying that is very apropos for last evening's events. 'Fools rush in where wise men fear to go.'

"Those four young fools were certain of their control of our ship. They thought they saw an easy ambush of a rich, defenseless holiday ship, ripe for looting. They could never imagine the guests included three passengers of surpassing physical competency…not to mention a god.

"Many young schoolchildren learn, painfully learn I must add, as early as kindergarten that playmates may be nice, but not to push them. They may push back harder than you would imagine."

"Yeah, M, I learned that lesson a long time ago," acknowledged Traveler. "But you still haven't explained what happened in the room when the door was shut."

"In a word, 'Theo.' The leader was suddenly living a nightmare when our big tabby cat became a twelve-foot tall Bast and held him over the river. When Theo brought him back inside, he instinctively curled up on the floor. The other three followed a similar path when they entered and met our resident god.

"I suggested, and Theo agreed, to teach the young pirates a lesson about the risks of an ambush. It was a lesson that will change their lives for the better. Former President Teddy Roosevelt is famously quoted as saying, 'Speak softly and carry a big stick.' Nobody's stick measures up to Theo's."

Pausing for another slice M continued, "Well, almost nobody. The fire creature host is the exception, it also carries a very big stick. Its stick first appeared in its ambush on Theo. Theo shared this story with me many centuries ago and he is ready to share it with you.

"Before I pass the storytelling to Theo permit me to set the stage.

"Our universe acts in many ways like a huge casino. The casino throws a wide net of randomness across the entire universe. Big and small bets are constantly being made. Many bets are placed following careful analysis, yet outcomes are often the result of chance. When an unexpected ambush occurred, Theo had to scramble to survive.

"Scrambling to survive was new to Theo. Theo and his brethren creators had never had to consider their survival before. They entered this new universe without concern for any possible risk to their own existence. They had always existed and believed they always would. After all, they defined existence.

"To them this was simply another universe they had created. How could there be a danger? But there was. To achieve the desired unpredictability, they had turned authorship of events over to the universe. In so doing they relinquished control of its actions.

"For those dark gods, centered within their black holes, their existence was unknowingly assured. The power of their enclosing gravitational fields provided protective shields against any threat. They never experienced a threat, they only observed.

"Unaware of the creature's existence, Theo was alone and vulnerable. His vulnerability to an ambush was greatly heightened. He was immersed in developing potential companions and this experiment held his total attention. As they say about knocked-out boxers, 'He never saw it coming.'

"This is a good time to pass the storytelling baton to Theo."

The giant cat proceeded to place itself between Glenda and Traveler. They instinctively placed hands on the thick fur and settled back for his tale. With a deep vibration Theo projected himself into the two teens' minds as well as M's.

"I was alone for the first time in my existence. While my observations of the developing star system and my planet captivated me, I found I missed companionship. Eons of earth time passed and even gods get lonely.

"I was pleased that the animal life was evolving, and I looked to it for possible companionship. As I hopefully studied the increasingly complex animal life, I sadly found that none would work. There was a diversity of powerful, massive land creatures but their brains could not adapt to the necessary changes." *Dinosaurs*, flashed through each teen's mind as Theo continued, "Nevertheless, I waited and hoped."

"This universe is so unpredictable. An unexpected event occurred that changed everything. A huge meteor moving through the solar system hit the earth. It was a random event.

It extinguished many advanced, dominant life forms, including the enormous land-based alphas. This extinction of the alphas became an opportunity for new and promising life to evolve.

"I watched evolution at work over many millennia. Finally, I saw there were potential companion candidates among the evolving human lines. I proceeded to experiment with selected candidates. I believe the computer term is to 'upgrade' them.

"Sadly, even the most basic upgrades destroyed the subjects. Either their minds or their bodies melted down with my most basic upgrade insertions.

"Fortunately, I am not hampered by time constraints. I continued to experiment, but with a great deal more caution. My early failures saddened me as I value all life, so my testing became more selective. I became much more adept at identifying potential candidates without destroying them.

"Eventually my search identified humans whose large, balanced brains and powerful bodies indicated they could potentially accept my changing their DNA. You have studied these early humans called 'Neanderthals.'

"I found the Neanderthals were the only one of various humanoid species that offered the potential to remain stable with my insertions. Even then I had only found two that could adapt to the upgrades. These two potential adepts were infants when I discovered them.

"With the initial upgrades accepted, I began to slowly expand their capabilities. The results fascinated me. They were acquiring skills and powers far beyond their fellow Neanderthals and human cousins.

"Interestingly, their Neanderthal bodies grew in both size and strength to match their brain growth. They were now giants in the true meaning of that word, both physically and mentally. They were a new species, and I modestly named them, 'Homo superior.'

"At some point in their growth, they moved from being interesting experiments to my desired companions. We could communicate. I was no longer alone.

"They viewed me as their father and I gladly accepted that role. Of course, I continued to monitor the planet but was deeply absorbed with the continuing development of my children. I was fascinated to see how far they could advance.

"It was that focus that blinded me to the fire creature's ambush.

"The creature launched its attack against me but also my children. A battle of powers began as my children and I defended ourselves.

"My children were committed to protecting their father and showed no concern for their own welfare. I experienced an emotion you call pride and renewed my efforts to protect all three of us. In hindsight the creature's error was diverting its focus from just me to include my children.

"As the battle progressed, I realized the outcome was increasingly uncertain, as the creature seemed to grow in power. Every battle also has a deciding point and they can come quickly. My battle strategy jumped from defend to what is commonly referred to as 'scramble.' Scrambling was not a skill I had any experience with. I had to scramble to survive.

"My actions were for survival, first for my children, then myself. I had a brief time to scramble as the host was preparing for a final blow against us. I placed my children in a deep state of hibernation inside a frozen mountain of ice. They would remain at rest until I called to them.

"I then fled to a structure I had built centuries earlier as an observation site. The structure was shaped like a reclining lion with the face of a man. I designed the shape to attract early travelers for my study.

"The structure still exists today and generates a constant source of speculation among archeologists regarding who built it." With a mental chuckle he added, "You know it as the Sphinx. The structure was placed near a large river, called the Nile. This was a fertile region where humans were already coming together to form early communities.

"Once within the structure I placed myself inside a thick lead box. The lid created a perfect seal, shielding my vibrations from the seeking foe. The host would find no vibrational trail leading to my resting place. Even so I needed to remain inside and dormant.

"I remained in the box inside the Sphinx structure for many millennia. While encased I reflected on the threat of the creature, and possible ways to defeat it. I knew I needed allies starting with my children; however, even if I upgraded my children further, I would still need additional allies.

"Finally, I re-entered the world of humans with great caution. To my relief the seeking host appeared to be gone. It was likely searching for me in other nearby regions of the galaxy. Of course, scouts and portals always presented a threat, but now that I was forewarned, I could avoid their detection.

"Once outside of my sanctuary I affirmed that I had chosen the statue's location well. I was surrounded by thriving communities of humans. My Sphinx was now worshiped as a god. The respect for the god was transferred to small felines, called cats, and they benefited greatly from their resemblance to my Sphinx. At the risk of making a bad pun, I was a godsend to cats."

"I dedicated myself to finding potential allies, M was the first and now both of you are with us. I will confront the creature at a time and place of my choosing; my ambush will be with my allies."

With the tale over Theo shook his thick coat and padded to the fireplace, becoming the cat at the hearth. Glenda and Traveler sat spellbound until Traveler ventured, "The Riddle of the Sphinx is solved. No archeologist will ever believe it." Glenda nodded back in agreement. Theo purred.

Chapter 20

Another Road Trip

With Theo gone, the three settled into breakfast. Each of them needed time to reflect on Theo's tale, eating was secondary. Even though M had heard it before he was still captivated. Finally, when the food and reflection time was over, thoughts were shared.

Traveler was the first to speak. "What an amazing story! Ambushes, even for gods, are a great challenge. You never know when the jinn will appear or how to defend against them. All you can do is scramble and hope."

Nodding, M added, "Ambushes often have unpredictable outcomes regardless of the attacker's planning. Last night's ambush resulted in an unexpected outcome for the pirates. In their case they did not get the expected loot but something much better, a life outside of Theo's mouth, and outside of prison where they were surely headed."

Glenda nodded. "We've got way too much ambush experience already. We barely escaped a jinn ambush in our entry alley. Then in the Dark Ages fortress we executed our own ambush. Our ambush was carefully planned and it did work out, but just barely. It only succeeded with the help of a giant. It could have easily gone the jinn's way. The good news is that we survived and advanced in terms of our ability to accept further book upgrades."

"Speaking of growing I believe the books are ringing the bell for class." Glancing at Traveler, Glenda added, "Race you to the alcove!"

As Glenda rose and was bracing to jump over the table, M looked at her and motioned to please sit back down. At the same time, a now tiger-sized Theo had risen from the hearth and padded over to join them.

A smiling M nodded at Theo. "Well, the main man has decided to rejoin us. Prepare yourselves, he has another message for us."

Glenda and Traveler simultaneously felt their bodies tense. An unexpected message from Theo always portended something scary was going to be dropped on them. They looked at each other and gave knowing winces and accepting shrugs. They waited for the Theo shoe, or rather the Theo paw, to drop on them.

M continued, "There is an old but true expression, 'History often repeats itself.' We are facing a dire situation that seems to be a most unwelcome ghost from Christmas past. Brace yourselves for a walk down memory lane."

Traveler was tired of bracing himself and blurted out, "Ok M, we know this will not be a pleasant memory-lane walk in the park, just throw it at us."

"Direct as always, Traveler. Thank you, that makes my job a bit easier. No need to sugarcoat anything with you two.

"You and Glenda must return to the same region of Transylvania, about twenty years after your prior visit. There is a darkness that is again rising from that region. Your old fortress is close to the source."

While Glenda was focusing all her attention on M, her hand was buried in Theo's fur for comfort. Her mind churned as bad memories flooded back. She remembered watching the jinn interrogate, then kill, a simple soldier. The killing was as impersonal as a farmer killing a chicken for dinner.

"Why do I think I know where this is going," said Traveler. "Are you telling us that the imprisoned jinn has escaped?"

"That is likely. However, there is a far greater concern than a single fire beast. There is a vibration arising that Theo identifies as a gateway portal that is now functioning."

Glenda tensed. "Does that mean there are now more of those wretched fire beasts to deal with? One was more than a threat. We only defeated it by ambushing it with our secret weapon, the giant Olaff. Without our giant, Traveler and I would not have had a chance."

Traveler nodded in agreement. "Glenda is so right, that fire beast is an absolute monster. There is not a trace of mercy in it, and it appears indestructible. At least for humans. Are you telling us that there is now a gang of them?"

"No, I'm not saying that. Theo does not know exactly what is there. Right now, all Theo knows is that a portal has been constructed."

M was studying each of them and their reactions to the threat. He saw that they were accepting the challenge without further pushback. His face reflected both respect and pride.

Sighing he said, "I am beyond pleased with each of you! You reacted as Theo and I had hoped to this unacceptable threat. You are both far beyond the two young students who first entered our sanctuary. You are truly proving yourselves to be the allies we have been seeking for many millennia."

As M praised the two, Theo's vibrations were a deepening presence that filled both mind and body of the two teens. The vibrations spoke of Theo's confidence that the two would meet and overcome the threats. As the vibrations continued, each teen felt their tension and fear disappear. There is nothing like praise and belief from a god to lift your spirits.

Watching the two teens, M saw both students were ready to move forward. He could now deliver the good news.

"Your prior visit to oppose the single jinn was necessary to advance your development, this is different. This time Theo expects you to return with your findings without a confrontation. On the contrary, information is the sole goal of this mission. Observe at the furthest distance you can. Keep stealth ready to hide from all threats, whether human or jinn.

"It is critical to your mission that you determine the status of the activated portal. Determine the degree to which it has already brought in additional jinn. Once you know the strength of the jinn's forces you may see a weakness. When you return you may suggest a strategy for Theo's attack.

"Theo understands there may be no such observed weakness. If Theo sees an opportunity to attack before the full host is deployed, he may take the offensive. What we cannot accept is an outcome where Theo attacks in error and is met by the waiting host. Your observations are critical to determining Theo's course of action."

Traveler was carefully absorbing M's message, and a frown appeared. "Please explain to us, why doesn't Theo do the onsite assessment himself? Why rely on lesser beings like Glenda and me when his very existence is at risk?"

M accepted the question with a nod of understanding, he knew Traveler was not trying to avoid a dangerous situation with a deflecting question. It was a valid question. Looking at both teens M replied, "In a single, overworked word, 'ambush.'

"These beings can sense Theo's presence just as he senses theirs. If enough of the host is present, then the jinn will lay a trap that Theo may not escape. This cosmic game of cat and mouse has been going on for a very long time.

"Time is different for Theo and these fire beings. Each side only needs to wait until there is a perfect opportunity to strike. Individual fire beings, or small groups of them, are a manageable foe for our mighty Theo; however, when their full host is present, it is unstoppable even for him. He only escaped once by the host diverting its attention, that won't happen again."

Glenda accepted this answer with a sad nod. "I'm starting to better understand why Theo needs allies. Somehow, I think the allies he needs should be far more powerful than simple scouts like Traveler and me. We got lucky last time with the jinn we subdued."

For the first time M visibly relaxed. He leaned back and gave a soft chuckle. "Rest assured, you are already much stronger allies than you think. Your development is ongoing. Your stealth is far more powerful. You are a master of languages without ever studying them.

"You are not necessarily aware of your continuing growth. Committed students in all disciplines grow day by day but frequently fail to see their progress. In sports, coaches keep daily diaries of these improvements.

"Your books are coaches as well as teachers. They recognize your daily efforts and growth. They inform Theo of progress at the end of each day. Theo views you as essential allies, you are invaluable to him and his survival. You are now more capable than you know."

Accompanied by a purring Theo, M concluded, "Equally important, he is very bonded to you. You are his children; your safety is paramount to him." Both students were now erect in their chairs and visibly basking in M's praise and Theo's purring.

Glenda finally broke the love-in with a quiet, "Well, my breakfast is pretty well-digested M, so I guess we should get on with the mission. Details please, and no sugarcoating."

Chapter 21

Details Sans Sugar

Settling settled back in his chair M took a slow, deep breath and began. "As I said, you are revisiting a region you know well. It remains as you previously found it, a heavily forested, mountainous region. While many parts of Europe have had forests cleared and converted into farmland and cities, the Carpathian Mountains remain largely untouched since the last ice age.

"The center of the portal-vibration is coming from an elevated area, possibly a mountain peak. That is the extent of what we know. You should proceed with great caution. Remember, dangerous natural forces are at work beyond the jinn. Forest beasts and human beasts are in abundance.

"You will arrive in a heavily forested spot that is near a river. The river will offer a frame of reference as well as possible transportation and, of course, drinking water."

As she listened Glenda had shifted acceptance gears, "Please M, we know the drill. Should we pack up some food supplies, blankets, and appropriate period clothing now?"

"Done and done. As the World War I soldiers' song goes, I have 'packed up your old kit bags.' The least I could do was to send you into the fray with basic survival supplies." M then pointed to a far part of the room. "The kit bags are resting over by the travel circle and await your departure."

Traveler cleared his throat, he was not quite ready to move out. "We know about the jinn threats, tell us more about the human threats. The Huns, led by Attila, were the great invaders last time. Who do we worry about now?"

"You are coming into the region around twenty years after your prior visit. Attila has passed away and his three sons rule the Hun Empire. The Huns continue to be a powerful, dangerous presence.

"Opposing the Huns is a gathering of Germanic tribes, notably the Gepids. The Gepids are a conquering tribe of East Germanic people closely related to the famous Goths. Both Huns and Gepids are dangerous, avoid both is my advice."

"Goths? Oh yeah, I know all about the Goths," laughed Traveler. "There was a Goth group in my high school that liked to darken their eyes and wear crazy spiked hair. We jocks poked fun at them."

"Well, nobody poked fun at the real Goths, or their cousins the Gepids. These were fierce, conquering people.

"The history of the region, we call it Romania today, reached its cultural apex under Rome. The Romans ruled the vast region for close to 200 years. They made Romania, or Dacia as it was known back then, a Roman province in AD 106. They ruled until they left the region in 271."

"Why did they leave?" asked Glenda.

"In a word, Goths. The Romans were locked into longstanding battles with various Germanic tribes for hundreds of years. To better protect the core of the empire, the legions were gradually removed from outlying regions such as England and Romania."

"So how did Rome manage to control this remote place for so long against those fierce Germans?" asked Traveler.

"Technology and discipline. The Romans were always outnumbered, they used their engineering skills to give them the advantage. Romans engineers could build with stone while the locals used wood. The Romans built impregnable stone fortresses that could fend off attacks from masses of barbarian warriors. Think of the Roman emperor Hadrian's seventy-three-mile-long stone wall. It was built in northern England to contain the fierce Scots. Parts of that wall still stand today.

"Once the legions left Romania, the entire region was up for grabs. There was a power vacuum and numerous warlords competed to replace Rome. The first winner in this regional game of King of the Carpathian Mountains were the Huns. Attila secured the region for his tribe."

"Yeah, we learned all about good old Attila in our last visit," said Traveler. "A nice guy who killed and plundered his way across a lot of Europe. He had his army ready to sack Rome before Pope Leo met him and somehow convinced him to go away."

M nodded. "Well, all empires fall sooner or later. Back in those days, as well as today, the declines were frequently the result of political infighting. Lots of leaders and their followers want that top position, and that is what happened to the Huns with Attila gone. At the time in which you are arriving, the region is an ongoing battleground between the Gepids and the sons of Attila. Don't get caught in the crossfire."

Traveler rose from his chair and headed toward his room. "I know this travel-drill M, let me get my period stuff from my room, visit the throne, and I'll be back in a jiffy." Glenda rose at the same time and headed to her room.

M watched them disappear past their study alcove. Turning to Theo he said, "We've done what we can, now it's up to them. Their books gave them a final boost of energy last night. They'll appreciate that boost with the challenges to come."

Theo watched his two allies as they disappeared. He agreed with M, their development was very strong, they reminded him of his two children from an earlier age. Theo was also pleased with the role his books played in training the two teens. The books routinely absorbed and analyzed all aspects of the teens' development, then presented their findings to Theo.

Beyond giving feedback, the books followed Theo's critical charge to advance the teens as rapidly as their evolving brains and bodies could adapt. *Keep them physically and mentally close to being overloaded every day, but not to a breaking point.* The books understood and complied; small upgrades happened every study day.

As the teens grew, the books were pleased to report that their naturally balanced brain halves were evolving into a single organ. The books confirmed that this ever-adapting organ now could learn and develop powers faster than was previously possible.

Theo was greatly pleased with this news. Their continued development was essential for them to reach the level needed to join him as powerful allies in the ultimate battle. The wild card in their development was the Casino and its randomness. Even Theo could not predict with certainty the highest stage they could reach. On the upside, if they continued their growth, they could become demigods themselves. Alternatively, they could short-circuit and burn out.

Even with powerful allies Theo knew that in this unpredictable universe he needed to accept that certain unacceptable outcomes could happen. Theo's reflections on his own possible fate quickly ended. Even gods do not dwell on those unpleasant possibilities.

Shaking his massive head, he padded softly to the travel ring to stand beside M. The two stood patiently, waiting for the teen travelers.

Traveler and Glenda returned from their rooms dressed in period attire. Beyond blending in, their outfits would help them manage the challenges of moving through the rough terrain. Durable boots were essential for walking on sharp-edged rocks and across chilling streams. Strong cotton and heavy wool garments offered warmth and protection.

Glenda was the first to step into the travel circle. Stepping up and over the elevated lip, she lifted her long coat with a little chuckle. "Feels like I'm wearing a suit of armor and heading into battle." Motioning to the arriving Traveler she added, "Time to climb aboard, this train is ready to leave the station."

M smiled at Traveler and nudged him forward. "Into the fray, young Lochinvar, your damsel awaits."

Traveler, the brave knight, knew that there was no time remaining for Lochinvar to delay. At the same time a little mouse-voice whispered, *Slow down, there may be more history you should ask about to be better prepared.*

Of course, he knew this voice of caution was just a nervous six-year-old boy venturing out on a dark Halloween night. Looking at a confident Glenda, he dismissed the six-year-old's voice and stepped over the lip.

Chapter 22

Not Quite Graceful Landings

Once Traveler was inside the knee-high walled circle, Glenda took charge. "I know you would secretly like to waltz with me in here, but this is a small dancefloor and your boots tell me to decline your offer. You may, however, hold on and imagine the music is just starting. Pretend we're taking a shot at doing the tango."

Traveler did as suggested. He took the offered hand and pressed it against his chest. Using his free hand, he pulled Glenda's heavy coat against his own greatcoat. Once they were pressed together they joined bracelets and their world changed as Theo worked his dimensional magic.

Both youths instinctively shut their eyes hard and clenched their jaws tight. M had assured them that they could relax and keep their eyes open, but primal instincts overrode his words. Stomachs seemed to be intent on crawling up and out of mouths, ears, and noses.

For the briefest of moments both wondered what their stomachs knew that they didn't. Could Theo have pressed the wrong buttons for time and place? Would they arrive at the bottom of an ocean or inside a mountain? Would they arrive in a world of hungry velociraptors as a tasty midday meal?

Time and space, as they experienced it in their day-to-day universe, was not what they were experiencing now. They were far beyond being disoriented physically and mentally. While they labored to keep heart and soul together, Theo the maestro played the cosmic travel song as only a creator god could.

Their awareness of real time and space returned with a jolt. Their boots arrived first, followed by their bodies. Both found their arrival position was lying flat on the greeting ground. Stomachs kissed the soft soil while minds kissed the journey's end.

At the end of the travel experience, they were happy to find they were still two human beings. They desperately needed to re-establish all normal frames of reference for mental balance and body balance. They needed to bring all five senses to bear to help their bodies acclimate to this reality.

The first returning sense was touch. That sense reassured them they were in one piece pressed against the ground. The next sense was sight and they saw they were in a dense forest, surrounded by huge ancient trees. The trees rose to block out the direct sunlight while promising protection from showers.

Quickly following touch and sight was smell. The surrounding forest was an ocean of drifting odors ranging from sweet pine needles to ground flowers. As noses explored they imagined being in a Christmas shop filled with incense sticks, scented candles, spice bags, and other olfactory delights that welcomed the holiday season.

Taste was not ready to be tested at the moment. That would come later when they sampled M's food offerings.

Sound was the last sense and it was a welcome one. They listened to the forest's musical symphony as birds of every size and temperament were shouting out their songs. Some songs embraced the day's glory while others were sending "come hither" calls to possible mates. A few of the loudest were the designated sentries giving shrieking intruder alert calls.

The birds reminded Traveler and Glenda of morning talk show hosts. Each host was a preening bird trying to distinguish itself from the other talking heads. "Look at me, listen to me, I am witty, wise, and glorious," was the message common to both birds and TV hosts.

Reflecting on the similarities between TV hosts and feathered forest denizens, Glenda laughed to herself as she thought, *Now I see where the terms "birdbrain" and "chatterbox" come from. Don't we share a lot of the same DNA with birds?*

Traveler remained motionless in body and mind. He slowly let all his moving parts come together. Finally, he began flexing his muscles, starting with biceps. Moving his left hand to his right arm he confirmed the bicep was nice and solid, it still jumped when flexed. *Muscles work! I'm OK.*

After his body confirmed it was intact, he thought, *I know how a wide receiver feels when he's tackled in midair by a rushing defenseman then finds himself lying on the ground. Message to self, make sure everything works and nothing's broken. Can I think clearly, what's my name? Did I hang onto the ball?*

Glenda was watching Traveler sort out his body and mind, then asked in a sympathetic tone, "Are you OK, partner?"

Traveler gave an assuring, small nod back with a sheepish, "All systems appear in working order, how about you?"

Glenda gave a soft laugh. "Same here. I think those yapping birds will give me a headache pretty soon, though. You know what they say, 'It's not the fall that hurts it's the sudden stop.'"

"Yeah, we need to discuss our landing with M when we get back. Can't he put a nice king-size mattress or two under us?"

He's fine, thought Glenda, *and I'm fine. We're like a tag team in wrestling. Both of us need to be in fighting form to face whatever is ahead.*

"What time do you think it is?" asked Traveler, "All I see looking up is a green ceiling."

"No idea. Do you think you can do another tree climb and see whatever is around us?"

"Can do, but first give me a few minutes to restore my equilibrium. Last thing we need is for you to be carrying me through the woods."

"For sure, take your time. I need some recovery myself, maybe a lot of recovery."

With a wincing shrug Traveler decided to stand. He rose slowly and gently shook his body. After a few shakes he leaned against the tree and stretched his leg muscles. He then did a deep knee bend, resting his fingertips on the soft forest floor. Standing again, he shook his arms and upper body. "Not to jinx myself, but I think the ape-man is ready to ascend."

Glenda rose and looked around. "Do you see the perfect observation tree?"

"Not right now, let me look around." With that he began slowly moving through the forest, carefully stepping over floor vines and around small thickets of thorny bushes.

Glenda followed closely behind. "Excuse me for staying on your heels, if we get separated, there are no cellphones to connect with." Traveler chuckled as he continued to survey the potential observation trees.

As they moved along, they each became aware of a soft background sound. Traveler instinctively moved in that direction. As they followed the sound it became increasingly distinct. It was neither loud nor disturbing, it was more like Lorelei's beckoning siren's call, "Come to me tired stranger, I will refresh your body and your soul."

Traveler stopped and pointed. "Hard to believe, but it looks like there is an opening ahead. Appears we have maybe stumbled upon M's river reference. Sounds like a large stream if not a river. I also see my observation tower, it's a Grandfather Oak straight ahead."

Glenda nodded as she stared at the enormous tree trunk. It was clearly a dominant survivor in the fight for sunlight and soil. Its lower limbs created a large shaded space around its trunk. It was a perfect resting spot as well as an observation tower.

Traveler walked toward the trunk then stopped to study possible limb-ladders. He studied not only the lowest of the limbs but also the limbs that rose above them. He needed his limb-ladder to first get above the ground, but then to offer continuing rungs for upward climbing.

Smiling at Glenda, he said, "This is definitely our lookout tower, and I see Tarzan's upward trail. It's time to join the clouds and look around. Guard our supplies, I believe I'll be a hungry guy after this trip." With that Traveler slipped off his carry sack and placed it on the ground close to the trunk.

"Don't worry wild bears won't dare touch our stuff. I'll protect it with all I've got. Bears beware!"

Travel braced his feet, then made a vertical leap that the books would be proud of. Resting on his first limb he looked down and grinned. "So far, so good."

Glenda grinned back at him. "Don't get a nosebleed up there, Tarzan."

Chapter 23

Good Views, Good News

Traveler ascended slowly. Caution was the word of the day. He was still slightly off-balance and a sudden slip of the foot could lead to hitting his head, and possibly a tumbling fall. A fall would spell big-time disaster. There was no 911 available, and the sentient books, Theo, and M were in a distant future world.

Ascending, Traveler frequently used his upper-body strength to assist his leg muscles by doing pull-ups. His progress was a testament to his hard, physical workouts. Whenever his back muscles, leg muscles, or arm muscles suddenly called for a timeout he would immediately pause. *This is not the time to test my endurance.*

As he rested on a large limb, he slowed his breathing then found himself studying the surrounding lush foliage. A large leaf caught his eye with its brilliant green hue. He realized this simple oak leaf was an emerald jewel compared to similar dusty leaves back in Charlottesville. *Wow, we have lost so much beauty and we don't notice since it happened over decades.*

He stopped his nature musings and refocused on the immediate mission. As he rose further through the tree's green canopy, he found sunrays were increasingly striking his body. Then his head emerged from the shade into a brilliant-blue, cloudless sky. His dilated eyes blinked hard.

Keeping a firm grip on a small limb at the top of the tree, he placed a foot in the joint of a limb and the main trunk. He began to survey the land below.

The land was a breathtaking green expanse. Robin Hood, resting high in a Sherwood Forest oak, would have appreciated the view. The visible forest bordered both sides of a wide rushing stream. The stream flowed briskly over protruding, jagged rocks, casting white foam from the collisions.

Looking out, Traveler felt like a sailor resting high in the crow's nest. There was a vast expanse of open sky above, and a green ocean far below. He let his mind float across the calm vistas and soaked in the serenity of Mother Nature. Finally, his mind snapped back to study the terrain across the river.

At the base of the tree, a tiring, still adjusting Glenda began twitching. *What's he doing up there? Why doesn't he call down? Is there a problem?* As her string of concerns was building, the ape-man's boot appeared above her followed by a descending body.

"Miss me, princess?"

Pleased with his return, she smiled back. "I assumed you had a lot to see and digest. So, what's the story?"

"Do you want the good news or the better news first?"

Laughing she quickly answered, "Start with any good news. Make me happy."

"Your wish is my command. The first piece of good news is that there is a lookout tower a short walk from here. We can get there and rise above the beasts of the forest while we eat and slumber."

Glenda's face lit up. "That sounds perfect, simply perfect. What can be even better news?"

"Brace yourself for this one. There are rising columns of chimney smoke coming from across the river and not too far away. I believe we are close to civilization. Well, civilization as this time period defines it. We can hike there tomorrow. I bet there's an inn we can use as our base camp while we scout this region. I'm thinking of fresh food and rooms with real beds."

Glenda's face was all smiles. "An inn sounds great! Let's hope no ill-tempered Throbbs are staying there."

"From your lips to the local god's ears. Sadly, I think there will still be Throbb relatives around for us to deal with, but we'll be quick to spot and avoid them.

"We can start to gather intelligence regarding the bad guys, human and jinn. The locals will know all about the Hun invaders. For sure they'll have stories regarding any demon fire beasts. If there is one thing these people worry about besides Hun invaders, it's demons."

Glenda nodded. "Let's get to that observation tower. It's getting dusky down here and forest sunlight disappears fast. I don't want to be tripping over stuff and banging into trees. Plus, it's way too easy to lose our bearings in the dark."

Agreeing, Traveler picked up his travel bag and moved in the direction of the river. In a short time, he slowed down, stopped, and began looking upward. "This is right where I saw the tower...I think. Of course, I was looking down and now I'm looking up. Sorry, things don't look quite the same from down here."

Glenda gave a quick nod. She followed Traveler's lead and began looking upward. She quickly found that constantly staring upward was stressful on her neck as well as confusing her still delicate balance. She dropped her head back to normal and took a few breaths. She noticed that Traveler was still staring upward using an arched back and deep breaths. *Our scout does know how to stay balanced.*

She began to think about how the lookouts would have accessed their hidden tower. *They must have a way to get there without the access being noticeable from the ground.* With this insight she began to carefully study the individual trunks. She instinctively ran her hands across them at shoulder level.

Traveler glanced over, smiled, and laughed. "I don't think patting them is going to get a tree to bond with you, but do things your way."

He returned to his slow, careful survey of the overhead canopy. With a disgusted grunt he said, "I guess I can always go up again if necessary. This climbing business is getting a little old." Noticing that Glenda was now beaming he asked, "You spot something, princess?"

Using her best modest tone of voice she answered, "I believe I may have found what we're looking for, take a look."

Traveler walked to her and saw she was holding a rope in her right hand. "Sometimes patting a tree works, it feels the love. Let's see what the rope is for." Holding the rope's end, Glenda gave it a whip-like snap. An overhead ladder came tumbling down.

As the ladder fell downward Traveler grabbed Glenda by her waist and pulled her out of the way. Glenda flinched as the falling ladder missed her by inches. Embarrassed and shaking slightly she quipped, "You have really fast reflexes, lucky for me. Thank you!" Staring toward the top of the ladder she added, "Very clever of them to hide this access."

"Very clever of you to problem-solve outside of my staring-up box. I could still be here tomorrow with a stiff neck."

Glenda reddened slightly with the praise as she felt a small glow pass through her. "Well, you did the heavy lifting and found this place. I just got lucky by doing some tree-hugging."

Traveler found a similar glow pass through him with the returning praise. "Well, we are a proven team. I mean, who else except us could have figured all this out? Let me test this ladder's steps to be sure we don't have a problem going up."

Traveler placed his right foot on the lowest rung, which was three feet off the ground. He took one of the higher rungs in both hands, then spread his body weight between the foothold and the handhold. Resting in place, he tested each hold, "It feels solid. I'm heavier, so let me go up first."

"You're definitely the climbing leader. I'll just stand here and watch you disappear into the wild green yonder."

Chapter 24

Above the Wooded Fray

After a few short minutes had passed Glenda heard a voice call down, "Tarzan here, Jane. We got lucky, come on up and join the apes."

Putting her right foot on the lowest rung she grabbed hold of a higher rung, and, like Traveler, tested each for its solidness. As her comfort level with the ladder rose, so did her ascension. She was quickly enveloped in surrounding greenery. It felt like moving through a jungle but going upward rather than forward.

Pushing down with legs and pulling upwards with hands and arms she finally saw a rectangular opening above her. Looking down, all she saw was a sea of green waves that slowly undulated as breezes stirred the leaves. Occasional glimpses of the ground confirmed it was still there.

A hand appeared, extending downward. "You've arrived! Let me give you an assist. Watch your head, I learned the hard way. The ladder's anchored above your head and sets you up for a nice bump if you're not careful with that last step."

Glenda held onto the extended hand and found herself being pulled through the entrance. *He does have ape strength arms*, she thought as she entered a small stockade. Once she was standing inside, Traveler quickly pulled the rope ladder up. He then replaced a nearby sealing board to close off the entrance.

Looking around, Glenda saw they were inside a small but sturdy wooden fort. The fort's sides went up about four feet, high enough to offer security from accidentally falling out but low enough to provide clear views.

Pointing to a corner, Traveler said, "Check out the pile of blankets. The lookouts left this place prepared with all the basic comforts of home. There's even a stone firepit for cooking, and heat in the winter." Pointing upward, he said, "Take a look."

Glenda looked up to see there was a thatched roof seven feet above them. The roof extended three feet beyond the perimeter of their fort's walls offering protection against heavy rains or snows.

A satisfied Traveler continued, "Is this place cool or what?! The thatched roof will spread out any smoke into the tree's canopy, it will just dissipate and never be noticed. Lookouts could have a fire up here without being noticed from the ground. How clever were these guys?"

Glenda acknowledged the builder's ingenious construction. "You're right; this is a well-designed lookout post. We can see out and nobody would ever spot us. I bet even the birds think this is some giant eagle's nest."

"More like a condor's," said Traveler. "But it's sure a great crow's nest. We'll hang out tonight with our feathered friends."

"Well, I'm ready to check-in right now with food, then check-out for sleep. Let's inspect M's menu for tonight."

The two placed folded blankets on the wood floor, opened their carry bags, and took out the offerings. They sat quietly, focusing on the satisfying meal. Suddenly Traveler stood up. "Rats, I'm thirsty. Between the smoked chicken and smoked ham, I need a drink."

"Well thank you for sharing that, now I'm thirsty. Let's go to that stream before it gets dark."

Glenda stood and tossed the ladder down. She shook it several times until it cleared the coverage below, then started down. Looking back up she said, "Shake a leg, Tarzan. Swing down, do whatever works best for the ape-man."

Travel ignored the good-humored jibes. "I'll do my best not to step on your head, Jane, as long as you keep moving."

Glenda didn't respond but found herself speeding up her descent. Once on the ground she looked up and noted that

Traveler was actually descending at a careful pace. *Maybe apes are more considerate than guys*, she chuckled to herself.

Traveler joined her and pointed to a path. "We're close. I believe we can follow that game trail to the stream. Animals are smart and follow well-worn paths of least resistance."

Following the path the two found themselves shortly approaching the stream. The path opened to a natural clearing that offered an easy slope to the moving water. Glenda was quickly down the side and beside the stream's edge. She stepped forward then knelt by a protruding rock.

The rock created a small, sheltering lagoon beside the flowing stream. She cupped her hands, thinking, *Resting water settles out the particles.* She slowly drank the refreshing, cool water. *Absolutely nothing beats water for quenching a thirst.* Stepping aside she motioned for Traveler to join her, he was there in a New York thirsty second.

His first intakes were gulps, he found it hard to slow down. The smoked meats required a quick drowning. Then he calmed himself and began taking slower longer sips. *Slow and steady, remember your boy scout training.*

Feeling satisfied, he was preparing to move aside to offer Glenda a second visit when he noticed her staring across the wide stream. "Traveler, I think we have uninvited dinner guests approaching from upstream. I believe we're dinner. Don't move fast but we need to get back right now."

Traveler was on instant alert. When Glenda called him "Traveler," it was often serious. He remained stationary while slowly scanning upstream. His eyes suddenly focused on a subtle movement along the edge of the opposing bank. The movement's source was staying hidden in the border brush while it was working its way downstream toward them. Stealth was being employed by using the natural foliage to its advantage.

Glenda whispered, "I believe what is coming is a wolf pack and they have bad intentions. You lead back, it's dusk, one tree looks the same to me."

Traveler whispered back, "Act natural, do not run. I don't know how much protection that water will give us but it should slow them down."

Traveler the scout instinctively knew where the return path was. He did a casual turn toward it and moved his legs slowly, giving no sign to the pack that he was aware of their presence.

"Casual is the word now Glenda. We're just two animals going to lie down for the evening. They will move on us when they believe we are settled for the night."

Just as Traveler's words of wisdom left his lips a sound broke the still air. It was the sound of heavy bodies smacking the water. The pack had hit the river at a run.

These wolves were not deceived by the casual human movement, not one little bit. If they could speak wolf-Latin, they would be howling, "carpe praedam," meaning "seize the prey," rather than their morning's call of "carpe diem," or "seize the day." Wolves enjoy a little alliteration.

"Run like the devil! I think they'll cross that water really fast."

As they rushed along the trail Traveler heard the first set of heavy paws hitting their side of the river's bank. "Don't use the ladder, jump to the limb."

"OK," was all Glenda could manage while running and doing her best not to trip on the underbrush.

Traveler was first to the tree, then turned to see that Glenda was closing fast. Moving faster was the oncoming pack leader. Its eyes were focused on Glenda, it was judging when to make its killer leap to take down the smaller prey.

Grabbing Glenda's hand, Traveler said, "Leap together like we did in the alley."

Glenda felt a moment of comfort from Traveler's strong grip, then she did her best prima ballerina leap, pulling Traveler upwards with her. The two landed on the first limb about twelve feet above the ground. Their feet established balance just as they heard a loud thump against a slightly lower limb, followed by the wolf's teeth snapping shut.

Through clenched teeth Traveler said, "We Road Runners need to go up another level as Wile E. Coyote down there collects himself. He can probably leap a little higher, maybe enough to grab an ankle or foot right here. Let's not give him a second shot at us."

The two immediately climbed up the next several limbs, reaching a safe distance. Looking down they saw the full pack was now with the leader. Red eyes looked up and they could feel the intelligence of the pack. The pack had them treed; maybe the prey would make a misstep. Dinner might yet fall into the pack's mouth.

Looking down, Traveler read what was going through the pack's mind. "Let's fade from their view. They are smart but being out of sight will lead them to find dinner elsewhere."

Glenda nodded. "Let's do it."

Before going stealth, Traveler took hold of the hanging ladder and started to pull it up. He found it was surprisingly heavy, with strong tension in the ropes. Looking down through the greenery he saw the pack leader had immediately grabbed on to the rising lower rung. The leader was looking up at him. If wolves could smirk this one had mastered the expression.

Looking at Glenda, Traveler chuckled. "I feel like Hemingway's fisherman in the story about the old man and the sea. I've caught a really big one and this guy just doesn't give up. He looks like he can hang there forever."

Feeling safe above the pack, Glenda was amused as she watched Traveler, the wolf fisherman, testing his wits against a very determined pack leader. *You don't become a pack leader unless you have a strong mix of brains and determination.* Laughing, she said, "Hang on there, fisherman, don't let go. I've got an idea." With Traveler hanging onto the ladder, Glenda climbed upward.

Traveler watched her rise. *So, what's the princess going to do? I bet she's never caught a fish in her life. Well, maybe she caught a few decent-sized Norwegian salmon but nothing like this guy. He's a small whale.*

Traveler and the wolf had entered into a staring contest. Both were determined to outlast the other. Both were showing off for the pack.

Traveler found he could slowly swing the ladder to create a pendulum effect. The wolf's body provided the pendulum's weight. At rest, the bushy tail just touched the ground with its rump a mere foot higher. Traveler began to gradually swing the ladder, making a wolf arc. Applying steady force, the arc extended further and further out. Soon the tail was well above the ground.

A few young wolves saw this swinging as potential fun. They thought for a moment about latching onto the tail. They were quickly discouraged by deep growling from the swinging leader.

The pack sat mesmerized as their leader was swinging freely in the air and apparently enjoying the ride. They noted their leader was enjoying the contest of wills. A few of the older wolves began a soft howl of appreciation which was picked up and amplified by the rest of the pack.

No longer able to stay controlled, younger wolves leapt up to brush against the swinging tail. Traveler found himself captivated by the show. *Glenda needs to watch this wolf trapeze act. Where is she anyway?*

As if reading his thoughts, she appeared beside him and was immediately captivated by the acrobatics below. "This looks like a starring act for an *Animals Got Talent* TV show. I think you and Wile E. are having way too good a time. If you were together in a pub, I bet you'd be buying each other eats and drinks while playing darts."

"Well, I guess you could see it that way. Never forget that my dart-playing buddy down there would make us the pub-eats for his crew given the chance."

Glenda nodded then yawned. "Enough wolves for this girl tonight. I've met a few street wolves in Oslo, but these are real wolves and a lot more dangerous. While I love the show, I'm ready for sleep. Let's bring the curtain down on this trapeze act."

With that she held out pieces of a sandwich. The leader's and pack's eyes shifted from Traveler to fix on the food. "First come, first served," Glenda called down and began dropping small hunks of M's delicious fare.

The first piece bounced off the leader's deeply scarred nose. One thing the leader could not do was hang on while snapping at the falling delicacy. A young wolf waited for the leader to swing out and instantly raced in and grabbed the morsel. The older wolves, either out of respect for the leader or concern for the swinging pendulum, simply watched the young wolf dart in to grab the prize.

The swinging leader fought an urge to lick its nose where the sandwich had left a most delicious smell. When Glenda dropped two more pieces the air show ended. The leader released its hold and seized one falling parcel in midair.

"This would be a good time to pull the ladder up unless you want more of tomorrow's breakfast down there…and I mean your breakfast."

Traveler nodded at the suggestion and quickly pulled the rungs up well above the lower limbs. "I'll bring the whole ladder up to the loft and give it some rest. We need to inspect the step with the teeth marks to see if it will hold our weight."

Resting in the loft Traveler proceeded to coil the ladder and then inspected the bottom rung. "It's amazing, the strength in that guy's jaws. He could have bitten right through the oak rung but was crafty enough to hang on by keeping the rung at the back of his jaw. Unlike a horse, he could get rid of this bit at any time but chose to wait me out."

Glenda added, "For sure, that is one very smart, determined guy. Reminds me of the old 1960s rock-and-roll song, 'The Leader of the Pack,' by the Shangri-las. It's a rousing fun song but let's hope we never meet that pack leader again. I bet he never forgets us. I bet he never forgives either."

"It's sleepy time now, give the ladder inspection a rest," Glenda said, as she began double layering the wool blankets. Once her mattress was prepared, she took her boots off. Finally, she pulled a blanket over herself, to make a cozy wool cave. "I don't know how long we've been up, but it feels like two long days to me right now. Wake me when the sun rises."

As a final drifting-off reflection she muttered, "Sleep well, Traveler, try not to dream of the big bad wolf swinging you on the bottom of a ladder."

Traveler smiled back, nodded, and then selected several thick blankets. The heavy wool promised a nice cushion for his shoulders. He picked a smaller blanket and folded it into a pillow. Following Glenda's lead, he took off his boots, then pulled a wool blanket over himself. He was a bear settling into a snug, dark cave for a long rest.

Traveler's deep sleep brought him back to their earlier visit. Buried memories returned, and the dream was disturbing. He remembered the large warrior called Throbb and his harsh encounters, first with a killer bear and later the killer mage. The dream was too clear and a restless Traveler tossed about within his blanket cave.

As he was close to waking he felt the dream's unpleasantness suddenly pass. Calm replaced the disturbing memory as his books took over. Even in his sleep the books were with him. They guided Traveler into a deep, refreshing, dreamless slumber. Shakespeare said it best, "Sleep that knits up the raveled sleave of care." The two teens had experienced more than their share of raveled sleaves in this first day.

Chapter 25

Revisited Places

Glenda woke, not to early sunlight, but to a feeling that she was being watched. It was early dawn, and its first rosy rays promised a bright day was coming. She was buried in the warm wool cave ignoring the light when her instincts prompted her to peek out. There was a soft rustling noise that piqued her curiosity.

Slowly her head emerged with blinking eyes. As she removed the mass of copper-colored hair from her face, she immediately reacted to a new presence. She was the subject of scrutiny from the largest owl she had ever seen.

The owl was sitting on the top railing across from her and seemed intrigued by her hair. Much of the tousled hair had been outside her blanket cave, and the bird was clearly captivated by the color. At that moment Traveler rolled onto his shoulder facing her, and she whispered, "Are you awake? We have a visitor."

Traveler made a low grunt that assured her that he was still sleeping, and would she please be quiet. Using her best sotto voice she whispered, "You will be disappointed if you don't see what I see."

Traveler found that trying to ignore an insistent Glenda was impossible. "This had better be good," he whispered back as his head peeked out from the covering blanket.

"Look across from us and tell me what you see."

The owl was now watching a second mass of hair appear. This mass was also longish and thick, but its natural darkness absorbed the light unlike the shimmering redness of the first. Traveler grinned as he studied the watching owl.

"What's it planning?" whispered Glenda.

"I think she is intrigued by your hair, princess. She sees a potential nest for her babies. I do believe she's pregnant, she's shopping around for a happy home for baby owls."

"How would you know that? I assume you're kidding."

"Not kidding," said a smug Traveler. "I studied birds, including lots of owls, for one of my scout merit badges. I know she's a female from her size. The female happens to be larger than the male. If she spreads her wings, and we really don't want her to, they go over six feet.

"She's one beautiful big bird. She is a Eurasian eagle-owl. You'll note that her ear tufts look like horns, and her eyes are a distinctive orange. These owls could have easily been named 'Devil Owls.'"

Continuing his morning owl lecture, Traveler said, "Disney created a wise companion owl named Archimedes for the future King Arthur in the animated movie, *The Sword in the Stone*. Archimedes always had a serious look, much like our friend here. In our friend's case we may need a different name since it's a 'she' not a 'he.' You do know the real Archimedes was a guy, a brilliant old-world scientist and philosopher."

"Of course I know he was a guy, but let's not get caught up with gender achievements. I say let's stick with Archimedes, it sounds like a fit for her. That work for you?"

"Archimedes it is!" Traveler agreed. "By the way, owls are naturally farsighted, they struggle with things close up. That's why she's staring at us right now."

Continuing he said, "Since she's pregnant she's searching for a suitable nest. Owls don't build nests they look for existing places. Our little tower platform would look like a perfect nest, it's up high and safe. Our wool blankets look just like perfect beds for her babies after they hatch. She's one cool, smart mother bird."

Continuing to stare at the owl Glenda answered, "I agree our friend is really cool. We'll give her our treehouse shortly, so let's not scare her away."

"Don't worry about scaring her away, she's not easily scared. She'll be quite aggressive in protecting the babies when they hatch."

"OK Mr. Audubon, after breakfast we'll move out and she can move in. Enough about her needs, right now I need to eat, I'm starved."

Glenda slowly sat upright so as not to scare Archimedes. Traveler followed suit. Watching them move, Archimedes' head rotated in a half-circle, as only owls can. The head stared first at Glenda, then at Traveler, then back again at Glenda. As Archimedes watched them, she ruffled a few feathers but appeared to be content. There was no apparent threat, so no reason to fly away.

Glenda reached inside her carry bag and removed the start of the breakfast fare. First out was a perfect large apple. M's choice of fruit was always impressive, and this apple was no exception. Thinking ahead, M had made deep knife cuts to the core. Individual slices were easily extricated by a simple twist and pull.

Holding a slice between her fingers Glenda took the first bite. A soft crunch came from the bite and she noticed the owl move her head forward. The owl's large eyes seemed to open even further. "See something you like?" Glenda asked as the remaining portion of apple disappeared into her mouth.

Glenda twisted off another slice of apple, brought it to her lips, took a small bite, and then held it out toward the watchful bird. "I wonder if she will eat apples."

Traveler saw the owl twitch and said, "Maybe, but she is a meat-eater. You know owls are raptors and farsighted. I would watch out; you can lose a finger. Your fingers probably look like tasty field mice or maybe long sausages to her, I'm just saying."

"No way my graceful fingers look like field mice or sausages, look at your own mitts, buster. Archimedes knows I am not teasing her. She can feel the love, can't you big girl?" The owl seemed to nod in agreement. *Best not to trust the love too far*, Glenda thought, and promptly tossed the slice forward. It landed below the owl's watchful eyes.

Archimedes shifted from one leg to the other. Two shifts and several head rotations later the owl dropped down beside the apple. The head bent forward while a powerful talon was extended to pick the apple up. The morsel was held up for the future mother's inspection, then the beak descended. The slice disappeared. The head straightened and wide eyes stared back at Glenda.

Traveler was amused as he watched the friendship dance between the owl and Glenda. Deciding he wanted to join the fun he reached into his bag and removed a croissant. This croissant had a ham filling, and the ham odor was immediately recognized by a twist of the owl's head.

"Let's see who Archimedes loves more, the girl with the apple slice or the boy with the delicious meat sandwich." Traveler tossed the morsel toward the owl who snapped it out of the air. "Wow, that is one fast bird."

"Well, now she trusts us and is certainly a hungry mother. I bet she makes her nest right here and expects us to supply more of the same delicious food."

"Probably right on both counts," said Traveler. "I wish we had the time to oblige her, but we need to get our show moving. Right now, she's a distraction from what lies ahead. I know how procrastination works with me, when I had homework I was a master at finding distractions."

Glenda grinned back, "I can relate. At the orphanage when it was chore time, I suddenly had a list of other things to do that were critical. Anyway, I agree it's time to let Mrs. Owl fend for herself."

Traveler looked at his carry bag, shook his head, and observed, "Breakfast is over too soon." With that he put the bag across his shoulders. "Ladies first," said Traveler, motioning to the hanging ladder. "Go slow, let's be sure Wile E. Wolf and his buds are gone. We should also avoid the last rung; it's likely to collapse after the chewing it got last night."

Glenda stepped over the side and tested the top rung before beginning her descent. She knew from cross-country running that going uphill is safer than downhill. While the ladder hung straight down, it was still a challenge as descending feet searched for rungs that wanted to drift away.

As the cloud of red hair disappeared over the side Traveler studied the surrounding forest. He saw how tentative Glenda was as she started her descent, he felt exactly the same. *It's showtime. Once more into the breach and I know the breach too well.*

Waiting to descend, Traveler remained the designated observer. It was his job to warn Glenda of any danger below. He knew that she was preoccupied thinking ahead about the day's journey and the coming risks, she could easily fail to detect dangers that were lurking around their tree.

As the observer he relaxed his mind, opened his senses to their maximum, and surveyed the forest floor. All was secure. Satisfied with Glenda's safety, he reaffirmed the location of the village. Breakfast-smoke was drifting up from distant chimneys as the village dwellers prepared for their long workdays. For these people the day started with a stout breakfast.

Satisfied it was a wolf-free safety-zone below, Traveler eased over the side. As he began to descend he took a last look back at a watchful Archimedes. Giving a small salute, he began his descent. *I swear I got a nod back.*

Glenda was relaxed as she waited for the descending Traveler. When boots appeared through the overhead greenery she called up, "Everything's good here, but watch that last rung. It's ready to break."

Traveler looked down at the mass of reddish hair and again thought what a great owl's nest it would make. He briefly studied the last couple of rungs then called out, "Geronimo!" and jumped the remaining distance. His gravity control was not as good as Glenda's, but it was adequate for the distance. After landing he grinned at Glenda. "Sometimes a guy's just gotta go with his instincts."

Glenda gave a slight nod of understanding as she thought, *No wonder guys get into a lot of messes, that's where "leap then look" instincts can lead you. Think what a twisted ankle would mean out here, big boy.*

Traveler stood still and relaxed his body, oriented himself, then pointed to a barely noticeable animal path. "There's our path to the river and to that village. Let's see where the wolf gang crossed, they did it fast and made it look easy. Once on the other side we'll walk parallel to the river, barring obstacles we should get there around noon."

"Lead on Geronimo, I'm right behind you."

Traveler stepped onto the animal path, ducked under a low-hanging branch, and moved into the dense forest. The walking was slow and deliberate as his eyes had to dart down to the trail, then up to the overhead limbs. Glenda followed, watching his body as it moved forward. She saw how he used his newfound walking stick to separate obstructing branches.

While it was now early autumn, with cooling breezes blowing from the north and west, the thick overhead coverage of still-green leaves acted as an incubator. The greenhouse effect kept the autumn forest warmer for a while at night but made the ground level heat unpleasant as the day progressed. Most daytime animals did their hunting and grazing early then found a place of coolness to settle down.

Glenda and Traveler had to ignore the rising temperature and continue moving forward. Finally, Traveler slowed, then stopped. Turning around to the trailing Glenda, he said, "I'm hot, thirsty, and a little leg and arm weary. All this careful step-by-step walking has taken more energy than I would have thought."

"That's how I feel and I know it's harder on you being in the lead."

"Thanks, I'm glad it's not just me. We'll be approaching our stream pretty soon and that's a good place to cool off and rest up a bit."

Fifteen minutes later Traveler paused again. "Hear that? Moving water. Stay here, I'll take a sneak peek before we go out into the open."

A returning Traveler was all smiles, "All clear, let's hit the beach. There's not really much of a beach but it's sandy, has moving water, and a place to cool off."

Emerging from the thick forest the teens saw that indeed they had a perfect resting spot. Straight ahead was a long, flat rock that extended from the bank into the wide stream. Sheltering the rock from the bright autumn sun was a leafy overhead oak limb.

Traveler was first to reach the rock. He moved onto it, sitting down with the limb above his head. "Love this place! Great sun protection, and a natural drinking spot." With that comment he quickly brought water up with cupped hands.

He drank several times then dribbled a handful down his back and front. Skin nerves welcomed the refreshing water and his body shivered. *Just like jumping into a pool on a hot day*, he thought and dribbled more water down. It was amazing how quickly the cooling water calmed his overheated body.

Glenda was immediately beside him, bending down for her own long drinks and dribbling the refreshing elixir down her front and back. "Water is the ambrosia of the gods," she said, taking another deep sip.

A serious-faced Traveler just had to add, "So true. My personal take on evolution is that when the gods were making their ambrosia, they had an excess amount. For amusement they poured it down on the pre-human fish babies. With a little help from above we grew flippers, lungs, climbed up on land and voila, here we are. All grown-up water babies."

A laughing Glenda gave a small clap. "Great explanation of a complex subject, much easier to understand than boring Darwin. You are certainly a master of science. Now we better get to the village before Ra the sun god decides to rest his chariot. Mache schnell, scout!"

Chapter 26

The Welcoming Inn

Traveler stood up, shook his body, stretched out the tight muscles from the forest walk, and pointed toward the wide stream. "I see a wall ahead, looks like a dam. Let's check it out, maybe we can cross over and keep our boots dry."

As they approached the dam, they saw it was a significant structure. The inlaid interlocking stones that formed the base and front of the dam identified it as Roman engineering. They noted both sides of the dam had stone retaining walls that angled out and away from the ends. The incoming waters slowed as they fanned out upon entering the reservoir. A nice-sized lake was the result.

Advancing Traveler leapt upward to stand on the retainer wall. Pausing, he motioned for Glenda to join him. "This is an easy crossing. It's plenty wide, not slippery, and gives us a great view of the lake."

With Glenda beside him he made a sweeping arm movement. "This is quite the Roman reservoir, look at the irrigation channels for watering crops. And it's a food supply, there must be tons of fish in the lake." Chuckling, he pointed ahead, "There better be fish, or else those guys are the village idiots holding poles for fun."

"You're right, we've got company! I never noticed them sitting there in the shade. Uh-oh, they've noticed us and they're not the village idiots. They're putting their poles down and picking up serious-looking spears."

Traveler immediately changed gears from humor to serious mode. "We need to act casual and slowly walk straight at them. I'll take the lead. Keep your hands in plain sight but be ready to run like a field rabbit."

As Traveler studied the standing men, he said, "They must be guards taking a break. Even in the heat those guys are wearing heavy leather. The good news is they won't run far."

Proceeding, Traveler closed on the three men and gave a friendly nod. He made direct eye contact with each of them, while at the same time making his empty hands obvious.

The men studied them with fixed expressions partially hidden by thick beards. What was not hidden were the spears gripped in thick calloused hands ready for quick thrusts. "Trust no stranger" was what their expressions, tense bodies, and gripped weapons declared.

"You look like escaped slaves," the tallest man said in a challenging voice.

Traveler immediately saw that these were Gepid warriors. Their heavy bodies, height, light-colored hair, and blue eyes identified them as Germanic in origin. They were physically the DNA-opposite of the shorter, leaner, dark-haired Asian Huns.

From M's short history lesson both teens knew that the Gepids and Huns were actively contesting this large region. Traveler used this knowledge to his advantage in responding to the challenge.

"You are partially right, sir. We are escaping but not as slaves. A band of Huns attacked our traveling group. My sister and I barely escaped. The Huns were on horseback and we ran into the thickest part of the forest to hide. The Huns stayed on the road. They either captured or butchered our friends, we never knew which. The Huns are a curse on this land."

The three warriors visibly relaxed. The tall boy and his tall sister could certainly belong to a Germanic tribe. While the Germanic tribes were frequently at war with each other, all opposed the Huns. The old saying "the enemy of my enemy is my friend" had created many tribal alliances following the arrival of the Huns. As the warriors studied the teens they noticed the lack of weapons, the potential for conflict seemed low.

As the men continued to study them Glenda spoke up. Holding herself in a confident stance she looked the lead man in the face then said in a calm, steady voice, "My brother and I have been running and hiding for three days. We are exhausted. Where is the nearest inn for rest and food?"

She received a direct answer accompanied by smirking looks. "You're in luck. There is a significant village nearby, we consider it a town. The inn you are seeking will be obvious. It is a Roman structure with many rooms and a large arena next to it. Follow the stream until you reach a wide road to your left. Follow the road and you will find the inn."

With a delayed final comment he added, "Good luck getting a room, this is fair week. Do whatever you can for your lodging." The parting advice was delivered from a leering soldier's face.

Ignoring the innuendo while maintaining direct eye contact, Glenda calmly answered, "Thank you, sir."

As the two proceeded past the three spear-holders the leader said, "When you meet Glaucus the innkeeper, tell him that Hans sent you."

"Will do," said Glenda with another sweet smile. Privately she thought, *Why are you telling me your name? Spare me, not another Hans.*

After they were a distance away a grinning Traveler said, "You're sure making friends fast. All the spear-carriers relate to you. You're their prom queen, lucky you."

Laughing, Glenda said, "Yeah, first Throbb, now Hans. When a girl is lucky, she sure is lucky. Wonder what he looks like under that beard? Think I'll pass on finding out."

A few minutes later Traveler pointed ahead. "There's our road."

"How did you spot it all the way back there?"

"Secrets of the boy scouts. Truthfully, when I was on the retaining wall, I saw the path ahead separate then widen. I figured there was a real road leading to civilization."

Moving ahead proved Traveler was correct. There was a wide, leafy tree-tunnel forking left through the thick forest. No longer a path, it was definitely a maintained road with a hard-packed surface. Whether traveling by horse or foot, passage was easy.

As he walked in the center of the wide road Traveler observed, "Man, those Romans really spent a lot of effort and money building their roads. The forest wants to reclaim the land and I bet Hans and friends are sent to remove little acorn sprouts every spring."

Glenda was half-listening as she kept her eyes focused ahead. While the road was accommodating for a brisk pace, the surrounding green wall made her apprehensive. *This feels like a prime place for an ambush.*

For a moment her mind unintentionally recalled Traveler's history lesson about the battle of the Teutoburg Forest. Three Roman legions were ambushed in a similar setting. The attacking Germans massacred nearly all the legionaries.

She tried unsuccessfully to forget Traveler's closing description. "Then they collected the officers and horrifically tortured them. They burned some alive and crucified others. It was a bad place and a bad time for a Roman army. Rome never again invaded Germany."

Glenda's mind was struggling to lose Traveler's graphic images when her mood suddenly brightened. "I see horses ahead! They're tied up to hitching posts in front of a large building, I bet that's the inn. We have arrived at the village, or town, or whatever they call it."

"Yeah, I see the inn ahead and it does stand out. It's not the Drake hotel but it's sure a welcome sight. Let's play the part of farmers barely escaping from the Huns, maybe pity will help us negotiate a room." With a reflective look and a shake of his head, he added, "Is there any pity in this time?"

As they moved toward the large building, they surveyed the surrounding structures. This was more than a significantly sized village, it was a small town. There was a visible range of services including stables, livestock enclosures, supply stores, and an operating blacksmith forge.

The paved main street was wide. It was filled with a large number of people moving briskly with the day's purpose. Mixed among the striding civilians were soldiers in protective leather wear. Officers stood out with their swords and iron mail. A few soldiers carried battle flags and banners on long poles to declare their allegiance.

The teens were nervous as they joined the flowing traffic. People glanced at them but without any reaction. Their clothing affirmed that they were likely farmers. The fact that they were on foot further identified them as simple folk. Horses were a significant asset and spoke to the owner's importance and wealth.

Once Traveler and Glenda realized they were not the focus of anybody's attention, they relaxed and surveyed the surroundings. The town was large enough that it clearly drew people from a wide region. It was a center offering necessary goods and services that were only available within a well-established town.

After making his initial assessment, Traveler focused on the large structure next to the inn. "Take a look at the place next to the inn. Those are stone walls, and that's a big deal in this neck of the woods. It looks like a downsized Roman coliseum. Let's do a little exploring before hitting the inn."

"Agreed. The more we find out about this place the better our chances of avoiding surprises. Forewarned is forearmed, and I have a strong distrust of everything and everybody around us. Those soldiers on a fishing break seemed off to me, they reminded me of the boat thugs. They made my skin crawl."

"Relax, they were just run-of-the-mill soldiers without much to do. A soldier is either preparing for a fight or recovering from one. Day-to-day they're bored, a pretty girl is big entertainment. You amused them, that's all. Take it as a compliment."

"Maybe," an unconvinced Glenda answered back.

They continued on the wide road and were soon at the entrance to the arena. The entrance was announced by large stone columns. The arena's purpose was clear, set into each column were shields displaying crossed spears.

Traveler motioned for Glenda to proceed. "Ladies first." Once through the gate they proceeded on a wide paved walkway that quickly took them to their destination. Entering through a short tunnel they walked up stone stairs to take in the full sight. The structure was built along the style of a Greek or Roman amphitheater. Centered below was a large, U-shaped sunken pit, this was the obvious event stage.

The sides of the pit were formed from vertical stone walls rising over fifteen feet. Spectator seats were long stone benches arranged in tiers that paralleled the enclosing walls of the pit. The tiered benches rose thirty feet above the enclosed pit offering clear views of the arena's ground level.

Studying the arena, Traveler concluded, "Looks like a packed dirt soccer field with bleachers made from stone." Pointing down he said, "The teams must come out of those big wooden doors in the center of the U."

"Gives me shivers," responded Glenda. "Somehow I doubt they play soccer down there."

"Yeah, you're right. Probably macho sports like boxing and wrestling. We'll find out when we get inside the inn."

Since there was only so much to see in a stone arena, they retreated down the staircase and out the tunnel. Once outside both gave quiet sighs of relief. "Maybe I'm paranoid," said Glenda, "but going into these places gives me the willies. I have a sense of foreboding about what constitutes entertainment to these Dark Ages people."

"Me too," said Traveler. "Not only are the people unpredictable and threatening, but so are the animals. I try to forget the giant bear who suddenly appeared, intending to make us lunch. As M said, 'trust nothing in this time period, neither man nor beast.'" With a slight grin he added, "The biggest risk back in Chicago was crossing a street filled with fast-pedaling delivery bikers and crazy cab drivers. If you wanted to see guys mix it up, go watch the Black Hawks hockey team."

Back at the entrance to the inn, Glenda ascended the wide steps leading to the main door. With a small bow she motioned for Traveler to lead the way in. "It's a man's world, I'll be the good girl and follow you in, my lord. I live to serve."

Lifting an eyebrow, Traveler looked back, winked and chuckled. He bit his tongue while thinking, *Sounds good to me.*

Knowing the weight of Dark Ages doors, Traveler put a firm grip on the door handle, pressed down, and eased the thick door open. *Feels a lot like Hermann's inn. These are real doors, and serve a number of purposes, starting with heavy protection from unwanted visitors.*

Standing inside, they let their eyes adjust to the semidarkness. "Where's the light switch?" quipped Traveler, trying to shake off his unease in the dark space.

As their eyes adjusted, they began to sort out the space. This room was much larger than Hermann's inn. It offered seating space that would accommodate a small army of drinkers and diners. Wide, heavy tables were grouped around large fireplaces. Groupings were further separated by wide support columns.

Thick oak benches were placed around each table. Ten large men could share dining, drinking, and discussion while being separated from nearby tables. The room's layout was no random placement. The innkeeper knew from past experiences that the best diners were those that stayed focused on their own table's conversations. Jokes made at a table would be kept there to avoid an unwanted fight.

Coming from the outside they immediately found the air heavy with the lingering fumes from glowing fireplace embers. A gentle overhead draft of incoming air struggled to improve the room's breathability. Looking up, Glenda saw louvered openings built into the first level dormers. Pointing upward she said, "It's Dark Age air-conditioned, sort of. I guess they recognize the need to breathe healthy while overeating and overdrinking."

Traveler nodded back as he surveyed the various nooks, crannies, alcoves, and exit points. "Let's check out the best places for quick exits before we engage the keeper. We need to pick a secluded eating place for tonight. Staying inconspicuous is key to minimize the risk of dealing with any Throbb wannabes and every one of these villages has at least one Throbb."

Chapter 27

Another Hermann

Their conversation was cut off when a short, lean man approached. His long dark hair was pulled into a ponytail that fell across the back of his neck. A trimmed front beard balanced the back ponytail. A fine, soft leather jerkin declared that he was a man of substance.

His large greeting smile declared that he was a hale fellow and totally trustworthy. Traveler and Glenda were well aware of deceiving first impressions. They gave controlled smiles back.

"Welcome to my fine inn, young travelers. I am Innkeeper Glaucus of the well-regarded Hermann family. This is our family inn. We offer safe lodging to all weary travelers. May I assume good food, drink, and safe shelter are on your minds?"

Traveler returned the keeper's Cheshire cat smile with his own. "You, sir, are a mind-reader. My sister and I look forward to lodging here."

"No mind-reader, young sir. Just a simple keeper who has hosted many travelers. Permit me to tell you about our kitchen's offering as well as our sleeping choices. We provide freshly-baked bread nightly. Our meats are from local livestock, and portions are generous. Our beer is from our own family recipe, and is in high demand."

Using his most beguiling smile, he joked, "You will find it difficult to rise after our dinner meal is consumed. Some have been known to sleep under the table."

The keeper's robust, welcoming voice changed as he softened it to a more intimate tone. "Permit me to ask, where have your travels taken you so far, and where are you going? Do you travel alone or are there more in your company we should prepare for? Please understand our inn is already filled due to the fair but possibly your coin can secure a small space."

In a confidential voice Traveler answered, "We are alone, Keeper. Ours is a pilgrimage to experience the world further away from our town. Our town fathers are sending young people, when they come of age, out into the greater world. We are expected to return with new skills and knowledge. Sadly, not all return."

Joining the conversation Glenda added, "We have no fixed destination. Our mission is simply to acquire new experiences as we travel. We will eventually return to our town when we think our experiences support such a return. Once back, we will serve as teachers and guides for others to go out and explore."

The innkeeper nodded and smiled at the merit of such a mission. "I believe your town fathers have a clever way to gather information. Information is essential for a person and a town's survival.

"While you are information scouts, fortunately, you are still youths. It's much to your advantage that you are obviously not military scouts. Any such discovered person is assumed to be a spy and is treated accordingly."

The keeper now asked an honest question. "I must ask, how is this scouting system working for your town? Possibly we should consider a similar program."

Glenda replied, "Well, it's still too early to tell. When we return our experiences will lead the way for others to follow with less risk.

The keeper nodded his head knowingly. "These are indeed risky times for all." With a concerned face he asked, "What happens if you do not return?"

"The town fathers understand the risks, as do we. Life has no guarantees for anyone. Being alive is a risk from day one.

However, if you never explore beyond your borders you never advance in knowledge. Threats exist everywhere, a town can become a victim from many sources."

Traveler picked up on Glenda's line of answers, he saw where she was going. Deflect attention away from themselves and focus on threats common to all towns including this one.

"My sister is so right. The biggest threat often comes from plagues. When we find villages that have experienced a plague we try to understand where it came from and how they survived. We determine whether they have developed curative medicines. If they have, we seek the medicine's source.

"My sister has a natural skill in understanding remedies for animals as well as people. We have earned our way so far by bartering her curative knowledge with farmers. My contribution comes from a strong back for hard labor."

With Traveler on board, Glenda slid into the negotiation process. "I suspect your inn likely requires a much greater payment than we can offer from our labor. We hope that we can barter a proven remedy for our lodging. Is that possible?"

The keeper's face developed a sly look. He was a crafty fox who has spied two naïve chickens wandering outside of their yard. "I would certainly consider the merits of a remedy as payment. Please describe your offer."

Looking at Glenda, Traveler said, "Sis, would you describe your remedy for headaches? It's a wonder." Looking back at the keeper, Traveler added, "As you know sir, headaches arise from many sources, including long hot days working in fields. Then there is day-to-day stress over crops and rain. And you know better than most the morning aftereffects when too much ale is consumed."

The keeper was highly intrigued. He fully understood the many ways aches of the head and body happened. He had experienced more than his own share of headaches while sampling the house-made beer. Looking at Glenda, he asked, "Do you have a proven remedy for headaches? The only certain medicine I know of is sleep."

Smiling back, Glenda's nod was one of absolute assurance. She was establishing her bargaining position. "Indeed I do! In my town the secret remedy is called 'aspirin.' The remedy has proven itself over many years from normal daily life to dire situations.

"We use aspirin to ease fevers, lessen pain, comfort the wounded, and reduce stress for all people worried about paying taxes. It is used by those in charge to clear their minds of the clouds of worry caused by the stress of their decisions."

The keeper was now a very eager fox. Greed was flashing across his face as he considered the riches that such a cure would bring him. "If your cure is indeed as you describe it then I can certainly barter lodging and food. Would three days be an acceptable consideration?"

Glenda thought, *Don't make your living playing cards. Your face is one big tell.*

Traveler knew that the keeper expected pushback from him. As the man he was the dealmaker. "Three days seems to be on the short side, sir. I think nine days would be a fairer offer."

The keeper smiled inwardly. He was prepared to offer a month's lodging at this early stage of bargaining for a cure such as this. Nine days was an easy trade to accept. Once he had the cure in hand, other bargains would be made.

Twisting his face to convey a painful acceptance he said, "Sir, you may be young and new to the world outside your town, but you are already a harsh man to bargain with. I will accept your offer since I intend to provide the cure to all in our town. I cannot think of how I will personally benefit in this bargain; however, I must consider all of our people, and how the whole town will benefit."

Traveler and Glenda immediately thought to themselves, *You intend to own this town by selling the cure. Your greed will be your undoing.*

The keeper quickly shook hands with Traveler, then with Glenda. The deal was now bonded. As each of their hands grasped the keeper's he felt a momentary shock pass through him. Their grips were both reassuring but also disturbing. *These two are strange.*

"When will you deliver the cure?" was the first question from Glaucus. This question was the essence of their deal.

"In a day or two," answered Glenda. "I will first need to write the procedure down in detail for your review. After that we can discuss any questions."

"Fair enough! I have a particularly good feeling about both of you. I trust you and you can certainly trust me."

Glenda and Traveler exchanged glances. Mentally they visualized the innkeeper morphing into a smiling fox with a chicken under each arm. They knew they were the chickens.

"Would it be fair to ask for a light afternoon meal?" asked Traveler. "My sister and I have had a full day of walking. My stomach is ready to leave my body unless some attention is paid to it."

"Of course! Where is my mind? What a poor host I am. Please be seated."

The keeper's mind's location was easily located. It was already busy calculating his pricing plan for this miracle aspirin cure. He would first buy the stables at the end of the street. These stables housed the visiting military guests who paid well for their horses' care. Naturally, he would raise the price for shelter and grooming care. The old man who owned the stable had not kept up with business dealings and had lost a small fortune in potential income.

Once the three were seated the keeper motioned to a waitress. "A sampler plate of tonight's cheeses Helga, make the best choices."

The waitress stared for a moment at Traveler and Glenda, then hurried away. *They must have much coin, he never extends a generous offer without heavy compensation.*

The waitress quickly returned with a plate laden with various cheeses and breads. The bread had steam rising from the crusted top. Trailing behind her was a young boy carrying full beverage steins.

"I hope these appetizers will hold you until the evening's meal is ready," the keeper said as he hoisted his stein in a welcoming salute. The three touched mugs in the universal greeting.

"My house-mixture. This comes from my family's secret formula." Smiling at Glenda, he added, "Like your aspirin cure, we have guarded our ale making process over many generations of Hermanns."

As they took their first sips Glenda and Traveler were aware of the impact that ale could have on them. They recalled a time when the bathroom floor and the throne were their best friends. *Not going down that road anytime soon*, they both thought as they sipped slowly.

Following the first sips both descended like wolves onto their selections. Bread and cheese had never tasted so good. There was a quiet time of cutting and chewing, then Glenda looked at Glaucus. "So Hermann is your family name?"

The keeper had just been thrown a layup pass. Smiling, he raced to score. "My common name among friends is Glaucus, while Hermann is a long-standing family name. One of the earliest Hermanns was an innkeeper. He began building inns to protect travelers hundreds of years ago. Our family learned the innkeeping craft and built on our early successes.

"This is our finest inn. It is a two days ride from the original one my father built. My father married late in life and I was an unexpected arrival. By the time I arrived Father was highly successful, and he created this inn as my inheritance.

"Since he had the first inn in the region, many interesting events happened in and around it. My father saw much and enjoyed telling tales to entertain guests. He became a local legend for his stories."

Chapter 28

Tales Told by the Innkeeper

Glaucus the innkeeper was clearly pleased to talk about his ancestor. When Traveler asked, "Any father-tales you can share?" the keeper quickly nodded.

"Some great ones. Of course, these are stories from the past so the skeptical person may decide what to believe and what to quietly laugh at. Call them father fairy tales if you please. I take no offense at those simply amused by my tales." Both teens were eager to hear the tales and sent the keeper encouraging smiles and nods.

"I'll start with a reasonably credible story; it is about guard dogs. Father's inn was in a remote area, several long riding days away from the great Roman fortress which guarded our land. While there were patrols sent out to observe and warn of invaders, these protectors were infrequent visitors to father's village. The inn's primary protection came from a pack of guard dogs.

"As the stories go, the alpha of the pack was a survivor from an earlier age. The alpha was enormous. He was a living member of an ancient strain of giant dogs called Molossus. Most of them had disappeared a long time ago. These were highly intelligent brutes used by the Romans in battle. They likely died out due to their deaths in battle. My father owned one of the few remaining beasts and he bred it to produce magnificent protectors for the inn as well as the local ruler."

Now that he was into his storytelling, the keeper paused to take several deep swallows of the dark ale. "Must prime the throat-pump to keep tales flowing. Now here is a tale that stretches the mind. You may well judge that it is a story made up to entertain. I believe it could represent real events, stretched of course, but still with some kernels of truth."

Glenda nodded encouragement as she said, "Our minds can stretch quite far, and we love tales of the mysterious. Please continue."

The keeper took another deep intake and settled back. His face for the first time lost some of its "fox in a henhouse" look and took on a reflective countenance. "Prepare yourselves for a very strange tale. It is a tale of mysterious travelers: some witnesses argue that magic was present.

"The tale starts with the appearance of two young travelers at the inn." For a moment his serious look vanished as he playfully said, "Much like you two. A beautiful, tall young woman and an even taller, very strong brother. The two travelers sought food and shelter but had no coin for payment." He slowed the story, studied them for a moment, and added, "Much like you two."

"They asked my father if they could work for their keep. My father was a shrewd bargainer, and he agreed that they could if they performed certain tasks. He later told guests that he never thought either youth could do their tasks. He thought he had bargained labor for a very low cost.

"The beautiful sister was given the dirty and unpleasant task of feeding the swine. The buckets of food were beyond heavy, and the girl was slim of build. Numerous trips would be necessary for her.

"The brother had to pull tree limbs out of an entangled pile, then cut them to size. Pulling apart the intertwined limbs required great strength. Father assumed the boy would never get past the untangling stage."

Glenda looked at Traveler with a veiled smile before asking Glaucus, "So exactly how beautiful was the sister? Did that beauty get her in trouble with the pigs?"

"Not with the pigs, but her beauty made her a target for a massive warrior named Throbb. His name is still recalled with respect as he battled a giant bear alone and saved his squad.

"Throbb approached her over dinner with bad intentions. My father had warned Throbb that the two youths were more than they seemed, but Throbb only saw what was directly in front of him. The brother was of no concern to the powerful Throbb."

Traveler sent a "back at ya" smirk at Glenda as he interrupted the keeper. "So much for her looks and pig-bonding. Tell us about the strong brother. He sounds like an amazing guy, how strong was he?"

"He was indeed of great strength. Amazingly, he defeated the massive Throbb at arm-wrestling. Before that contest, he had separated then cut the entire pile of entangled limbs into stacked firewood. My father claimed that he had the strength of Hercules."

A strange look flashed across the keeper's face and he blurted out, "My father told guests that he wondered if these two were gods." Looking at Glenda, he continued with a hesitant smile. "You are not the same beauty from that distant time…or are you?"

As Traveler was still basking in his own legend, Glenda responded with a humorous answer. "Sir, are you insulting me? Do I look like I am old?"

The keeper immediately relaxed and returned her smile. "Not a day over sixteen. Of course, goddesses never age. Keep doing whatever you're doing in the coming years to retain your beauty. Marrying rich is a sound approach."

Looking deeply into Glenda's eyes he added, "Many young women have learned, to their great satisfaction, that successful innkeepers bring much to the marriage. There is always food, shelter, protection, and servants. Wives are never bored as they enjoy the company of notable, accomplished guests. It is a rich exciting life." Glenda gave a sweet smile back.

Glancing at Traveler, Glaucus added, "You, I presume, are not Hercules." It was clearly a humorous, rhetorical remark.

Feeling that his tasks of strength and courage were not receiving as much credit as they deserved, Traveler simply nodded. "So, whatever happened to these two travelers of mystery?"

"That is the strange ending to the story. They left the inn the next day. Throbb arrived the following day with a squad of horsemen and hounds. He had declared that the brother was a demon and had presented this as a fact to the regional nobleman, called the duke. The duke was not considered a man who believed in demons but to support his men he told Throbb to capture or kill them if he could.

"While the soldiers searched for many days the two were never found. Of course, the forest is huge. They likely decided to simply avoid the fortress road and pursue other travel routes." With a soft shrug the keeper closed with, "But who knows. Maybe they returned to Olympus, or Valhalla, or wherever they came from."

Glenda gave Glaucus a glowing smile. "Keeper, that is a great story. I am very much complimented by being compared to the beautiful girl of mystery. I wish we had time to stay and learn more of the local history, but we may need to move on after delivering the promised aspirin. If we do not stay the full nine days, you will have the better end of our bargain."

A shadow slipped across the keeper's face at the news of an early departure. Was it caused by losing a marriage opportunity? "I strongly encourage you to stay long enough for our harvest fair to begin. The fair attracts many wealthy nobles and merchants from a wide region. It is an exciting time in our small town. My inn has many rooms reserved and guests are continuing to arrive." Winking at Glenda he added, "It is a good time to be an innkeeper or an innkeeper's wife."

He continued to expand on the merits of their staying, "Many come for the entertainment, for meetings with old friends, or the abundance of food and drink. Naturally, many come to gamble. The main draws, however, are the exciting contests held in the arena. Wagering on outcomes is a passion, with fortunes made and lost.

"Selfishly, I seek out the best lodgers to attract my share of the freely flowing coin. Your presence as distant travelers will draw attention to my inn. A beautiful young lady appearing at dinner adds an increased level of enjoyment to those dining in her presence. Who knows, a nobleman, tribal chieftain, or possibly a wealthy innkeeper may begin to court her."

Blushing at the innkeeper's bold suggestion and Traveler's wide grin, Glenda bit her tongue.

"You make a compelling case for staying," said Traveler. "We'll stick around a little longer then and enjoy all the fair has to offer. Maybe we'll make a small wager or two to see if the gods of chance favor us."

The keeper's face brightened with this response. Visibly relaxed, he extended his hand to Traveler. "This is a wise decision; I assure you that you will never forget it."

As he studied the smiling keeper, Traveler thought, *That sounds suspiciously like a double entendre. Exactly why won't I forget it? Spider senses are on full alert. This guy strikes me as a cross between a fox and a weasel, with the weasel being the dominant side.*

Glenda had the identical reaction as she listened to the keeper's sales pitch. *He's a weasel who thinks he's a fox.* Smiling back at the keeper, Glenda added, "I can't wait to enjoy the fair, it sounds really exciting. I'm so happy we found your town with your great inn." Pausing a beat, she added with a smile, "And you, of course."

The beaming keeper felt his chest expanding as he gave a short bow then pointed up the staircase. "Yours is the first room at the top of the stairs." Turning toward the kitchen access hallway, he closed the conversation by saying, "Please excuse me now. Many plans to make, and as usual not enough time to get everything in order. I'll see you at dinner tonight, it's the beginning of our feast week. Roasted ox and pig are both offered, I suggest you try both."

Once the keeper was out of sight Traveler turned to Glenda. "Well, that smooth talker could be a carnival barker selling sideshow admissions. I wonder what his game is." Suddenly laughing, he said, "Well, his opening game was aspirin money but now it may be charming you."

Ignoring the "charming you" comment, Glenda said, "His game is easy, it's still money. He has greed bubbling right below the surface, you can see dollar signs in his eyes. He wants any other cures I may have."

"You're probably right, we'll get out of here before the fair starts. He'll be busy with the incoming guests and we're masters of leaving Dodge City before the cowboys settle in. We'll stay the night, enjoy a final, hearty meal, sleep in a real bed, and slip out before the sun appears."

"That's the plan. Right now, let's head out and do some serious recon with the locals about strange happenings and possible demons. With people coming in from all parts of the region we should be able to get a good idea about where the jinn threat is located."

As they prepared to step outside Traveler glanced at Glenda's oversized pupils struggling to see in the dim room. Laughing, he quipped, "As I live and breathe, it's Betty Boop! Or maybe Miss Archimedes, not sure which. Can you help me out?"

Blinking back at the self-amusing jester, Glenda replied, "You really don't want me to go there, funny boy, I can make it Betty Bop instead of Betty Boop."

Deciding he did not want to match verbal wits with Betty Bop, Traveler grinned back. Like every jokester, Traveler knew when to take his witty one-liners and get off the stage. "Let's go outside and check things out."

Chapter 29

Hail to the Chief

After adjusting to the bright sun, Traveler and Glenda casually walked along the main road. There was a steady stream of travelers continuing to arrive on horseback. A few were being hitched in front of the inn; however, most were queuing up at the large stable.

Rich leather saddles, jeweled halters, and colorful horse coverings declared each rider's importance. The afternoon sun captured the rich coverings and reflected off colorful threads of inlaid silver. The visual effect was a moving kaleidoscope of changing colors and geometric designs.

Surveying the horseshow, Glenda commented, "Horse outfits straight from the Dark Ages fashion houses in Paris and Rome." As she studied the milling parade, she added, "But they are beautiful. Must cost a small fortune."

Nodding, Traveler added, "Horses rule in this time. They get dressed up and showcased, just like new cars. In tournaments their protective coverings display their coats of arms. Their riders, even when enclosed in protective leather and armor, are easily identified.

As they observed the waiting stable queue, an enormous black horse covered in a knee-length dark blanket moved through the waiting line of riders. The line immediately parted, permitting horse and rider to enter the stable. Observing this,

Traveler said, "Rank has its privileges. No waiting around when you're Mr. Big."

A few minutes later the rider emerged. Chainmail covered his chest and hung to his knees. Glenda and Traveler stared at the man then Traveler observed, "Well, he is certainly Mr. Big. That explains the size of his horse. Another Throbb coming off the Dark Ages assembly line."

Nodding, Glenda said, "He is clearly somebody of importance. Those other men are important, but they are all looking for his acknowledgment. They look ready to genuflect when he passes."

Nodding, Traveler quipped, "It's good to be the big chief."

As the two stood there watching the attention being lavished upon the mail-clad leader, they suddenly realized the man was staring at them. Moments later they saw he was striding toward them. Before they could fade into the crowd, he was in front of them. He was a chainmail fence cutting off any exit.

Traveler studied the man standing before them. Traveler saw the man was definitely taller than him despite the heavy protective coverings pressing down on his body. *Don't step on soft ground; you'll sink to your knees.*

Traveler next noticed long, reddish-blond hair coming down to the chainmail-clad shoulders. The hair framed a pair of piercing green eyes. *Unless I'm mistaken, he and Glenda must be cousins. Definitely some shared Viking DNA there, just a thousand years apart.*

Standing in front of Glenda, the warrior's face transformed from that of a serious leader into that of a still young man smiling warmly toward a beautiful young woman. His eyes conveyed the same warmth as his smile. He removed a gauntlet, then extended his hand to Glenda and made a small, formal bow.

"I am known as Ardaric, chieftain of the Gepids." Pausing to study Glenda, he asked, "And who do I have the pleasure of meeting? I have never seen you before and I would certainly remember. What is your name? Do you travel alone in these dangerous times?"

Glenda felt a slow redness creeping up her neck to her face. She gave a practiced curtsy in return. "I am Glenda, a traveler accompanied by my guardian brother. We happened upon this town by accident just as the fair was beginning. We were fortunate to secure lodging at the inn."

Pausing, Glenda remembered a favorite old song lyric, and she added, "We have a long way to go and a short time to get there."

The tall chieftain was relaxed as he studied her while giving her his best, "it's all good" smile. His followers wisely stayed back to avoid intruding into his talking space with the young woman. They recognized focus and purpose in their leader.

"I like the sound of that phrase, 'A long way to go and a short time to get there.' It could be my battle motto. I believe I will have it placed on my banner, it tells my men all they need to know." Glancing at Traveler, he asked, "And what would your name be? I like your size and bearing. Exactly where is it that you and Glenda are in a rush to get to?"

Traveler carefully considered his answer. This man was Throbb in size but projected a much stronger presence of intelligence and purpose. Lying would be a dangerous road to go down. Then inspiration hit him. He could kill two birds with one stone. A carefully crafted answer could possibly solicit information regarding the location of the jinn.

"I am called 'Traveler' after my father's lifelong love of travel. He was fascinated by what lays beyond each mountain, so he rarely stayed in one place. My sister and I became accustomed to life on the road and have seen many places and people."

The chieftain studied Traveler, then said, "I understand your name. Now please answer, where are your travels taking you in such a hurry?"

Traveler inwardly winced. *This guy has no problem detecting a verbal deflection and pushing back. I need to think faster.*

Glenda, seeing the rising nervousness in Traveler, interceded. "My brother spoke of our travels. We have heard rumors of an unusual place that seems to absorb any who venture in. The location of such a place could help us in our travels." Pausing, she continued, "Of course this could be a myth created by scared farmers. Any information you could share would greatly help us have a safer journey."

Ardaric inwardly smiled. *She is indeed worthy. She sees her brother stumble with a simple question and replaces him. Perhaps he is a little dull. She, however, is far from dull. I will get to know her much better during this fair time.*

Reflecting on Glenda's question, the chieftain visibly straightened to his full height and squared his shoulders. He was back as the Gepid leader, his answers were intended for his surrounding captains. Looking around at his men, he raised his voice. All were hanging onto his words as he shifted his attention from the girl to the Hun foe.

"You're correct, my lady, about the forest from which none return. The dangerous region is deep in the Carpathian Mountains. It will likely be a place where the fate of all Germanic peoples will be determined.

"I believe there is no great mystery there. No hidden monsters are at work. The danger is the Hun and their brutality to any who venture in. The ruling Hun brothers sign treaties then break them when they see an opportunity. They view a treaty as a sign of weakness.

"They intend to maintain iron-fisted control over the vast region conquered by their father, Attila. I was a strong supporter of the great Attila, both on and off the battlefield. However, his sons are another matter."

Ardaric's face was now clouded, his voice rising into a battle call. "None of the sons are Attila! They have no honor! They would make all Germanic tribes slaves despite our past support.

"My Gepid chieftains will be joined by other Germanic chieftains to contest them. There is no Hunnish force, absent Attila, that can stand against our combined might! We will seek out the Hun. We will break the Hun!" The surrounding captains were beaming at their leader. They believed every word.

As suddenly as his battle face had come, it disappeared. He was again the young man speaking to the young girl. A twinkle in his eye joined his youthful smile. "My lady asked a simple question. I will not be your brother giving an evasive answer but a direct one. We Gepids are known for our directness in conversation, war, and of course," pausing for a moment, "love." Glenda's cheeks immediately betrayed her as their color deepened.

The chieftain pointed up the road then motioned to the right. "Several hard-marching days ahead of us is a long-deserted stone fortress that was built in Roman times. To the east of that fortress is a dense forest that is near impassable for horse or cart. Travelers need to move on narrow paths, passage is difficult.

"Indeed, many of those that have entered this dense forest were Gepid scouts. All have disappeared. Some local farmers claim that forest demons are protecting the privacy of their domain from man. Others claim that the fortress houses a demon who absorbs any being it finds in its territory. I believe that the fortress is an abandoned stronghold occupied by the Huns. Whether demon or Hun, you should avoid this region and the fortress."

Directions and warnings over, the chieftain continued smiling brightly at Glenda. "We cannot lose you to the Hun barbarians. I will act as your protector, and hopefully as a dinner companion during this weeklong fair."

His smile faded as he added, "Sadly for me, I must excuse myself. My duties include reviewing the lodgings the innkeeper has prepared. My captains expect much from the inn, and it is my job to ensure their stay is rewarding for them. They will have a demanding battle in the coming days, all need to be at their peak of readiness. Each man accepts that their remaining days may be limited, this fair will be the last chance for many to enjoy all this world can offer."

Exchanges finished, the chieftain turned and walked toward the inn. Armed followers formed a protective wall around him. As he stood in front of the inn's open doors he turned and raised a gloved hand to Glenda. Redness reappeared on her neck and cheeks as she gave a returning wave. She watched as a confident, charismatic Ardaric disappeared inside.

"Wow, I believe we have just met 'The Man,' ruler of the Gepids, scourge of the Huns. Interesting that he supported Attila but turned on his sons." With an easy grin Traveler added, "I believe he was quite taken with you. Smitten is a word that comes to mind.

"Be warned future Gepid princess, Throbb was nothing compared to this guy. He is a bear disguised as a friendly, protective mastiff. What he sees and wants he takes. Better keep out of sight and hide your dance card before you find you're Queen of the Gepids. You'll be living in a dark forest eating lots of half-cooked food."

Shaking her head Glenda said, "Yeah, I see me as the queen bee of the Gepid hive. Flattering, OK, but I'll take a pass on that queenship. It's clearly in our interests to get out of this town ASAP. Tomorrow is the kickoff to the fair so we should be able to exit without drawing any attention.

"We'll chow down tonight, refill our carry bags, and move out early. I'll leave a written note for the keeper about how to make aspirin." With a sly grin she added, "I'll end the note with 'questions answered when we meet'."

"Sound like a solid plan. By the way, what do you make of the stories about a stone fortress? Think that's our old stomping ground?"

"Probably. However, it seems weird that it would be deserted. I bet it's still got normal people inside, just keeping a low profile. They probably spread the demon story to discourage people from coming in. It's their sanctuary and they don't want to share it. I think we can relate to being sanctuary dwellers ourselves."

Smiling back at Glenda's reference to their own Chicago sanctuary, Traveler said, "Right now our sanctuary is this inn. It's getting dark so let's head to our room and get the first seating for dinner. With the size of these Gepids, you don't want to be in line behind them."

Chapter 30

Settling In

Once inside the inn they saw that the fireplaces were now blazing. Torches in wall sconces further lightened the large room casting dancing shadows across tables and floors. Their eyes again adjusted to the changing light while they surveyed the dining scene.

The heavy tables were being actively set up for dinner by the young serving staff. Each place setting had a large pewter plate accompanied by a large ale mug. Dancing on the ceramic surfaces of the mugs were a range of wildlife, notably horned bucks and long-toothed boars. Circling the mug's surface were scenes of wildlife being pursued by hunters gripping spears and notched bows. The inscribed etchings made it clear that hunting was a celebrated pastime for warriors.

As the teens moved toward the staircase at the far corner of the room, Glaucus called out. "Wait a moment please my favored guests! Good news!"

Traveler paused on the first step with Glenda until Glaucus reached them. Outwardly smiling but inwardly cautious, Traveler said, "Good news is always welcomed news. What is this good news, Glaucus?"

Answering Traveler while smiling at Glenda, Glaucus said, "Your sister has made a striking impression on Lord Ardaric. He asked me about her in the most serious manner. He made it clear she should receive the best room my inn has to offer. Of course I am happy to comply. That would be the last room at the end of the hallway.

"He also thought Traveler looked like a potential warrior. I assured him you were not a warrior. I told him you were the brave young man sent by your village elders as a necessary companion for the sister. She would be lost without a strong man to protect her. He still thought you appeared capable of growing into a warrior even though you seem reluctant."

Traveler felt his chest expanding from the chieftain's assessment. *I'm more a warrior than you, little man, and the big man could ever imagine.* He saw Glenda was giving him a small headshake and he quickly answered back, "Thank you for that truthful description. I sure don't want to get drafted into the Gepid army." Laughing, he added, "Wouldn't know which end of a spear to hold onto.

"Now it's time for my sister and me to retire and prepare for dinner. We want to be in the first serving if possible."

As Glaucus was turning to leave Glenda asked, "Is there a bathing facility?"

A beaming keeper answered, "Of course! We adopted the Roman custom of bathing pools. The pool is found behind the inn. Simply leave past the kitchen and follow the short path.

"There is more good news. Our bathing pools are only available to the lords; their men would quickly darken the waters with their body dirt. The pool was recently cleaned for the fair, and you," he motioned to Glenda, "will have the first private use.

"We also have a sauna for use before the bathing pool. This sauna is kept hot to loosen the dirt on the skin. Scraping tools are available to remove skin soils. There are tubs of soap for use after the sweat is scraped off. First visit the sauna, then the cooler bath waters. You will come out filled with great energy and clarity of mind, and very hungry!"

"Sounds perfect," said Glenda. "Any chance of having towels or robes for the visits?"

"Already in your room. A set is there for each of you. Dinner will start and your table is by a far fireplace. You'll know it by the carved wooden statue beside it. The statue is of my early ancestor, the first Hermann who defeated the Roman legions."

As the keeper was turning again to head back to the kitchen Glenda asked, "Glaucus, is there any way that my brother and I could have our dinner in our room tonight? We're both exhausted and want to have lots of energy for the opening day of the fair. Please heap our plates, my brother eats like a horse."

Glaucus laughed and gave Glenda a bow. "Of course. You take care of your bathing needs and I will have the food brought to your room. Tomorrow will be a special day and both of you want to be rested.

"By the way, Lord Ardaric extends his apology for this evening. He has matters that require that he dine with his captains. I am to tell you he would far prefer your company and he looks forward to hosting you in all the coming evenings."

As they headed up the heavy wooden staircase Traveler quipped, "My sister, the future queen. So many good things happen when the big chief has her in his sights." Glenda just shook her head.

Once inside their room they looked around and found themselves more than pleased. The room was large and inviting. Glenda was indeed being treated as an important person who deserved the best the inn had to offer.

A three-person bed captured the back wall. A thick, red patterned quilt covered the bed. A folded green quilt lay across the bottom. Three heavy wool pillows marked the suggested head locations. By each side of the head of the bed were carved wooden nightstands. Resting on the stands were bronze candle racks, each with four thick candles. On the side closest to the door were stacked bathing robes and heavy woolen towels.

An oversized fireplace was centered against the outside wall. It was already lit and was justifying its presence by sending out waves of warmth and light. To the side of the fireplace was an iron bowl with stacked replacement logs. Standing beside the fireplace was a metal rod with a replaceable wood tip, this was the fire-starter for the candles and the wall sconces.

In the center of the room, across from the fireplace, was a heavy oak table surrounded by four carved chairs. The back of each chair presented a Roman face. Resting on each head was a laurel wreath. These once-famous men were now long forgotten. If alive they would truly understand the Latin phrase, "fama est labilis," meaning, "fame is fleeting."

"Wow. This inn is something, this keeper must be a shrewd businessman. I'm so lucky to know such an important person as the future princess. Try to remember we little people when you are Queen Glenda ruling your Gepid hordes."

Glenda failed to laugh, instead she looked pensive. "I'm a firm believer that there are no free lunches. There is some price for this hospitality, and we don't want to see the bill. Early tomorrow is better. We need to put a lot of distance between us and these people and their fair." Brightening, she added, "Right now I need that sauna hothouse and bath."

Scooping up the robes and towels, Traveler said, "I agree about free lunches and an even early departure. My spider senses are tingling from this room and that plastic smile from Glaucus. He's the cat that's ready to swallow the canary. I like Ardaric, but we don't want him to focus on you. He could assign guards to protect you and we'd be stuck here."

Opening the door, Travel gave a hand gesture. "Let's take the back staircase, it likely comes out by the rear exit door. The less we're seen the better. We'll use it tomorrow and be out of Dodge well before the sun's up."

Descending the staircase, they heard the noise of the kitchen staff in full cooking and serving mode. Pots boiled, pans simmered, and cooks shouted at staff to hurry. They paused for a moment and savored the cooking odors as Glenda said, "We'll feast tonight, and again on the leftovers tomorrow. Right now these smells are driving me crazy. Let's get out of here."

Traveler opened the exit door and stepped outside onto a formal pathway. "Looks like a red brick road leading to the land of clean bodies." Pointing ahead he said, "How cool is this, there are torches showing the walkway."

Following the torchlit path they were quickly at a wood-framed structure. They noticed steaming vapors escaping from the chinked logs into the cooling twilight air. Opening the door, they felt a blast of pent-up heat strike them as they entered the small common room. Inside they saw arched doorways on both sides. To the melody of an old Scottish tune, Traveler sang, "Oh ye'll take the left road, and I'll take the right road, and I'll be in sauna afore ye." Glenda grinned.

They quickly changed in their separate rooms then entered the sauna's main wood-paneled sitting room. Arriving at the same time they looked at each other and laughed. Traveler immediately began a chant of, "Toga! Toga! Toga!"

Glenda picked up the chant, then added, "When in Rome dress like the Romans. Actually, these are pretty snappy outfits and perfect for a sauna. Let the sweating begin."

Sitting on the thick wooden bench, they welcomed the heat. As the heat crept into all parts of their body, each retreated into a quiet place in their mind. Relaxation of body and mind deepened as they felt the stress of the day flow out of opening pores.

With sweat-dripping bodies each took a hanging curved blade and pulled it across their limbs. Looking at the scrapings on her blade, Glenda said, "Yuck! Double yuck!" and rinsed it off in the nearby water tub.

Traveler looked at his blade, wrinkled his nose, and added, "Where are the sauna slaves to do this?"

Once scraped, Traveler reached over to a long-handled, deep cavitied wooden spoon. He dipped the spoon into a clear water bucket, then spilled the water across the iron rack that held the red-hot rocks. A thick cloud of steam erupted from the rocks and the room's temperature rose.

Glenda was stretching her arms and legs when the burst of steam greeted her. She winced for a moment, then laughed. "This is going to be a very bad hair night."

Traveler nodded in agreement as his own hair was plastered across his neck and face. Sweat was freely flowing down his face and all he could say was, "Sweat in the eyes. Can't really see your hair, princess."

"Wipe and scrape again. Trust me, you need it."

When their body thermometers declared that both were fully baked, they looked at each other and nodded. "Time to exit this lava pit. I think we can stay in our togas and go straight into the cooling bath waters," said Traveler.

"Lead on scout, but go slowly. My legs feel like stretched rubber bands."

"Mine too. That heat pulled energy as well as stress out of my body. Glad we have an easy night ahead. Eat, sleep, then rise before the sun and head out."

"Good news," said Glenda as she pointed, "I see the bathhouse ahead. There are big torches on each side of the entry pillars. Last one in is a slowpoke. You run ahead and jump in, let me know how the water is."

On cue, Traveler sprinted through the pillars, then opened double bronze doors. He entered the long-pillared room, then stopped to take in the pool-house interior. It would make Rome proud. The ceiling had carved crossbeams supporting a tiled roof.

Enclosing mosaic walls were set well back from the pool. Along the walls were long, padded tables clearly intended for massages either before or after swims. Clusters of padded chairs appeared along the perimeter with adjacent small tables. The message was obvious, sit with friends, talk, and enjoy mugs of ale or wine. Life was good for the rulers.

While Traveler was studying the room's design Glenda passed him and descended the inlaid steps. She was quickly immersed in the soothing waters. Looking back, she called, "This is perfect! The temperature is warm enough to soothe but cool enough to counter the sauna's heat." With that she ducked under and began to swim the length of the pool.

Traveler dove in headfirst then fast-stroked to beat her to the far end. As Glenda's head broke the surface, she faced a grinning Traveler. "Feels like old times crossing the lake inside the fortress, but this water is so much nicer. Hope you're not too tired to get back."

With that he went under and pushed off the wall. Staying under, he sped through the water using cupped hands to pull the water joined by powerful dolphin kicks. Approaching the wall he blew out his lungs as he shot to the surface with a final snap of his legs. "Neptune rises!" he shouted.

Neptune found himself facing a red-haired mermaid who was paddling in place waiting for him. "Got caught in some weeds down there?" asked a serious-faced Glenda.

"Up and back," said a challenging Traveler as he placed his feet against the wall for a push-off. "Let me know when you're ready."

"I'm ready but you should take a little head start to avoid my wake."

With the race-gauntlet thrown, they pushed off with full strength. Both bodies came out of the water as they skimmed the surface. Speedboat racers call this riding on the water's surface "planing." Powerful arm and leg engines push their chest bows above the waterline.

Kicks and pulls powered each of them to the far end where they twisted together for the return. Traveler made a classic mistake by pausing to see where his competitor was. A foot slammed down on the water in front of him and a resulting stream connected with his face. Sadly, he had just been taking a deep breath when the strike arrived. Coughing, he plunged forward into a mini wake. He heard Glenda laughing as her crawl stroke lengthened. The race ended before Traveler reached the final five feet.

As he touched the pool's edge, he saw long legs now standing above. "You are very fast," he acknowledged. "Care for a replay?"

"Now why would I do that?" answered Glenda as she was wringing out the toga's water. "Anyway, I think we need to get back and secure our room. I'm tired and famished."

Traveler quickly moved to his piles of clothes and the towels. "I'll give you some privacy and go change outside."

"Thank you, sir, always the gentleman."

Once Traveler disappeared through the bronze doorway Glenda shrugged out of the clinging toga, toweled off, wrung out the toga, and put her garments back on. She called out, "Ready or not, here I come."

Glenda saw a slightly red-faced Traveler finishing up. "Don't know about you but that toga was like plastic wrap. It was really clingy," Traveler said.

"Don't feel bad, we girls learn at a young age how to change quickly inside a store's changing room. We learn how to slip clothes off and on without tearing anything. It's just another female skill."

"I accept you're superior at changing. As a guy we don't change much. Jeans on and jeans off." Laughing, he added, "And sometimes slept in."

Fully refreshed, they double-timed the walk back. They entered the same back door, confirmed the staircase was free, and quickly ascended. Once in the long hallway they were a few long strides to their room's door.

"Let me check it out first," said Traveler. He slowly opened the door then stepped inside. "All's clear! Come on in."

After Glenda entered she pulled the heavy door shut behind her. "Be sure and bolt it," said Traveler.

Slightly annoyed at the comment she retorted, "No, I think I'll leave it open."

"Sorry, didn't mean to insult you," Traveler said apologetically, "It's an ingrained habit. Stuff we say without really thinking."

Giving him an appreciative smile for his apology as she motioned to the center of the room. "Look at our table."

"Come to Papa!" said Traveler as he sat down to study the feast. As he rapidly filled his plate, he announced, "Houston, I have fork liftoff! All eating systems are a strong 'go.'"

Glenda naturally took more time with her choices. Acknowledging her dining wisdom, Traveler slowed his chewing.

The dark bread welcomed the sweet spread choices, prompting Traveler to say, "I'm torn between the honey and the jam. We don't have honey like this in the stores. What do you think?"

"Love the honey. I think the bees were different in this time and their honey is more natural. Personally, if I had to choose, I'd pick the jam. Can't figure out what the ingredients are, mystery berries I guess."

Finally, with a heavy sigh Traveler leaned back. "I'm stuffed and sleepy, plus that sauna dehydrated me. I can't believe we drank the whole pitcher of cider. If it was the hard stuff, I hope it was diluted. It went down so easy without a kick, but the kick may be coming in a while. It's OK if it kicks while I sleep. Right now I'm starting my sack-time so we can get out of here early."

Glenda sighed, "Yeah, that sounds good, but I still need to write out the instructions for making the aspirin."

"You are so honest. He's a weasel but I guess we don't want to skip town without paying." With a smile he added, "Besides they might even come after us chasing the aspirin cure."

As Glenda wrote the instructions, Traveler shook his tired head. "There is something off about him. I get a bad vibe despite his weasel smile."

Glenda nodded adding, "I agree one hundred percent but we'll be out of here tomorrow before any sneaky plan he has gets put in motion."

With heavy eyelids Traveler saw Glenda was wrapping the generous remainder of their feast into their hand towels. The wrapped food was then carefully placed in their backpacks. Pausing for a moment, she went over to the apple bowl and placed a few into each backpack. Satisfied, she placed the packs next to the bolted door. "We can get up, put our packs on in the dark, and be out of here."

Watching her preparations, Traveler had a sheepish look. "Well done Glenda, sorry I didn't think of that. Smart to place our packs there, we don't want to make noise poking around in the dark. And we don't want to light candles to alert anyone passing by that something is going on in here."

Glancing back, Glenda said, "Believe it or not, I'll sleep in my boots. When I get up I want quick feet on the ground, ready to roll."

Traveler nodded. "Leaving our boots on will also help to keep us from sleeping too long."

With the wake-up tactics finalized, Glenda rolled in to find the welcoming thick pillow. She saw Traveler had his share of the red quilt tucked around his head and she did the same. The fire was now a bed of embers and the night air was establishing itself. For a brief moment she considering getting up and adding a log then dismissed the idea. Morpheus watched the two relax and brought them a deep resting sleep. They needed to be ready for the early start.

Chapter 31

Too Much Sunlight

A greatly refreshed Glenda was experiencing an enjoyable REM dream. Her dream was upbeat as she stood reviewing her recent purchases of holiday outfits. A long day of shopping with Virginia, Traveler's mother, was a big success. She and Virginia were always spotting showstopper outfits for each other. One set of searching eyes helped the other.

As happens in dreams, the scene changed for no reason. Just as she strode from her sanctuary bedroom to show off a terrific holiday dress, her wakening nose began to warn of a big sneeze. *How annoying, nothing breaks a royal entrance more than a sneeze.* Her still-asleep hand instinctively came to her face to scratch, missed the nose, and hit her forehead. *How embarrassing, where is my nose?*

An eye slowly cracked open to look for the missing nose. A dancing sunbeam jolted the eye back shut while continuing to annoy the nose. *What time is it? Why is there light? It should be early morning and dark.*

Keeping her eyes shut, Glenda moved a leg across the wide bed to prompt answers from Traveler. The leg brought no answers from an empty blanket.

Jerking awake, she sat up and confirmed she was alone. *Just me and my boots*, she thought as she pivoted on the bed then stepped onto the wooden floor.

Glenda considered the situation. Clearly this was the next day. Sunbeams and her body told her it was morning. Calling birds were clearly happy with the clear day. She frowned as she was forced to accept that a sunlit day had already arrived some time ago.

Being fully dressed, she took a minute to stretch and reflect on the situation. *Traveler must have slept in also. Bet he decided to go down for breakfast and plan out the rest of the day. He'll have a new exit plan when I meet him.*

Heading for the door she was startled when a knock sounded, followed by a chirping voice, "Rise and shine, noble lady. Fair Day is here, your presence is requested." Glenda was annoyed at the upbeat voice. *I'm rising but not shining.*

Opening the door she saw the smiling innkeeper holding a garment. Beside him was a serving girl holding a tray of steaming food and a decorated beverage vessel. Two inscribed dancing cows declared this vessel offered milk. "Food and dress offerings for my lady. May we enter?"

Glenda nodded as she stepped aside.

Handing Glenda the garment the keeper continued, "The great Lord Ardaric hopes you find this dress acceptable. He apologizes that the selections are limited to those found in our humble town. Personally, I believe you will still stun the attendees." With a wolfish grin, he added, "And, I am confident you will stun Lord Ardaric as well."

Still waking, Glenda held the dress out in front of her. She found herself fully awake as she studied the dress. Her dream had just entered her waking world. She hesitated before saying with great sincerity, "It's beautiful!"

Then her mind left the dress. "Do you know where my brother is?"

"Already at the games. He is an early riser and wanted to secure the best viewing place. Excitement is in the air and the arena is almost filled. Lord Ardaric is already there preparing to open the games. Now our fair will not begin until you are seated in a place of honor beside the lord. Please dress, eat, then join me downstairs. Clara here will stay and give you any assistance necessary." With a theatrical hand flourish and bow, Glaucus left.

Clara immediately brought the tray and ornate milk vessel to the table and carefully placed them down. She put a deep pewter mug beside the plate. "May I pour, my lady? It is chilled and most delicious with the added cream."

Glenda ignored the question. Her mind was racing. How would she find Traveler in the seated crowd? How would they be able to escape without being noticed when they were marked people? Then her stomach made a suggestion, *Eat first. With food comes clarity of thought. Trust that Traveler has a plan and will certainly find you, he won't leave town without you.*

Glancing at the serving girl, her good Norwegian manners immediately prompted Glenda to say, "Please be seated, Clara, and join me. Even my brother could not finish this feast." A look of surprise passed over the serving girl's face. Nobles never invited staff to join them. In fact, nobles barely noticed the serving staff at all unless an error was made, then the notice resulted in most unpleasant reactions.

Clara bowed, then cautiously sat in Traveler's chair. She hesitantly added some of the food to her plate. Looking at the small portions Glenda said, "Please take more, a lot more, and enjoy the creamy milk. We girls need to stick together."

Invitation extended, Clara's rigid face softened and was followed by a sweet smile. She proceeded to fill her plate and mug. Both young women immediately began to eat. Once finished, Glenda saw the girl was far more relaxed than when she first entered. It was a good time to begin seeking information.

Her mind replayed Glaucus's comments about her being a guest of honor. *Once I'm in the arena I may be trapped. It may not be easy to extricate myself from Ardaric and his nobles. I need information that will help me slip away without anyone noticing. I'll need some way out of the arena other than the main entrance. Once outside I know Traveler will meet me.*

"Clara, I'm wondering about this arena. I've only entered using the main gates. Are there other ways in and out, maybe ways used by servants, that are not normally available to the spectators?"

Clara gave the question some thought then her face brightened. "At the closed end of the arena is a staging area. Participants enter the staging area from outside passageways, their arrival is a surprise to the spectators. Part of the games' excitement is not knowing what is hidden."

Great, thought Glenda, *I can participate in the game.* "Nothing else?"

"Well, there is an exit at the far end of the arena. It is a wooden door and is usually blocked, but it is a way to leave the arena floor and go directly outside."

"Why is the door blocked?"

Clara gave Glenda a puzzled look then said, "So participants cannot simply flee their contest. The contests require bravery. Cowards are punished by the crowd and the sponsor."

No help there, guess I'll need to improvise. "Thank you, Clara, now please give me some privacy. I'll dress quickly, I can hear Glaucus twitching outside."

Clara gave a graceful bow, left the room, and shut the heavy door. Glenda picked up the garment, unfolded it, and held it to her chin. A surprised smile swept across her face. *Beautiful! It's beyond beautiful, it's a stunning work of a master dressmaker's art. Virginia would love it. And it's clean, yippee!*

She quickly got out of her peasant clothes and donned the dress. As she began to slide it down her long frame, she studied the high collar. The extended collar was perfect for her long neck as were the extended cuffs for long arms. She smiled at the inlaid gold and silver threads circling the cuffs and the high collar.

While there was no mirror in which to admire herself, she saw the incoming window light reflecting off even more silver threads. These threads were woven vertically down the dress and accentuated her long body. *This was custom-made for me. I'll be a swan among the arena ducks.*

Looking down, she saw that the dress fell to her upper ankles, leaving her feet and leather boots complete freedom of movement. *A tailor would drop this hem down another three inches, but this is perfect. I can run if need be…hopefully, I won't need to.*

Finally, she put both of their bags on the bed. Opening them, she folded her clothing and blankets around the food. Squeezing the air out of the thick wool she had just enough space to fit it all in. *Can a girl pack efficiently when she needs to? Oh yeah.*

Opening the door, she motioned for Clara to come back in.

Clara stared at Glenda and exclaimed, "My lady will leave the arena warriors breathless! Lord Ardaric will bask in their envy." Pausing, Clara added a truism, "Great lords appreciate being envied as well as feared."

A beaming Glenda accepted the compliment with a modest nod. "Why thank you, Clara, what a nice compliment." Glenda thought, *I'm dressed like a prize horse that Ardaric's going to show off to the crowd. Well, I guess it's not much different from being a prom queen. And who doesn't want to feel special? I sure do!*

With that thought Glenda wrapped a strap around each hand. With the bags hanging from each arm she headed down the hallway to the stairs. As she descended into the main room Glaucus was there to greet her. Looking up at the bags his face flashed an almost scared look. He quickly extended his hands toward the bags. "May I carry the lady's bags?"

"The lady likes to carry her own bags to wake up. Maybe when we get closer, but thank you."

Glenda saw that a rebuffed Glaucus immediately looked sulky and definitely scared. *He's concerned that Ardaric will take him to task for not carrying my bags. I'll let him worry for a while then take him off the hook once we're there. Besides, I don't want to make my grand entrance looking like a pack mule.*

Accepting the rejection Glaucus simply said, "Let me know when I may assist my lady." He quickly brightened, "May I lead us to our seats, now?"

"Of course, lead on please."

Chapter 32

Act One

The two walked quickly out of the inn and onto the wide path that led to the arena's entry gates. At the gate Glenda handed her bags to a nervous Glaucus. Relief swept over his now sweating face.

When Glenda was approaching the gates her ears were the first sense to be assaulted. The noise level matched the wildest rock bands. She heard trumpets blaring and drums being pounded adding to the sounds of a large, boisterous crowd. The sound was momentarily muffled as she passed through the short entry tunnel, then the bedlam returned.

Upon entering the stands, she saw the crowd was a mass of warriors, highly animated with the anticipation of the games. They were shouting to each other and yelling playful insults across wide spaces to friends. For friends on the far side of the arena, shouts needed to carry the distance. Big lungs were up to the challenge, but sore throats would pay the price the next day. The resulting blend of ear-deafening, cacophonous noises resembled a marching band that was warming before a big football game.

The next sensory impact hit Glenda's skin. While the walk over had been cool, with a brisk breeze blowing across the walkway, the impact of the heat radiating from the massed crowd arrived. Over a thousand large, excited men were radiators throwing off body heat due to their close contact and exuberant animation.

The final sense to suffer was smell. If the seated warriors had bathed in the last month, it was a well-kept secret. *When did we start using deodorant? This is worse than any locker room filled with sweating jocks. Not that I was ever in one of course, but I can imagine.*

For a moment Glenda tried to ignore the sensory assaults then accepted the onslaught waves of odor, heat, and noise. *I feel stinky, and this dress is already too hot. It may look designer cool, but it's stadium hot.*

With Glaucus ahead carrying the bags, she glided along a wide aisle. As she did her best runway model's walk she became aware that the crowd noise had dimmed. She noted that a thousand pairs of eyes were tracking her entrance. She knew how a lion-tamer felt entering the cage with only outward confidence and a whip to command respect. *Show no fear, act the queen.*

Maintaining a confident model's stride, with head held high, she arrived at her place of honor. A towering Ardaric had stood to greet her. He dismissed Glaucus with a flick of his hand. He gave his guest a welcoming honor bow before motioning her to the waiting seat.

Glenda paused before sitting. Her seat had an ornately carved backrest and a thick tapestry pillow for resting on. She noticed that Ardaric's seat resembled a throne with an elevated padded seat and a higher backrest.

The crowd was now virtually silent, their next queen had made a grand entrance. The warriors stared as they took her in. The first entertainment of the day was provided by the paired royalty. Warrior eyes could not move off the couple.

Still standing, Ardaric made an upward motion with both hands followed by a nod toward Glenda. Every man rose as a single group to show their respect. A cheer erupted that scared resting birds everywhere into hasty flight. Glenda jumped despite herself and knew a watching Traveler had to be containing a laugh.

With another downward motion the warriors sat again, released to resume their gossip. These exchanges differed from those before Glenda was seen. This was the sound of large men enjoying whispered speculations about their lord. Glenda's face was already pink and would have been an even brighter red if she heard the nature of the discussions.

Ardaric addressed the crowd. "Welcome, my Gepid lords and warriors. This fair will entertain us before our task of clearing the Hun from our lands begins. Our coming battle will be challenging, have no question about that. Know I do not doubt our victory!" A roar of approval erupted across the arena. Heavy feet stomped on the thick stone surfaces, returning birds were again sky-bound.

Smiling at his warriors, Ardaric gave a powerful shout. This was the voice that was heard issuing orders across battlefields. "Let the games begin!"

Ardaric sat down, then turned to Glenda with a soft voice and a soft smile. Leaning into her at a suddenly close distance he started to speak only to find he had to suddenly clear his throat, a frog seemed to have taken up residence there.

"I know it is loud and uncomfortable for you here. Forgive my speech making but it is my duty to instill battle confidence into the warriors. This greeting was a warmup. I will be far more commanding when we face our enemy. The warriors must pulse with anger and courage when the battle begins." Glenda returned a knowing, accepting head nod.

"Now permit me to start over. Welcome to the fair! You grace all here with your presence. I was amused watching as you held my rough warriors spellbound with your entrance. That whispering you hear is warrior gossip. It tells you what a strong impression you made." Smiling again while looking deeply into her eyes, he added, "Of course you note that I am also whispering right now, which is rare for me."

"You flatter me Ardaric, but please use your normal voice. With the crowd noise I strain to hear everything you say, and I certainly want to."

Basking in her thoughtful response Ardaric answered back in a normal voice. "I obey your wishes, my lady." Both settled back. The initial exchanges were finished, and it was show time in the arena.

Subtly glancing down Glenda confirmed the bags were at her feet tucked beside the throne. The keeper had done well and Ardaric had never noticed them being place there. Like his warriors, he too had been captivated by the approaching girl.

As she leaned back Glenda began carefully scanning of the opposite side. Her mind was focused on identifying Traveler among the seated, hulking men. Her careful scanning resulted in no sight of Traveler. *Well, he's not across the way so he must be on this side. That's fine. He knows where I'm seated, he'll come to me when the time is right.*

Comfortable with how they could connect, she prepared to enjoy the arena's offerings. She was focused on the opening stage doors when she felt a hesitant hand on her left elbow. It was Glaucus crouching beside her. *He lurks* came to her mind.

"I trust you will appreciate my efforts to secure your future with our lord. Today's events will ensure that you become his queen. Please remember me when you ascend to royalty. You will, of course, always be my queen in thought and deed."

Feeling his charm was working, he continued. "All here know your presence is what matters most; however, the dress I selected brings out all you offer. The gold and silver threads have captured the sun. They try and compete with your glowing hair but come up short. Your height is perfect for the dress's length. Might I add that our lord appreciates tallness in women."

"Trust me I will remember you," answered a smiling Glenda. *Better you pray I forget you, you slimy toad. And I am offering nothing to your lord. He seems like a good guy, but this is the last he will ever see of me.*

Misreading her smile, a confident Glaucus strutted back to his position as the game master. His place was directly in front of the wall's lip and offered a perfect view of all that would happen in the arena.

Looking down, he congratulated himself. Each scheduled event was of his own careful design. All present knew there was a great battle looming on the horizon and each of the day's events would deliver a powerful message of courage to the assembled warriors. He anticipated a large reward from Ardaric, as fitting his inspired game choices.

Seeing that the crowd was ready to watch the first event of the day, Glaucus gave the signal to begin. The crowd saw his signal and there was a sudden hush. All waited for the first contest to begin. The only sound was from the massive paired doors creaking as they fully opened. The crowd held its breath. Anticipation ruled at the moment.

Dozens of young men ran out, carrying bales of straw. They stacked the bales about seventy-five feet from the door. The stacks rose a foot over a man's head and twice his width. Stacking complete, the youths ran back into the enclosure.

Six men strode out. Each man walked toward a stack, bowed first to Ardaric, then to the crowd. They backed against the stacks and turned to face the open door. Coming out were six archers carrying bows in their right hands and quivers in their left.

Each archer stood a measured twenty-five strides away from a stack while facing his partner. The archers first bowed toward Ardaric, then to the man directly in front of them. Their final bow was to the seated crowd. The crowd returned a polite clapping of large hands.

A set of trumpets made a calling blast and a single man entered the arena. He was dressed in the uniform of an archery master. "My lord," he called toward Ardaric in a deep voice that carried to every seated warrior. "The Huns believe their horsemen are the best archers that the world has ever seen. They respect no one else. Perhaps they should. You decide our skills.

"The first test of an archer is accuracy." He nodded toward the six archers, and each notched an arrow. Each archer assumed a braced leg position facing their opposite. The standing targets took large melons from the sacks at their feet. Each melon had a thick stem protruding from the top. The men held the target melons at arm's length.

The master nodded a second time and the archers drew and aimed. His "Release!" followed immediately.

Six melons were each split by an arrow. The small explosion of fruit brought cheers from the crowd. Ardaric nodded his approval. *Nice aims*, thought Glenda.

The master simply nodded, then said, "Now, those melons were the size of a man's head. I would like to imagine them as a Hun's head." A roar of approval erupted.

"Let us test our aims with a smaller target, perhaps the size of a Hun's curled hand as it prepares to draw his bow." Again, the crowd roared its approval.

The standing men now selected fruit the size of an apple. Placing the fruit on a flat palm, with arms outstretched they stood motionless.

"Notch," said the master. Six archers notched and braced. "Aim. Release."

Six apples exploded plumes of juice, seeds, and bits of meat. The crowd rose to its feet with shouts of approval. Ardaric gave a stronger nod while Glenda thought, *Now that's very impressive. They would be Olympic gold medalists.*

The master addressed the crowd. "Now, a Hun is a tricky target, so don't expect him to stand still. To hit him takes multiple fast shots, three will do the job.

"When I call out 'release,' each of you warriors should immediately count rapidly to yourself. Now, for those of you who cannot count even slowly, I suggest you have a friend check your bill at the inn." The crowd roared, and many pointed fingers at Glaucus while laughing.

While the master was talking, the six targeted men had each picked three apples out of the bags at their feet. They placed the largest apple on their head, and they held one in each extended hand, resting on open palms. Heads erect, arms extended to both sides they stood as statues.

The audience was motionless. They had gasped when the third apple was placed on the head. The six archers were in their braced positions. Bows were held in their left hands. Their right hands now held three arrows.

"Notch," commanded the master. "Draw."

"Rapid fire!"

The six archers performed like a well-practiced ballet company. Their arms and hands moved together as puppets moved to a master's hand. Few members of the audience had even started counting when the right-hand apples exploded. An instant later the left hands dripped juice and seed. The last apples' explosion was the pièce de résistance. Relaxed smiles passed over the standing target men, despite juices dripping down foreheads into dark beards.

There was a stunned silence. Then Ardaric stood and robustly clapped. All warriors came up as one body and the cheers were deafening.

The master permitted waves of cheering and clapping to continue before motioning that the show was not yet over. "Raise your hand if your count got to the number three." There was silence. "Now raise your hand if you forgot to count."

Ardaric and Glenda were the first to raise their hands, followed by a roar of laughter sweeping over the arena as two thousand arms shot skyward.

"The final consideration we face is what to do when the Huns shoot at us. One choice is to move as fast as your scared feet will permit: of course, Gepids do not run." Again a robust cheer arose. "Another choice is to stand still and meet your ancestors." The crowd was totally into the master's humor as well as the skills he had perfected among his champions.

"There is an alternative possible. I don't suggest it works for everyone." Motioning to the standing targeted men, he simply said, "Brace and extend."

Each man extended a right foot forward, followed by a right arm held forward with a slight angle to the elbow.

"Archers, prepare." The archers assumed their normal firing positions. Archers and their targets exchanged looks over the 75 feet separating them. "Notch and aim."

After pausing a brief moment, the master commanded "Release!"

Six arrows flew toward their targets. Six arms whipped out to strike the incoming arrows. Six arrows hit the ground. Two arrows were buried in the ground with fletching appearing above the ground. The remaining four arrows were lying flat with heads buried in the arena's dirt.

In the moment of hanging silence, the master made his final quip to the seated warriors, "I suggest shields as a suitable alternative to fast hands."

Wild cheers erupted while a thousand men stood to shake their heads in disbelief. As the warriors cheered the keeper was a puffed-up bullfrog. The event, with the master's frequent humor, had put the Huns in their place as simply another foe.

The archery display had shown the Gepid warriors that their own bowmen would be a deadly weapon in the battle. Glancing back Glaucus knew these lessons were well-noted and appreciated by Ardaric. His expected reward was increasing with the best to come.

The twelve men and their master came together and formed a single line. The master was in the center. The line first bowed to an applauding Ardaric and his queen, then to the cheering warriors.

Glenda turned to a cheering Ardaric and simply said, "I see but don't believe!"

"What we have seen is unsurpassed skill but even greater bravery. They train every day from their youth. Sometimes they are the archer, and sometimes the target. They learn the skills necessary for both sides.

"I have seen this performance from the master in prior years. I recognize that the targeted men out there are not the same ones I saw in the past." Pausing, he concluded, "I hope each of the past targets retired above ground.

"You may want to stretch your legs now before the next contest begins. The innkeeper tells me it will be exciting and much to my liking. It is a test of one warrior's cunning and fearlessness. I look forward to this one-man contest. I have experienced a few of those in my own life. Believe me, things are far different when you stand alone."

Glenda gave an appreciative smile. "Thank you, Ardaric, for your thoughtfulness. I do indeed need to stretch my legs. I'm excited about the next contest although it's hard to see how that one could be bested. I believe I will walk around now to the opposite side for a few minutes. I'll be back for the excitement." Ardaric smiled and nodded.

Glenda found that a path opened for her wherever she went. Many heads bowed in respect as she passed by. More eyes followed her, thinking, *It's good to be Ardaric.*

When she had reached the opposite side she carefully looked back at her side. Traveler should be there. She looked for a signal such as a hand wave. After several slow, unrewarding searching passes, she realized that the next contest was waiting for her to return. Heads were now looking at her with encouraging nods to rejoin Ardaric. She quickly walked back.

Once she sat down Ardaric nodded to Glaucus to begin. Glaucus stood and gave a clap to a large man waiting by the entrance doorway. The man stepped forward and was followed by a dozen young men carrying large bales of straw. The previous, smaller bales had been removed.

The man proceeded to a center point fifty long strides from the entrance then motioned for the bales to be placed by him. The men placed the bales into a random pile then ran back into the building. A moment later they appeared with a second load of bales. They threw these on top of the existing pile.

All returned to the entrance and looked up at Glaucus. Glaucus gave a clenched-fist salute back and the men disappeared inside. The crowd's eyes followed the retreating men and continued to stare at the open passageway. A tall stooped man hesitantly appeared.

Chapter 33

Act Two: The Main Event

Glenda stared down at a hunched over, slow-moving Traveler as he emerged out of the dark entrance. He seemed disoriented and confused. His eyes were dilated from the backstage darkness and were rapidly constricting in the face of the bright sun. His body was swaying as it tried to find its balance. This was not her Traveler. Strong emotions rushed through her.

Then a man appeared above the entrance and moved forward to the end of a wide platform that extended over the passageway opening. The platform reminded Glenda of a high diving board at a swimming pool but with a safety railing around the sides and end.

The man was short and chubby. If he ever did a dive it would a cannonball. His entrance walk reminded Glenda of a penguin's waddle. He appeared fat, but how fat was difficult to determine. Much was hidden with the loosely hanging, elegant robe. *He's vain about his weight. He thinks clothes make the man, he's so wrong.*

Neither vanity nor weight, however, detracted from the voice. He could announce football games without a microphone. His loud, clear voice filled the arena to reach those seated furthest away.

"This is a traditional Gepid contest of man pitted against beast. More precisely, multiple beasts. The beasts will arrive shortly. Savage they are by nature and hungry they are today.

They were captured recently in their wild domain and brought here for your enjoyment.

"When they appear, the combatant can run to the door at the far end and attempt to exit. Of course, the beasts will see his movement and the race will be on. Very few have ever won the race. Actually, none.

"Even if he reaches the door it still must be opened. The door is slow to open due to its own weight and the stacked bales leaning against it from the other side. Still, it is a possible way to escape. Of course, the beasts can follow through an open doorway so even that victory may be short-lived.

"Another possibility exists. A few warriors have built an elevated platform by stacking bales and remaining on top. If they can stay there until dusk, we remove the beasts and the surviving man is declared a victor. Surviving combatants receive generous gifts when dusk arrives."

With a telling chuckle, he added, "Of course the beasts are quite smart and may decide to shorten the day by playing 'attack the stack.' Sadly, all gifts have remained unclaimed."

Looking dramatically up at the bright sky, he closed by saying, "It appears we have a long day ahead. The day will become warm so enjoy the free ale as a gift from our Lord Ardaric." The crowd again roared while stomping their feet at the mention of the free ale. It would be a great day to be in the stands, not so much to be in the arena.

As she listened Glenda felt an overwhelming anger surge in her. Spinning toward Ardaric with a reddening face, she was an attacking mother-bear. "That is my brother down there! Is this your idea of how to impress me?"

Ardaric was stunned. He had no idea what Glaucus had set up as a game. This was far from being an entertaining game to the person beside him. The young woman was no longer the calm, clever, sweet beauty he had been pursuing. This was a tall wolverine in attack mode.

While he feared no man on a battlefield, he found himself backing away from the incensed beauty. There was a power coming out of her that had him holding his breath. *How am I cowed? Who is this? Have I incurred the wrath of a Valkyrie? How do I correct this injustice?*

Unable to look a furious Glenda in the eyes, he found his response was caught in his throat. When he finally did speak, the words were faltering and the tone subdued. "Not my will, my lady! This is absolutely not of my making...certainly not with my approval. I would never have done this to your brother...much less to you."

Beginning to collect his thoughts he turned toward a smiling Glaucus. "The innkeeper has overreached himself. He determined that your brother is an impediment to my courtship. In his stupidity he has tried to please me. He is a self-centered fool, to presume my thoughts. He is wrong."

"Well, please me right now. Get my brother out."

Ardaric nodded in hasty agreement and started to rise, then sat back with a heavy sigh as the crowd roared. The game was underway.

* * *

Traveler's arena journey had started when he was pulled from his holding cell and forced to advance through a stone tunnel leading toward a sunlit opening. His legs were unsteady, and his stomach cramped. He was forced to bend over as he moved. He felt like a drunk seaman trying to cross a tossing deck. His head was doing cartwheels, sending mixed messages to his body. *Sit down please*, his head pleaded, but long spearpoints poked him forward.

Now I know. Yes, there is light at the end of the tunnel! flashed through his slowly wakening mind. He shook his throbbing head thinking, *That feels like gallows humor, I'm in big trouble. The cider was drugged, and I've been shanghaied. What did they do to Glenda?*

His left foot caught the corner of a raised brick, and he stumbled. Naturally a curse came out. *Brain, tell the legs to get a grip, and do it right now! I need to be ready for whatever is coming.*

As he neared the wide opening, he saw a dozen men, including archers, standing in the shade watching his approach. *They look like I'm walking to the gallows. Not a promising start for whatever is coming.*

As he reached the opening, the spear points backed off. He was permitted to stand for several minutes to collect himself. As his eyes adjusted to the sunlight his ears responded to an announcer's voice coming from above him. His brain was rapidly clearing and going to full alert. His mind understood the arena crier's message. His eyes confirmed the message when they spied a pile of straw bales straight ahead.

For a moment he had a flashback. It was a fun memory of him and Glenda in the haylofts of the fortress stable, playing among mountains of deep straw. They burrowed into it, threw it at each other, and jumped down into it. For a moment he laughed out loud as he recalled Glenda struggling to remove the straw from her hair and sneezing.

The memory disappeared in an eye blink. His brain sent an urgent message to his feet. *Run! Escape!* Far ahead, at the opposite end of the arena, he saw a dark door. It promised an exit if he could reach it.

Studying the distance to the far door he became aware of the crowd of warriors looking down at him from their elevated seats. They clapped and cheered him on. As warriors they wanted to lift his spirits before his adversary arrived. He was the entertainment and they wanted a good show. Ignoring the noise of the crowd, he made a decision. First he would move quickly to the bales, identify the game and the opponent, then possibly race to the door.

He bolted toward the oasis of safety, the piled straw bales. He had just reached the pile when his "beware" instinct commanded him to look back. Some battlefield sages advise to never look an enemy in the eye or listen to their war cry. Traveler had learned from hard experience that he was at his best when he faced a threatening adversary head-on. He was not built to ignore a threat, he was built to confront it directly.

The arriving threat had similar instincts. From a smaller opening beside the exit tunnel, a long snout slowly emerged. The snout tentatively sniffed the air, then a grey body slowly moved into the sunlight. Squinting red eyes began adjusting to the bright sunlight.

The massive head began to study the arena. Like Traveler it ignored the crowd's cheers and jeers. It only glanced up once and immediately understood it could not leap to the top of the containing wall.

Traveler quickly saw that the first adversary was not alone. It was the lead scout ensuring the pack could safely follow, and follow the pack did. As the grey wolves came out, they emerged in order of size and age. The younger and smaller were first. None were small except in comparison to the adult giants that followed them. Age and experience had earned the adults the right to study their opponent before engaging.

The alpha entered last, then moved forward to assume the leadership position. The pack patiently waited for a command from the alpha. The alpha carefully studied the arena, the height of the elevated crowd, and it drooled. It wished it could reach the stands but concluded the same as the scout. Stone walls were too high. Man could be a tempting but elusive meal.

The alpha gave the equivalent of a shrug. It knew there was a purpose to being here, but the purpose was not yet clear. It slowly rotated its head as it studied the open arena and sniffed the air. Its olfactory senses were partly lessened by the enclosed aroma of the seated warriors. Its eyesight, however, was not dimmed. It studied the space for any movement. Movement was the trigger for its next move.

Traveler had immediately crouched down when he had seen the scout entering the arena. As the pack had emerged it was clear they had not yet seen him. He remained hidden prey.

Then he focused on the alpha. A shiver ran down his back. The alpha had a long scar running down its snout. He recognized the scar and the alpha; he had swung it on the ladder for many long minutes while locked in a staring contest.

The alpha would certainly remember him once he was spotted. He recalled Glenda's words that it would never forget nor forgive. The alpha would be a wicked foe seeking revenge.

Traveler again studied the distant door at the end of the arena. He knew a run to the far door would trigger the pack's pursuit. He had seen the speed with which the alpha had moved when chasing them to their tree post.

He considered using his gifts but that would alert the crowd that he was not a simple farm-boy. He needed to keep both his and Glenda's identities hidden. The jinn could never be alerted to their presence.

As he considered his options, he spotted Glenda and felt relief. She was present and being honored. He gave her a brief subtle wave of acknowledgment and she returned it. He was beyond pleased to see she was furious. Recognizing her mood gave him a jolt of positive energy. A second jolt followed from the book's departing energy gift. His body shrugged off the lethargy of the drug, he was fully charged. Traveler was back and was in a fighting mood.

While the pack was still entering, he began to mentally organize the bales into a stable column. He counted thirty-six of the large bales and noted the dimensions. They were consistent in their heights, widths, and depths. That was as good as his luck could be. It was time to build.

Like all builders, he respected symmetry for its promised stability. His middle school geometry provided a guide for optimizing the greatest, stable height. He immediately saw how to build a well-designed base with interlocking bales. He began slowly making the base without creating any motion to alert the pack. With the base prepared he began the dangerous task of building elevation.

He took his time. He saw the pack had settled down awaiting a move by the alpha. Younger wolves began a friendly tussle among themselves. They were a distraction to the alpha and other adults. Maintaining discipline among the young is difficult, ask any middle school teacher.

As he built his ascending tower he carefully remained out of the pack's sight. Keeping his body movements behind the rising bales he slowly lifted them and placed them in the desired order. *When I can't use magic, good old math still works*, he smiled to himself.

As he was placing the final bale upward an elbow briefly jutted out from behind the column. The scout saw this human arm movement and growled. The alpha immediately saw the scout's focus, then the movement.

Communications were immediate within the pack. The alpha understood this was the hiding place of a human prey. A sharp bark told the pack to listen up. The alpha leapt forward. *Man is a tricky prey*, thought the alpha, *but my pack has tricks of its own.*

Traveler saw the oncoming charge and instantly ascended the straw column. He used his arm strength to lift himself upward while maintaining the stability of the tower. He was resting on top, stretched out on his belly for greater stack stability, when the pack arrived.

As the pack reached the straw column it immediately spread out, cutting off any possible path of retreat. The man was isolated. The only consideration was how to bring down the feast sitting above them. Young wolves leapt up and snapped in the air to no avail. Traveler was positioned in the center of the stack and offered no target for seeking jaws.

The crowd was torn between cheering for the wolves to knock down the structure and respecting Traveler for the stability of the construct. No other man had ever been able to use all the bales in a design capable of withstanding the leaping wolves. None had ever been controlled enough to build their structure while remaining unseen.

Fear had always been the undoing of past men. This man had retained his wits in the face of a killer wolf pack and the warriors respected that. They knew from personal experiences that the best warriors retain their training in battle regardless of the threats coming at them.

Now that there did not seem to be an immediate end to the contest, the warriors settled into their favorite pastime. The pastime was betting on the man's survival time and was accompanied by the consumption of copious amounts of the free ale. Motivated servers rushed down stone aisles as loud, bearded men shouted out at them.

Betting purses clanged as they changed hands while metal mugs bumped together in friendship. Backs and shoulders were slapped with the sound of large hands striking leather. This was a great day of entertainment for the seated crowd.

Glenda's eyes never left Traveler and the pack. She watched as the crafty alpha studied the situation. The alpha was sniffing the air with a snout pointed upward. *Impossible. It's the same guy, and he remembers. This fight is now personal. That alpha wants more than a meal, it wants revenge. This is just what M told us, how random chance shows itself at the most unexpected of times, nobody could have predicted this.*

The younger wolves' early leaps were not an effective attack. The alpha would not denigrate itself with a leaping failure. As it watched, several of the large adults made their own leaps. Before leaping they snapped at the younger wolves to move aside so they could get a running jump. Their leaps were not successful, but as their heavier bodies hit the side of the structure the alpha saw the column move slightly.

The alpha knew that movement was good. That which moves will eventually be caught. The alpha could not coordinate the hits, but it encouraged the large adults to leap and hit. The pack now saw the resulting movement. Traveler and Glenda both saw the wolf strategy and understood the end it would bring.

Glenda prepared to use her powers to help Traveler. *He needs to use his true power, and do it before he's on the ground. There are too many of them even for Traveler.*

Chapter 34

Glaucus Flies, Traveler Runs

As Glenda stood up and prepared to leap toward Traveler, she saw that Ardaric had also risen. His face had the battle-rage that opponents knew too well. He had found his answer regarding what he could do to redeem himself with the Valkyrie beside him.

Moving past Glenda, the huge man stood behind the innkeeper. Glaucus was standing beside the retaining wall, totally absorbed in the coming demise of the girl's brother. He was cheering the pack as it hit the column.

He was lost in a fantasy regarding the upcoming reward he would receive. The keeper anticipated a great reward from Ardaric for eliminating the dull-minded brother. He had planned this event carefully from the moment he had met the girl and seen Ardaric's great interest in her. Crafty planning was his special talent. With the brother torn apart by the pack, the woman would mentally crumble. She would have no protective support other than from Ardaric. He was a king maker or rather a queen maker.

The keeper's reward came faster than he had imagined. He found himself being lifted skyward by massive arms. He was a child being raised overhead by a powerful father. Sadly for him, this was not his father. Before he could speak or move, he found that he had covered the distance down to the arena floor in a short second without gravity control to lessen the impact.

He landed hard with a sharp exhale and loud grunt. His bright blue, air-filled toga contrasted with the dark brown of the arena's packed dirt as it deflated back onto his frame.

The entire pack momentarily stopped to stare at the new arrival. It sensed a second offering was being made. While one prey was still above their heads, they knew it could not escape. The stack was ready to fall after additional attacks were launched. At the same time, they saw the second prey was just beginning to rise slowly. Slowness meant one thing, a prey that could not quickly escape. Their decision was instant.

Glaucus was on his feet and realized he was being studied. He looked to the entry doors with the archers watching the contest. He made a fast hand motion for the archers to send their arrows into the pack. The archers ignored him, looking to their lord for direction.

Ardaric stood motionless. For a passing moment he considered mercy then dismissed the thought. In a commanding voice he called out to the entire arena, "Innkeeper! You chose to decide the brother's fate. That was my decision. This is never the decision I would have made. I welcomed both brother and sister to our fair and you dishonored me. Now make decisions for your own fate."

Glaucus turned pale as the blood left his face. He instantly lifted his robe and began to sprint toward the guarded gate. His motion triggered an immediate reaction in the pack. While Glaucus had the shorter distance, his speed was a fraction of the wolves'. Wolves can approach forty miles per hour while an out-of-shape Glaucus, even running scared, was far, far slower.

The pack broke into two groups. The first group ran toward the open entry doors to cut off any possible escape back into the tunnel. The balance of the pack, led by the leaping alpha, fell on Glaucus in seconds. Glaucus immediately went down and curled into a tight ball. His move to curl up was instinctive, much as those being attacked by a bear will do.

The wolves knew the defensive move. They were accomplished at opening up any curled prey. Long snouts worked their way under chins and legs. Arms were pried away and legs opened. Then the biting-attack began.

Arms instinctively tried to push jaws and teeth away, only to create greater openings. A whimpering voice made a final desperate call for help. An exposed neck drew the swift attention of the alpha. In moments, the brilliant blue toga was transformed into a glistening red cloth. Consciousness fled while legs twitched for a few more moments. Then all went still.

The arena was silent. The warriors had been focused on the man on top of the bale pile and were awaiting final attacks when suddenly their eyes shifted. They were mesmerized as they watched the innkeeper desperately run for safety before being brought down on the arena floor.

The keeper's frantic final cry was one they had all heard on battlefields too many times. The memory of those cries kept them focused on the keeper as he was torn apart. Each warrior briefly wondered whether they could have made the safety of the doors. All were glad that would remain an unanswered question.

Traveler saw the scene in slow motion. He realized his exit path was suddenly unguarded. He leapt down and began his sprint toward the far exit door. Glenda saw his move and instantly followed with a bag in each hand. Jumping onto the top surface of the containment wall she began sprinting toward the far exit door. The bags provided balance as she ran, she never felt their weight.

The seated warriors were still captivated by the innkeeper's demise. Nobody tried to interfere with Glenda as she ran along the wall's ledge. She arrived above the door a moment before Traveler and called down, "Look out below!" She used her gravity control to lessen the landing shock. The brilliant dress flew above her for a moment then settled back down to her ankles.

Traveler was already pushing hard, but the door barely moved. "We have a blocking problem here," he said. Looking over his shoulder he saw that the alpha had noticed his escape sprint. The full pack was coming toward them at their fastest speed led by the alpha. "Push with all your power right now! Don't look back!"

The two pushed together on the edge of the door for maximum force, and the stacked bales on the other side went flying. The door swung partially open and they squeezed through. Both immediately put their backs against the door and pushed it closed just as the alpha's heavy body slammed into it. There was a moment of grace time as the alpha collected itself. "I'll hold it shut and you stack bales against it."

"Of course!" Glenda said while grabbing multiple bales and shoving them against the bottom of the door. She raced to gather the closest bales and had them back in moments.

With the door momentarily secured, Traveler joined her to gather the remaining bales that were further away. As they stacked the bales in an interlocking pattern against the door, they heard repeated harsh thumps and clawing noises. The pack was in full attack mode and furious at the prey's escape.

With the retaining wall of bales restored, the door remained sealed. Their safety was secured, at least for a breathing spell. As they stood gathering their breath and their emotions, Glenda said, "What do you think all this straw is used for, besides holding the door shut?"

"Blood," answered Traveler. "The Romans brought in straw after each match to soak up blood and keep the arena floor stable for footing. My guess is these contests involve battles that generate a lot of the red stuff. This is a crowd of warriors and they love bloody fights. I bet this arena has seen many captured Huns pitted against other Huns as well as against wild beasts."

Glenda grimaced. "I think you're right. Some of these bales probably had your name on them. Now Glaucus's blood will claim your straw. I like that trade, thank you alpha wolf. "

"Better yet, 'Thank you, Ardaric.' I saw the big guy give Glaucus the heave-ho into the arena. Without that distraction I would have been Humpty Dumpty after a few more wolf attacks. Those wolves learn fast and that alpha is an orchestra conductor. The pack all watch him and perform to his bidding."

"Well, I agree Ardaric did a good turn, but he's the reason Glaucus started this whole affair. It's a classic example of how a sycophant messes things up when trying to please the boss."

"Agreed," said Traveler. "But that's equally true in our time as it was in centuries past. Everyone wants to please the person wearing the crown of power. It's human nature." He paused a moment before saying, "However, most ladies, even in our time, would see Ardaric's attention as a big compliment."

Chapter 35

Plan B

The analysis and trauma of the arena ended as Glenda said, "Let's forget Ardaric. It's time to go with a new Plan B. We need to get out of Dodge as fast we can. I see a yellow brick road leading down to the river, it says, 'Follow me, escapees.'"

As Glenda started to move toward the path Traveler held up a hand. "Maybe there's a better choice. Ardaric will send a lot of men here to find you. He's not going to let his princess escape. He's a guy who gets more determined when he's thwarted."

Looking around, he smiled. "Let's not rush off. I think they will expect us to run toward the river. That path is just too promising a way out. Why don't we do the unexpected? We can hide in the straw pile. I think we can burrow in, try not to sneeze, and enter the arena through the door when they leave."

Glenda shook her head. "We'd be trapped if they found us. Let's go vertical. They won't have hunting dogs right now sniffing for us."

Traveler immediately nodded in agreement. "Solid thinking, that's a much better choice. Without dogs our stealth works. I'll pick our tree if that's OK." Glenda nodded.

Traveler scanned the nearby trees then pointed. "Big oak beside the arena wall. There are no lower climbing branches, nobody will think of us being up there. As our teachers and coaches frequently say, 'Rise to the occasion.' Let's do it."

Traveler walked below a large overhead branch. He crouched down and then he gave a strong upward leap. He barely reached the thick limb with his outstretched hands. He dangled down for a moment then asserted his arm power and chinned himself up. Once his feet were secured on the thick limb, he grabbed an overhead limb for balance, then motioned for Glenda to follow.

Glenda made a final look around. After confirming they were still alone, she crouched and then launched herself toward Traveler. Her hands were unnecessary as her feet landed on the limb holding Traveler.

"You've still got it, princess. I thought that heavy dress and the bags would slow you down but you're a skyrocket." Stepping toward the thick trunk, Traveler pointed upward to a natural resting spot where branches intertwined. After climbing up, he said, "Throw me the bags and join me." Glenda was fast with both requests.

Seated, the two looked at each other and were torn between laughing and sighing. They did both. "Wow," said Glenda, "you were once again cornered. This time by wolves, not jinn, but those wolves were so very dangerous."

"Yeah, but why me? I'm feeling like General Custer at Little Bighorn. I keep asking, is there a little dark cloud that likes following me around?"

"The only cloud following both of us was that treacherous keeper. Once again, you kept your cool. I loved how you built your tower of straw and were on the top when the pack woke up and charged you. These wolves may not have been able to huff and puff your tower down, but they sure intended to knock it down. That alpha was one smart leader."

Traveler was preparing a witty little piggy reply when voices and hoof sounds filled the air. "Stealth time!" said Glenda just as riders wheeled to the recently vacated spot.

Ardaric was the lead rider. Reining in his horse, he pointed to the straw pile. "They are clever, very clever. They expect us to chase them to the river, make sure they are not playing hide and seek in the stacked straw."

Two warriors instantly dismounted and began throwing the bales away from the stone wall. In a short time, the door reappeared and they were able to confirm that there were no hidden escapees. Satisfied, Ardaric nodded. "Well, that would have been too obvious, and they are clever. They are running hares, so the chase is on."

Glenda gave Traveler a short poke in his side and a big grin. Traveler smiled back and whispered, "I was just testing you with the straw idea."

"Sure," was her whispered reply.

Ardaric was now surrounded by over two dozen riders, and more were arriving. He pointed at the path leading to the river. "Eight to the river. When you arrive, four cross over and search up and down. The other four do the same thing on this side.

"Stay in sight of each other and call out any sign of their direction. They may try submerging themselves using reeds to breathe through. Look for any unnatural movement."

Looking at the large remaining group of arriving riders, he commanded, "Spread out into a search line. Each rider, stay in sight of the rider on both sides. As you move forward always look up. They may hide in the thick foliage above your heads. Look for bird movement, that could indicate their presence."

Glenda and Traveler sat listening to the orders. They had the best seats to listen and observe. Their stealth skill was once again justifying the effort required to master it.

As the riders departed for their respective search missions, only Ardaric remained, accompanied by his squire. Looking down at the lord they studied his face. He looked perplexed. Something was bothering him.

Indeed, he was bothered. He had seen the young woman race along the top of the wall then leap down to the floor. He had studied her fall expecting she would likely break a foot, or certainly twist an ankle badly. She should have been very slow in rising. Somehow, however, her fall seemed too slow. She landed more like a child's blown dandelion ball, gently descending in still air.

The boy's running speed was not right either. Ardaric was an experienced judge of warrior speed. Battle nerves give a body enhanced power and quickness, but the boy was simply too fast.

Finally, the door should never have yielded to their effort. The stacked bales would require time and effort from many powerful men before the door could open outward. Yet the two seemed to simply push on it and it opened.

Who are these two? the battle lord wondered. *Why are they here? They are certainly not Hun spies studying our plans. They appear to have little interest in our approaching battle. When they are found, I have many questions.*

Whispering in Glenda's ear Traveler said, "He reminds me of that jinn in the great hall when we were watching from the crow's nest. It knew something was not quite right but never figured out what it was."

Glenda nodded, whispering back, "He is the lord for more reasons than just size. He's smart and observant, much like Attila was when confronting an enemy. We need to be very cautious."

They only relaxed when Ardaric swung his horse's head around and trotted back toward the inn, followed by the mounted squire. They listened to the receding hoofbeats until they knew both horsemen were well out of hearing distance. Feeling secure they dropped their stealth covering.

A smiling Glenda said, "I think we need to rest up right now. We're stuck here until the scouting parties return. Last thing we want to do is head out and run into them."

Traveler nodded in agreement. "What if we drop down into the upper deck of the arena? That's the last place they will look, and the riser steps will hide us if we lie flat. Sleeping on stone is not my first choice but I think Morpheus will help us out."

"Lead away, I'll follow you out on the overhanging limb." Pausing, she grinned. "May I say we're going out on a limb with this idea?"

Laughing back, Traveler quipped, "Watch monkey boy's moves. Monkey-Glenda see and monkey-Glenda do."

Glenda gave him a grunting sigh back, then an exaggerated side scratch followed by a monkey's "uh uh uh" sound.

The two moved effortlessly out on the thick limb. Traveler was first and he carefully surveyed the arena floor as well the empty stone benches. "The coast is clear," he said before he dropped down. He moved quickly out of the way as Glenda landed beside him.

Secure on the wide stone aisle, both stretched their legs out from the cramped tree position. Bending down, Glenda opened a travel bag and slowly removed the wool peasant dress that she had worn before being dressed as a princess. "Give a girl a little privacy, please."

Traveler obeyed and turned to study the tree limb they had just used. He waited a few moments and started to turn back. "No peeking please, make your mother proud. This expensive robe is a work of art and I don't want to rip it with fast moves."

Traveler grimaced at the need to continue twisting his neck, *Women can be so slow. Dad has told me that the best way to learn patience is to go on a shopping trip with a woman.*

Glenda was now seated. "OK, you can unkink your strained neck, too bad you don't have some owl DNA in you. And lose those 'slow women' thoughts that are running through your reptilian brain."

How did she know that? Traveler wondered.

Handing Traveler a bag, she said, "Take out the food supply and use the empty bag for a pillow. I'll use the robe as my pillow, it is so delicate it deserves my soft skin and never your rough face stubble." She hesitated then asked, "Shouldn't you be approaching that time in life when you'll need to shave?"

Traveler accepted the playful jibe while inwardly thinking, *She's right. When is my beard going to start coming in? Has living in a time-controlled sanctuary stunted my manly appearance? Where is my Russell Crowe gladiator look?*

With the resting arrangements decided on the two stretched out on their backs with pillows supporting their heads. As Glenda was drifting off, she thought, *Great, the smell of my old sweat is back.* Before she could mentally complain further Morpheus had her join Traveler in a deep resting sleep.

Chapter 36

Roads Less Traveled

Their peaceful sleep ended abruptly. They stirred at the same time, as the sound of slow-moving horses alerted them to approaching company. Traveler was the first to attempt rising and was the first to groan. "My back has a steel rod down the spine, I can't bend."

Glenda rolled onto her side and placed her head on a hand to elevate it. She moved very slowly before whispering, "I met the same blacksmith and have the same steel rod. Slow movement is the answer, bend the rod gently."

Traveler followed her example by first bringing his knees to his chest, and then using an arm to elevate the head. He rocked back and forth to get up while biting off a groan. "Never again. Stone is not my friend."

Glenda followed suit. Finally sitting up, she lifted her arms to stretch high in the air. "Try this, it helps open the chest and the neck muscles. The good news is I really slept deeply and have energy for moving out."

Traveler did the suggested stretches, then slowly rose to his feet and confirmed that his balance was intact. He then went to the back edge of the wall and in stealth mode peeked over. A large congregation of sweaty horses and riders were resting in the shade.

Glenda squeezed Traveler's arm. "Someone is coming, and coming fast." They saw Ardaric approaching at a gallop. He rode into the center of the group. Those on the ground quickly moved out of the way while the mounted riders wheeled their horses away to create an open circle.

In a commanding voice Ardaric ordered, "Give me your reports. I don't see our two runaways. I assume they ran faster than our horses or did they lie down in thick grass while you thundered past? Could they have developed gills and stayed underwater for an hour? I am more than disappointed." Giving each scout a hard stare, he quietly asked, "Where are they?"

Silence passed over the large group. The only sounds were the contented chewing noises of the horses masticating and swallowing. Not one warrior, either mounted or standing, returned the lord's stare. Heads were down and eyes focused on feet.

Ardaric waited long enough for his men to be more than uncomfortable, then he pointed to a young mounted rider. "Geoff, you were my leader for the river group. What did you find? Rather, why did you find nothing?"

As the young warrior began choosing his words, he saw Ardaric begin to scowl. The lord did not want a diplomatic answer expressed in meaningless, placating words. Geoff understood he had best give an accurate, honest accounting in his own words.

Straightening in his seat, looking his lord directly in the face he answered, "My lord. We trotted down the pathway in single file toward the river. Our lead riders moved with speed while studying each side of the road for any hiding spots. The followers moved more slowly reviewing the same ground.

"With sixteen eyes searching we were sure we had not passed them by nor were they hiding. Once we arrived at the river we broke, as you ordered, into two groups. One group stayed on this side and the other went to the opposite side.

"Our lead riders in each group advanced at a faster pace to ensure the runners were not ahead of us. The trailing riders were deliberately slower and studied the shore for footprints. They also studied any potential hiding places among reed beds."

Gaining confidence as he saw Ardaric's face begin to soften, Geoff continued. "Birds flew up in haste with our arrivals, they had not been disturbed by any runners. We went further than any runner could have gone then we turned and repeated the search on the way back. The two could not have eluded us. We are sure they never came along the river route."

Ardaric studied the eight river riders and saw they were nodding in agreement. These were honest, open-faced warriors, they were not covering up any error in judgement or lack of effort. Each was dedicated to their lord and wanted to please him.

Accepting the response, Ardaric continued, "So they must have escaped through the forest." Turning to an older warrior he called him by name, "Fritz, describe your picket line and how you searched."

A standing Fritz straightened and lifted his eyes to his lord. "My lord. We are experienced forest scouts. We have many times pursued those trying to escape from a battle or hide from your justice." Pausing he said, "While we lacked our hunting dogs their absence did not impair our search."

Ardaric gave a nod to show that he appreciated this honest answer. No excuses were being given.

Similar to Geoff, Fritz warmed with the nod and continued. "We are the largest group and we spread our line as wide as possible. Our line had eyes on a width that was over a mile. We moved our steeds slowly around the larger trees to ensure they offered no hiding spot. We constantly search the upper limbs.

"Once we were further out than any runner could have gone, we split ourselves into two groups for the return. As each group came back, we further spread the arc of the search and added half a mile on each side.

"Going and returning we banged our swords and called out to each other. The forest rang with our calls. We drove many deer ahead, a dozen or so boar, and three very annoyed bears. Nothing had disturbed the wildlife except us. We do not believe two runners could have taken the forest pathways."

Encouraged by Ardaric's accepting nods, Fritz gave a slight smile. Looking Ardaric in the face he concluded with, "Lord, our throats are sore from a day of shouting. Is there a possible remedy?"

Ardaric began to laugh and his men visibly relaxed, "Indeed Fritz, I believe we can find an appropriate potion to relieve your sore throats." Looking at the river riders he added, "And of course your efforts are appreciated and deserve a similar reward."

Turning his horse back toward the inn he closed the conversation with, "Let's return to our lodgings and think about the day. Possibly one of you will have a sudden idea on where they may have gone or where they may be hiding. They are indeed very clever. To escape the arena's test is nearly impossible. At first, I first thought the young man a bit dull, I see I was mistaken. He hides his wit behind a bland face."

Glenda gave a playful grin to a frowning Traveler, only to be ignored.

"Now it is time, my searchers, to feast and recover. The cooks will have our food prepared and the tables set. My guess is that the fate of the innkeeper will motivate them to prepare the best feast possible."

To a man, each warrior suddenly found his mouth watering with the prospect of the upcoming meal. Dry throats were already anticipating long intakes of cool ale.

The men on the ground quickly remounted. The entire company followed their lord in a long, orderly line around the arena's stone walls and out through the pillared entry gates.

When the last hoofbeats were gone Glenda turned to Traveler. "He is a smart, fair leader. When they returned emptyhanded, they trusted him to listen and be reasonable. And he was. He responded by rewarding them tonight. He also knows he needs them to make their best efforts for him when they face the Hun. Leaders and followers must have mutual trust."

A "get even" look suddenly passed across Traveler's face. The undeserved "bland face" comment and Glenda's amused look would stay with him for a while. He jabbed back with, "You're right. He is such a wise leader, he could make a great ally as we figure out the threat we face. Maybe you should rejoin him and pledge yourself as queen. That would give us a real army if needed."

Glenda simply looked at Traveler and snorted, "Very funny, Mr. Bland. Feeling a little dull today? Perhaps your head is suffering from lying on the stone for too many hours."

Then her voice turned serious as she said, "Traveler, forget the slight, of course he's wrong. Now this is a perfect time for us to head out. The big man and his minions will spend the night drinking and be slow-moving tomorrow. We will be a fading memory. Besides, they are here to plan their attack on the Hun armies."

Traveler was instantly brightened with Glenda's reply to his being Mr. Bland. "As usual you're right. We have our escape window right now, the big question is, exactly where do we go?"

"I've been thinking about that. I'm sure something nasty is in the dense forest to the east of the old Roman fortress. There must be more going on than a massing Hun army. The jinn are likely there and in control. I think unfortunately that's where we head. What do you think?"

Traveler nodded. "We go east, but first we get to the fortress. Assuming it's abandoned we can use it as our base camp."

With the destination decided upon, they stepped onto the rim of the wall and did their controlled glides down to the ground. Traveler paused for a moment. "Would it make sense to go back to the kitchen from the rear entrance? We could use stealth and take more provisions."

Glenda thought, then frowned. "It could work but more likely not. The kitchen staff will be on edge and hustling, someone could bump into us and set off alarms. Not worth the risk."

"Yeah, you're right, but it was worth considering.

Glenda noted that the sun was now behind taller trees. Dusk would be closing in on the forest shortly, with total darkness following. "I think we need to hustle and put distance in pronto while we can still see. Let's stay on this maintained path for as long as possible. Lead on, my scout."

Fortunately, the path was wide and well maintained. While they did not move as fast as a horse, they had high energy and long-legged strides. Their determined pace quickly separated them from the town.

Despite their ground-covering pace dusk arrived too quickly, the path was no longer lit by fading sun rays. The only light now came from a bright three-quarter moon. Surprisingly the moon's rays did an acceptable replacement job with falling beams reflecting off specks of quartz in the gravel.

The reflecting effect produced a walkable path that shimmered in the soft moonlight. It reminded the pair of sparkling salt on Chicago streets. While far from the bright yellow brick road of Oz, it did extend a sparkling "follow me" beckoning of its own.

With owl-eyes held wide open, and pupils fully dilated, they focused on the glistening road at their feet. After several hours they saw the path that had run along the river was now gone. Hearing the murmuring river flowing close by, they increased their pace and in a few more minutes arrived at the river's edge. Their prior moonlit path was replaced by a hard-packed dark riverbank.

Before starting their journey on the bank, Traveler stopped and bent down beside a calm side pool and began drinking. A satisfied look crossed his face. "Just as cold as I remember it."

Lifting his head, he glanced at Glenda. "I feel like this is déjà vu. Been here drinking before. The only thing missing is being chased by Throbb and his hound pack." Quickly beside him, Glenda nodded in agreement as she slowly drank from cupped hands.

Thirst satiated, the two stood up. Traveler said, "We could follow the riverbed all the way to the fortress. The bank may be dark but it's hard-packed and we don't have to worry about nasty forest brambles and tripping vines. Alternatively, when we're far enough away from the town we can head back to the main road but do it in daylight. Right now this river bank feels like the best way to travel." Glenda agreed.

The two settled into a moonlight walk. The flowing river made soothing sounds while nighttime denizens barked back and forth. As she walked Glenda reflected, "Sounds like the foxes are having their own arena games. Run softly, rabbits!"

Listening to the fox calls Glenda said, "At first I thought those were some weird dogs with laryngitis. So that's the sound of a barking fox. Any scout experiences to share?"

"Indeed I do. We have a lot of foxes in Virginia. I've seen them sitting and barking by the woods around my house. My guess is they are calling for a mate, or maybe trying to scare a rabbit or field mouse out of hiding and into a meal."

"Well, let's hope we don't hear wolf howls. Foxes are cute, wolves not so much. I'm tired of being the first course on a pack's menu."

The conversation quickly ran its course, and they walked silently beside the river. Occasionally there was a slapping noise as a fish jumped high and returned to the moving water. Bullfrogs were a constant male orchestra as they made their loud chug-a-rum calls to would-be mates.

Traveler was the first to suggest a break, "Mr. Brain is telling me a stop is needed and maybe some traveling food. How are you feeling?"

"Agreeing with Mr. Brain. I see a nice sitting spot ahead, close to the river with moss growing like a blanket." Glenda was the first to reach the moss blanket. Sitting down she began placing travel food on top of the cloth wrap.

"Ladies get first dibs," said Traveler as he joined her. "As they say, 'an army marches on its stomach.'"

"Who is 'they'?" asked Glenda, partly out of curiosity and partly to slow Traveler's food intake.

"The quote goes to either Napoleon or Frederick the Great. Since Frederick predates Napoleon by fifty years my vote goes to him, but whoever knows the real authors? Likely it was first said by an overworked cook somewhere and then credited to a noble's wit."

Sitting on their haunches they finished eating then slowly drank their fill. Finally, they stood, stretched, and accepted that the march needed to continue. Looking ahead Glenda offered, "Want me to carry the heavier bag? You've had it the whole time."

"Just try and take it. This is what we guys do best, we're two-legged mules but thanks for the offer. Did you know a typical Roman legionary walked twenty miles a day while carrying everything he needed on his back and belt? And those guys were pretty small compared to today's soldiers, around five feet seven and 140 pounds". As an afterthought he added, "Small maybe but huge in battle."

The trek went onward as miles passed under their feet. To their hiking pleasure, the riverbank continued to provide an easy walking surface. At last a morning ray snuck through the top of a tall tree, striking both in their faces. The ray was a wakeup call to the forest denizens, it quickly prompted an outburst from birds greeting a new day.

Blinking into the rising sun, Traveler said, "I think it's time to call the night march over. We need rest. Well, I need rest. My dogs are barking and I don't want to deal with blisters when we start up again."

Chapter 37

Welcome Back Home

Glenda had a tired smile as she leaned against Traveler. "Thank you, my scout, I'm done in. Do you see a nice resting treehouse somewhere?"

Traveler started to shake his head "no" then found himself staring ahead at a high riverbank. "Am I imagining things or is that possibly our old riverbank cave ahead? The opening is all covered up by tall weeds and reeds, but my memory says it could be. I'll check it out."

Glenda watched as he parted the covering greenery and then disappeared. When he reappeared, he was a Cheshire cat grinning from ear to ear. "Guess what? The hiking gods are with us. If you ever question déjà vu, the evidence is right here."

Glenda moved rapidly to the thicket, bent down, pushed the tall reeds to the side, and looked into an opening. "Unbelievable! I don't know how you ever spotted this but it's our old stone cave built into the bank. Give me our bags and I'll set stuff up inside." With that she pushed the front reeds aside and disappeared inside.

Waiting outside, Traveler heard a voice echo within the small cave. "It's exactly as we left it! I don't know why it's not home for bears, wolves, or foxes but it's our home today."

A minute later she called out again. "Coming out." Once outside she smiled at Traveler. "I left our food inside and the bags are empty to carry whatever we want. I think soft moss beds would really be great. Can you remember where the moss was?"

"Absolutely. This mule remembers every plowed furrow and every bed of nice thick moss. Hand me the bags and I'll bring a load back."

Bags in hand, Traveler headed downstream to find where he had found the moss on their earlier visit. He turned into the forest and let his instincts take over. He didn't need to force a memory, he just let his feet do the recall. Shortly he found the thickly regrown moss bed.

As Traveler began carefully cutting out chunks of moss using a sharp-edged river stone he thought, *This is so much easier with daylight. I remember last time it was dark and Glenda had to find me and torch my way back. The sun is my friend right now for cutting but the cave will be nice and dark for sleeping. It's the best of two worlds.*

Knowing he had plenty of time, he carefully cut the moss into wide squares. The cutting required focus and a definite effort. *Don't want a rock cut, take your time boy scout,* and he did. When his load was ready, he lifted both bags and returned. *Maybe that was twenty minutes,* he thought. *Takes me that long to make my bed and straighten my room.*

Once back he called down into the opening, "Are you inside?"

"Yep. Just pass the bags in one at a time." As requested, the bags went into the cave. In a few minutes, two empty bags were returned.

The echoing voice called out, "Are you getting another load? We're probably OK right now, it depends on how tired you are."

"This mule doesn't know what tired is. Besides, I want to sleep like Rip Van Winkle. See you in a few." With that he turned toward the cutting bed.

Traveler was quickly back at the cutting ground and settled down to make a second full load. *Another twenty minutes and I'm greeting Morpheus.* The second cutting came in on schedule and Traveler lifted the two loads.

Standing up, he felt the strain of cutting and carrying. *I'm a tired puppy.* Smiling to himself he thought, *Part puppy, part mule, I'm a weird mixed breed.* As he emerged from the forest he froze. His spider senses went to full alert. Someone or something was in the flowing river. A shimmering body had suddenly disappeared underwater. It stayed submerged until slowly reappearing.

Squinting due to the sunlight reflecting off the flowing river, he stared at a long neck. *Not the Loch Ness monster. Swan? Mermaid? Water nymph? Lorelei?* Long, flowing reddish hair said it could be a Lorelei. Of course, it was Glenda. Being a gentleman, he called down, "I'll leave you and put the loads inside."

Head now above the water, Glenda called back, "Just leave them by the opening, I'll place them. Right now, I suggest you join me. You can keep your filthy clothes on and let the river do its washing job."

Traveler placed the two loads beside the cave opening, then took his boots off and placed them beside Glenda's. He walked quickly to the river's edge and started to look for the best way in.

Glenda saw him searching and she pointed upstream to a series of descending rock ledges. "Use those. They're manmade for easy entry. You'll be in a nice-sized pool and it's surprisingly warm. You're a natural otter so have fun." With that she ducked under, only a floating red tail disclosing where she was.

Once down the steps Traveler embraced the pool's inviting water. The pool was clearly manmade. Dug out of a side bank, it was protected by an encircling rock retaining wall. The water entered the pool slowly from a lengthy side-channel coming off the river well upstream. Once in the pool the water was nearly stationary. It benefited from the sun's rays as it absorbed energy and created warmth for the bathers.

Traveler, the ever-curious otter, paddled out of the pool and into the river. His return to the pool was fast. The contrast between the pool's warmth and the river's chilly water was pronounced. Teeth chattered in the river while body limbs could relax in the calm, warm pool. *This has to have been built by the Romans. Probably legionaries who missed their heated baths. Not quite a hot tub but close enough.*

Glenda dog paddled toward him from the far end of the pool. "Pretty great, isn't it. Not exactly the bathhouse, but still a great experience. I knew I needed to bathe when I finished making the first layer of the beds. The cave is great for sleeping and protection but not much air movement. I thought, 'What stinks in here?'" Grinning, she continued, "I was ready to blame you except you were outside. Now enjoy getting clean!"

Traveler was a happy otter paddling around. The pool was fairly deep. He jackknifed in the water to shoot down and touch the bottom. Once there he rolled into a ball, rotated upward, kicked his feet hard against the sandy bottom, and came flying out of the water. Bursting from the surface he shouted out, "Aquaman surfaces!" He knifed in the air and plunged back into the deep pool.

Amused, Glenda watched the calming surface, thinking that Traveler was more like Otterboy. Again the surface exploded, "Aquaman searches for his trident!" He was indeed a fun-loving otter, amused at his own water hijinks.

Otter boy took in deep mouthfuls of the clear water, swallowed some, and made volcano eruptions with the rest. With a sly smile he ducked his head and swished it around, then he padded closer to Glenda. Putting a serious look on his face he asked, "Did you see the classic John Belushi movie, *Animal House?*"

"Of course I did. Why?"

"Trivia question. What did Bluto do in the cafeteria? Maybe you need help remembering." With that the otter ducked its head to quickly emerge with full cheeks. Two hands immediately slapped the puffed cheeks together. The exploding jet hit Glenda full on.

Glenda's squeal was something between the beginning of a laugh and the call of a dangerous Lorelei. Knowing he was now the prey, otter boy instantly submerged and paddled away to escape the vengeful river goddess.

Finally, the otter surfaced while gulping in air and laughing. "The answer is he was a zit if you…"

His witty answer was stopped midsentence by a powerful stream of water delivered by a nearby Lorelei. With water up his nose and throat he coughed, sputtered, and then rolled on his back. "You have killed the innocent otter who is just nature's little clown."

"I am so sorry, Mr. Otter. When winter comes all my Norwegian friends will admire my fur scarf and ask what happened to the sweet little otter. I'll tell them I found him sadly drowned in a faraway pool.

"Now, Mr. Otter, I am going to dry off and I suggest you do the same. I'll go upstream to a grassy patch, get out of this garment bag I'm wearing, and dry off in the sun. There is a nice spot further down that has your name on it. This wool is like an absorbent paper towel. I suggest you wring out your garment bag as hard as possible and let Mr. Sun do the heavy drying. We'll be nice and dry and clean in under an hour."

Traveler knew when the high school dance was over and the teachers were wrapping things up. "OK, princess. Be careful not to get sunburned."

"Same to you, Otter Boy," answered Glenda as she moved up the steps heading for her sunning spot.

The two were quickly at their respective drying spots. As Traveler began to get out of his clinging garment, he quickly found himself annoyed again. This time the annoyance took the form of wool that was determined to stay with him.

He felt like Br'er Rabbit wrapped up with the tar baby. Like Br'er Rabbit, his mood jumped quickly from frustration to annoyance, to anger. It was his time to sunbathe and the tar-baby garment seemed determined to deny him his respite.

Looking upstream he saw that Lorelei was now comfortably stretched out, welcoming the sun. Her tar-baby garment was clearly well-behaved and was sunbathing beside her. He was already behind in the drying-off race.

How do girls do this clothing stuff so easily? Mine was fine in the water, I barely knew I had it on, and now it refuses to come off. I'm very close to tearing it off. Taking a deep breath, he said to himself, *Calm down Traveler, you're the otter, have fun.* The message worked. He took another deep breath, relaxed his tense body, and suddenly found the wool was his friend. The clinging challenge was over without a tear.

He proceeded to wring the garment out with both hands and was amazed at how much water the garment had absorbed. Then he spread the garment out to let the sun work its drying magic.

Stretched out on soft grass in the warming sun he had never felt so relaxed. Traveler was a happy clean otter basking in the warmth of the friendly sun. He was in the sweet state that exists between conscious daydreaming and sleep. His mind was imagining himself as a young otter chasing other otters down a waterfall slide. He heard their gleeful barks calling out to him, then he realized the barks were from an approaching Glenda. "I'm coming, get decent."

Traveler scrambled for his clothes. The wool was now sun-soft and warm. It slid over his head with ease. Arriving, Glenda was looking at him and laughing. "What's funny?" he asked.

"Look down at my dress and down at your pant legs."

Traveler's eyes immediately went to Glenda's hem then to his own pant legs. Both had risen at least two inches. He started to chuckle. "My mom was right. Again. Clothes shrink when not properly washed."

"Your mom's right about a lot of things, shrinking is the least of them. On the positive side we can run faster if need be. There was too much looseness before, my fit feels much better now. It's a definite improvement, and we smell much better. Trust me you will be happy once we're in our cave."

When they reached the cave Glenda bent down and entered the dark opening. After a few minutes she called out, "Hand me the bags, please."

Traveler passed both in, "Now the boots, please." Finally came the invitation to enter. "Feel free to hibernate with the bears. We are due a long sleep."

Before entering Traveler swept his hands back and forth across the tall reeds. With the thick grasses again covering the entrance he bent down and backed inside, "Weeds and reeds, weeds and reeds, our camouflaging friends."

Smiling at his singsong words Glenda replied, "Weeds and reeds, weeds and reeds, that's the poet hiding in you. Now it's sleepy time, lay back and relax."

Stretching out on the soft bed of double-thick moss Traveler sighed saying "It's so comfortable in here, and dark thanks to our weeds and reeds blocking the sun. How will we know when it's dark outside and time to move on?"

"That's not something to fret about, Mr. Otter. Let's trust our bodies to recover from the ordeal of the last two days. They'll wake us when it's time to move ahead."

"I like that answer. This otter is on his way to Morpheus land. See you when I can't see you... hopefully 'cause it's dark again outside."

Glenda smiled back. "Sleep well, I'll race you to Morpheus land."

Morpheus watched their deepening breathing and decided their race was a draw.

Chapter 38

Apples for Barter

Stress moves at its own pace. Sometimes it flies away, other times it seems determined to stand still. The cave gave stress all the leaving time it needed as hours passed unnoticed. Finally, Glenda opened one eye.

Her folded gift dress had served well as a soft pillow. Due to its length she had been able to pull down part of it to cover her eyes. The only light she expected to see when she woke was from the golden sphere of a harvest moon.

Squinting with one eye, she saw that the weeds and reeds projected a soft, rich green color. Their color was the result of the sun encouraging the development of more chlorophyll before winter arrived. "Store up your energy while you can," was the sun's message.

Glenda snapped awake. *It can't still be daylight. I feel totally refreshed.* With a gentle poke to his back she said, "Traveler, time to wake up."

"Why? I'm in REM sleep and having a great dream. Morpheus is my friend."

"Well, say goodnight to Morpheus. Roll over and look at your weeds and reeds."

A reluctant Traveler slowly rolled from his right side to his left. Like Glenda he opened a single eye. His second eye snapped open. Sitting up he exclaimed, "We could not have slept through a day and a night. That's impossible." After a pause, he added, "Isn't it?"

Glenda sat up, basking in the relaxed, recharged state her body was in. Smiling she said, "I think our bodies knew what to do, and our minds let the body take over. I feel great. How do you feel?"

Traveler was smiling. "More rested than I can remember. Even in the sanctuary I never slept like this. I was always aware of what I had to study the next day, and the books worked my mind while sleeping." He paused, then added, "And besides, there's always the stress of competition. I didn't want you getting ahead on the study schedule."

"I understand and have all the same reactions," Glenda said.

Sitting up she reached behind herself and brought out a small, thin blanket. Opening it she displayed a round loaf of dark bread, a slice of smoked ham, a wedge of cheese, and two apples. She tore the bread in half then split the cheese and ham into multiple pieces. Traveler was now sitting and staring at an unexpected but very welcomed breakfast.

"You are definitely the magic woman. This has me super excited about today. I get a great sleep and now a surprise breakfast. To paraphrase Clint Eastwood's detective Dirty Harry, 'Yes, I do feel lucky! You've made my day!'"

"Consider this the reward for a little delayed gratification," said Glenda as she took her half of the bread loaf. "We could have eaten it last night, but I think it's better now."

With a mouth full of bread and cheese, Traveler mumbled, "It's Christmas in the cave. This is everything a Christmas morning breakfast should be. My stomach votes you the perfect elf." He ended the sentence reaching for a red apple.

Smiling to herself Glenda mentally affirmed his elf remark, *I know I have petite little elf-ears, they are so cute.*

As he bit into the rosy apple its juice escaped down his chin. Wiping the dripping escapee away he said, "Those are unbelievable good apples. They look like decorative plastic fruit in a furniture store." Pausing, he added, "I thought we had finished them off already."

"Your memory is fine. While you were getting the second load of moss, I did a little reconnoitering and found a winning fruit tree. It was inside a thicket of thorn bushes, protected from small animals and deer. And I agree they're great. They remind me of the magical apples of Idunn, our Norse goddess. Her apples gave the gods their immortality and energy and so do these."

With the discussion of fruit finished, they proceeded to eat the remaining breakfast. Finished, Traveler leaned back with a satisfied expression and patted his belly. "The apples really made this a feast. They delivered the sugar I needed and lots of juice. Thank you, Glenda! Now I'm ready to head off."

Standing he stretched, then bent down and went through the opening with the bags. Once outside his eyes slammed shut against the bright sun. "Ouch! Watch out, it's like a floodlight in your face. Squint hard coming out, I'll clear a path through weeds and reeds for elf girl."

He heard a muffled "OK" that was followed by an emerging mass of red hair. Glenda's eyes remained slits and she turned her back to the sun. Slowly opening them, her pupils returned to normal size. "Boy, are you right. I felt blinded coming out."

Traveler nodded, then pointed to the river. "We need to fill up and pick our route. If we leave the riverbank and head toward the road, we've got hours of moving through the forest. Big question: do we stay on the river course or head into the forest toward the road?"

"I vote to follow the river. It's already late morning, there's less than a day of sunshine left and we can't go through the forest at night. Let's just get more distance from the fair today. Tomorrow we can go through the woods and get back on the main road."

"Sounds good. Our immediate mission is to move fast while staying clear of Huns and Gepids." As an afterthought he added, "I still feel like a convict on the run."

As they added miles to their journey, they found it increasingly necessary to stop and rehydrate as well as to rest tired legs. As he took a deep drink, Traveler chuckled. "Haven't heard a search hound all day but my own dogs are barking."

Glenda gave him a puzzled look. "You've said that before. I'm curious, what are your barking dogs?"

"American expression used by marching marines. 'Barking dogs' means your feet are tired, complaining, and want a rest."

Smiling back, she quipped, "Should I say you have gone to the dogs with this little factoid lesson?"

"Very clever, now I'm worried your biting wit will be snapping behind me all day."

A smiling Glenda growled then said, "Let's wake up the dogs and get moving. Are you ready to roll out?"

"Yeah. If I sit too long, I won't get up."

Stressful or not, the day was glorious for hiking. Both were in a walking groove that permitted the miles to flow easily under their feet. There was no barking dog either two-legged or four-legged bothering them. Finally Traveler asked, "Is it my imagination or is the sun beginning to set?"

"Yes it is, thank goodness. I do believe we are approaching the end of a great hiking day. I think we should begin looking for nourishment. We have apples left but they could sure use some company. Maybe some sweet berries." As an afterthought Glenda asked, "Could we catch fish, Mr. Boy Scout?"

"Easily done in the movies. In real life, not so much. Maybe if we had a net, otherwise no."

Glenda frowned, accepting their stomachs' sad plight. "Well, we can keep going until it's dark, then find a place to hole up and eat a few apples. Tomorrow we should reach the fortress and I'm hopeful that there will be something edible there."

Traveler nodded, told his stomach to shut up, and leaned into the hike. *Don't think food, just move* was the message he gave himself.

Time sped up with the sun's now-rapid descent as dusk darkened the forest. Suddenly Traveler stopped, lifted his head, and scanned the woods. Glenda tensed. "What does my scout hear?"

"Not hear, smell. Do you smell anything?" asked Traveler.

Glenda relaxed. Given the question, no threats were likely. Smells are rarely indicators of danger, with forest fires and annoyed skunks being the exceptions. Sniffing the air, she nodded in the affirmative. "I do, it smells like chimney smoke."

Pointing ahead into the forest, Traveler said, "That's our new direction. Even though it's getting dark, I think we can follow the smoke trail. If we can't find the source pretty soon, we'll go upstairs to our usual treehouse lodging."

Glenda nodded, "Lead on, we'll follow our noses."

Once into the twilight forest the encroaching darkness was determined to trip them up. Stumbling along they opened their eyes as wide as possible. They again resembled Archimedes as they searched for the smoke's source.

Searching was slow. This was an old-growth forest. Huge tree trunks rose from the fern and moss-covered floor. Traveler used his walking stick to avoid collisions. In a light tone Traveler said, "Stay close and listen to the grunt when I run into something."

"I can still see a little," said Glenda. "Want me to lead?"

"I'm OK right now but we could use some bat sonar." Swinging his stick ahead in an outward arc, he said, "Let's see how we do."

After many more challenging forest minutes passed, Glenda said, "I am sure the smell of burning wood is much stronger. Let's look for light."

Chapter 39

Wisdom of the Elderly

Glenda had just finished speaking when Traveler stopped again. He motioned for her to join him then whispered, "Your nose is spot-on. I believe I see a cottage straight ahead in a clearing. What do you see?"

"I see the moon lighting up a thatched roof. I see a window with light. Better yet I don't see any threatening movements."

Traveler gave a hand motion to advance to the edge of a clearing then stopped again. "I think you need to be the first presence at their door, I could scare them. Use your sweetness on them. I'll stay here on the edge of the woods; I'll be there fast if anything threatening starts to happen."

Glenda nodded, then stepped into the clearing that surrounded the cottage. She approached the single door, deliberately making herself as visible as possible from the front window. *No skulking. Skulking is a big danger signal.*

Glenda reached the wooden door and paused to calm herself. She studied the one-person entry door, it appeared as a single sheet of solid oak. The oak was a statement about protective strength. It suggested not testing it with weapons, weapons would just get stuck. *These old doors were truly the guardians against uninvited entry, not the flimsy stuff we call doors today.*

In the center of the door hung a thick iron bolt. The bolt was clearly a knocker. Glenda lifted it and let it fall back. The iron kissed the oak, and a responding echo came from inside. The echo was followed by chairs scraping on a wooden floor. The next sound was a determined scratching to get out. A gruff voice ordered the scratcher to get out of the way. The door opened slightly then stopped.

A wet nose inserted itself into the opening and a brown ear flopped on top of the nose. Above the nose a thickly calloused hand held the door firmly in place as narrowed, cautious eyes looked out. Then the door slowly opened a few more inches. Glenda stepped slightly forward so she was better lit up by the interior light. She gave her most winning smile back at a grizzled face that was taking her measure.

"Yes?" said a raspy voice. It sounded like a longtime smoker's voice but was likely the result of living in wood-smoke-filled rooms.

"My brother and I are travelers following the river. We missed the path that connects the river to the road. In the darkness we got lost then we smelled the smoke from your hearth. Our joy was great to think civilization was close by before the animals of the night took us for their dinner."

"Open the door Ivan, she is just a young lady and no threat to you." The man opened the door further and the old hound did his expected inspection. He sniffed and snorted until Glenda finally reached down and petted a graying head. While the hound was old it could still sort out friend from foe. Glenda passed muster as a friend and it licked her hand.

Ivan's wife moved him aside as she took over the greeting protocols. "Where is your brother? Is he armed? Is he a threat to two old people and an ancient hound?"

Smiling, Glenda answered, "No threat. He is shy, and easily intimidated." She then gave a come-out wave to Traveler.

Traveler walked slowly from the woods to the door aware that his size could be off-putting. Once there he stood meekly beside Glenda in the light, permitting the couple to size him up. He slowly turned around, making it clear he was unarmed.

When facing them he kept his hands open and flat. He kept a "first day of school" smile on his face. His face did its best to make it clear to the inspecting teachers he would never be a class problem. Teachers knew better of course.

The dog was once more the guard at the gate. Coming out, it again did the sniff-and-snort sizing up. Traveler waited patiently then patted the head and long droopy ears. Having fulfilled its second inspection and guarding duty, the dog licked the hand then returned to the fire.

Satisfied that the two presented no threat, the couple motioned them to enter.

Once inside Ivan removed his hand from a large iron sword that had been resting behind the door. Noting the weapon Traveler recalled President Reagan's famous line about nuclear disarmament with the Russians, "Trust but verify." In this case it was, "Verify then trust."

Ivan motioned to the woman and with a raspy voice said, "My wife. She is called 'Frau.'"

Later Glenda said, "He is certainly a man of few words. He calls his wife 'Frau,' which means 'wife' in German. One word does it all for him."

The wife, regardless of how she was called, was clearly the family leader and she took on the shrewd look of a bazaar merchant. "I assume you seek shelter and possibly food, is that correct? What can you offer in exchange? Do you have coin?"

Since the woman ran this household it was fair for Glenda to act as their leader. Traveler relaxed and enjoyed watching Glenda become the bazaar buyer. The two women began matching wits and negotiating skills, the two men were merely bystanders.

Glenda nodded then said, "We have no coin but something better. We have the apples of Idunn. These apples are perfect for pies but are also perfect dipped in honey. Reaching into her bag Glenda selected a perfect, bruise-free, ripe red apple and held it out.

The apple glowed in the firelight. It was a special fruit and would command a premium in any bazaar. The old woman raised an eyebrow at the offer. She took it in her hand, stared at it, studied all sides, and nodded her head.

Chuckling to herself, Glenda thought, *I'm feeling a little guilty right now. I'm like Snow White with the old woman but in reverse. I'm the one conning a nice old lady with some forest apples for a full meal and lodging. She probably can't even see it well enough to appreciate it.*

Glancing over at Traveler, then at Ivan, she thought *I can see Ivan is already salivating at the prospect of a pie.* She noticed Traveler was quietly giving her a "thumbs up" signal in appreciation of her shrewd bargaining.

The woman smiled at Glenda, "You are such a sweet girl. So well-mannered, so considerate of your elders. Please follow me for a few minutes of discussion without the men."

The woman walked to the door and opened it. As the cool night air entered the warm room, the sleeping hound lifted an eyelid and sniffed. Satisfied that all was well, it closed the eye. Perhaps it had understood the word "pie" and now had a dream-pie between its paws. Who knows what a dog's happy dream is about?

The woman moved through the doorway and gave Glenda a beckoning nod. Glenda understood the deal would be closed in privacy and away from the men.

Once outside, Glenda followed the woman around the far side of the cottage. A bright moon made walking easy; they were soon standing in the rear clearing. Glenda gave an encouraging smile to the woman indicating she was ready to close the bargaining for the apple/food exchange.

Returning Glenda's smile the woman pointed her arm forward. "Focus straight ahead my dear. Let your eyes adjust and tell me what you see."

Glenda was puzzled but accepted the woman's charge. As her pupils fully dilated the trees ahead took form, then distinct shape. Hanging on the branches were red balls that caught the moon's rays and bounced their rosy color outward.

The decorated trees reminded Glenda of Norwegian Christmas trees that lined the streets of Oslo. Unfortunately for Glenda these red balls were not ornaments but fully ripened red apples. Glenda felt herself shrinking as the woman smiled at her.

"Let's go back inside, dear. This chill is more than I need. We can continue the conversation in more comfortable surroundings." Glenda could only nod.

Once inside the woman led Glenda to a small dining table near the fireplace. After they sat down the woman removed a brightly colored cloth from a wooden bowl in the center of the table. Pointing to the bowl's exposed contents the woman smiled, "Our orchard produces the best apples in the area. We sell them each week at the outdoor market for a pretty penny… or two. Apples are our livelihood. What else can you offer?"

Glenda felt like a little girl during show and tell in the first grade. Her offering did not measure up and her classmates were snickering at her embarrassment.

Traveler was torn between being amused and at the same time ravenous and exhausted. He saw that Glenda was rapidly losing the barter chess game. The old woman had her close to checkmate. Then he saw a potential winning move. "Glenda, I believe you have something in your bag that our hostess may find most desirable."

Glenda felt her mind snap out of her *I've been bested* funk and back to the present moment. Smiling, she answered, "What you suggest, dear brother, has a value far beyond food and lodging. Anyone who views it feels instantly compelled to have it. It's not fair to these nice people to show them what they cannot have."

The woman was now staring at the bag. What could these two coinless youths possibly have that she would covet?

Keeping her bargainer's poker face, Frau said, "Alright, your brother has cleverly teased me with the bag's content. I have seen many valuables in my lifetime so I seriously doubt that whatever is in there will mesmerize me. Please bring it out and satisfy my curiosity. Trust me, I will contain myself."

Glenda reached into the bag, paused for a dramatic effect, then slowly lifted out the gifted dress from Ardaric. As the dress slowly emerged the woven threads in the high collar first caught the fire's light and burst into ribbons of flashing silver and gold. The threads following in the cuffs added a second level of sparkle and eye-commanding focus. Finally, the long-hanging garment presented itself fully.

Viewers would be torn between staring at the wearer's face above the collar, the ornate sleeves, or the long, silvered sides of the dress. The wearer would appear as a jeweled queen.

The woman's poker face cracked, then vanished with an uncontrollable smile. She visualized herself as a noble lady hosting lords of the land. She imagined the respect and jealousy that other noble ladies would feel in her presence. She would be a queen by dress, if not by title. Neighbors would give respectful bows when she came to market.

"May I please hold it?" was all the woman could say. Glenda knew the "must have it" hook was firmly lodged in the woman's mouth. Now was the time to reel the woman in. She handed the dress to the woman while smiling encouragingly.

Traveler watched the woman hold the dress up to her chin while letting it drop to the floor. "It's made for you," was all he had to say.

Ivan nodded while working hard to close his gaping mouth. Whatever facial-control skills he had were long gone. Ivan was staring at his wife like she was a twenty-year-old princess. He saw her again in the glory of her youth. The damages of time had disappeared from her. He wanted her to wear the dress for his own viewing pleasure.

"I cannot offer enough for this, yet I truly want it, just as you foretold. Is there any barter possible?"

Glenda put a thoughtful expression on her face and finally answered. "Yes, there is. Seeing the pleasure it will bring you and your husband, I am in a generous mood. I believe good deeds come back to the giver, so permit me to make you an offer.

"My brother and I still need food and lodging. In exchange for the dress we will stay here overnight with a warm meal. Then you will provide two bags filled with your best foods in the morning. Is that an offer acceptable to you?"

The woman's eyes began to water. She could only nod her head in acceptance. Wet eyes showed that she was at a loss for words. Clearly the girl was nobility and the frau found herself kneeling before Glenda.

How and why she was here was a mystery, but her generosity was clear. The woman would tell this tale of noble visitors for many years to come. The proof of the tale was the dress.

Ivan now stepped forward and bowed low to both Glenda and Traveler. He grasped his frau's hands and assisted her to her feet. Once she was up, he circled her waist with his arm and held her close. He was dazzled by the dress but also by the visitors.

Like his frau, he knew these two young travelers were special. He had never met their kind before nor, he knew, was he likely to in the future. Only the hound appeared less than impressed as it continued its sleep.

Bowing his head again he said, "Permit me, noble guests, to welcome you to our humble home. I apologize for my earlier lack of hospitality. We have a most comfortable guestroom through that door. It is there for our children when they visit. We keep it clean. The bed is large and accommodates all four of our children.

"The two of you are very tall but will have sufficient stretching room and plenty of quilts to assure a warm night. Please allow me to show it to you while Frau starts the evening meal."

Ivan pointed ahead then stepped aside to encourage the two to lead the way. The man was well-aware that nobility leads, while the lesser follow. Glenda and Traveler walked first down the narrow hallway.

At the hallway's end was an arched door with a carved face that stared up the hallway. Possibly it was a guardian god offering protection to entering guests. Flanking the god's face were carved forest figures ascending the sides and across the arch. Unlike the figures in Olaff's ceiling, these remained fixed. They were charming in their constructs but had no apparent magical movements.

Wow, thought Traveler as he approached the entry. *This outwardly simple cottage has craftmanship inside that is well-hidden from the outside. Smart way to avoid making yourself a target.* Ivan opened the door and stepped to the side, permitting his guests to enter first.

"There is wood in the fireplace. I can start it now if you like."

"Please do, and thank you," said Glenda.

Ivan then pointed to an open window, saying, "We keep the window open for fresh air, but the room becomes quite cold at night. Shut it as you desire."

"We like cold air," said Traveler "We'll leave it open for now. If it gets too cold, I know my sister will get up and close it. Right, princess?" Glenda's look back answered that silly question.

So they are a prince and princess. I knew it! Frau will have the best tale to tell for years to come. "I'll leave you to settle in. Dinner will be ready in less than an hour and I'll knock to let you know."

Ivan remained a moment longer talking with Glenda about dinner while Traveler inspected the interior. Like the doorway it presented a multitude of carved treasures, some were part of the furniture and some were free-standing statues. Each carving was a small jewel presented to entertain guests as they relaxed and fell asleep.

Children would be mesmerized by the wooden figures. Older children could build stories about them and entertain their younger siblings. There was no loss from missing modern-day electronic devices. Imaginations were developed in this room.

Chapter 40

Dinner Tales

With their privacy secured, Glenda said, "Traveler, that was really fast thinking on the dress. The frau owned me at the bargaining table, what a shrewd lady. And I still liked her even when she outfoxed me.

"I feel really good that this couple will treasure the dress forever. I saw how happy Ivan looked when his wife held it up to her body. They may be too old for children but who knows what magic is in that dress. Old in this time is youthful middle age in ours."

Traveler nodded in agreement with all of Glenda's thoughts. "You are right across the board. I feel we have done a very good thing for Frau and Ivan, our karma should be nicely stepped up. And the practical upside to the bargain is that we will have days of food to take with us. A food supply gives us a time advantage to scout for jinn without constantly searching for our next meal."

Glenda relaxed in bed while Traveler talked. He noticed her eyes were beginning to shut so he said, "A nap may keep you awake later." The response was a soft inhale. Traveler discovered his own eyes were drooping. He quickly lay on top of the bed and a nap followed.

It was an hour that felt like a minute when a soft knock came on the door. "Dinner's ready. Please join us while everything's hot."

Traveler's head twisted toward the door and he struggled to sound awake. "OK Ivan, we'll be right out," was the best that he could muster. Feeling groggy from the interrupted sleep, he gently poked Glenda. "Rise and shine, princess, foods await us."

Glenda tried to shake herself awake, then settled back on the soft pillow. "What year is it? Boy, was I out."

Lying there forcing their bodies to rise, the wafts of cooking odors coming under the door did the trick. Stomachs motivated legs into motion. They were up and out the door in short order. Once back at the main room they paused to take in the table setting.

The frau had pulled out her best dinnerware for honored guests. At the center of the table were fresh-cut, late-season flowers. The bouquet was held in a colorfully painted, tall pewter bowl. The vertical bowl was shaped like a standing bear. It was another craftsman's work of art.

Circling the bear were platters of steaming foods. It was a feast that M would have approved of. The two quickly took their seats and were joined by Ivan and his wife.

"I wanted to wear my gown but was afraid I would soil it. Not that I'm a messy eater but a dinner table is not the place to risk a beautiful dress." Pausing and then pointing, Frau said, "Even though it's not on me right now it's still with us."

The gown was indeed on display. Hanging from a display rack, its silver and gold threads sparkled from the nearby candles and fire lights. It was an original showcase piece whether presented on a New York, London, Rome, or Paris runway model. It seemed content resting on a Dark Ages wooden rack.

"It is beautiful," said Glenda, "and will be even more beautiful on you. You and Ivan have many years to show it off and enjoy it here in your home."

Traveler joined the compliment circle. "It is indeed a wonder but so is this feast. Rarely have I seen a more beautiful or bountiful dining offer." After pausing a moment, he asked, "May I start?"

As the serious business of eating began, conversation ended. Four sets of arms, hands, and mouths descended on the various choices. Eventually, Glenda saw the first round of intake was ending. *This is a good time to start a little information scouting.*

"We understand the great stone fortress is deserted. Is it really empty? And if so, why?"

Traveler was still helping himself and was pleased he could listen without interrupting his meal. Glenda noticed his questioning look and gave him a nod to continue eating, she would do the verbal scouting.

Accepting the question after a slight hesitation, Frau said, "Yes. The great fortress which guarded this region from the distant time of the Romans has been reputed to be empty for many years now."

"Why was it abandoned?" asked Glenda. "Did the Hun invaders capture it then occupy it? If it's not occupied why don't people simply return?"

Ivan was closely watching his wife answer the girl's question. He had heard tales among the older working men in the region regarding the empty fortress. Their tales seemed to be built on some mystical happening. He had chosen to avoid discussing these stories with his frau. There was no purpose in scaring her. Now he was curious to hear what women thought of the fortress's condition.

The frau gladly accepted being the center of the questions. More than acceptance, her face indicated she was relieved that she could talk about something that had been long repressed. She had never shared this story with Ivan. *Why upset him?* she had thought.

"My mother had friends that worked in the fortress kitchen. Two of them arrived unexpectedly at her cottage. They arrived frightened beyond reason, out of breath, with red faces from running and crying. Far beyond being disturbed, they were terrified. They were hysterical as they attempted to talk.

"At first none could speak clearly, their sentences caught in their throats and they had to calm themselves before they could start to speak. My mother gave them some strong ale to settle them. They calmed enough to tell a terrifying tale.

"They claimed they were preparing to clean the quarters of the fortress lord. He was called 'the duke,' and he was reputed to be a true giant of a man. Typically, they carried the food tray along a walkway tunnel then up a steep set of stairs. At the top, the stairs opened onto a floor that wrapped around the duke's suite of rooms.

"On a normal day they would place the tray to the side of the entry door, knock, and return to the kitchen. It was not their place to see the duke early in the day." Glancing at Glenda, she added, "Noble men are sleeping bears, slow to wake and grouchy when they do.

"This visit, however, was far different. They had brought up brooms and other cleaning tools and were preparing to begin when they froze in place. An ear-shattering sound came from around the corner. They described it as a piercing, grating sound, much like a heavy rock being pushed across other rocks, or dull writing chalk being scraped across slate surfaces. The sound was an early warning to all in the fortress. Sadly, none knew that at first.

"Following the sound, dark air rushed past them like a great storm. Even sheltered by the sidewall of the duke's quarters, their hair was blown about and turned grey. The grey came from the thick dust carried by the wind.

"Rather than investigate the source of this sound, they simply stared at each other then ran for the staircase. Without buckets and brooms they flew down the stairs and raced into the kitchen. They were breathless but alive.

"They described the sound and the wind to all within their tale's range. A number of the young serving men immediately rose and raced to the duke's quarters. Only one returned. His eyes had rolled in his head and his hair had turned white. His whiteness was not from the dust but from great fear.

"My mother's friends said his speech was so garbled it was not understandable. An older cook tried to calm him but to no avail, he raced through the kitchen shouting out gibberish and disappeared outside.

"Later we understood he was trying to call out a warning, but his mind could not bring the correct words to his voice. People who did not know him would have viewed him as a person with an addled mind. Later we realized his mind was indeed addled, but from a terrible experience.

"Since the morning meal was well underway there were other men present. A number of warriors, as well as some older stablemen, armed themselves and raced toward the duke's quarters. Only three returned: two warriors and one stable hand. They each told a tale that froze all of us. After hearing their story, fear spread throughout the fortress like a raging forest fire.

"The stableman went to his fellow workers who had begun the morning's chore of brushing and feeding the mounts. He told his tale and it was believed. They immediately began releasing the horses, but too soon they had to abandon this effort for their own survival.

"The two returning warriors, after giving their tale, bravely returned to the fortress calling out warnings to flee. After seeing the fear on the returning warriors' faces and hearing their tale, the kitchen staff left their posts and fled to the outside courtyard. A few had the presence of mind to take food with them, but most simply ran. It was as though the kitchen was on fire and escape was all that mattered."

Traveler and Glenda were spellbound as they heard the story. "Did your mother herself ever see what had caused the panic?"

"No, but she later heard similar stories from others who had witnessed the happenings and lived. The stories were all consistent, so she accepted them as the truth."

"Did she tell you the stories?" asked Glenda.

"Not at first. Years later my mother told me the tales when I said I was going to explore the deserted fortress with my friends."

Motioning toward Glenda, she continued, "I was about the same age as our princess here when I heard mother's tale. I was already committed to marrying Ivan who was a strong, protective young man. I had felt safe exploring the fortress with Ivan as my knight. Being young and curious both of us wanted to find what was inside." As he listened to his wife's story, Ivan's heart soared to hear of his wife's faith in him.

"After I heard my mother's tale, I instantly decided not to involve Ivan and myself in an ill-planned adventure. I told Ivan I had simply changed my mind as young girls were permitted to do.

"While still young I was gaining wisdom. We have avoided the fortress to this day, I believe that was a wise decision."

The frau saw questioning looks still on Glenda and Traveler's faces, and she realized she had not yet fully explained her decision. "Sorry to take a bit long to answer a simple question but you needed to understand the seriousness of the tale.

"This was not some mother's tale told to keep a young girl in line. This was a sincere tale of demons. Possibly only one but if there was just one it behaved like a multitude in the evil it spread."

"How did this evil manifest itself?" asked Glenda.

"Those in the fortress who heard the early cries and wails from the dying fled their posts. There was no time to consider responsibility or duty. Of course, a few brave ones did stay: out of duty, curiosity, or the lack of an escape route. Those that stayed and survived had the following description of events.

"There was a red cloud projecting multiple arms which constantly varied in size and length. The cloud passed through people. Once struck by the cloud the people lost their senses. Many immediately collapsed, dead, while others became unresponsive to any word. The unresponsive stood in place with the blank look found on cattle. Those who tried to withstand the red cloud were instantly silenced. The only option was to run.

"Running to escape produced a flood of people desperate to flee the fortress to the open fields and forest. The fortress was quickly empty and has remained so to this day. Even warriors refuse to enter."

As Glenda and Traveler listened in silence, they each felt a tightening in their stomach and a tremor in their mind. When the frau had finished, Traveler asked, "Were there no hero warriors who could stand against this cloud? I understood there were two giants that protected the fortress. Or is that a tale to frighten invaders?"

Pausing, the woman took a breath to collect herself from the tale. She had never before presented the story in the depth she did now. She saw Ivan was sitting frozen in his chair, she felt guilty over giving him the story. Once calmed she answered, "Yes and no.

"Yes, there were two huge men that were described as giants and protectors. Of course, people exaggerate size a lot. From tall to giant is just a big stretch, particularly if you are short yourself. I have never seen a true giant. In my experience they exist solely in children's stories.

"Giants or not, the two large protectors were not in the fortress when the cloud descended. Legend says they were together exploring a threat from the east. Possibly they were seeking information about the Hun invaders. Those Huns have also been described as demons even though they are human.

"Personally, I believe the best explanation of the fortress demon is a plague. Plagues arrive unseen, and they strike and kill before people are aware. As people begin to die of no apparent cause, group fear arises.

"Fear is a plague in its own right. With fear comes a loss of reasoning. Those who see the effect of the mysterious deaths may well have addled minds and imagine demons are among them. Flight is the ultimate cure taken by those under the plague's threat."

With this explanation the frau saw Ivan visibly relax. He understood the terror brought by sudden plagues and could accept this cause for people abandoning the fortress. He knew that once a village or city was evacuated people rarely returned, at least for many generations.

Traveler and Glenda were pleased as they listened to the frau's tale. They were beginning to gain information about the jinn threat. Unlike the frau's speculation regarding the cause of the evacuation, they knew from personal experience that demons did exist. They also knew that giants existed.

The demons were the jinn, and the giants were Olaff and the duke. Of course, there was no reason to share these truths with the two older hosts. Silence was best in this case.

Smiling, Glenda said, "I agree with you, Frau! Demon red clouds and giants are tales intended to scare children and the curious away from a possibly disease-filled place. Unseen disease is a true evil. When it is not understood it is often called a supernatural force."

Traveler leaned back in his chair and nodded his agreement with Glenda's comments. He then shifted the conversation toward their travel needs. "Will we pack our food now or in the morning? I would like to pack now if possible. We have left a great feast on the table and this may be the time to bundle it up for our days ahead."

"Please wait a moment," Ivan said, and as he rose. Smiling, he said, "I needed to get up and move around after my frau's story. For a moment she had me seeing demons and giants, and I am far too old to believe those tales. What I do believe in is the importance of fulfilling a promise." He disappeared into the kitchen, returning a few moments later with two large leather water pouches.

Handing them to Traveler, he said, "I suggest you pack now. Please take this table food as well as any in the kitchen you want. Frau and I may be asleep when you young people are on your way. I remember being young and moving about early; however, the older you become, the more sleep becomes your companion."

With a sharp grin he added, "Feel free to visit the orchard and take as many apples as you can carry." Looking at his wife he said, "Now, my lovely frau, I believe we can retire. Please tell me a pleasant story for my restful sleep."

The woman was on her feet, smiled at her husband and motioned toward their private part of the cottage. "Husband,

I will tell you a story of good-natured, generous, traveling nobles who helped a poor forest family. Both of us will sleep much better with this tale. There is no need to dwell on scary old legends from the distant past."

With the couple gone, Glenda and Traveler began an organized packing. They carefully placed similar foods together: meats together, cheeses together, and separated from the breads and apples. When they were finished each bag bulged. "Can we eat all this?" rhetorically asked Traveler.

Glenda looked at him then laughed. "Maybe not you, who is such a dainty eater. Trust me to step up, I know days' worth of feasting when I see it."

Traveler gave a grin back, "Yeah, I already see dueling forks in our future."

Chapter 41

On the Road Again

The next morning arrived with stealthy rays of soft light filtering through the wool drapes. The sun was barely peeking above the horizon, roosters were not yet declaring the day's arrival. "I feel great!" said a waking Traveler. "Mache schnell, princess."

Turning over, he saw an empty bed. The pillow still had the indentation of Glenda's head, indicating she had slept there recently but was now gone. *Mache schnell, me*, he thought. Downstairs, he saw a seated Glenda enjoying a morning apple. "Try one. Fruit first thing gets your motor running."

With a sheepish look he asked, "Been up long?"

"Just an hour or two." Then she laughed. "Maybe ten minutes. Eat that embarrassed look away."

Noticing there was an unpacked loaf of raisin bread remaining, Traveler picked it up and placed it into a large pocket. Watching him, Glenda went into the kitchen and returned with a small wheel of blue cheese. "We'll feast on the road. Let's head out before we wake the sleepers. Always leave a party when people want a little more of your time."

Traveler acknowledged the wisdom of this, opened the door, and gave a courtly bow and hand sweep. "Ladies first." Glenda gave a returning smile and bow.

The hound lifted his head as cool outside air came to him. He sniffed, considered getting up and going out, then reconsidered. *Later* went through his mind as his head fell back on a soft paw-pillow.

They had only walked a few minutes when the goodbye call of Chanticleer the rooster followed them up the road. "I think he misses us," said Traveler.

"Better we hear him in the distance than through the bedroom window. Like Mr. Chanticleer, I'm feeling great, I'm ready for a strong day. How about you?"

"Ditto," said Traveler as he lengthened his stride to keep up with Glenda.

They settled into the glory of the early morning. The sun was a welcoming source of both light and warmth. The road was now fully visible, the chill of the night was rapidly disappearing, and the air came in refreshing breezes.

After an hour of fast walking, Traveler paused to look at the surrounding trees and calling birds. "This is so pleasant. No threats, just nature in all its beauty. As they say, 'I wonder what can go wrong?' You know, the expression, 'Too good to last' has its roots in many sad outcomes following joyous times."

"Ixnay, big boy. Don't suggest that bad stuff may happen, that's a sure way to invite it. That's like welcoming a vampire into your house, just don't do it. Think positive thoughts. We make our own fortune. Well, mostly. This morning is working for me right now. I'll tense up when I need to."

Traveler gave an understanding smile back. "When you're right, Glenda, you're really right. Forgive me for being Mr. Worry Wart. What could possibly go wrong on a day like this?"

Glenda's returning look said, "Did you listen at all?"

As they hiked briskly along they saw a sharp bend ahead. Traveler motioned to slow in the event of an unexpected threat that could be waiting around the bend.

Coming first around the curve Glenda excitedly pointed, "There it is! It's even bigger than I remember!"

Traveler instantly lifted his eyes from the road and felt a shiver pass through him. The enormous stone fortress had suddenly appeared when they rounded the sharp bend in the road. It was huge. Beyond huge, it filled the skyline. It was a stone guard declaring its dominance over the surrounding countryside.

As they approached it, the fortress became less intimidating. It was like an unpredictable acquaintance from their distant past with both good and bad sides. *Which side will present itself today?* they wondered.

Standing in front they studied the dark entrance tunnel. The entrance was separated from the road by the rushing waters of the river. A wide wooden drawbridge offered passage to the opposite side bank. Once across the bridge the gate beckoned them to enter the dark tunnel.

As they inspected the stone giant in front of them, the bridge reminded them of a tongue protruding from a god's open mouth. Was this a hungry god or a welcoming god? Before they could determine the god's mood, Glenda flinched and turned to Traveler. "Tell me you don't feel the ground trembling."

Their morning was now delivering answers to Traveler's rhetorical question of "What can go wrong."

Traveler's attention left the dark entrance and focused on the increasing vibration rising from his feet and up his legs. "Rats, that feels like racing horses. It's the charge of the light brigade and it's heading for us. My guess is that Ardaric's men are on a search-and-recover mission, and you're the mission. We need to move inside right now!"

Without a word, Glenda came out of her walking stance like an Olympian leaving starting blocks. She was instantly ten feet ahead of Traveler, heels kicking down hard with strong push-offs, elbows swinging sharply at her sides. Traveler became a trailing sprinter copying her form but not her speed.

They flew across the bridge into the dark tunnel. Once inside they stopped to regain control of their breathing. They pressed themselves against the stone walls of the tunnel and entered stealth mode just as the lead riders rounded the road's sharp curve.

The charging horses slowed as they approached the river and their riders reined them in. Once at the crossing bridge the group of six riders sat in their saddles and studied the open tunnel. One rider advanced to the edge of the bridge, rose in his saddle, and carefully studied the dark tunnel. "I can see all the way through. The tunnel is empty." Looking to the lead rider, he asked, "Do we enter?"

The lead rider was pondering this question. He advanced his horse past the questioning scout and proceeded over the bridge. At this close distance the tunnel's interior was clearly visible. Soft sunlight illuminated the passageway and confirmed the tunnel was indeed empty. The leader had to decide whether to enter.

Through the tunnel, the sun offered a partial but clear view of the interior. The courtyard appeared as an open green field, thick with overgrown weeds, bushes, and small saplings. The large space had reverted to nature many years ago. Nowhere was there evidence of footprints from man or beast. Horses could navigate it but at some risk from cutting bramble thorns. Nothing called for further investigation.

Satisfied with his closeup observations the leader turned his horse around. "No one has entered here for many years. The saplings are well over ten years old. The ground growth is a mess. The many thorn bushes would make bad passage for our horses.

"We have done our duty. We will return to Lord Ardaric and confirm that this road is a dead-end and the fortress empty. The lord will likely request we begin a search on other roads but that is his decision, not ours."

Chapter 42

Fortress Time

As Glenda and Traveler watched the riders' faces, they saw the barely concealed relief that swept over each one. There was no appetite to enter the fortress. Each of them had grown up hearing the stories of the red cloud demon, none wanted to test the veracity of the tale. All turned their steeds and followed their leader on the road back toward the safety of the town. Huns they could face, demons not so much.

When the horsemen disappeared around the sharp curve both Traveler and Glenda slipped out of their stealth camouflage. Traveler was the first to speak. "Wow, that was close. Did all your boyfriends chase you like that?"

Laughing at the compliment Glena answered, "Not Norwegian boys. Their mothers watch them like mother hens when a girl is around."

"Mine too," grinned Traveler. "Of course, nobody ever chased me except in a dream or two."

Now that both were collected from the close encounter, they proceeded through the tunnel. As they entered the enormous courtyard, they stopped to study how the setting had changed.

The first thing they saw was that the large fountain was still bringing water down into cascading layers of vertical catch basins. Roman plumbing and aqueducts continued to perform as designed. Without hesitating they sat beside the fountain, cupped hands, and took cautious sips.

"It's still wonderful!" exclaimed Glenda as she brought a water-filled hand to her mouth. "Water is one less thing we need to worry about."

Nodding back, Traveler said, "I may cool off in it before dinner."

"I may join you as long as there is no splashing otter. Right now, I want to explore the old familiar places, starting with the kitchen."

Traveler took a final look around. "The lead rider summed this place up pretty well. It's been deserted for a long time. It's clear nobody has worried about maintaining this as a staging area for mounted warriors. No horse droppings anywhere, ergo no horses. Notice there is ivy growing up the walls. This place feels like it could be a deserted university somewhere in New England."

Glenda agreed with his reflections while heading to the kitchen. The large entrance from the courtyard into the kitchen was open. Its heavy wooden doors were pushed to the sides, warped, and secured by rusty hinges. The lack of repair spoke of sudden departures a long time ago without a return visit.

As she walked past the open kitchen fireplaces she called back to Traveler, "Good news, we can heat our food. Some stoves were set up but never lit. The wood will be dry as tinder."

Traveler entered and surveyed the kitchen scene and then the large dining area. He imagined himself as Sherlock Holmes as he studied the deserted space. *Read the clues, Sherlock*, flashed through his mind.

Sherlock called out to Glenda, aka Watson, his now-imagined sidekick, "Look at the tables! Some of them still have plates and glasses right where the diners left them. Notice how the silverware is scattered around, even the precious knives were left. Note the mold growing inside many of the steins as the ale continued to ferment. This reminds me of my high school biology lab with petri dishes gone ballistic."

Looking more carefully at plates, he added, "Mice have no fear of demons. They descended on the tables, chewed their fill of food, and nibbled plate edges."

Glenda stood beside Traveler and took in the state of the dining tables. Grinning at him she said, "I know that look, you're Sherlock Holmes looking for clues. Those dirty dishes remind you of something. I bet you were a master of stacking them unwashed in your sink. All I see is clear evidence that people got out of here as fast as they could. What do you see?"

With Glenda's fast take on the evidence, Traveler found he had suddenly morphed from Sherlock into Watson. Traveler quietly answered, "Let's visit the stables."

The two went back to the courtyard then entered the stables. The wide, wooden stable doors were also open. One door was lying on the ground while the other clung at a sharp angle held by a single weary hinge.

Glenda observed, "These doors were left open to the winds and have slowly been destroyed. The stablemen were so protective of this place and their charges, they lived for the wellbeing of the horses. They would never desert it like this. I feel really depressed about what happened here."

Passing into the large stable, the two separated to walk down parallel corridors with horse stalls on each side. Traveler stopped at the end of one connecting aisle. "Glenda, take a look at this."

Coming across the aisle, Glenda joined Traveler. She saw a pained look on his face as he pointed into a stall. "You need to see this."

"What is it?" Then her face betrayed what she saw. She quietly said, "It's the skeleton of a horse, a large one."

Traveler was slowly nodding as he reflected on the scene. "They loved their horses; only great fear would have them ever leave a single one. Even with a fire they would have taken them all out. What could scare them even more than fire?"

Looking at each other, they answered together. "A demon."

As they finished their inspection tour and met at the end of the stable Glenda asked, "How many skeletons did you find?"

"I counted twenty-five on my side."

Nodding back, Glenda said, "That's about what I found. The stable boys never got to this end to open the back doors. I think they saved as many as their fear and wits permitted, then ran like crazy. The poor horses had no chance to escape."

Trying to break the depressing mood, Traveler pointed up. "Want to visit the land of hay and straw?"

Relieved to get away from the horse cemetery, Glenda was more than on board with the suggestion. "Sure, jump away, nobody is watching."

"Ladies first." As Glenda did her Michael Jordan leap, Traveler marveled at how easily she did it. *She's got an extra leg-spring built in there somewhere.* He leapt, but with more effort, to land beside her.

As they looked across the long loft, they saw all the feeding hay had long ago deteriorated into straw and dust. "Nothing here except dead hay. Let's go up another level."

The two were quickly on the highest loft. They had simultaneous memories of the fun straw fights with its accompanying sneezing. Traveler studied the sad remains of previous straw mountains, then he pointed. "The good news is our passageway entrance is easy to spot now. I'll push on the entrance block."

The sealing stone slid easily back on its iron runners and Traveler crawled partway in. "We need light, I forgot how dark these tunnels are. There used to be wall-torches, let me see what I can find."

When Traveler's head met stone Glenda heard a loud grunt and muffled words best not spoken in mixed company. Then a light illuminated the entrance. She bent down and used a soldier's elbow-stomach crawl to get inside. Once inside the hallway she saw Traveler rubbing his head. "We always had a torch when we came here."

"You OK?" asked Glenda with sincere concern in her voice and face.

Traveler held back what he would have answered for mom-sympathy. Instead he said, "Yeah, I'm fine. Just feeling stupid that's all. Let's light the torch and roll the wagons."

They began the familiar walk back to the hallway's opening in silence. When they arrived at the junction point Traveler said, "Don't know about you but I'm getting flooded with memories. A few good and many scary."

"I feel the same way. I think they are memories but also warnings about what we are walking into with our mission. We're inside the deserted belly of the jinn beast. The beast may be gone but there is a residual stench of evil here."

"Yeah, that's the smell that makes me tingle. Let's get out of here and go to Olaff's sanctuary."

Glenda nodded. "Let's hope there is still a skiff to get us across. I definitely don't want to swim in that freezing lake. Been there and done that."

Chapter 43

Olaff's Safe House

The second tunnel brought them to the massive door that led to the landing steps. The door was the final barrier to reach Olaff's sanctuary and was typically locked. Traveler braced himself, then pushed against the door. He sighed in relief as the oak door swung inward on its hinges.

Standing on the inside landing, Traveler pushed the door shut and locked it. The torch he carried did its best to light up the dark space, but it was a struggle. Looking down the dark staircase Traveler said, "It's hard to see even with the torch. Be careful. Remember how deep each step is, they were built for Olaff's giant legs."

"Thanks, but how could I ever forget? Particularly climbing up."

The two proceeded downward with as much speed as the curving staircase, flickering torch, and good sense permitted. Halfway down Glenda said, "If this had a straight drop we could use our gravity control and float down. Why didn't the books give us a skill for this kind of descent? It's all leg muscles and balance, it's exhausting." Pausing, she grinned in the torchlight. "OK, I'll stop complaining now."

Traveler didn't answer, his focus was on his feet. Heavy boots were great for a forest hike but not so much descending the steep staircase. He had to stay focused on his balance or face a bone-breaking tumble down the stone staircase.

Once at the bottom Glenda pointed into the darkness beside the clear lake. "There's our skiff."

"Eyes of an owl," Traveler said.

Holding onto Traveler's extended hand for balance, Glenda boarded the boat. Traveler threw off the mooring rope and quickly stepped aboard. Lowering himself into the rower's seat, he gripped the mounted oars. He recalled his scout experiences with rowboats, *rowing is tricky*. He focused hands and back muscles into getting the skiff safely off the jetty's edge.

Once away from the stone pier he began slowly moving the skiff into the lake. He recalled from summer camp how to pull the oars toward him then rotate the oars ninety degrees to feather them forward on the water's surface. "You navigate and I'll row."

Glenda opened her eyes as wide as possible and thought she saw a lighter shade of gray across the way. "I think I see where to go, but not too fast. We don't want to ram the stone side." She pointed a guiding finger and Traveler began making powerful, even strokes.

Both kept their eyes wide open as they stared ahead into the darkness. From his seat, Traveler could only see the departure landing, which quickly vanished. After five minutes of steady rowing, the opposite side remained a dark wall. When the torchlight suddenly reflected against the dark wall, Glenda made a jerking downward arm motion as she called out, "Stop!"

Traveler instantly rotated the oars and pushed back. The skiff settled in the water before gently nudging the landing.

"That was too close Traveler, so sorry. I'll do better next time."

"We'll blame the torch," was Traveler's humorous retort.

Glenda was out first and anchored the prow to an upright post. Traveler was more cautious in climbing out. He had more body weight to rock the skiff. His concern was banging the skiff against the stone wall. When he felt the skiff had settled firmly against the dock he quickly climbed out and secured his end.

Once on solid stone he shot his arms in the air, "Lafayette, we are here!"

Glenda had a puzzled look, "Who is Lafayette? He is most certainly not here."

"The Marquis de Lafayette was a French noble and a hero of the American Revolutionary War. As a young nobleman he left his privileged life in France to join the American army. He became respected by Washington and many other founding fathers. Jefferson put a bust of him on display in Jefferson's plantation home, Monticello, in Charlottesville, Virginia.

"Anyway, in France when America had just entered World War I, there was a ceremony by Lafayette's tomb led by the American commanding general, Black Jack Pershing. The ceremony was to honor Lafayette. The famous phrase 'Lafayette, we are here' was made in a speech by Colonel Stanton but the general got credit for the quote."

Pausing, Traveler added, "I guess with us the more fitting phrase would be, 'Olaff, we are here!' Just like Lafayette, Olaff was our hero without whom we could not have defeated the jinn."

Glenda smiled. "I like both quotes, now let's explore Olaff's domain."

They entered the large kitchen/dining area and immediately lit a wall sconce. With light bouncing off high walls they lowered the massive candelabra. Thick candles were still in place. Once lit, the entire room brightened.

As his eyes adjusted, Traveler said, "Let's check out the pantry and see if the mice have left anything."

Once there they quickly found that kegs of honey were intact. Glenda beamed at the treasure. "Honey withstands the test of time. We'll have sweet honey for our dessert."

Traveler had moved to the large kegs that were resting above the floor on heavy, wooden supports. One keg had a protruding tap in the base. Holding a nearby stein under it, Traveler slowly opened the tap, and a dark liquid flowed out.

Closing the tap, he lifted the stein, sniffed, then put a tongue carefully into the liquid. "Not sure what it is. Tastes good but kicks like a mule. With water added it will be more than acceptable."

Putting the mug down he changed tasting gears. "What's this?" he asked while pointing at a covered bulk. Peeling back the cloth the two stared at a large ham. Bending over Traveler gave the ham a sniff and declared, "It's old but has been smoked. I think it's OK, it's been preserved and is in a cold storage place."

Shaking her head Glenda warned, "Sadly, no. We Scandinavians know about preserving food by smoking, and that ham is way past its expiration date. Like a lot of semi-preserved foods, that may still look and smell good but trust me, even the wolves would leave it."

As Traveler was leaving the pantry ham with a sad look Glenda added, "Think positive, big boy! All of Frau's food is delicious, and we now have an added treat of honey. Now excuse me, I'm going to see if the shower still works."

A few minutes later Glenda came bouncing back to find Traveler in the kitchen beside a rebuilt fire. "Good news, we've lucked out! Everything is intact and works as well as when we left." She paused, then added, "I'm calling dibs on the shower."

Noticing the blazing fire, she smiled. "Nicely done! Warm dining room to go with a hot shower then food. We are two lucky ducks right now. By the way, there are still plenty of Olaff's giant-size towels in there. Pick any one, they're still clean."

Traveler grinned back. "You go shower, leave a little hot water for me."

Glenda needed no encouragement and was quickly inside the bathing room. Clothes flew off and she rejoiced at being back under the familiar shower. As the hot water flowed over her, she felt it carry the stress away.

She tilted her head back, and the cascading water fell on her face. She turned her body slowly to receive a water-massage. The water induced a state of semi-euphoria, and she embraced it.

Toasty-warm and clean, she soaped her thick hair using the powerful overhead falls to wash the suds away. Disappearing with the soapy lather went the accumulated forest deposits of leaves, dirt, and other uninvited hitchhikers. Staring at the drain she realized another lathering was in order.

Finally, she shut off the hot and switched to cold. The Norwegian Valkyrie in her embraced the chilling cold. She felt her heart step up its pace but in an energizing way. *Contrast is a very good thing in so many ways* she thought as she stepped out.

Once the oversized towel had absorbed the wetness, she wrapped it around several times into a toga. Toga wrapped, she padded toward the warmth of the dining room.

Entering the dining room, she saw the dinner offerings were setting on the massive table with plates conveniently placed. Ale cups were filled with Olaff's mystery drink greatly diluted by chilled water. Traveler glanced up at her entrance and pointed to the chair by the fire. "Enjoy Olaff's fireplace. You can dry out your clothes by the rack.

"You look so clean it's embarrassing; now I'm feeling really dirty. I'll return a better man. You can start if you need to." Looking at the dining spread, he gave a sheepish grin. "I almost started but decided I'd enjoy this more when I'm clean. Of course, company always adds to any meal."

"I agree, dining is best when there is good company to enjoy it with. Go take your shower. Heads up, though: the water is coming down totally cold. Believe me you don't want the Arctic hitting you. Oh yeah, double-wash your hair." Glenda immediately moved to the drying rack and proceeded to hang up her clean clothing.

Traveler double-timed it to the bathing room. He was quickly out of his wool travel clothing. He stuck a hand into the falling water, and then pulled it out. *Yep, that's Norwegian freezing.* The hot lever quickly balanced the flow to a soothing, beckoning warmth and he stepped in.

This is a tonic for body and soul. Thank you Olaff for being the best host, even when you're not here. He quickly scrubbed both himself and his clothes. Like Glenda he saw the accumulated debris in his hair disappear down the large drain and double-washed his head.

After a brisk body and hair rubbing, he assembled his toga, using a cloth belt to secure it. His stomach hastened him back to the dining room. After hanging up his clothes he joined Glenda.

"That was pretty fast! Don't you feel one hundred percent better."

"Yes, and I feel one hundred percent famished. Pardon me while I start."

The two settled into controlled feasting. After the second helping Traveler pointed to a deep bowl. Reaching into it with a spoon he said, "Here's our discovered honey. Put it on the raisin bread and make dessert." Glenda needed no encouragement. The raisin bread welcomed the honey and her first bite declared success.

Finally satiated, the two settled back in their chairs. "Maybe it's the shower, fire, or the food but I am exhausted. I'm heading to Olaff's giant bed, I call dibs on the side by the door."

Rising, Glenda said, "Race you."

As usual Glenda was first and she leapt onto the far side. Pulling the heavy, giant-sized wool blanket to her chin, she said, "I love how chilly it is in here. No central heating but perfect for sleeping."

Lying on his back Traveler stared at the ceiling. The images he remembered were still there. Fleet-footed Pan was still chasing a number of gleeful, beckoning nymphs while a unicorn patiently watched the demigods at play. "I love this ceiling art. Look carefully and the characters move, they really do. Can you see their…"

Before he could finish Morpheus took him to a land of dreams that transcended the ceiling art. Glenda's soft breathing indicated she was already in that dream world.

Chapter 44

Hard Departures

They slept until Morpheus nudged them awake with internal body pressures. Traveler was the first to be aware of the need to rise and permitted his eyes to slowly open. The room's darkness made the opening of eyes an easy step. However, the softness of the bed and the pillow encouraged him to roll over and continue the sleep. Sleep was not in the cards. "Wake up!" his lower body insisted.

He slid out of bed with the heavy toga wrapping him like a mummy. Once up he was instantly on the way to the bathing room. Glenda felt the far side of the bed release his weight and her own eyes snapped open. Then her mind demanded, *Move fast big boy, I'm already standing in line.*

Once out of bed Glenda headed to the dining room and put on her clothing from the rack. The warm wool absorbed the chill of the room. Noticing the fire had burned down during the night she added a log.

Traveler entered the dining room just as she had put on her boots. He nodded in the direction of the bathroom. "I moved as fast as I could, I know how frustrating sharing a single bathroom is."

Glenda gave a small smile in return. "Thanks." To herself she thought, *Try living in a dormitory.* Her exit was immediate.

Traveler quickly changed and prepared their breakfast. As he refilled the honey jar he slipped a finger in and licked the goodness. He quickly took a second, deeper swipe into the golden mix. *Sweetness from real honey, this is the best sugar boost ever.*

Glenda came striding in, energy pouring off her. Traveler saw her obvious vitality, "Somebody got a great night's sleep and charged their battery! Have some breakfast, I recommend the honey on everything."

The two settled down to enjoy a meal that they knew would have to last them through the day. When both plates were empty Glenda said, "I guess we know where the first stop is. Can't say I want to return there but we have no choice."

"I'd like to avoid it but you're right. We need to return to the scene of our ambush and our close escape. On the positive side let's remember how well we did together. Of course, I'd sure like to have Olaff with us right now, but he's long gone."

Nodding, Glenda said, "That's so sad, he and the duke are just memories now, but such great memories. They will always be with us whenever we remember them."

The two quickly arrived at the moored skiff and Traveler offered Glenda a hand as she climbed in. Slipping the rope off the pier's holding struts, Traveler stepped nimbly into the skiff and put his back toward the far shore. "OK navigator, I'm ready to row. Just point the way."

As he rowed across the placid lake Glenda said, "We were smart to light that bottom torch, I can easily see the dock. I'll give you a better heads-up this time."

After a few minutes of Traveler's powerful strokes, she said, "Now!" Traveler dug an oar into the far side water and pivoted the skiff. The boat rocked as it slid sideways with inertia, easing them against the dock.

Traveler was first out. "You lead. Take the torch up the staircase. We'll leave it at the top and bring it back when we return. Be careful, I remember how draining these stairs are going up. Dangerous going down and tough going up."

They ascended slowly and carefully but still found they were taking frequent deep breaths when they reached the upper platform. Wiping his forehead, Traveler said, "I swear this staircase gets longer and steeper with every trip."

Grinning, Glenda said, "Yeah. I started out climbing like bouncy Tigger, now I feel like sluggish Eeyore." Traveler answered back with a soft bray.

Once they had their bodies back under control, they opened the massive door and proceeded down the interior walkway to the hallway exit door. Standing in front, Traveler slowly opened the heavy door. They remained still and listened. Neither wanted to think about how much the place felt like a tomb.

Traveler stepped first into the hallway and looked around. "All's clear, let's check out the great room then go to the kitchen." They walked quickly down the long hallway without the need to conceal their footsteps. Their leather boots remained ninja quiet as they kissed the floor.

As they passed the open vaulted doors for the great dining hall, they stopped and looked in. Without speaking they stepped inside. Thoughts of the chilling encounter between the warrior Throbb and the mage came flooding back. They saw the mage, with the jinn living inside his body, interrogating poor Throbb.

"Guess we don't need to dwell in this place," Glenda said softly.

Traveler looked sad. "Yeah, this was a room filled with fear. The jinn inside the mage projected evil and the warriors sensed it, even though all they saw was the old mage."

"The only good news was we saw the face of our enemy. We saw its total disregard, worse, its disdain, for human life. It's all about gaining knowledge at any cost with the jinn."

Glenda remained quiet as she stared up at the elevated stage. She suddenly found there was moisture collecting in the corner of her eyes and she forced the horrific memory into a deep recess in her mind. "I understand why Theo had sent us on the mission to kill, or at least, contain this monster. Looking back, I'm still amazed we pulled it off." Shaking her head she backed out of the doorway, "Let's get out of here and head to the kitchen."

Once back in the hallway an echo of terror followed them. Proceeding away with quick steps they fought the urge to break into a run. Reaching the entrance to the kitchen they paused to confirm nothing had changed. Reluctantly, they moved to the walkway leading to the duke's private chambers.

Chapter 45

Haunted Places

Walking with nervous strides they were soon at the foot of the staircase leading to the upper suite of rooms. The heavy iron gate that could seal off upward access was open, and they began to ascend.

The ascent was much easier than the staircase to Olaff's sanctuary. The risers were built for normal serving staff and permitted easier climbing. Nevertheless, they still reached the top with elevated heart rates. Their hearts were not racing from the climb but from vivid memories of a dark evil that had dwelt here. This upper floor was the battleground where they had confronted the jinn residing in the mage's body.

Immediately in front of them was the door to the duke's private quarters. It was open and Glenda made a tentative first step into the chamber, Traveler followed slowly behind. The hairs on his neck were rising and he had to shake his head to clear his mind and mood.

Once inside the large room they stood and surveyed the surroundings. Traveler took several deep breaths then said, "I feel like Carter when he first entered King Tut's tomb. There is something mystical here that speaks to our deepest fears."

Glenda nodded. "I know. There is a vibe about this room that makes you just stop and react. I can imagine how early man first stepping into a mountain cave would feel. He would see hanging stalactites of all sizes, shapes, and colors. He would see rock crystals embedded in the walls sparkling in the sun's rays. It would feel magical, it could be where his gods would dwell or worse, his demons."

Adjacent to the central room was an open archway. They passed through and began exploring. The archway had led them into a room that appeared to be a study. It enjoyed wood-lined walls, built-in bookshelves, heavily beamed ceilings, and a grand fireplace. Centered in front of a colored glass window was a massive wooden desk. The desk was flanked by several leather-covered chairs.

They were drawn to the desk with its neatly organized papers and colored maps. Pewter figurines were used to hold papers flat to keep them from curling up or being disturbed by an open window breeze. Making a cursory inspection of the papers, they found nothing of interest, then moved through the next arch.

This arch was the entrance to a short walkway which led to a grand bathroom. The shower was well over twelve feet high with a series of water heads running down three sides. An elevated, wooden bench was centered as the focal point of the water jets.

Looking in Glenda said, "Reminds me of our sanctuary home." Remaining motionless she suddenly exclaimed, "I miss the excitement of Chicago's Christmas season. Shopping with your mom, the snow, and the music! I even miss the wind off Lake Michigan. Such good times!"

Nodding in agreement Traveler said, "Me too. I sure wish we were back. I miss M and Theo. I even miss studying."

With reminiscing over, they proceeded to the bedroom. The bed was the size of the one they had slept on last night. A family of four could easily fit on the bed. Sleepers could comfortably toss and turn without annoying each other. The family dog could be welcomed at the foot of the bed.

Each room they visited had at least one ornate fireplace framed by exotic facings carved with images of mystical creatures and their secret activities. The bedroom was no exception. A person's head resting on thick pillows could watch the carved figures move in the flickering firelight. As the fire's flames rose then gradually fell, the figures' movements would follow. It was a graceful, relaxing minuet between flame and figure. Sleep would quickly follow.

In all the rooms overhead beams secured massive hanging chandeliers. The chandelier's light came from large candles resting within bronze figures. Adding to the room's lighting each room had at least one large window. The windows captured the sun's daylight as well as the moon's radiance. Incoming moonbeams added to the glowing radiance cast by the multitude of candles. Their combined radiance spread soft shadows across furniture and walls.

Once they had completed their tour they were back in the entry chamber. Traveler made a sweeping arc with his extended arms. "This entire suite is contained within a single high turret. Every room has at least one picture window. The resident lord could see in all directions and survey his domain at will. He could be an advance scout without ever leaving his personal suite."

Glenda was standing by a wide window, taking in the idyllic countryside. "It's hard to believe, looking out at this beauty, what evil was residing here. I wonder where the evil is hiding right now." Pausing, she frowned. "Silly me, of course that's our mission."

Traveler moved to the doorway. "I guess we know where we need to go next. Brace yourself for more unwelcome memories." Glenda followed him out.

The two walked out of the entry chamber's door, then moved slowly around the corner to face the surrounding platform. The left side of the platform terminated with a high stone wall. Along the right side were large alcoves. Each alcove was a dark cave suggesting mysteries inside waiting to be discovered. At the far end was another stone wall holding a large iron sconce. The sconce was built as a webbed basket serving as a large torch. The torch was not lit.

Carrying their own torch they proceeded slowly toward the back wall while studying each alcove space as they approached it. They were tense as they peered into each alcove before entering. Each inspection was reassuring, all was as they remembered. Their confidence climbed as they continued their tour toward the platform's end.

Then the two scouts froze and grimaced. Their torch had illuminated the front of the last alcove. The light identified hunks of crumbled stones scattered outside of the alcove's entrance. The torch's ever flickering light cast dancing shadows behind the sprawling debris. The floor almost seemed to move as the shadows danced.

Barely breathing they stood in front and took in the full scope of the devastation. The inside brought to mind a building blown apart in wartime. A powerful hand grenade or possibly a mortar shell appeared to have exploded inside. Destruction was everywhere.

Traveler motioned for Glenda to wait as he advanced into the interior. As he slowly moved forward he had to carefully place his feet around scattered piles of bent, torn metal and rock fragments. Sharp edges were everywhere. After a few minutes his voice called back, "Come on back Glenda and go slow. I'll hold the torch up high, watch your feet and look out for sharp objects."

Glenda followed slowly. She had studied the debris outside and now she studied the destruction within the alcove. Bad memories of this place and of her role in confronting the mage came charging back. The flickering torch only added to the scary recalls. After calming herself, she permitted her eyes to take in the scene in greater detail.

Resting in the rear of the alcove, in front of a large jagged opening in the stone wall, was a scattered pile of twisted, sheared thick lead plates. Scattered among the warped lead plates were piles of stones of varying sizes. The debris was a testimonial to a small apocalypse coming from an explosion behind the thick stone wall.

As they studied the ruins, they understood that the force of the explosion had to be enormous. The dense stone used to construct the back wall had been over four feet thick. It was solid rock and had been blasted into pieces.

As they continued to absorb the destruction, they studied the various stone fragments. Some fragments were as large as basketballs, some were the size of softballs, and some were hourglass sand. Regardless of size, many were now the composition of glass. Immense heat had altered their molecular structure, they resembled desert sand following a nuclear blast.

Standing in place Glenda finally said, "Now we know. We have only seen its power when it occupied and destroyed humans. This destruction tells us that its power is vastly greater. Our bodies must be like tissue paper to it. The lead encasement was really strong as was the stone wall, yet once freed it blew all that away with ease."

Traveler nodded as he slowly said, "I've seen enough. More than enough. I think the less we focus on it the better. I don't want us to get so intimidated we freeze up if confronted. We're forewarned and that's our advantage."

With Traveler's quiet reflection Glenda found herself standing straighter. Head and eyes that had been downcast became increasingly level and clear. Her heart slowed and her breathing deepened. Glenda the Valkyrie was returning.

"I agree Traveler. Let's track this monster and let it know the big dogs are back. We're two Beowulfs and it's just Grendel. Fear us, Grendel!"

Traveler gave an encouraging smile back. His companion had recovered and was now in a battle stance. *She's morphed into a berserker warrior. I need that confidence and aggression.* "I love it when you take the Grendel-monster by its horns. We're going to make it wish it had stayed in its hiding place."

Chapter 46

Leaving Time

It was still early morning when the two made a return trip to their Olaff sanctuary. They packed the remaining food and returned to the moored skiff. Looking back at the torchlit opening into Olaff's home, Glenda said, "I feel sad leaving this place. We're going to miss our showers and giant-sized bed."

"Yeah, I feel the same. But we both know we need to get moving. It's just too comfy in there. It reminds us of our Chicago sanctuary, it makes us feel safe. The alternative is facing the jinn world, and who wants that?"

As Glenda stepped into the skiff, she raised a clenched fist and called out her challenge. "Once more into the breach! We're coming, Grendel."

A smiling Traveler manned the oars and they were shortly moored by the opposite pier. They took their time going up the staircase to conserve energy for the challenges ahead.

Once in the main hallway they walked quickly into the courtyard and sat by the fountain. "Fill-up time," said Traveler as he placed the water pouches under a cascading stream. The two took a final look at the courtyard then proceeded to the entrance tunnel.

Once inside the stone tunnel they advanced far enough to study the road and the forest on both sides. With a clear line of sight, they proceeded to the entrance, gaining a wider view of the outside with each step. Once outside they paused to confirm no Gepid or Hun scouts were lurking around.

Looking at the road ahead, Traveler pointed to the left-hand branch. "We know the road we came in on and where it leads. We need to go left, and head north-east. That's our road of destiny. What do you think?"

"We only have one choice, let's get on with it."

With their route determined, they passed over the connecting drawbridge and veered left onto a wide Roman road. As they distanced themselves from the fortress, the road took them through once-cleared fields that were rapidly converting to new growth trees. The forest was reclaiming the farmland. The road's pushed up surface stones confirmed that nature had its eye on the road as well.

As the two walked, they observed more of nature's encroachment. "Looks like the cleared farmland has not been cultivated for many years, and nature is reclaiming it. I bet if Chicago were deserted for forty years the skyscrapers would have vines going all the way up the sides. Mr. Hancock would see his grey tower as simply a very tall green protrusion. Civilization is a thin veneer over nature and requires constant maintenance. Plants always win, ask any gardener."

"You're right. Human clearings are a nuisance to nature, nothing more."

The further from the fortress they went, the more the forest was establishing itself. The road, which was once wide enough to offer smooth dual passage for horses and wagons, slowly narrowed into a single lane. The once carefully laid stone surface was now potholed and rutted by rainwater and seasonal icing.

Overhead, tree branches on both sides reached toward each other to create a canopy of shade and roosting places for birds. Chirping noises and sweet calls came from the overhead limbs. "It's like an orchestra tuning up just above our heads," said Glenda.

Nodding, Traveler said, "Yeah, and the players are really shouting it out right now. Sounds like jazz." Smiling, he added,

"It's all good, I like how the birdbrain band puts a spring in my step. Reminds me of the old fifties rock song, 'Rockin' Robin.' It's perfect for hiking."

As they continued, they were increasingly surrounded by tall weeds on both sides. The ever-narrowing road was rapidly degenerating into a forest trail. An ambushing floor vine caught Traveler's tired foot leading to a hard stumble and a muttered expletive.

Glenda's hawk ears caught the oath and she playfully said, "Did I hear our scouting leader chastising his path? Shame, shame. Treat the vines as fellow travelers on the road. Don't hurt their feelings." Traveler's answering grunt told her how he felt about unwelcome guests hanging onto his feet.

After a few more hours, Glenda stopped. "I think we've come quite a long way from our fortress, and I'm pooped. We need to secure a safe place to rest overnight. The sun is sinking and my Archimedes eyes are opened as wide as they can go."

Traveler's enthusiastic nod said he was with her. Looking around, he said, "Yeah, definitely time to stop. I've been looking for a good campsite. So far all I see is a forest, nothing calls out to me. The good news is we're still on a definite people trail, let's go a little further. Maybe we'll luck out and stumbled onto an old hut."

Glenda grimaced, "I'm not saying 'no' to further walking, but if I collapse please feel free to carry me."

Smiling, Traveler said, "More likely you'll have to carry me. Let's just go a little further but not too far." They accepted the forward challenge and tried to ignore their now howling dogs.

As the overhead canopy became a darker umbrella Traveler stopped. Glenda was immediately beside him and followed his eyes. "Do you see what I see?" he asked while pointing up.

Glenda squinted hard and forced a tired head to look up. Then she smiled, relieved. "How did you ever spot that?"

"Honestly, dumb luck. As scouts we're taught to look up as well as down. When we walk through woods all our instincts are on the ground and straight ahead. If you look up you may see things that are helpful. In this case my head jerked up after I tripped on another vine and I saw our tree hut. Just dumb luck."

The elevated platform was nearly invisible even as the two studied it. It circled a giant oak trunk and was resting on thick limbs. The limbs supported and enclosed it. Lower branches encircled the platform and masked it from an easy view.

With further study they saw a series of subtle steps that were carved into the trunk. A skilled climber could access the platform using toe placements and hand grips. The two teens had easier ways to access heights.

"You found it, Mr. Scout, so permit me the task of investigating our crow's nest." Dropping her bag beside Traveler she lifted her arms above her head, crouched down, then sprang up. She had picked her landing limb with care and was positioned to continue the upward climb.

Placing a foot into a carved-out step, she elevated further and entered the platform's opening. Once inside she cautiously walked in a circle testing the supporting floorboards. She disappeared around the trunk then emerged with a big smile. "You found a winner. The floor is solid, as are the knee walls. Grab our bags and join me."

Traveler studied the landing place and considered his two loads. He didn't have Glenda's leap. "I think I better toss these up first. Ready to catch?"

Glenda leaned over the knee wall, looked down, and punched her open hand like a catcher's mitt. "Show me your best pitch, big boy!"

Traveler tossed each bag up into outstretched arms. Both were easily caught and secured. "Better hustle up here before I eat everything."

Traveler studied where Glenda had landed, braced himself, then pushed down hard with tired leg muscles. To his surprise he went up like a bottle rocket. He landed feet first and grabbed onto an overhead limb to steady himself. Once his balance was secured, he used the built-in footholds to enter the platform and join a sitting Glenda.

In a short time it was pitch-black. A chuckling Traveler quipped, "Lucky we got to our food in time. Another ten minutes and we couldn't see it, I'd have sunk my teeth into a hand I was so hungry."

"Well, I think the darkness has a message beyond eating. It's slumber time and I am one very exhausted girl. Make a pillow out of your bag and wrap the scarf over your ears and head. You'll be snug as a bug in a rug."

The two wrapped themselves tightly in their warm wool coats and scarves and tried to ignore the wood floor. While softer than stone both quickly found it was far from being an acceptable mattress.

Traveler was like a settling dog. First, he found that lying on his left side, using an arm to further cushion his head, seemed the most comfortable position. Then he tried the other side. A few hours later he found that the best position was being back on his first choice. While turning over again his errant elbow bumped a sleeping Glenda, she automatically reversed her side without waking.

Chapter 47

A Long Road

Surface hardness continued to dictate sleeping positions. Both teens ended up on their backs, then sides. No position offered comfort for very long. Finally, the early morning light ended their sleep suffering. "Are you awake?" asked Glenda in a soft voice.

A tired, grumpy voice answered, "No. I am going to stay here and prolong the suffering. Where's my air-mattress when I need it?"

"Well let's get this circus rolling. The good news is that I think we are heading toward our destination using this trail. My books are giving me a kind of directional reassurance. The bad news is my dreams were worrisome, we are going toward a very big threat. I'm sure it's Theo's source of worry."

Sitting up, Traveler said, "You're not alone, I had troubling dreams that had my poor toes curled up. I chalked it up to sleeping on wood, but you're right. The discomfort is a lot more than the wood floor, it's knowing what's waiting for us ahead."

With an agreeing nod Glenda said, "Definitely. We're getting the same book message. I think the threat is still a distance ahead, but we need to be ready for quick hiding. We'll keep our stealth-powder dry for quick use."

Breakfast was quickly consumed and the bags repacked. The two floated down and made immediate use of the many private forest bathrooms.

Meeting back on the fading trail, they swung travel bags across shoulders and leaned forward to start the day's journey. The usual chirping orchestra did its best to brighten their day but could not compensate for the night's restless sleep. Both were more than grumpy and walked in silence.

The morning passed without incident. Their travel route was now little more than a separation of brambles on each side of a traveled path. Traveler was forced to constantly study the ground to make sure they stayed on the correct path. A low hanging limb slapped his head and Glenda saw the air turn blue with his muttered expletives.

When the overhead canopy was at its brightest, with scattered rays hitting the path, Traveler said, "I think it has to be after the noon hour. Notice the light rays. They're slanting at an angle through the leaves, the sun is no longer directly overhead. I say let's stop. You good with that?"

"More than good. Use your scout eyes to pick us a nice clearing to rest in."

"As you command, my lady. I already see where to rest and it's better than just a clearing."

Traveler stepped off the path and headed toward a cluster of brambles. Glenda had a questioning look before she saw the brambles both hid and protected a berry bush. The bush shone with clusters of red fruit.

Heading toward the beckoning fruit Traveler used his walking stick to create a pathway. "We're in luck. The brambles have kept the deer at a distance. Sorry deer, no sharing today." He motioned Glenda to stay back while he forced his way into the berry patch.

Following in his wake, Glenda pressed against the thorn bushes until sharp edges declared "far enough." She extended the open bag and watched as the gathered fruit flowed into it.

Traveler became a two-handed harvesting machine. He moved with purpose, rapidly plucking the ripe treasures then placing them softly into the waiting bag. Both teens were anxious to sample the fare but neither broke their coordinated gathering rhythm.

Feeling the bag's weight following a final large deposit Glenda said, "That's plenty, my arms are exhausted. It's time to dine!"

Dine they did. With sweet berries accompanying bread, chicken, and cheese they found their energy return. A sudden need for napping came with full bellies. Sleep was immediate.

Somewhere in the back of their minds, an internal wake-up clock buzzed too soon. While the nap seemed over in a moment, it had been a solid hour and had recharged their bodies. Traveler stretched his long body and slowly opened his eyes.

Glenda was already standing, bending into a long stretch to touch her toes, then bending further down she placed palms flat on the earth. Holding her stretch she smiled at an awakening Traveler. "Stretching is good to wake us up. The muscles need a little time before we put them back in the harness."

"Yeah, I know. I tended to skip stretching, particularly after a race, and I paid for it later. By the way you look like you're Plastic Man from the comics. Even on my best day I could never stretch like you. Can you touch your elbows?"

Glenda felt a familiar redness creeping up her neck and immediately finished her standing leg-stretches. "Let's get moving and see where the path less traveled is leading us. I'm feeling a book-vibe saying we need to keep stealth ready."

"I've got the same book-vibe warning. I'm feeling like a cavalry guy with General Custer racing into Sioux Indian territory thinking, 'This is so easy, what can go wrong?'"

With bags secured across their backs, they once again leaned forward into the path's gentle slope. The rising path increasingly demanded more effort from the two. A tiring Traveler had gradually slowed the pace as his tired legs and path-clearing arms demanded a break. A trailing Glenda had felt the energy drain of the last several hours and was beyond happy to see him pause to catch a breath.

She was ready to congratulate him on stopping when he pointed up. A big smile appeared on a tired Traveler face. "Well, lucky us! Another lookout tower, can you see it?"

Staring upward she said, "I do now but would never have seen it if you hadn't pointed it out. You've got the great eyesight of a searching eagle, no rabbit can hide from you!" Pausing she added, "This entire trail may be lined with lookout posts. I'm thinking there will be more ahead, at least I hope so. You're the eagle-eyed scout so I trust you to see them."

"I'll do my best. It would be great to find another treetop shelter before we stop." As they continued moving ahead at a slow but steady pace, Traveler said, "Are we heading uphill or are my legs giving out?"

"I think uphill but it's a little hard to judge after all this hiking. My legs are flat out road weary. But yes, I do believe we are going up."

Traveler nodded. "Feels that way to me. I remember my treadmill workouts too well. Running coaches loved to increase the inclines. Speaking of going up, I think it's getting cooler."

Glenda felt a sudden shiver. "You're right. I'm sweating from hiking but standing still I can feel the cooler temperature."

After another hour passed they were relieved to see the setting sun declare that their hiking day was ending. Finally, Traveler had stopped. Staring at him Glenda started to laugh. He reminded her of a water dowser but in reverse form. His clasped hands were pointing toward the sky rather than the ground. "Do you see what I see?"

"Yes I do! Well done, scout." Cocking her head, Glenda said, "I think I hear running water ahead. Do you hear it?"

Traveler's focus shifted from visual to audio. "You're right, that's the sound of moving water. Let's find it before going upstairs."

The two followed their ears. As they advanced, they heard the sound gathering strength. Coming around a bend in the path they found themselves standing close to a waterfall. It was small but still magnificent as sunlit waters cascaded down nearly twenty feet into an accepting pool.

Traveler was quickly beside the bank, putting a hand into the water. Yanking it back he exclaimed, "Cold! Cold! Great for drinking but not bathing. Don't think about going in there."

Glenda had indeed been considering the merits of a cooling bath in the pool until she put her own hand in. "Ouch! You're right, that would give us frostbite. I guess we just stink tonight."

Traveler moved away from the fall's churning bottom to begin filling the empty water pouches. Once filled he tilted one downward to pour a refreshing jet into his mouth. "This is so good, try it."

Glenda took the offered pouch and let a stream of the chilled goodness strike her mouth and throat. After several, too fast long swallows, her face suddenly reddened. Coughing, she exclaimed, "I've got an icicle in my brain."

Traveler gave a sympathetic nod. "Been there, felt that. It's a 'too cold' brain-freeze, don't worry it'll pass quickly." With a little smile he added, "Well, it usually does."

Nodding back, Glenda took a smaller mouthful, held it a moment then swallowed more slowly. "Wow. Brain-freeze or not, it's so refreshing." She then refilled the pouch and put in the stopper. "Shall we ascend to our penthouse?"

They backtracked to the hidden platform. Keeping her bag on her back, Glenda was the first up. Looking down she waved to Traveler and then continued upward. Keeping the designated landing limb in sight Traveler was quickly beside her. "So, what's for dinner?"

"Let's check our bags," was the reply.

Reaching into his bag he found he seemed to have lost an extra slice of ham, chicken, and cheese compared to Glenda's bag. *I swear I only matched her...well, maybe not.*

Watching his sad, puppy dog expression Glenda finished pulling her food out saying, "Remember, we share." Traveler's face brightened as he reacted to the word "share." "And remember our sweet berries for dessert." Traveler's puppy dog tail was in full wagging mode.

By now the forest was all darkness surrounding the treehouse nest. Birds of the night announced their presence with short hoots and muffled squawks. On the ground a keen ear could detect scampering herbivores seeking out night meals. Occasionally a cut-off squeal announced that a stalking predator had also found its dinner.

Secure in their elevated treehouse, Glenda and Traveler stretched out. Tired legs appreciated the stretches and promised to be on board with the next day's hiking agenda. With bags again offering head support, the two accepted the coming sleep. Traveler's final comment was, "It's weird to be camping under the stars but without any stars in sight. Weird, I say."

Glenda tried to make an agreeing sound but found Morpheus was whisking her into dreamland. Morpheus could multitask and Traveler was quickly brought into his own dream world as well.

Chapter 48

The Hun

The next morning, rapid eye movements behind closed lids reflected their dream states. The eye movements suddenly stopped; dreams vanished as lids unwillingly opened. Human voices announced they had company below. Somebody was already up and starting the day.

Glenda and Traveler went into stealth mode as they peered down over the knee walls. "Hun foragers," whispered Glenda. Traveler nodded and then cupped his ears to listen. The translation magic of the books showed itself. The two were able to clearly understand the short Hunnish barks.

The scouts below were moving on their small ponies around and through the thick forest. These horses were bred for mobility and stamina. They had navigated many rugged terrains as they crossed vast distances carrying their riders. By contrast, Western warhorses were bred for the size and strength necessary to carry large armored men on forward charges.

Hun horses and their bowmen riders were the heart of the Hun army. Hun horses gave their riders a fast-moving, mobile archery platform. They easily darted between opposing, slower warhorses. The highly skilled mounted Hun archers could release deadly arrows while their mounts made sharp turns in response to jabbing heels.

The accuracy of the mounted Hun archer was legendary. Hun horse and rider behaved as a single unit. Many observers viewed them as centaurs with the Hun archer seemingly married into the body of the pony.

The emphasis on speed and sharp directional turns had given the Huns a great advantage on the battlefield. Armored knights chasing the elusive Huns found their giant warhorses quickly tired. "Stand still and fight," shouted frustrated knights, while the Hun's reply was, "Catch me if you can, slow man wrapped in iron."

A sudden twang below announced the release of a Hun arrow. Glenda and Traveler tracked the flight and watched a large buck collapse. The shooter's companion said, "Well-aimed through the trees. I always welcome you beside me on the battlefield."

Traveler whispered, "Some part of the Hun army will dine on deer steaks tonight. My Hun history claimed that meat was frequently placed under the saddle, cooked or not, and was available as the moving rider needed a meal. Of course, that may be an ugly rumor planted by their civilized enemy." Rumor or not, Glenda grimaced at the mental image of eating meat only warmed by the heat of a saddle.

Traveler pointed to the disappearing riders. "Let's eat fast and follow these guys. They'll take the deer back to their camp; it may be the main camp. Ardaric mentioned that the Huns are massing for a major strike, this area may be where they are grouping."

Watching the riders as they rode away, Glenda said, "We'll follow them but let's give them some distance first. There may be other patrols around."

"Yeah, we've arrived in Hun country and stealth is the word of the day. I bet they know where the jinn are operating, we'll follow them to their camp and listen in. Easy peasy."

Glenda grimaced with the "easy peasy." *Nothing ever is, be careful about jinxing us, Traveler.*

When they saw that the foragers were disappearing from view, they quickly descended to the forest floor. Once down Glenda said, "You lead, I'm right behind you. We can double-time it until we catch up."

With the leader bit in his mouth, Traveler moved quickly ahead. He saw that the foragers' trail was easy to follow. The night's dew had not yet dried up and hoofprints stood out on the softened ground. After less than half an hour passed, he gave Glenda the universal hand signal to halt.

Pointing ahead, he indicated a gathering of horsemen no more than two hundred feet away. The riders were engaged in rapid conversations punctuated by big hand motions. Both Glenda and Traveler were instantly in stealth mode.

They crept forward until they were close enough to fully see and hear the discussions. As they listened, they identified the earlier deer hunters but saw that other riders had joined them. The new riders appeared to be older horsemen.

As they listened, the group's primary mission became clear, they were to capture any stranger who came into their region. Strangers were expected to be spies who would provide information regarding the Gepid forces. From their frustrated comments, no captures had been made so far. The slain deer was little consolation for failing to capture a lurking spy.

One warrior, whose face projected a wicked frown, shared his frustration as he lamented the lack of trespassers. "This morning's hunt was disappointing. We usually flush out a Gepid or two trying to spy on us. Once they're spotted, they run like scared rabbits. Bringing one down with an arrow to the leg is most satisfying."

The two stealth listeners advanced slowly to a large tree. Staying behind it, they picked a thick overhead limb and ascended. Once they were resting on the landing limb, they ascended further, using the thick trunk for concealment. When they reached an opening among the canopy limbs, they moved around to better study the group.

As they watched, they saw additional riders join the group. Glenda cupped her hands around each ear to create a sound funnel. As she concentrated, she realized her enhanced listening skill was bringing the Hun conversations to her as though she was in the group. She motioned to Traveler who immediately followed suit.

The miracles brought by the book's enhancements once again justified their study efforts. They heard and understood the conversations. The Hunnish grunts and rapid language chirps were instantly converted into English.

Watching, as well as listening, they saw the frustrated looks on many younger faces. Proper conversation protocol was being observed, age and experience dominated. One older rider said, "Our captains are concerned. I have observed it."

"Concerned is too soft a word," replied a man beside him. "I say they move and speak with uncertainty. Uncertainty may arise from the rumored schism among Attila's sons. Ellac, the oldest, was chosen by great Attila to lead. Now with Attila's passing, Dengizich and Ernak each insist they are entitled to a portion of our vast empire. Who now commands the captains and the Hun host?"

Joining the discussion, another aged rider added his thoughts. "I do not believe it is our place to be concerned over a possible divide in Hun leadership. We always unite with battle. My concern is the rumor of a rising leader uniting the German tribes.

"Rumor says that the leader is Ardaric. This Gepid lord was our great Attila's strongest ally, both on the battlefield and off. Many nights they passed out together from drinking strong kumis in Attila's tent. More than a trustworthy ally he was a true friend to Attila and the Huns."

The respected speaker was being given his time to speak without interruption. He continued, "Something has changed his allegiance to the Huns. Rumor again is that he strongly disagrees with the sons' intentions toward the Germanic tribes. This Ardaric claims well-established treaties are now being broken without cause.

"The sons are reputed to view the tribes not as allies but as slaves. They feel that Attila was overly generous to these tribes. They intend to greatly increase the annual tribute... as is a master's right."

Another rider had been patiently waiting for his turn. "I believe this Ardaric has lost his loyalty to the Huns for his personal gain. Our leaders see this and properly have no patience for a traitor. It is likely the traitor believes he sees an opportunity while the Hun leadership appears split between brothers.

"Despite past battles, he still does not know our true strength and skill. Now he believes himself lucky and will test us on a battlefield. He is a great fool. He was protected in battle by Attila. Facing us as an enemy he will be crushed."

Finally the oldest rider spoke. "Like you I have heard similar rumors, how could I not? However, be advised before you accept rumors as truth, that horsemen have nothing better to do at the end of a day's ride than gossip like women. Know that this Ardaric does not depend on luck. I have seen him on the battlefield, he made our Hun forces even stronger.

"Our captains are not unsettled or divided. They are concerned and recognize this is a time of change. They are showing great judgement to wait until all change has been observed. This is a mark of wisdom, not hesitancy. Our captains have seen the error of fast judgement on past battlefields by our enemy. As Attila told them before each battle, 'First study the enemy's moves and only then commit to strong decisive action.' Battlefield patience and observation were Attila's great genius."

The final rider to contribute was the most recently arrived. Looking at the oldest warrior, he said, "I agree with all you have said. You have the advantage of great experience and insight. I agree this Ardaric could be a threat. However, he is not yet a proven threat. We must observe him before we act.

"Beyond a Germanic challenge, there are other great concerns to be considered. There is something strange taking place in this region. This is not rumor or gossip. I have returned from our command center, where I saw many warriors diverted to act as common labor.

"Experienced riders are forced to move rocks of great weight from a distant quarry. Warriors are treated as beasts of burden. Many horses and men are committed to this task. When I asked a captain about the purpose of this effort his eyes flared red. Truly red. My heart stopped, and my breath would not come.

I felt fortunate to be sent back to patrol. Not all threats are as obvious as this Ardaric. Not all is as it should be."

The experienced warriors absorbed this new information then decided to drop the conversation. They feared these speculations could create negative karma among them. They understood that the strength of the Hun was to act as a single unified force. To divide that force in any way would be a signal of weakness to their opponents. This was a time for the Hun warrior to avoid idle political gossip. The wise warrior trusts his leaders and fights as directed.

The young riders had quietly listened to the exchanges. Their opinions were not welcome. As the lowest units in the army, their role was to listen, learn, and serve the experienced riders. Later, when alone, they would freely gossip, speculate, and complain about how the older warriors didn't show them respect.

Chapter 49

Scouting Time

"Methinks there is confusion in Hun City," said Traveler. "There are multiple rumors causing dissension in the ranks. Brothers fighting over the spoils of their dad's empire, a German ally turned against them, and some unknown force at play. I bet the unknown force is the jinn. If so, the Huns are in big trouble, then again so are we."

"They certainly seem conflicted," agreed Glenda. "It's interesting that the younger riders are not encouraged, or even permitted, to voice their thoughts. Silencing the young is a road to future trouble. As the expression goes, 'Out of the mouths of babes comes wisdom.'"

Glenda paused, then continued. "Perhaps what comes out of their mouths is simply unfiltered truth as seen by the young. They should be listened to if for no other reason than to give the young a sense of being valued. We're both young, but M and Theo listen to us. And we sure feel good to be able to express ourselves."

Traveler nodded back. "I agree. We express ourselves and always feel respected. Speaking of being listened to, do you think we should continue to follow them?"

"No, let's leave them alone now. I don't think we'll learn any more from them as they continue scouting. I think we should take the path that the last rider came from. He just came from the main camp and was able to give us a clue about what the jinn is up to."

Nodding, Traveler said, "OK, makes sense. Did you notice exactly where he came from?"

Pointing, Glenda said, "Think so. Pretty sure it's to our right and along the river. I bet Mr. Scout will spot hoofprints, broken blades of grass, and all those other scouting clues." Laughing, she added, "Probably you'll spot horse droppings and can test their interior warmth to confirm how long ago he passed by. I've seen that trick in lots of Westerns."

Smiling back, Traveler answered, "You get dibs on testing any droppings, you seem pretty informed. I'll stay with the broken grass."

With the playful exchange over, Traveler walked to the indicated path and confirmed that it was indeed the trail. The path was easily followed since horse and rider had recently passed through. There was no need to study broken grass, as the depressed hoofprints were easily spotted. Fortunately, there were no droppings to start a debate over who would read the dropping's interior clock.

Hours passed and the path was now widening into a traveled trail. Traveler stopped and motioned for Glenda to come beside him. "This is a well-traveled trail, almost a dirt road. We need to slow down and listen for scouts; we need to spot them before they spot us. Maybe it's time to do a vertical climb and see what's around us."

"Pick your scouting tree and don't worry about what's down here. I'll stay and listen for trouble."

Nodding at this sensible approach, Traveler was quickly a tree-monkey moving upwards. Glenda was right, he had to focus on going up while she stood sentry below. Going up turned out to be no easy climb, this tree seemed to resent his presence. The tree apparently viewed him as the legendary timbering giant Paul Bunyan and sought its revenge.

Too frequently a small limb, bent out of the way, returned to give him a sharp, whipping smack. The tree apparently felt the need to constantly remind him who was the tree and who the intruder. He was an unwelcome visitor and must pay the tree's toll for bending its branches.

Despite the whipping, his choice of an observation tower proved to be worth the lashes when he reached the top. After steadying his body and breath from the climb, he began a slow 360-degree inspection. Looking back at their path he confirmed there was nothing behind them. *We picked the right direction*, he congratulated himself. Looking forward he saw the river had made a number of turns and was now running parallel to their path.

He also saw billowing clouds of thick dark smoke. The smoke was coming from countless cooking fires spread over a large area. This was indeed the major Hun encampment.

How big is this army to require this many cooking fires? The mathematician in him began to count the flickering dots of fire and quickly found there were far too many individual fires to count. *Time to use statistics and make an estimate. Our book-magic rules, but math is a great backup. Thank you, Albemarle, Virginia math teachers.*

To make his starting estimate he laid out a mental grid over the umbrella of smoke. He estimated the number of smaller grids within the entire smoke covered area. He then counted fires in just one grid.

When he found a hundred fires in the single grid, he did mental arithmetic to estimate the army's size within that grid. *If each fire would cook for at least 20 riders that means around 2,000 riders in one grid. The total area looks like it holds between 20 and 30 grids so this could be an army between 40,000 and 60,000 men. Wow, this has to be the main Hun army!*

Traveler was excited to share his discovery and descended hurriedly. Many of the small branches remembered him going up and greeted him going down. He received a second round of strong smacks to his legs, chest, and arms. *Who would think a tree would have a memory and hold a grudge? I'm bruised from ankles to neck. Glenda was smart to avoid this ill-humored sun-blocker.*

When he made his ground appearance Glenda was there to greet him. "Who punched you out? Looks like you ran into a door or a street gang. Are you OK?"

"Just one nasty, mean-spirited tree. It must have confused me with a lumberjack. Anyway, climbing up was worth it. I hit the motherlode of scouting information. The main Hun army is camped along the river. I estimate between forty and sixty thousand men."

Glenda listened, shook her head at the size, and asked, "You couldn't have counted noses, so how did you make that count?"

Traveler described his grid and the method of making a mathematical guess. "It's just an estimate but I think it gives us the order of magnitude. Ardaric would sure like to know what he's facing. It's a massive force looking to crush any Gepid insurrection."

Glenda had listened to Traveler's estimating technique and simply said, "Our magic books make us so advanced, but you still have a really solid, logical mind from schooling before the books. I never learned that estimating trick. Well done, Mr. Math."

Traveler found the bullfrog in him had his chest expanding. For a moment, a loud "Look at me! Chug-a-rum!" was on his tongue, then he bit his lip. *Be modest, that's what she respects.* "Probably something I was taught in high school statistics and happened to remember. Kudos to my teacher."

Glenda beamed, *Modest response.* Then she said, "Well done, Traveler! Now we know where our spying destination is. All we need to do is get inside the hornet's nest and avoid an army of potential stingers."

Chapter 50

Huns Debate

They proceeded forward on the widening trail. Even though the dense forest gave limited visibility, the trail was clearly leading toward the Hun camp. Using his mental compass Traveler was able to keep his sense of direction regardless of the trail and obstructing trees. If the trail began to move away from the camp, he would sense that and adjust their approach.

The trail did not divert away. In fact, it was joined by more trails and soon widened into a serious transport road. The need for a serious road was no surprise. Given the army's size, foraging was not nearly sufficient to feed it. A constant stream of supplies was brought from outlying towns and villages. Fortunately for the teens this movement of men and wagons was easily detected well in advance. The two spies could quickly disappear into the dense forest before being spotted.

After several more hours of cautious walking, Glenda asked, "How close do you think we are to the fringes of the camp? When should we get off this road and camp for the night?"

"I think we've come far enough. This is a busy road, the longer we're on it the slower we need to go, even then we could still stumble onto resting supply lines and scouts. Let's not press our luck, it's time to move off the road to the less beaten path." Glenda nodded in agreement.

With his clearing stick in hand, Traveler entered the dense foliage. Trail distance passed slowly as Traveler cleared the way. When his arms and body were close to exhaustion, he heard Glenda call out.

"Is that a lookout platform straight ahead?"

Traveler lifted his head and wiped the sweat from his face and eyes. Managing a tired smile, he answered, "Well done! It is indeed. You are now the official troop leader. I would have missed it for sure, I was too busy swatting vines and looking for deer droppings."

Glenda sent an appreciative look back as she said, "You've been clearing our path since the road. Your arms must be exhausted, I could not have done that. I was able to look up since walking behind is a lot easier. Let's adjourn to our penthouse."

Traveler felt his energy flowing back with the praise. *She spotted the platform in the middle of these trees, yet gives me credit, I really needed that boost!* "You head upstairs, I'll follow after I get my breath back."

Glenda leapt upward followed shortly by a tired Traveler. His legs struggled to find the strength to push off, but the recent praise provided the necessary jolt of energy.

Once they settled onto their lookout post they realized what a terrific roost Glenda had spotted. Looking out they had lines of sight all the way to the smoke-covered Hun camp. They could see the various paths, trails, and roads that all converged at the expansive site. Smiling, Traveler quipped, "I guess not all roads lead to Rome. They did lead to Rome for Attila, but not for his sons."

Glenda had already surveyed the terrain below and announced, "I'm going up higher to see what else we can spot. We need to find a good way to get into the camp and spy on the leaders, maybe I can spot it. I know you're exhausted so feel free to stay here."

Traveler simply said, "I'm with you. Let's go vertical."

As they ascended, they found their tree was well above the surrounding trees. It had claimed the land early on and had grown higher to capture more sunlight. It also proved to be an accepting tree for climbers, no harsh smacks were offered as they ascended.

Pausing in the climb, while already above many surrounding trees, Glenda observed, "This tree is a survivor. Not as naturally large in diameter as others, it compensated by early height. I bet when you are at the river and looking back you will see our tree's top is well above the other tops."

Resting below while clinging to the dwindling trunk, Traveler responded, "Good for our tree. Let's get to the top before my nosebleed starts."

The final ascent was done with caution. Once they were above the surrounding foliage, they felt a brisk wind hit them. Their high crow's nest was swaying, each gust demanding stronger grips from both hands and legs. Clear views in all directions confirmed the camp's location within the forest and its proximity to the river. As they studied the access roads, trails, and animal paths, many choices for a stealth approach appeared.

Looking out from her swaying perch Glenda suddenly felt the beginnings of vertigo. Glancing down at Traveler's head, she said, "I hate to say this, but I may get seasick. I feel like I'm bouncing on the end of a bungee cord, way too much swaying. Most unsettling."

Traveler was enjoying his own view and was unbothered by the swaying trunk. While feeling a bit of sympathy for Glenda he was enjoying his roller coaster ride. *We boys love riding the bronco and the bull! No vertigo for this cowboy.*

With intended humor he just had to say, "Yeah, I know what you mean. It's like being stuck right at the top of a big Ferris wheel. Back and forth. Back and forth. You can feel the seat swaying up and down. You can feel the dizziness climbing up after you. Whatever you do, don't look down. Don't think about our seat snapping off with the wind."

Realizing he was having fun with her discomfort Glenda looked down, put two fingers toward her mouth, and said, "Please keep up the Ferris wheel story, I'm really fascinated with your take on this swaying. If I can't control my stomach contents, any chance they may hit you? I'll sure do my best to aim away and hope the wind cooperates."

Accepting her humorous chastisement Traveler grinned and changed gears. Pointing outward he said, "We have a clear view of the river and the open land on the other side. It looks like a huge field that's gone back to nature. Maybe when Attila came through his horses ate whatever was grown, then trampled what was left."

Glenda shifted her gaze outward to the large open field. It appeared to offer an extended clearing between the river and the surrounding forests. It could easily contain many football and soccer fields with lots of bleacher space to spare.

As she focused on the field, she felt her stomach tremors subside. She knew Traveler was helping her get through the nausea by having her focus in the distance. *OK, first he's the pranking otter now the helpful doctor. Surprisingly, I'm feeling better. Thank you, doctor, for making a treehouse visit.*

She looked away from the field to study the sprawling site. As she took in the layout with the interior connecting roads her eyes locked on to three prominent tents close to the river. The tents' sizes stood out from all neighbors and declared this was where the Hun leadership was housed. The center tent flew Ellac's flag and was flanked by the tents of his brothers, Dengizich and Ernak.

Glenda noted all three tents were equal in size and thought, *Each son considers himself an equal of the other two. Leadership over the Hun empire is far from settled. A divided Hun leadership is good news for Ardaric, if and when he confronts the Hun horde.* Her attention returned to Traveler, who was studying the encampment. She asked, "How do we access those main tents to listen in on the brothers?"

Traveler shook his head. "Not obvious to me. Lots of possibilities but all have issues, let's get back to our platform." With that he began the slow downward retreat. Once he landed on the platform he quickly moved to the side as feet and long legs came down past him. A mass of wind-tangled reddish hair arrived last.

"Bad hair day, princess. Sorry about that."

"Least of my problems. Bad stomach is what was happening. By the way, thanks doctor for your advice up there, it helped a lot."

Traveler's teasing grin immediately morphed into a comforting smile. "I make crow's nest house calls when needed." Reaching into his sack he removed a loaf of dark bread, tore off a chunk, and handed it to her along with a water pouch. "Bread and water. Best medicine for rumbles in the tummy."

Glenda took a small bite, chewed slowly, and washed it down with a sip of the cool water. She smiled, nodded a thank you at Traveler, and repeated the process. After a few minutes she grinned. "Got my sea legs back, let's eat."

They carefully paced their intakes, realizing that either of them could have a delayed bout of seasickness. Fortunately, their stomachs were settled and accepted the offerings without further tummy threats. Recharged from their meal they relaxed as twilight settled around them.

Traveler yawned, and asked, "Should we try to formulate a plan now or do it in the morning? How do you vote?"

Catching his yawn and feeling her own coming on, Glenda quickly answered. "Definitely tomorrow. I'm whipped from hiking, scouting, and riding the upstairs Ferris wheel. Worrying about how to sneak into a Hun city with tens of thousands of potential killers takes way too much thought. Besides just the idea would keep me worrying all night."

She proceeded to layer her blanket for padding then rolled the carry bag into the faithful pillow. Now on her back, peeking out of the blanket, she added a final comment., "You do some great thinking right before sleep, please let your mind look for solutions. Tell me all about them in the morning."

Traveler had reached the same conclusion and was rolling onto his back. *Tomorrow is better. Maybe Morpheus will inspire me. I know he'll inspire sleep and that's really needed for this tired puppy.*

Chapter 51

New Day Brings New Answers

Like all treetop mornings, their waking up process began with birds noisily greeting the day. Songbirds were joined by darting sunrays that were working hard to come through the overhead canopy. With the thick cover of overhead green foliage, none of the seeking rays hit their faces, however, they successfully brightened the small lookout platform enough that the two deep sleepers woke up.

Both were still on their backs and gave long stretches before facing the waking world. With a muffled groan Glenda said, "I'm afraid to sit up. Overnight there was another steel rail implanted to replace my spine. Steel doesn't bend, so how can I sit up?"

"Don't ask me. I'm riveted to the boards. Even my arms are useless."

When their morning wake-up complaining was over the two finally sat up. Looking around, Glenda observed, "The good news is it's a brilliant day. A tad frosty, but bright and beckoning. Let's breakfast while we brainstorm the spying mission. Did you get inspired last night?"

"A little, but I don't think you'll like any possibilities."

Glenda bit into a morning apple, then smiled. "Lay it on me. Everything looks possible in the morning."

"Well, I considered a lot of options and only see two choices. Plan A is that we sneak in at nightfall on one of the trails then weave our way through the camp using stealth as necessary. Hopefully there won't be any guard dogs who sniff us and start yelping but that's unlikely. It's a big risk if they do.

"The camp is huge, and we would need to cover a lot of ground and avoid a lot of guards and dogs. If we're detected an aroused camp would alert a lot more guards and dogs but worse it may signal the jinn to our presence. We'd no longer be stealth observers but running convicts chased by dogs, Huns, and jinn. Escape would be very unlikely. Even if we escaped, the jinn would know of our presence."

Watching Glenda's reaction to plan A, Traveler paused. She was clearly hesitant. Sniffing dogs worried her a lot. Dogs and Huns alone would be a handful but add in jinn and the land route was more than perilous. After a bit more reflection time she said, "OK drop the other shoe. What's Plan B?"

"Brace yourself, it's a water route. The brothers' tents are set up close to the river. That minimizes the amount of land to be covered, which reduces the risk of camp dogs."

Glenda's face immediately reacted as a variety of emotions swept across it. "You're right, I'm not thrilled about any water route, I'm scared silly. I still dream about being forced to go deep in total blackness to get under the fortress gate. Nightmare is the word for that experience."

Traveler gave a sympathetic look back. "I understand, but we're not going underwater. If it helps, I still have my own painful flashbacks about going under the gate, the total darkness and burning lungs. This water option is challenging but not life-threatening."

As he assured her, Glenda began to relax. With emotions coming under control she gave a weak nod back, accompanied by her best "Lay it on me, I can take it" face. "OK, partner, keep it going, please. The sooner I hear the details the better."

With his audience now prepared to listen, Traveler forged ahead putting a tone of quiet optimism into his voice. "We'll head to the water, using the forest to get close to the riverbank. The river is moving along at an acceptable pace, not too fast and not too slow. We'll find suitable floating debris that camouflages us while we ride along.

"We'll wait until dusk, then, as the expression says, we'll 'go with the flow.' We'll float close to the brothers' tents then hit the shore. Spotting them, even in the dark, should be easy. They're the biggest tents by far, plus there will be a lot of open fires around them.

"Once ashore we'll scoot into the woods, circle around, and get to their tents. We'll slip inside, stay in stealth mode, and listen. We'll leave when they pass out from drinking. Easy peasy."

With a wry smile, Glenda responded. "Easy peasy again, oh yeah. What could possibly go wrong? I'll try not to think too hard about that. I know any approach has lots of downsides. With sniffing dogs and Hun scouts everywhere, not to mention jinn, the land approach has too many ways to get discovered."

Giving a small, accepting sigh, she concluded, "Like it or not, I guess the river route is the best course. The upside is if we do get discovered the water may give us a little edge in trying to escape from the jinn."

Finished with her rumination she suddenly gave Traveler a wink and big smile. "By the way partner, big congrats! You have again come up with a plan that's as good as the circumstance permits. Well done!"

Traveler's puppy dog tail was wagging with the praise, he needed a booster vote of confidence. He was naturally pleased that she saw the options the same as him, he knew it was clearly the better way to go but needed her to buy into it on her own. This seemed the best of their bad choices. He thought his book agreed.

With a grin he said, "Thanks for that vote of confidence! I trust your judgement and we're on the same page. Now if something bad happens feel free to blame me."

Pausing, he pointed downward, "And there's no time like the present to get going. Shall we start to work our way downstream and find a spot to hitchhike?"

Glenda gave an accepting nod. "History guy, tell me again, what did the gladiators say when they entered the arena? Perk me up please."

Traveler laughed. "This is not the best pep talk expression, but the Latin was 'Ave Imperator, morituri te salutant' meaning, 'Hail Emperor, those who are about to die salute you.'"

Glenda started to laugh, and she said, "Not exactly the inspiring send-off phrase we want. How about, 'Hail, Theo! We who are about to river ride salute you.'"

A grinning Traveler replied, "Your motto is so much better! OK, let's move out."

Chapter 52

Did Huck Finn Do This?

It was a clear day for hiking. By noon they heard the sounds of the moving river. Even slow-moving water creates murmuring sounds as it flows and cascades across jutting rocks. The closer they came, the more pronounced the call of the river. Advancing slowly, they emerged from the surrounding forest to find they were on a small bluff leading down to the flowing waters.

As rivers go, this one was more a tributary. It was wide enough to technically qualify as a river but appeared to have limited depth. Lurking underwater rocks occasionally rose from the river's floor to challenge passing waters and surface riders. Their upcroppings declared their presence to any observer. "I could see a Rhine maiden sunning herself on that flat center rock," said Traveler, pointing.

Glenda snorted. "Well, you wish you could. Be glad you don't see a Hun resting there."

"Touché, princess. Actually, I don't see anybody, this could be where we wait for our ride."

Time flowed slowly to match the river's gentle pace as both looked for a suitable ride. Glenda's eyes went from the river's oncoming offerings to possible offerings along the nearby bank. The bank held nothing. Small debris floated past but nothing suitable for riders. After a while her frustration surfaced. "We got nothing. Maybe you can float or swim that far, but I can't. How are we going to get there?"

Traveler gave her a sympathetic look. "Fear not, I'm in the same boat as you. I'm no long-distance swimmer and need to hitch a ride myself. Let's go down to the bank and scout around. There's bound to be something that's washed up that we can use. We have lots of time, it's still daylight and way too early to start anyway."

The two moved slowly down the side of the bluff to the flat, sandy riverbank. Once there they paused to ensure nobody was around. After carefully studying the opposing banks, Traveler said, "Let's search further upstream, away from the camp. The odds of stumbling onto some Hun scouting party will decrease the further away we get."

Eeyore gave a skeptical response. "OK, maybe we'll get lucky."

They walked along on the edge of the bank, staying close to the forest above them. If a Hun suddenly appeared, they would scramble up the side and lose themselves among the bordering trees.

After walking another hour, Eeyore looked increasingly unhappy. "This sounded like a good idea a couple of hours ago but the further we get away from the camp the less feasible a water approach seems. Maybe we should rethink a land approach tomorrow, besides the wind's increasing and storm clouds are coming our way."

Traveler looked up and nodded but wanted to stay with the river option for a while longer. He attempted some delaying humor. "Personally, I love a good storm. I bet thunder and lightning scare these Huns silly since they live in the open in flimsy tents."

Glenda was not prepared to be humored; she was preparing a "Woe is us" response when she froze in place. Pointing ahead, she whispered, "Do you see what I see?"

Following her pointing arm Traveler broke into a relieved smile. "Do I ever! Our ship has come in!"

Ahead of them, on their side of the river was a large dock extending from a manmade break-wall. Moored to the dock were rafts of varying sizes. Stacked on each side of the dock were piles of stones of diverse sizes and shapes. This was the Huns' loading and transportation center.

Glenda's darkening mood had instantly brightened. Eeyore was now Tigger with a bounce in her voice. Beaming, she said, "We're back in the spy business! This is the loading dock to move those stones downstream. And we don't need to float in the water hanging onto a twisting log. I'm a happy camper!"

"And more good news, nobody's around." Looking upward to the darkening sky, Glenda said, "I bet they knocked off early with those storm clouds coming. They're too smart to be on the river when there's a storm approaching, I mean who would be out there?" Grinning at Traveler, she added, "Well, almost nobody would." An agreeing grin and nod came back.

The two energized youths strode confidently out to the dock and inspected the moored rafts. "Simple design. Simple, but very functional," said Traveler. "They have bound logs together with vines and put a sturdy rudder at the end. The dock extends far enough out so the rafts get swept into the center of the river when released."

Glenda was studying the available choices. "We've got our pick of sizes. I think the smallest one would be best for us. It looks like a forward scout raft, maybe it steers the big rafts past water obstacles. What do you think?"

"Yep, small is better for us. Let's take possession of this one and celebrate our good fortune with an early cruising dinner. This is going to be a long afternoon and night so let's pamper ourselves." They stepped onto the raft and noticed how stable it remained. The logs were thick and securely bound to accept jolts from unavoidable, jutting rocks.

Glenda sat down near the center and Traveler beside the rudder. Placing an arm across the rudder's heavy oak steering bar he imagined himself as Huck Finn rafting down the mighty Mississippi. Carry bags were opened and each picked an evening meal. A soft wind came up the river, cooling the day from the sun's heat.

As they slowly ate, an occasional fish came out of the river to belly smack on the flowing surface. Traveler motioned at a loud smack off their starboard side, "It's either showing off for us or it's running from a bigger fish, maybe a nasty pike."

As Glenda finished, she lifted her eyes then raised an arm skyward. "Is it my imagination or is the breeze turning into a real wind? Are those lightning flashes coming our way? We need to get moving, partner!"

Traveler's answer was to stand up and remove the holding ropes. The raft immediately headed into the river. "It's getting dark fast, let's try and stay ahead of what's coming. The good news is we'll be invisible and the storm will send the Hun guards and dogs running into their tents."

Traveler quickly sat down by the rudder and steered the raft into the center of the river. *Fewer rocks, I think. At least, I hope.* Looking upward he made a challenging face as he called out to the increasing wind, "Is that all you've got? Huck Finn has seen far stiffer breezes on the mighty Mississippi."

Grinning at his seaman's bravado, Glenda moved from the front to sit beside him. "Who's this Huck Finn?"

"Only the greatest young teenage adventurer in American literature. In my opinion, the best American author of all time was Mark Twain. He wrote fiction stories about the adventures Huck and Jim had rafting down the Mississippi River. Huck was a teen orphan and Jim was an escaping adult slave who joined Huck on the raft. The two became fast friends over many shared adventures."

Glenda nodded. "Remind me to read about them when we're back in our sanctuary. Right now, I'd prefer less adventure." Looking at the front of the raft, she saw that it was beginning to move slightly up and down. "Captain, is it me or is our boat starting to tilt a little with the waves? Should I start to worry?"

Traveler's challenge to the storm was already regretted. His confident smirk was replaced by a furrowed brow. This was not the time to get motion sickness. He didn't remember whether Huck got sick with wave motion, but he recalled the great Lord

Nelson always got seasick when first on board. "Yeah, this is not good. No need to worry right now but please sit forward and look for oncoming rocks. Give me hand signals when you spot trouble."

Staying on her hands and knees, Glenda moved to the front. Once there she sat cross-legged and focused on keeping her balance. As she placed a hand down on the log surface for stability, she discovered a short thick post rising six inches from a center log. A similar post was quickly found on the other side. She realized that the raft builders had placed these handholds so that a forward observer could remain secure while guiding the rudder man. Relaxing a bit, she could direct with either hand as necessary.

Looking over her shoulder she called back to Traveler about the handholds. They were invisible in the growing darkness. He heard her and moved a hand around beside him, then shouted back, "Great heads-up! I found my left-hand grip, the rudder is my right-side hold."

Glenda turned back to stare ahead just as a small, rising plume announced a rock near the surface. She gave a fast "go right" hand motion and Traveler adjusted the rudder.

The two quickly synchronized as navigator and pilot. Glenda held the post tight with her left hand and signaled with the right. Although they were only fifteen feet apart visibility was increasingly dimmed as a determined rain was now falling. Traveler was braced in his sitting position staring at Glenda's back. Her mass of reddish hair was his lighthouse focal point.

When an occasional hand signal came it was accompanied by flying hair from the brushing arm. "Call out as soon as you can!" shouted a soaked Traveler. Nerves had him tense, he knew disaster would happen if they hit a large rock head-on. Glenda waved her hand in acknowledgment.

The storm was now fully on them. The river's water flow increased as did the raft's speed. Fortunately, with the rising river level, this stretch of water seemed deep enough that dangerous submerged rocks were infrequent. A few times their raft unexpectedly hit the tip of a submerged rock and shook the raft and the riders. Due to careful construction the logs remained tightly together as their bindings held.

After a jarring bump Glenda was always quick to call back, "Sorry!" Traveler always gave a smile in return and a fast, left-handed thumbs up. He understood the small hits were unavoidable. His navigator was doing a fine job, despite the wind driving gusting rain into her face.

As they moved forward at an increasing pace, Glenda shifted eye contact from river rocks to shore. Traveler's eyes likewise shifted away from "Glenda the Red Lighthouse" to the shore. Both searched hard for early signs of the Hun camp.

Another exhausting hour passed, feeling like ten. Necks were sore from rapid twisting; eyes were blurring from constant squinting. Then twinkling fires were spotted.

Chapter 53

Among the Hun

Contrary to Traveler's conjecture, the Huns were highly experienced dealing with strong winds and heavy rains. Nature's anger had little effect on them. They had quickly erected hide-covered protectors for themselves and the fires. The overhead covers had extended sides going halfway to the ground. The sides were tightly moored by deeply driven iron stakes.

The overhead covers and side buffers permitted campfires to operate. The vertical sides broke the impact of gusting winds and prevented sideways-driven rains from dousing the fires.

The red glow of fires appeared as distant lighthouse beacons flickering in the driving rain. When first spotted, the beacons lifted the rafters' spirits, their destination was approaching.

Their initial relief was dampened as the rafters grasped the size of the camp. At a treetop distance, it had appeared as a brown open space residing in the green forest. Now it appeared as a huge tent city holding tens of thousands of warriors. They had to choose the correct landing spot or become lost in a city without street signs.

As the rafters continued moving toward their destination, an increasing number of twinkling lights broke the darkness. The multitude of fire lights now resembled swarms of summer fireflies hovering over large open fields. The growing brightness and density of the firefly lights indicated they were approaching the center of the Hun encampment. Where to land continued to be the critical decision.

Glenda repeatedly wiped her face and shook her head. Her eyes were slits from constantly squinting into the pelting rain. She was close to exhaustion with a raging headache when a standout encampment suddenly appeared. Focusing through tired slits she first sighted a massed grouping of connected windbreakers. Then she saw much more.

The windbreaking wall protected three large tents. It curved around to provide additional buffering for a large center firepit with adjacent blazing pits. With the light cast from the grouped firepits, she saw the outlines of a nearby storage enclosure. The fenced enclosure was apparently the supply depot serving the three central tents. They had found the compound of the three brothers. This was their landing site.

"We're close to being there," she mouthed as she pointed to the left side. "We need to abandon ship and head ashore."

Nodding in agreement, Traveler released the rudder and quickly crept forward. "On my signal you go in first. I'll be right behind you. Throw me both backpacks, I'll bring them in."

Glenda tossed both bags to Traveler, then went onto her belly to the side closest to the Hun camp and called back. "Ready when you are."

Traveler quickly cross-wrapped the bags on his back creating a taut X on his chest. Looking at Glenda, he cupped both hands to his mouth. His "Now!" barely reached Glenda but she understood. Traveler waited until she rolled over into the river. He rolled immediately after her.

The river grabbed both with bad intentions, it would sweep them forward as flotsam and jetsam. Traveler fought the river's force by giving his strongest sidestrokes. He was immediately beside a struggling Glenda. "Another bad hair day, does it ever get better?"

Glenda managed a weak smile. She was fighting hard against the river's flow, using strong leg kicks. However, every time her legs stopped kicking she was pushed forward by the river.

"How can we land?" barely came out before she was gulping and coughing.

"Get behind me, grab onto a backpack, and keep kicking hard. I'll do my thing. It's all good." Glenda responded without hesitation; this was otter boy's world.

The two had extreme power in their legs and arms, working in tandem they moved sideways against the river's strength. One pair of feet was always kept secure on the bottom while the other pair kicked. They moved slowly toward the shore while looking for the best landing spots. The closer they got to shore the less force the river had. Traveler raised his right hand and pointed. "There's our spot, hang on and kick like crazy."

Both legs began kicking as hard as they could until they suddenly felt their boots hit a sandy bottom. Still feisty the river remained eager to pick them up and carry them away, but as they advanced it finally accepted that it had lost its prey.

Leaning back against the pushing river, they dug their boots into the bottom and slowly walked to maintain their footing. Heads stayed just above the water while disappointed choppy waves did their best to enter gasping mouths. The river was a bad loser.

Glenda saw that Traveler was heading toward the nearby fenced enclosure and released her hold on his carry bag. Once they reached the shoreline the two crawled on their stomachs across the wet, sandy ground. In a few minutes of salamander-wiggling, they were beside the fenced site. They immediately confirmed no guards were protecting the stored contents.

Looking through the fencing they saw stacked boxes of varying sizes. "Perfect!" said Traveler. "This is a supply depot for the big chiefs." As he briefly scanned nearby labeled containers, he said in an admiring voice, "Saddles, blankets, arms, and containers of food. Everything's organized for speedy access. Everything the Hun did was organized to maximize speed. Speed was their edge over every opponent."

As she recovered her breath Glenda had a harsher take. "Agreed, they are speedy. Speedy killers. Let's forget their organizational talent and start our recon.

"We can approach any one of the tents using the shelter of the storm. Lucky us, there aren't any guards around, they'll be hunkered down around their firepits with their dogs. Man and beast will stay close together in this storm."

With her mention of firepit warmth, Glenda found she was starting to shake and tugged on Traveler's arm, pulling him beside her. "Cuddle time big boy, I need some warmth. If hypothermia sets in, I'm useless." Without further explanation she placed Traveler's arm over her shoulder and pressed into him.

Traveler was nonplussed for a moment, then accepted the logic of shared warmth. In a short time, he found the reciprocating warmth was a very good thing, as his own shaking quieted down. He also found the sharing process was more than acceptable.

When both had their shivers under control Glenda shrugged and leaned away. "Thanks for the lift, big boy, I needed that. Let's start our spy campaign. I hope the brothers are a babbling fountain of jinn information after all this. Which tent do we try first?"

"Let's start with the older brother's center tent, that's probably where they'll meet."

The two crept to the edge of the enclosed supply depot while surveying the open ground and surrounding forest. Glenda motioned to her right, whispering, "I think there's good forest camouflage that way. Let's get into the trees and circle around." Traveler nodded, and the two salamanders crawled fast to the nearby tree line.

Once inside the forest they slowly stood up. As they looked around, they saw how the hard-gusting winds were contorting limbs, treetops, and tent sides. They knew nature was giving them a green light to proceed using the storm as a major distraction.

The distraction continued as the center of the storm appeared to be resting overhead and content to remain there. Regular lightning flashes lit the open camp spaces. No Hun was seen out braving this demonstration of power by the God of Heavens.

A crackling fireworks-lightning display suddenly lit the heavens followed by a deafening thunderclap from Thor. The two teens instinctively jumped, then moved quickly to the side of the center tent. Dropping to their bellies, they slowly lifted a flap several inches to create a peeping window.

Looking in they saw there was a roaring fire inside a deep pit. Flames and smoke rose to exit from a center opening. Glowing red coals sent heat radiating out to warm the tent.

Adding to the interior comfort were heavy rugs spread many layers deep across the floor. Thick silk cushions were placed for comfortable seating. This was far more than a simple shelter; it was a magnificent enclosure that spoke of the wealth and entitlements of the ruling brothers.

With a grin Traveler whispered, "Not exactly like my boy scout tents."

Smiling back, Glenda replied, "Nor my Norwegian camping shelters. A girl could sure adjust to this place. All it needs is an indoor shower and throne room."

Traveler studied the large interior then focused on the small group sitting close to the firepit. The group was being served a series of foods and drinks from silver platters and jeweled cups. These were the three brothers dining together in apparent comradeship while assuaging their hunger and thirst.

Looking through the lifted flap they saw intricately woven baskets stacked around nearby carved benches. Resting on the benches were piles of additional rugs, cushions, and furs. The seating area by the firepit could easily be expanded to accommodate a much greater gathering. Stacked at a distance from the firepit, the benches and baskets offered a perfect hiding place for their spying mission.

Traveler studied the distance to the closest bench and decided it was near enough for a rapid salamander approach. "We need to get inside to hear better, but we need to do it fast. This flap opening will blow cold air inside, someone may notice. Not the brothers by the fire, but a sharp server could feel a draft."

"You're right, I've been thinking the same thing, it's also way too loud out here to hear them. I'll head in first and settle behind that bench on the right side. Stay here until I'm in. You'll need to lift the flap up a little more, then pull it back down as soon as I'm inside."

"OK, I'll lift when you're ready." For a moment Traveler found he was sitting back in his first-grade reading circle holding a primer book. Patting Glenda on the head he said, "Go, Spot, go." His wit earned him a mock bite before she motioned to lift the flap. She was a very fast salamander scooting inside, once secure beside the bench she gave a thumbs-up.

Without hesitating, Traveler lifted the flap and rolled inside. He dropped the flap, then demonstrated his own salamander scoot. He was instantly beside Glenda, joining her to study the servants as they moved around the brothers.

There was no change in behavior among the servers, nobody looked their way. Their entry had been fast, and the servants were totally focused on the brothers. The two intruders relaxed and began their spying operation. They quickly realized the thick tent offered not only warmth but also soundproofing. The brothers' conversations were clear.

The spies were immediately captivated as they listened to the rapid conversations among the brothers. The brothers were highly animated in voice and hand movements as they hovered over a large map. From the heated discussion it was clear the subject was the sharing of the Hun Empire. Each brother argued the case for his desired region and the residing tribes.

The back-and-forth bargaining over lands and tribes highlighted the conflicts between the brothers. The intense bargaining reminded the stealth observers of playing the Monopoly game. Each player tries to outwit their opponents with proposed trades. Trades only happen when each player thinks he got the better deal.

As the brothers continued to argue over the distribution of the empire, the parallels to Monopoly became even clearer. One critical issue was the amount of tribute that would flow to the ruling brother. Just like in Monopoly, the tribute was a form of rent. Unlike Monopoly, if the tribe failed to pay the rent when due, the landlord would arrive with an army to collect. Rather than going to jail, the overdue renter would suffer a far greater penalty inflicted by a Hun sword.

Listening to the demands, offers, and counteroffers, Glenda and Traveler grinned at each other. They were getting insights into the realities of the Hun Empire. The conquered peoples were viewed as little more than domesticated animals. They were discussed in terms that sounded like an auction for horses, cattle, or other livestock. Nowhere was there a recognition that these were humans.

As the evening progressed, the arguments recycled many of the same offers and conditions. Whispering to Glenda, Traveler said, "This is like the definition of insanity. Saying the same thing over and over in a louder voice and expecting a different result. Alcohol certainly contributes a lot to the bargaining logic." Glenda gave a returning smile.

Occasionally a brother would rise and leave the tent for a nature call. The moment he was gone the two remaining brothers quickly entered into a discussion of how to more fairly divide the empire. Brotherly affection came in a distant second to personal gains.

Of course, when the next brother had to step outside, he was aware of the bargaining ploys that would happen in his absence. Gradually it became clear that this was not only a division of spoils but also an enjoyable contest of wits and bargaining. Assessing a situation for a weakness, quickly followed by aggressive demands, was part of the Hun culture.

There was an unspoken acceptance among the brothers that no matter how flagrant a claim or how insulting an offer, it was made in the spirit of a betting game. Without this spirit of acceptance, bargainers could die at the table. In contrast, five hundred years later, Viking lords were quick to raise a sword over some perceived insult. To their credit, the Huns were controlled in their heated discussions, at least at the gaming table.

As the evening wore on and the brothers' words became slurred, Glenda and Traveler began to doubt that their spying risks were going to result in useful information. Looking at each other they acknowledged that their great effort appeared to be a waste of time. They accepted that they would need to retreat shortly. They could hear that the storm was losing its assault on trees and tents, and Hun guards would shortly begin a perimeter patrol.

Chapter 54

Servants Know

Just as Traveler was starting a suggestive hand motion to leave, three of the servants came to sit on a nearby bench. The two teens instantly went into a deeper stealth mode, praying the servants would not come around and step on them. The casino's random chance factor favored the hiding youths. The servants sat down on silk cushions without ever moving toward the hidden teens.

The servants were clearly tired physically and mentally. Their voices betrayed frayed emotions. To serve the brothers was an honor but also a deadly challenge. Each servant had to anticipate a brother's needs and satisfy them before being asked. If a brother had to break his conversation with a request the servant would be unhappy with what followed.

Now that the three brothers were enjoying their full cups of kumis, they were beyond immediate needs and the servants could relax. With deep sighs their bodies began to shrug off the stress of serving. With pillows placed on rugs and platters of food resting in front of them, they began to discuss the day's events, warrior gossip, and what it all meant to the army. More importantly, what did it all mean to them?

Age did not prioritize or limit servant conversation as it did with the warriors. Older servants knew that younger servants were nearly invisible to the rulers, they often overheard the choicest of discussions. As the two older servants commenced eating the youngest began. "Which is the greater threat to us, the anticipated German attack, or being used to help transport the stones? I fear both possibilities."

The servant beside him paused, bringing the yogurt-covered bread to his mouth. "You should fear either possibility. The Germans have been treated like cattle to be herded, used, and sold. They are a fierce people; we are fortunate that they fight among themselves. If united they would be the most dangerous of foes."

The third servant swallowed then joined the conversation. "Personally, I would prefer contesting the Germans. Our warriors have conquered all we have faced. The greater threat is being conscripted to move the heavy rocks downstream."

The second servant nodded. "Yes, that is true. I have heard the heavily loaded rafts are known to break their bindings when they hit buried river rocks. Stones are often stacked too high and a tumbling stone immediately crushes anyone in its path. Rumor is we have lost dozens of warriors so far, and many more have been crippled."

The oldest servant continued with his thoughts. "Even worse than the dangers of transporting is not knowing why our leaders are building a structure in this land. For what purpose? Huns never leave permanent monuments. We capture cities, we destroy cities, and then we move on. We never remain in place. We never build."

The youngest continued to probe for possible answers, either from fear or curiosity. "Where is this building structure placed? Few seem to know the location. Why is it a secret? I have wondered if it is a key to locating a hidden treasure."

With the mention of a treasure horde, all three began to speculate on the possibility and the size of such a treasure. They all agreed that if they knew how to find it there may be a day when they could return and claim it. Visions of wealth captured each servant's mind.

The oldest servant acknowledged the possibility that the monument was a treasure locator. "I think the monument's location is indeed a carefully managed secret. It may well be the means to finding a treasure. I would, however, prefer to fight the Germans than build a monument. Treasures remain secret since the lords eliminate all the workers when the building is complete."

The youngest servant nodded his head indicated an insight. "I definitely think there is a treasure involved since workers disappear and get replaced. While none of the construction workers have returned to camp, I have an idea of how to find the treasure." The other two servants were now hanging on his words. The stealth spies were equally captivated.

"I have heard raft pilots say that they continue on the river until they reach a great waterfall at the base of a snow-covered mountain. They unload at that point. Ponies are waiting to move the rocks once they are removed from the raft. The monument must be under construction somewhere up the mountain past the falls.

"I would not want to know the exact location by working there, but I believe the site could be found. I believe the pilots speak the truth regarding the transport of the rocks. They are all very nervous men because of their knowledge. They are no longer fierce warriors, something has them living in great fear."

The speculations over hidden treasure continued until there was motion from the three brothers. The servants quickly stood and brought platters of spiced dates to the seated brothers. It was dessert time.

Chapter 55

A German Storm Approaches

The brothers were beginning to devour the dates when the large entry flap was pulled aside. A grizzled captain entered, did a short bow to the seated brothers, then declared, "One storm is easing while another approaches. Our scouts report a large group of Gepid warriors approaching on the other side of the river. They are dressed for war."

The oldest brother, Ellac, immediately rose. Swaying slightly from the kumis, he responded in a commander's voice. "They want war; they shall have it. It is time to crush these faithless vassals. Their loyalty pledges mean nothing."

The second brother, Dengizich, was also on his feet. "I also tire of these Germans. The Hun world needs far fewer of their impudent lords. Let us reduce the noise coming from these bearded barbarians. Slaves should live to serve, never threaten."

Watching the interactions, Traveler whispered to Glenda, "It's amazing how these guys shrug off the drinking. I remember it took us over a day's sleep, and another day's rest after Olaff's ale… and we still wobbled."

Whispering back, Glenda said, "I remember all too well. Now let's get out of here while they're focused on the Germans."

Traveler immediately crawled back to their exit flap. He rolled onto his side, peeked out to confirm that nobody was guarding the back, and slipped out. Once outside he held the side up. Glenda was again a fast-moving salamander and joined him in seconds.

Inside the tent a servant caught the motion of a tent-side moving, but immediately dismissed it as being torn loose from its mooring stake. No warning shouts came from inside as the two youths faded back toward the storage area.

Once at the storage depot Traveler paused, "Let's take a minute to resupply." He proceeded to pull the top off a nearby wooden crate. "We hit the jackpot!" he quietly exclaimed as the pleasant smell of smoked meats and fresh breads wafted up to his nostrils. He began rapidly filling his bag with fresh supplies.

Glenda was equally enthralled with her own discoveries. "Unbelievable," she whispered, "We have oranges." Opening an adjoining box, she added, "Sugared dates layered on pita bread and goat cheese. We'll feast like M is serving."

Traveler's head suddenly jerked upward as a series of lightning flashes crossed the heavens. Following the flashing lights came a series of breathless grunts and exhales that resembled those of a startled deer. Rising quickly to his feet, Traveler placed his carry bag on his back, then looked at a grinning Glenda. "What's up?"

She pointed across the depot's holding fence. A wide-eyed Hun was staring from the far side. "Boo!" said Glenda. With a visible jerk the guard got control of his body and proceeded to run as fast as his bowed legs could carry him.

Laughing, she said, "I think he just learned to levitate without our book's help, first with me, now with you. I had just stood up when that lightning fireworks came. I guess all he saw was a mass of red hair and green eyes staring back. And I'm a foot taller than him. Then giant boy appears out of nowhere. His scared little yelps got translated as 'Demons! Demons!'"

Traveler joined Glenda's amusement over the poor guard's shock. "A redheaded demon, oh yeah! Sounds like you passed for a jinn. Better yet a big efreet. It's nice to know the fearless Huns can be scared. Right now, though, I think we'd better leave Dodge and the supplies pronto."

"Agreed. So sad to leave all this, but we need to head out before anyone takes him seriously. These Huns are paranoid about Gepid spies. Despite his demon hysteria, spies are what cooler heads will think."

Their whispering stopped abruptly as they heard running feet and shouting orders. They fell into a fast, silent jog.

Chapter 56

Allies Arrive

A mounted Ardaric rose in the thick metal stirrups to study the long lines of incoming warriors. War flags and colored banners identified the gathering tribes. With their battle flags held high, Ardaric easily identified warriors from the Goths, Rugi, Alans, and Heruli.

He was pleased to identify many smaller groups of individual chieftains who brought their personal guards. These chieftains were all noted warriors. Some would advance to become tribal leaders if they survived the pending battle.

The incoming Germanic tribes were of varying numbers. Ardaric's own tribe was significant in size, however, larger tribes were always needed. More warriors are necessary in a pitched battle, and this battle would be one for the ages.

He reflected on the size of the much larger opposing army and consoled himself, thinking, *The Huns have not faced our united force. Numbers matter, but so does an individual warrior's experience and courage. We are gathering a formidable army of experienced warriors. This is our land. Our warriors will fight as a cornered wolf pack.*

In the midst of his somber reflections a welcomed face appeared. It was Theodemir of the large Ostrogoth tribe. *As promised, he has come.* Riding to greet the Ostrogoth lord, Ardaric removed a gauntlet to grasp the extended hand. Exposed flesh and callus greeted flesh and callus as the two lords sealed their meeting with powerful handshakes.

Theodemir spoke first while presenting a slight smile. "I understand you are preparing to chase the Huns back to their lands in the east. I have heard you intend for it to be to the very far east. We are here to provide whatever meager assistance you may need. Not that the great Ardaric needs any help."

Ardaric started with a booming reply which broke into a thunderous laugh. "Double what we have, and more would still be welcome. You grace us with your warriors. They are renowned for their bravery, as are you! Welcome, my friend, you are sorely needed. I am pleased at your arrival more than you may imagine."

Theodemir gave a modest smile in return. "One way to consider the unfavorable numbers is that there are more of their spirits for us to send in defeat to their version of hell."

Ardaric nodded at the small boast while looking at the continuing flow of Ostrogoth warriors. "Have I missed your king Valamir, or is he still waking up from last night's drinking? Perhaps he considers this battle too easy for him, and he only sends you. If so, we have gotten the better end of that bargain."

Theodemir gave a thin smile to acknowledge the compliment, then said, "You have not missed him. Our King Valamir is a cautious fox. He keeps a foot in both battle camps. In our war council we were divided. As you see, many joined me. Valamir chose to join the Huns as a reserve force. I have the better followers.

"As we parted company, Valamir boasted that following the Hun victory he would save those among us who lived. His parting words were, 'Regardless of the battle's outcome, the Ostrogoth tribe will survive under my leadership.'"

Ardaric frowned. "Your king may find his own survival is in doubt, either on the battlefield or after. Following our victory, I believe the Ostrogoths will demand a new king, and I see my own choice."

Nudging his horse forward toward the open expanse of the battlefield, Ardaric said, "Let us examine the contest field. I have thoughts of how to lessen the Hun advantages and want your thoughts."

Chapter 57

Roles Are Decided

While Ardaric, Theodemir, and their captains scouted the battlefield, the Hun brothers debated.

"We should attack at once," an excited Dengizich said, as he slammed his mug on the map table for emphasis. "Our scouts say that there is a long trail of Germans marching through the forest to join those already by the field. Other scouts have confirmed Ardaric as the commander. We should first cut off the snake's head then slice up the snake's body as it tries to advance."

The youngest son, Ernak, gave a silent approving head nod. His unspoken allegiance was typically with Dengizich. Dengizich knew his brother's character and played upon its weakness. Ernak's pledge of loyalty had been secured by promising him a portion of the empire; he was too easily bribed. With Attila gone, Dengizich had shrewdly created a manageable ally in youthful Ernak.

Attila had recognized his youngest son's weakness and was hesitant to recognize him as an equal to the other two. Blood ties finally convinced Attila to bring Ernak into the small ruling group of brothers. Attila was more than aware that a Hun leader could never have too many sons. Pitched battles often determined which son survived to lead.

After permitting Dengizich his say, Ellac stood and patiently lectured both of his brothers. "Our father never rushed into a battle until he had considered all possible strategies. I understand the value of swift action, but only when it is correct and found to be the best possible action.

"You have both seen me on the battlefield and know my prowess and bravery are second to none. To pause at this moment and reflect is proper thinking. It will ensure that our action will prevail."

While the two younger brothers were always annoyed at Ellac speaking to them like they were children, they recognized he was a fierce warrior with many followers. He had also received the greatest training from Attila, which they had to admit was an advantage.

Dengizich slowly nodded his head in acceptance of this "wait and study" tactic. "I will wait brother, but only so long. When I feel the German forces are most vulnerable to a sharp attack I will engage. I know each of you will join me."

Ellac smiled at the brother, saying, "We agree. When we attack, I will lead our central force. Dengizich, you will be my right flank, and Ernak my left flank."

Inwardly Dengizich was pleased. He knew the right flank was always the hammer that struck the anvil of the central force. Glory came to the hammer.

Ernak nodded at his role. The left flank was a reserve force and waited in safety. The reserve became significant after the hammer and anvil had prevailed. With fresh warriors it became a rested killing force. It arrived as a pursuing storm of death sweeping into running foe. Few runners escaped the storm.

Chapter 58

Final Decisions Are Made

While the Hun brothers debated tactics over many cups of kumis, the German leaders had continued to scout the battlefield. They observed that since the heavy rain had stopped, the river and field now permitted massed horse crossings. The Hun would come soon, and they would come fast.

They studied the open terrain for best troop placements. They rode their large battle horses on a number of the wider trails to confirm which trails permitted horses to move quickly. They confirmed how many horses could ride side by side. They accepted that swift Hun horses would soon be charging across the wide expanse and discussed how to best defend.

Over the day a great deal of information was brought to Ardaric, along with numerous suggestions. As he listened and assessed, he shared his thoughts with the reporting commanders. Each commander appreciated Ardaric's insights and his respect for their findings and opinions. It was a long, busy day for all leaders.

All commanders accepted that Ardaric was responsible for combining the gathered information and suggestions into a single battle plan. They trusted his judgement; he was the best among them. By the end of the day the battle plan was clear in Ardaric's mind. He reviewed it to the nodding heads of the gathered leaders. Discussion time was over.

With twilight descending, the commanders surrounded Ardaric for a final fellowship bonding. Looking at them Ardaric knew they needed inspiration. The leaders had all observed the massive Hun camp across the river, each had estimated the enemy's size. While the estimates varied, even the smallest described a massive army that greatly outnumbered them.

Knowing their concerns, a confident Ardaric rose in his saddle. With a sweep of his arm toward the Hun encampment, he said, "I know your thoughts. They are the same as mine. Yes, we are greatly outnumbered. Yes, we know tomorrow's battle will be beyond difficult. Yes, many will die. Yes, if Attila were leading this army I would fade back into the forest.

"However, his sons are not Attila. I know each of them, and I am confident we will defeat them. Permit me to tell you why.

"Ellac is the best of them but he is still less than his father. He leads, but cautiously with concerns about his brothers taking his orders.

"The other two are less of a threat. Dengizich views himself as the strongest leader. He questions Ellac's decisiveness. His weakness is to attack too quickly. Once he commits, he lacks the flexibility to adjust as the tides of battle change.

"Ernak is the weakest. He commands their reserve force. He is not a coward but is overly cautious. All warriors watch their leader, in a pitched battle he will fail their test."

Smiling, he brought a mailed fist to his own chest. "I am well aware that Germanic warriors also watch their leaders." Each commander smiled back and nodded in agreement. They knew and accepted their battlefield roles.

"Our advantage is that they may not act as a coordinated unit. Each brother wishes to establish himself as the successor to Attila. Of course, they may surprise us and coordinate their separate armies. That is why battles must be fought to determine outcomes.

"Each of you will lead and determine our shared fate. I will sleep well tonight knowing I am in your company. Return and join your forces, let them see your confidence. Sleep well brothers, tomorrow's sun and our shared fate will be with us soon."

Ardaric's obvious confidence and description of the brothers' weaknesses provided the needed inspiration. Confidence is contagious, and Ardaric's spread across the gathered commanders. *We can and will prevail* was imbued in each heart and mind as the commanders returned to their tribes.

As the group dispersed Ardaric called his own captains to him. "Light fires along the length of this river. I believe it is called the Nedao. Post sentries with horns.

"The river is no longer deep. The Huns may consider a night attack, we should discourage that. Attila would consider such an attack to rattle and tire our men; however, I doubt the sons have the stomach for leading a night assault. Fires will tell them we are waiting and offer an excuse not to attack. Both sides need tonight's rest."

Chapter 59

Battle of Nedao River: The Dice Are Thrown

The next day saw an early but subdued sun rise in the east. While the heavy storm had ended the day before it left many thick, dark clouds. Daylight was slow in coming. Warriors on both sides were pleased for the additional time to wake and prepare.

Men in both camps moved quietly, lost in their thoughts. Both sides knew this would be a determining battle. The Hun Empire hung in the balance. The fate of Germanic servitude would be determined for many generations.

Observers on both sides looked upon the stage that nature had prepared for their contest. The Nedao had been initially swollen from the storm's rains but the water flow had greatly slowed. The surrounding sandy riverbanks appeared ready to accept mounted horsemen. The river itself was now low enough to permit mounted riders crossing without fear of losses.

While the field was still visibly wet in spotty places, its elevated height facilitated natural drainage. The surface was rapidly stabilizing to accept charging horses.

Each army now had direct access to the other across the large open field. With a sense of urgency, men assembled into their battle formations. Leaders on both sides pondered the opening move. Which adversary would show confidence and throw the opening challenge?

The Hun warriors were now mounted and forming into their three battle groups. Confidence was high. There was an anticipation of the coming battle that charged up both horse and rider. They had been in the camp for many months, and this was an army built to move and fight. The captains were in place, focused on their leaders, the three brothers.

The brothers rode together to the edge of the river and were pleased to see the banks offered a wide, gentle, downward slope access to the river. "I like the conditions," said Dengizich. "This river has greatly receded, we can cross in massed units with the firmed slopes."

Wanting to establish his presence, young Ernak added, "The river crossing is promising. It will wet our riders but only to the middle of their bellies, and not to their bows. That is acceptable. All bows will remain dry." With a smile, he added, "Many need a bath, their stench alone should scare the Germans."

The two older brothers chuckled at the humor to show their support for their youngest brother. In this battle they were committed to each other. Monopoly would be played again, but only after the Germans were defeated.

As the youngest brother received smiles back, he was emboldened. He affirmed to himself, *I will show my brothers my courage. Father Attila, high above with the sky god, will see that his son is the warrior he wished for.*

Dengizich turned to the oldest brother, then pointed to the moving mass across the field. "I believe they continue to flow in. They must be struggling to form battle lines. With so many different tribes, keeping units together must be impossible.

"Many of these tribes fight each other. They will not stand together as fighting units. They will fail to commit to each other when personal sacrifice is needed. Is this the time, brother, to cross and sweep these traitors from our lands?"

Ellac had been in deep thought. He was still undecided about whether the time was right for the massed charges. He saw the land was still wet, but Hun ponies were lighter than the large, heavy armored German warhorses. Additionally, the Hun warrior was a smaller, less armored man. Less weight would help offset the slippery footing conditions. *Field wetness is to our advantage today*, he concluded.

Ellac reflected again on Dengizich's analysis. He frequently disagreed with his headstrong brother, but on this day he accepted that there was battlefield wisdom in it. The Huns had a long tradition of facing alliances of various tribes that had joined together simply for a battle. The coalition always collapsed when Hun-pressure started the casualty tolls. Each tribe fought for its own survival while Huns fought and died only for Huns.

Ellac recalled his father's oft-repeated battle strategy. "Attack the strongest tribe first. This is typically the center force. You will see they share a common banner on shield and pole.

"When the center falters and splits open, the flanking sides will lose heart and run. Your ponies will swiftly track down a running man and spear him in the back. Kill them all to avoid meeting them another day. The sky god is watching, let him be pleased with his warriors."

Ellac's concluding thought was that if he failed to lead now, his brother may cross first, with Ernak joining him. Alone, Ellac would appear as the tail on the dog. *I am no dog's tail.* Without saying a word, Ellac motioned for his banner to be raised. He pointed across the river.

His center roared their approval. These warriors enthusiastically followed Ellac. They knew he was the oldest, and Attila's favorite. He had led them to victory in many battles. The center felt they were following Attila himself; all knew the oldest son was the reincarnation of the father. Attila's spirit and wisdom resided in Ellac.

Pleased with his brother's decision, Dengizich raised his own banner to lead his force across. His force roared their approval. They knew they were the battle hammer that would smash the foe on the center's anvil. They knew Dengizich was a battlefield master as he personally created openings in opponent lines. "Follow Dengizich" was their battle cry.

The brothers were united! Brother Hammer and Brother Anvil would win the coming battle. Brother Reserve would bring swift death to all running rabbits. Germans would cower for many generations.

Ernak held his force back while the tens of thousands crossed first. He accepted his role as the reserve. He glowed with the inward confidence that came from knowing that it was the reserves, in a pitched battle, that carried the day. He was also relaxed knowing this would not be a pitched battle. His brothers would utterly destroy the facing force. His glory would come in leading the killing storm.

Ernak's suppressed thought was, *Dying in battlefield glory is good, but the sky god also values survival. I will survive. Will I be the only remaining brother? Will the empire be united under my sole command?*

Chapter 60

An Early Manassas

The two sleepers were awakened by heavy vibrations coming from below. The sounds and tree vibrations of a vast army moving around them chased dreams from their minds. The morning's usual bird calling was absent. All wildlife remained silent, hiding in place. Human predators were walking the land.

Peering down, they saw the Hun army attired for the coming battle. Thick leather vests wrapped around each rider. Most riders wore metal caps on their heads with thick protective attachments that covered necks. Many caps displayed long horsehair plumes honoring their mounts.

Neither teen spoke as they watched the riders assemble into three massive groups. Looking to the riverbank they watched the Hun forces as they spread out, preparing to cross. Across the open field they saw colorful German war banners waving in a chilling morning breeze.

Traveler first spotted Ardaric and pointed him out to Glenda. "I see your boyfriend over there. He's the man alright. You chose well. Hope he's around to escort you to the prom. The Huns look like they are ready to have his head on a pole." Watching the confident Hun brothers, Traveler said, "I feel like I'm watching a replay of the First Battle of Manassas."

Glenda's face wrinkled as she said, "What's a Manassas?"

"Not a 'what', but a 'where.' Manassas is in northern Virginia and it is where the first major battle between the North and the South took place.

"It was 1861, and war had been declared between our states. We call it our Civil War. It was by far the deadliest war America has been in. More American soldiers died during the four-year civil war than in any of our subsequent wars, including World War I, World War II, Korea, and Vietnam."

"I didn't know that," said a quiet Glenda. "What happened at Manassas?"

"A Northern army entered the southern state of Virginia to end the secession of southern states from the union. Virginia was a powerful and historic state. George Washington, the first American president, arguably the greatest, was a Virginian.

"The North was very confident of victory. They had the numbers and the equipment. They were so confident that many Northern supporters came out of the Union's capital, Washington DC, to watch the anticipated Northern victory. They set up picnic spots to eat and enjoy the action close-up, using opera glasses."

"I get it," said Glenda. "We're the picnic people. Sitting here enjoying our breakfast while a battle is ready to start. So how did the Manassas battle turn out?"

"Not well for the Northern army or for the picnickers. The South won decisively. The Northern army was routed, and picnic baskets were abandoned. The real war had just started.

"It took four years and over 600,000 deaths before the Civil War ended. It was a war of attrition, and eventually the North won due to a larger population and a stronger industrial base." Glenda was trying to imagine the number of casualties and could only shake her head.

Looking out again at the crossing Hun army, Traveler reflected, "Invaders often find their defending foe is a more difficult challenge than expected. Invaders typically have the advantage of greater numbers, not always, but usually. Defenders are frequently in their own land and are fighting not only for their own lives but also for the lives of their families and their community.

"At Manassas, the North was the invader and the Southern troops were defending. Here, the Huns are the invaders and are the numerically superior force. The Germans defend. The invader may be surprised at how this battle will go." He paused, then quietly added, "Or not."

The two sat back to watch the unfolding drama. Stomachs tightened. Both were subdued over the anticipation of the carnage that would shortly begin. The battle-dice were in commanders' hands and were ready to be thrown.

Unlike Ellac, Ardaric was the sole commander. He recalled the great Roman general, Julius Caesar. As Caesar committed to crossing the Rubicon river to enter Rome, he said to his legions, "Alea iacta est," meaning, "The die is cast." Ardaric watched as the advancing Huns made the first cast of the die, they crossed the Nedao. Now it was his turn.

As Attila had taught him, Ardaric took his time, watching the Huns as they flowed across the Nedao. He had earlier considered advancing to confront them as they began crossing. *Attack while they are bunched together in the river.* This was a worthy strategy, but he discarded it. *This could be an opening move to lure us from our defensive positions. They could reinforce their crossing and attack while we are spread out.*

When it was clear there was no feint intended, Ardaric accepted that the opportunity for a river attack had passed by. He accepted this with calmness. He had always expected that the confident Huns would lead a massed horse charge across the wide field. He was content with his defensive strategy.

With Theodemir beside him, he said, "Well, they seem intent on charging us with their fast ponies. They have given us the field position of our choosing; let them pay in blood. Our fields need nourishing for our fall crops."

Theodemir smiled. "They are too eager and have erred early. They failed to study the field, a sign of overconfidence. I will see you, my Battle Lord, on the field. Now I join my mounted warriors, they are eager to shout our insults even though the Huns won't understand them." To himself Ardaric smiled thinking, *Oh, I believe they will fully understand your insults.*

Wheeling his horse away from Ardaric, Theodemir raced toward a mass of mounted cavalry resting in the center of the forming line of spear warriors. Joining them, he rose in his saddle and motioned to advance. As they moved forward, they spread out in a wide line facing the advancing Huns.

Theodemir's warriors and their mounts were prepared similarly to the Huns. They knew the field ahead was still wet and that weight was a disadvantage. Both riders and mounts were lightly armored. Riders carried small shields on their left arms and bows on their right arms. A pair of arrow-filled quivers were strapped close to both sides of their mounts' necks for quick access. In all battles speed matters.

The advancing line beat swords on shields as a first challenge. Large Germanic bodies began loud shouts of warrior insults. Ardaric was correct. The Hun understood the insults and were eager to return the verbal insults with arrow strikes.

Coming behind Theodemir, at a fast trot, were massed warriors preparing to create the fronting shield wall. These were older, powerful warriors who advanced with their thick wooden shields and long heavy spears. Younger warriors followed behind carrying even longer sharpened spears to reinforce the front line. It was a mix of defensive strength against horse charges combined with offensive spear thrusts at riders. The mass of men resembled a long, spread-out Greek phalanx wall.

As the lagging massed footmen advanced, they suddenly split into three units. The units moved to form shield wall groups on the left side closer to the Nedao river, the center, and the right side of the open field near the forest. In front of the advancing shield wall units, the German cavalry was closing to within arrow range of the Huns.

The Hun advance was controlled and steady. In the center rode a confident Ellac. He was Attila, his father, demonstrating his control over battle-hardened riders. This demonstration of battlefield discipline had proven itself against all foes. He knew the approaching German riders would begin to tremble in anticipation of the Hun's killing charge.

Chapter 61

The Battle Is Joined

The right flanking Hun hammer, under Dengizich, was advancing as a fast-moving mass across the open field. His mounted warriors were eager to engage the opposing shield-holding Germans. The stationary Germans looked like archery practice to the approaching Huns.

Rapidly advancing, Dengizich observed his distant brother leading the anvil forward at a controlled pace and smiled. *The Germans have foolishly split their forces to contest the entire wide field. A serious error.*

While advancing, the anvil-center Ellac saw that his brother's hammer was moving quickly, as planned. The hammer would soon reach the opposing shield wall. The wall did not have the necessary depth to withstand his brother's charge. The Germans had chosen to strengthen the center wall, hoping the flanks could hold.

A serious error, Ellac thought. *Dengizich's hammer will drive through them to come behind their larger, thicker wall. Their wall will be under Hun attacks from the front and back. An impossible situation to defend. Those in the center are useless. No shield wall can fight on two fronts. Father Attila is again correct, attack and crush the center.*

As he continued to move forward at a controlled pace, he carefully studied the German movements. He knew Ardaric was a capable commander who would follow each move his opponent made.

Ellac saw that the thick center shield wall was continuing to be strengthened. He knew these walls were the backbone of the German infantry. He saw the long spears being prepared to halt charging horses. He had no intention of charging into the spear-wall.

Ellac knew from experience that the best way to defeat any shield wall was to pressure the center with arrows launched from the front while attacking from behind. His center would force the shield wall to remain in place until the hammer arrived. Shields could only protect in one direction. The massed German wall, regardless of thickness, would be cut down by arrows from two directions.

Ellac knew the battle god was with him. The field was too wide for the German shield wall to reach the river. While there were many Germans, the field's width was too great for the required thickness. Ellac saw how Ardaric would make his final stand within the concentrated center.

Watching the German strategy as it unfolded, Ellac understood Ardaric had committed the approaching horsemen in an attempt to disrupt his brother's hammer advance. Ellac gave Ardaric credit for knowing he could not have the Huns behind his shield wall as well as in front. His error was in misjudging the power of the hammer.

The oncoming German cavalry was advancing in an uncertain and slow-moving line. It was not a fearless charge. Despite brave insults, they were clearly unhappy about engaging the Hun horsemen. Ellac saw the hesitancy of the lightly armored German knights. *They cannot fight without their armor.* He heard his father's voice, *Once studied, never hesitate in battle.* He raised his banner upright, then swiftly lowered it. The countercharge order was given.

The Huns in his anvil center roared with their battle lust. They had been waiting too long, this is what they were born for. Their ponies were equally incensed. Man and horse were one and seemed to lift from the ground with their charging power. Each rider picked the German horseman that they would skewer, first by arrow, then finish by sword if necessary.

A series of loud German trumpet blasts crossed the field following the Hun charge. The slowly advancing German cavalry line turned and suddenly raced back. They flowed evenly between the three separate German shield walls, then wheeled to face the Hun. They instantly lifted their bows, notched arrows, and released when a second horn call sounded.

The Huns' speed was such that the German cavalry had barely notched and fired a second volley before the Hun forward line reached the center wall. Long spears immediately stopped the charging horses.

The Hun center turned quickly and began their own returning volleys at a safe distance. The pointing spears met no targets. Powerful Hun arrows struck the thick shields, with many arrows finding openings to fell a shield-holder.

With a motion from Ellac, Hun arrows shifted to create a falling rain into the German cavalry. The Huns staggered the trajectories, with waves coming down into the mounted knights as other archers picked at exposed shield and spear holders. The wall held only due to the depth and courage of the defenders.

Another trumpet call announced a second German offense. Flowing from the forest were men carrying large wooden walls. Behind these walls were the main German archers. These archers carried multiple quivers, and a firestorm of arrows fell on both sides.

Ellac was impatient. His brother should have already flanked or crushed the German wall closest to the river. The hammer should be approaching from the rear. *Could my brother betray me?* flashed through his mind. The answer arrived from a racing Hun messenger.

"Dengizich cannot pass the shield wall. There is a swamp between the wall and the river. He has repeatedly tried to charge through, but the surface causes our horses to slide and collapse. Then heavily armored foot Gepids race from behind the shield wall and kill our horses and riders. After many charges there is a wall of dead horses and riders. We cannot attack our way through.

"Dengizich asks permission to join your center and combine with you to smash between the two shield walls. What is your command?"

Ellac understood how his brother had failed to adjust to the conditions. He had attacked too many times and had blocked his own passageway. *My dear, brave, headstrong brother. Still unchanged after all of Father's teachings.*

Ellac accepted the changed conditions. This battle would not be determined by indecision or an unnoticed swamp. Cursing last night's storm, he said, "Tell Dengizich to join me immediately. I will attack now. He can lead into the gaps I open and get behind the shield wall. Take a fresh mount, return quickly."

The rider nodded, jumped onto a fresh pony, and galloped away.

Ellac called his captains to him. "We must push between the two shield walls, there is much space. Get into close formation and charge on my signal. Those who pass close to the Germans must show their valor. When we break through the wall it will collapse. Tell our archers to shoot only when they have targets."

The Hun captains quickly reformed the mass of riders. The captains noticed that the volley of German arrows was still thick, while their own riders were now carefully reserving their remaining arrows. Many captains thought, *We have wasted too many arrows killing wood, not men.*

With their formations set to charge, the Hun center mass had positioned itself to enter the most vulnerable space between the two shield walls. There was a significant space but also many Hun horsemen. Hun discipline would be critical to limit their losses from hand-to-hand combat. Ellac gave the command for a full charge. Horses again rushed forward.

Ellac was in the third wave and saw how riders approaching the openings suddenly slid out of control. This entire center field proved to still be water-soaked ground that offered slippery footing to charging horses. Sideways movement led to falling mounts and men. Riders from behind plowed into falling horses, and a series of collapsing horses paralyzed the center's advance.

Piles of obstructing horses and riders began to build up. These built-up piles generated an opportunity for the Gepid shield wall warriors. Behind the front line were masses of warriors eager to move forward. These unengaged warriors now saw their opportunity. Without weakening the wall, warriors toward the rear flowed out on the flanks to engage the Huns.

Slowed Hun riders were greeted by bearded giants swinging long swords and battleaxes. Both edges of the Hun anvil became a killing zone for the German foot soldiers. The ever-falling horses and riders continued to narrow the passage for the massed riders pressing behind them.

Years of pent-up rage over subjugation and humiliation had bloodlust driving the shield wall warriors. Increasingly, warriors moved out to engage Hun riders. Hun mobility and speed were rapidly disappearing in the narrowing space.

The Huns were fierce warriors, even on foot. Those on the center's edges leapt out of saddles to engage with their swords. Ellac stood in the center of a protective circle many Huns thick, shouting commands to hold and advance. He was a brave leader refusing to yield to the closing pressure of his opponent. The Huns took heart as they saw Attila was again leading them.

The attacking German battleaxes, fueled by rage, continued to shrink his protective circle. Ellac knew that his reserves, under his brother Ernak, should now be coming. *This is the time in battle when reserves are most needed. Is my brother blind?*

Surrounded, Ellac's luck suddenly changed. A great roar went up as his collapsing center heard the trumpets call out Dengizich's arrival. Fresh Hun riders were again target shooting German soldiers who were no longer protected by the shield wall. The momentum had shifted to Ellac.

Exhausted German warriors began to waver, while their captains shouted orders to re-join the shield wall. Shouting captains were recognized as leaders and immediately drew Hun fire. As identified targets, captains began falling under the barrage of Hun arrows. German warriors wavered as they saw their leaders fall under the fresh assault.

Battle fates are similar to the fates of poker players. The best analysis and plan can be destroyed by the turning of a single card. Dengizich's arrival was such a fortune-changing card. The momentum of battle had shifted sharply to the Huns. The hammer was now descending on the anvil as planned.

Watching the changing fortunes in front of him, Ernak was energized to join his brothers. His earlier hesitancy was gone and he prepared to order his captains to attack the Germans' wavering flanks. He would commit his reserves as the decisive trick.

But not all cards had been dealt. The next card that appeared was the Ardaric card. When it was added into the German hand the battlefield odds shifted again.

Ardaric suddenly appeared behind the massed Hun armies. His army was made up of thousands of heavily armored knights on huge warhorses. The mounted knights advanced in three lines. Each line had spaces between riders that permitted the back rows to flow through. Standing high in the stirrups, Ardaric gave a commanding call. "Forward, Gepid knights! Death to the Hun! Victory!"

The charge came on the part of the field that was not water-soaked. The heavy warhorses and the massive knights were in their battle glory. This was the vaunted charge of iron men and iron horses. The charge came as an iron fist driving into the massed Huns. The Huns were now an anvil receiving blows from the German hammer.

The first line's hammer blow struck, and Hun riders reeled from the impact. Many tried to turn to face the new threat when the second hammer struck. The open spaces between the first two rows closed as the third hammer line struck. With each hammer blow the Hun were forced closer together. The three Germanic lines formed an iron fence closing on the trapped mass of Hun horses and men.

In front, the Huns faced the blocking shield wall whose long spear thrusts were now reaching horse and rider. Behind were the ever-descending hammer blows from the mounted knights. Ironclad warhorses constantly pushed forward. Brave Hun horses could not stand against the pressing massive warhorses of the knights. Contained Hun warriors could not stand against the hacking giant Germans.

Huns caught in the center mass could barely move. There was no escape. The Huns became the trapped Roman army at Cannae. Hun speed and mobility were gone. A managed retreat was lost, only survival mattered.

Ardaric cut his path toward a besieged Ellac. He respected the son's bravery and was preparing to accept his surrender. Then he saw a massive Gepid foot soldier swing an enormous sword with two hands in a wide arc. The sword was a horizontal guillotine. Ellac never saw the stroke coming. His head was quickly impaled on a German spear. The Huns' final resistance collapsed.

The reserve force under Ernak remained as observers. Ernak stared in place as he saw the arrival of the heavily armored Germanic cavalry. He remained frozen as he watched the death of his older brother. Shaken to his core, Ernak was unable to launch a heroic charge. With lowered heads, the reserve faded back onto an escape road that headed east. Ernak prayed the Germanic forces would not pursue his retreating reserves.

Chapter 62

Battle Sickness Then Recovery

Glenda and Traveler were stunned. They sat for long minutes, transfixed by the scene. Neither could talk. This was a real-life killing field, Hollywood movies paled. The battle overwhelmed their senses. The sight and sounds of wounded horses and dying men crying out stunned their bodies and minds.

A shaking Traveler finally stood and offered Glenda his hand. He needed to put his body in motion to throw off the waves of emotional shocks that continued to hit him. Glenda took the extended hand, rose up, then hugged him as hard as she could, whispering, "That was beyond terrible. I saw the jinn kill poor Throbb without pity, this is far worse."

Still holding Traveler tight, she said, "The jinn is a different creature, and we are not beings that it relates to. This battle was between humans who could have been friends, yet the killing was impersonal. Aroused humans may be as dangerous and pitiless as the jinn."

While standing Traveler found he was slowly regaining his composure. Giving Glenda a final long hug back, he stepped away. "You're right, of course. We are indeed a dangerous, scary, and unpredictable species. At the same time, the jinn are an existential threat to all humans and maybe the whole universe. Let's stay focused on the jinn as the ultimate bad guys."

Glenda felt a loss of comfort as Traveler separated. Regaining her own composure, she said, "Of course you're right. We need to focus on the jinn. At the same time, I'm glad the Huns finally met their match. They have been a destructive killing force for too long. They behaved like the jinn too often to those they conquered."

Traveler was strapping on his carry sack as he said, "The positive side is we have the Hun camp all to ourselves right now. Let's resupply, then explore downstream. From what the servants said, that's likely where the falls and the jinn are." With that he began the descent toward the empty forest below.

Glenda quickly followed. Once beside him she said, "The bad news is we lost our raft. I guess we hoof it and follow the river."

They walked quickly through the deserted Hun camp. Any Hun survivors were long gone in their frenzied escape, and the German victors had not yet arrived. Glenda picked up her pace. "I think we should jog to the brothers' supply depot and help ourselves. The Germans will be here shortly, eager to sack this place."

The two jogged to the supply center. Both went for oranges first, then supplies of smoked meats, cheeses, and breads. Dates were dropped into open spaces to settle around the larger supplies. In a few minutes both had bulging bags.

With an acceptable supply of food, Glenda noticed an ornately carved ebony chest. She lifted the lid and exclaimed, "We sleep tonight! Look at these blankets and robes, I see sleeping cushions. Tie a few of each around your body, trust me you'll be a happy camper when we lie down." With that she removed a heavy blanket and a thick woolen robe.

Traveler was quietly grumbling about lost time but knew she was right. *What's a little extra weight to carry?* he thought. Settling down later to sleep he found the carry-price was more than acceptable.

Glenda stood and pointed to a wide path that ran parallel to the river. The thousands of tramping horses in the Hun reserve unit had cleared a trail that was easy to follow. "Too bad this doesn't go all the way to the big bend and the falls."

Looking ahead, Traveler nodded. "I like that there is still a thick line of trees between us and the river. Germans will be arriving shortly; we don't want to be spotted. I think your boyfriend would be eager to claim you as his victory prize."

"Yeah, yeah," replied Glenda. *That joke is a little long in the tooth.*

After several demanding hiking hours passed, the easy walking trail was far behind. When they finally emerged at the open riverbank both were exhausted. Looking around, they dropped their bags and extra clothing, removed boots and socks, and walked slowly into the water.

They cautiously tested the river's bottom. The wide, slow-moving river offered soft footing. When they put their full weight down, fine sand oozed between toes. The water was a soothing balm over ankles, it promised even greater relief for the entire body. Mother Nature soothed both. The river flowed around and over them, and the sun warmed them while the forest provided a comforting solitude. Germans, Huns, and battles faded.

Basking in the river they watched the wildlife resume their normal routines. Across the river they saw a large heron strike a slow-moving fish and swallow the prize without moving. Parallels to the battle popped into their minds and were quickly discarded.

Glenda finally stepped out and put on the Hun robe. "We need to find our resting place while there's still light. Mache schnell, big boy."

Glenda's "Mache schnell" had Traveler grinning. *I've created a monster.* Seeing that Glenda was ready to go, he moved fast. In a few minutes he was ready to search for their night's lodging place.

Chapter 63

A Raft Returns

The sun was well below the tree line as the two moved out. The moon was slowly rising to upstage the remaining red glimmers of the sinking sun as it placed its silvery radiance on the river. As their visibility was rapidly disappearing Traveler stopped, pointed, and exclaimed, "Tell me you see what I see!"

"Unbelievable!" said Glenda. "I do believe it's our old trusty raft, and it appears intact. Apparently, the last sharp turn sent it to our side of the river, let's check it out." Lifting her robe away from the water she waded to the raft. Hopping on board, she waved for Traveler to join her.

Once on board Traveler acted as a raft shipwright. He first inspected the rudder, then the raft's log bindings. A smile confirmed the raft's reliability. "It looks river-worthy to me! I think a morning push-off is the way to go. I say we spend the night right here. The last thing we need is to run into something nasty in darkness, and I'm tired of treehouse living." Glenda nodded back in agreement.

While Traveler had been doing his inspection, Glenda had explored the raft's surface in greater detail. "I never noticed before, but people obviously slept on this raft. There are smoothed log surfaces in the center giving flat areas to lie down on. Even Hun don't want to sleep on a washboard."

As she ran her hand over a smooth surface her finger caught a protruding metal clasp. She slowly pulled up on the clasp and removed a squared surface board. Once the sealing board was put aside, she looked down into a blackened pit. "I believe there is a firepit built in. All the comforts of home, take a look."

Traveler walked to the center where Glenda was sitting. He knelt and studied the depression in the large center log. Putting his hands into the cut-out bowl shape, he confirmed, "You're right, this is a firepit." He inserted a hand into the pit and slowly explored the bottom and sides. "There are doubled brass bowls inside. They made the second inside bowl to insulate against heat. Solid Roman engineering."

Moving his hand further around the inside he lifted out blackened fingers. "There are charcoal briquettes at the bottom resting on a bed of kindling. The pit was already prepared for a fire but never got lit. We stole it before it made its next downstream trip, lucky us."

Glenda nodded while contemplating the evening, "We have a safe harbor for tonight and a firepit ready to light up. Let's set up some drying racks in front and back of the pit. Our clothes are soaking and need to be dried out. I don't want to start tomorrow's trip wearing wet clothes."

Traveler was instantly on her suggestion. Setting his bag down, he stepped back into the river. "You stay here, I'll find some racks for drying."

Glenda knew a good offer and smiled back. "You're our Paul Bunyan, logs are your game."

Traveler moved rapidly to the nearby forest edge. He quickly spotted potential drying racks. Several small trees had recently been cut down but not yet delimbed. Green limbs extending from small trunks suggesting they would make great drying racks.

He dragged two saplings behind him to the edge of the river. He lifted one over his head and waded to the raft. Glenda watched him coming and lifted the clothing rack onto the raft. Traveler returned with the second rack, handed it over, then climbed aboard. Glenda quickly positioned both racks near the firepit placing them in front and back.

Once on board the first thing Traveler noticed was the red glow coming from the firepit. The tinder had been sufficient dry for the charcoal to quickly ignite, and now the glowing briquettes were warming the surrounding space. The warmth was more than welcome as the chilling night air was descending onto the river.

The two Huck Finns placed their wet clothing on the racks. Socks were pulled down over narrow green stems while the heavier wear was stretched across multiple larger limbs.

Traveler placed his bag beside his smooth resting area then triple-folded his heavy blanket across the surface. Next, he removed his blanket from the bag. He proceeded to place a selection of the Hun brothers' dinner supplies beside the pit as Glenda added her own selections. Dinner was served.

Glenda motioned toward the covered drying racks. "You found perfect racks. Using saplings with those springy limbs was a smart idea. After one side is dry, we'll just rotate the rack and dry the other side."

Traveler accepted the compliment with a slight shrug. *Stay modest.* "Well, they'll do the job. As a bonus they'll also cut down on the night breezes. I bet sleeping on the river will be a frosty experience. Let's thank our firepit for being a well-needed heating system. It's like a sunken Rumford fireplace."

As she was enjoying their dinner Glenda found she wanted to eat, not talk. *I'll let Mr. History do the talking right now.* She threw him a layup. "Who or what is a Rumford?"

"Rumford is the most efficient wood burning fireplace ever invented. It was created in 1796 by Sir Benjamin Thompson, Count Rumford, an Anglo-American physicist. His specialty was the study of heat. The fireplace is named appropriately after his design."

He rose and felt the garments benefiting from the heat. "I believe these sides are dry already. I'll turn the racks, you just sit and relax."

"Your wish is my command." Patting her belly, she quipped, "Not sure I could get up right now, so a big thank you."

After turning the racks, Traveler returned to study the next round of intake. He discovered, to his surprise, his hunger seemed mostly placated. As he pondered the need for further eating, he noticed a small pile of folded, thin bread strips. He took one, and his face lit up as he chewed. He swallowed then said, "These are great! I mean M quality great! Try one."

Glenda took a piece and bit off an end. She instantly grinned then noticed her sticky fingers. "Thick sweet honey with ground nuts inside, this must be the original baklava. The Hun brothers knew their pastry." She quickly took two more of the delicacies.

With dinner over, both rafters were stuffed and sleepy. Traveler stood and inspected the racks, confirming that both sides were warm and dry. "Our great meal is followed by more great news! Mr. Rumford did the drying job. We have more bedding for our sleeping comfort. Since all the garments are warm, I'm putting mine on the bottom to hold the heat as well as to provide more padding."

Glenda felt her own warm clothing, then finished making her bed following Traveler's suggestion. A look of contentment spread over her face. "My back is so happy with the extra padding and the warmth."

The two were stretched out, lying on their backs and looking up. "The stars are so close I can almost reach them," said Glenda softly.

Traveler was also fascinated by the clear night sky. The Big Dipper and North Star were easy to spot. He noted that some constellations seem to have shifted a bit from his science class pictures. *I guess things moved around over fifteen hundred years. Plus, I'm looking at them in the Carpathian Mountains instead of in Charlottesville.*

The rising river fog began to dim the star show. As the fog thickened, it increasingly clung to the river's surface, bringing in more chilling night air. Ever present and doing his job, Mr. Rumford resisted the fog and kept their space almost cottage-cozy. Both were soon fast asleep resting on thick warm padding. Huck Finn never had it any better.

Chapter 64

By Land or by River?

Sounds carry far on water. When they woke it was to the sound of a beaver slapping the water. Multiple loud slaps became an unwanted morning alarm clock. Both grunted at the intrusion into their sweet REM dreams. The beaver had earlier left his own dreams behind in his river lodge to become the busy animal he was known to be.

"Please shut him up!" grunted Glenda, still wrapped in her over-the-head blanket.

"I'm thinking beaver pancakes," answered Traveler from deep in his own blanket-cave.

The two had slept all night on their backs, and now both rolled to the side facing the still warm pit and each other. Two heads emerged to find the early fog still surrounded their raft. The lingering cold night air was now dominating the fireplace, and neither wanted to leave their warm beds. Unfortunately, nature called, and both accepted the need to return to the shore.

Glenda was the first to rise and step into the slow-moving water. Her loud yelp caused the beaver to pause in his chores. "Yes, it's cold! Make sure you hold your robe out of the water when you get in." With that warning she was across to the bank and into the woods.

Reluctantly, Traveler swung out of his bed, stood up, stretched, and slow-walked to the edge of the raft. Just in time, he lifted his robe before stepping in. He bit back a number of bad expressions, followed by a few pitiful whimpers as he moved to the shore. *There should be ice on this surface*, he thought.

He crossed the soft river bottom and up the bank to the tree line. Calling out he said, "I'm coming so look out. It's still really dark and foggy so don't walk into me."

"Thanks for the heads-up but don't worry, you make as much noise as that beaver. I'm heading back to our raft, see you there. I'm thinking of those baklavas, I'll try to save a few."

Traveler didn't really need any prompting, but the image of the depleted baklava plate sped him up. He was shortly back to the bank, calling out, "Save at least one for me."

Back on board, his face fell, looking at the empty baklava plate. A seated Glenda was watching him with a wry smile. "I'm sorry, I started on them and just couldn't stop myself. I'm embarrassed."

Watching the sad puppy dog look she began laughing. She reached behind herself and placed a pile of the sweet treats in front of them. Traveler knew an accusatory look had come over his face and now he was embarrassed. *Where is my trust?* he chastised himself.

Pride had him hesitating to take a piece. Glenda laughed, took the largest piece, placed it in front of him, and said, "Eat right now or I will." A second command was unnecessary.

Finished, Travel asked, "Do you think we should stay on the river, or move by land? There are pros and cons to each."

Glenda reflected on his question. She knew this was a big decision, so she decided to spell out the pros and cons that she saw. "Part of me wants to ride the raft to the falls. It's easy and my body needs some rest. It promises to be a great day, and it would be nice to have some time to enjoy the land we are passing through."

Continuing, she said, "When we hike there's no relaxing. Furthermore, there's nothing to look at except brambles, tripping roots, and Hun stragglers. On the other hand, when we're hiking we're never out in the open. On the river we're a visible moving target...So that's my quick take on our choices, what do you think?"

"You nailed it! I can't add anything. I'm thinking that a river cruise would be a sweet way to travel. I can see us cruising, enjoying the scenery, eating, and napping whenever the mood hits us. We'll be like old Huck moseying along as the river takes us. Besides, we deserve rest before confronting what's coming."

"That's my choice also," said a grinning Glenda. "We'll be two Huck Finn river travelers enjoying the trip."

They were loading their bags with the dried clothing when the Huck Finn rafting plan changed. The first thing they noticed was the sudden stillness of the forest. Birds were quiet, and no slapping sounds were heard from Mr. Busy Beaver.

The sudden quiet was shortly explained by muffled shouts coming through the lingering fog. The shouts, accompanied by loud grunts and various curses, were spoken in thick German. Rafts were following the course of the river.

While still some distance away, they would shortly come around the bend. "Big rats!" they said together. *Best laid plans of mice and men. Why can't we catch a break?*

"So much for our holiday," said Traveler with a sullen tone. Glenda's frown mirrored Traveler's voice. "Let's get our stuff and then clean up the raft. No reason to alert these guys that anyone used it recently. I'll get rid of our drying racks and you put some water on the firepit."

Glenda was already a step ahead, as she was dipping part of the heavy blanket over the side. Returning, she rung it out over the still-warm embers and watched a plume of white smoke rise. She quickly returned to the side, soaked the same end, and repeated the drenching. No smoke rose with the second drenching. She replaced the cover board and stood up.

Traveler had already jettisoned the first drying rack off the front end of the raft. The sapling was immediately caught by the river's current and disappeared downstream. Glenda was ready to ask Traveler why he wasn't jettisoning the second rack but paused. Traveler had a scheme in mind.

"Time to go, we can dress once we're in the woods," said Glenda.

With the thick blankets secured across their shoulders and held in place by the bag straps, they lifted their robes and stepped onto the river bottom. The cold water again gave a shock, however, this time it was anticipated. Its impact was further ignored due to their focus on the sounds of the approaching rafts.

Wrapped in heavy coats, blankets, and backpacks, the two resembled bloated sea creatures leaving the water to test the land. They demonstrated their evolved land skills by quickly ascending the bank's side to the safety of the forest. Trailing behind Glenda, Traveler used the second sapling's limbs to swish away both sets of footprints. *Always planning ahead, clever lad* she thought.

Safely inside the tree line, they stopped to catch their breath. Hearts slowed as the immediate threat of discovery was gone.

Glenda removed her bag, then placed the heavy blanket beside it. She opened the bag and pulled out the dry clothing. She turned her back and shrugged, and her robe fell to the forest floor. She began putting on the well-used hiking wear. Traveler followed suit and the two were once again Transylvanian peasants.

Lastly, they sat down to pull on heavy hiking socks, and finally their leather boots. Standing up, Glenda twirled around. "This is the latest fall style to show off the feminine look in the Dark Ages. How do you like it?"

"It's functional and eye-catching for any time period," replied a smiling Traveler. "You certainly caught Ardaric's attention wearing it." He was amused at the redness creeping onto Glenda's cheeks.

The two placed their robes back into their bags, draped blankets across shoulders, and lastly secured their bags with retaining straps. They were ready for rapid movement in any direction just as they heard the rafters coming around the bend.

Two rafts broke into view and were moving in a line. The front and sides of the large rafts held spaced vertical posts.

Braced against the posts, large men stood with long poles, ready to push the raft away from obstacles.

"Those are the big boy rafts," said Traveler as he studied the approaching rafts. Each raft held ten fully armed warriors. Six warriors held poles while two warriors were lookouts at the front and two managed the rear rudder.

In the center was a four-foot-high stall containing a horse. This was not an oversized warhorse but a smaller, lean scouting horse. There was a pile of hay inside to keep the horse distracted.

Flanking the rudder on each side was an open supply chest filled with the usual armaments of warfare including heavy shields, spears, bows, and multiple arrow quivers.

The rafts and crews reminded both teens of Viking raiders. As she studied the small flotilla, Glenda concluded, "These warriors are an advance force, probably looking for any Huns who slipped away. The horses are there to get messages back quickly." Traveler nodded, that was his thought also.

They watched as the alert men in the lead raft spotted their raft and motioned for both rafts to approach and land. The men on the rudders and side pushers were adept. The two rafts immediately headed toward the shore. Once out of the main current the rafts slowed, and the polers kept the rafts in place with little effort.

Two large men stepped off the lead raft, swore as they hit the water, then moved to the deserted raft. They climbed aboard and began an inspection. They studied the floating platform, obviously looking for any sign of recent occupancy. The men remaining on the back two rafts studied the shoreline. There was nothing to indicate that Huns had recently left the raft to go ashore.

One man knelt and removed the cover from the firepit. He placed his hand down into the pit, noted there was no heat, and shook his head. Standing up he said, "No escaping Hun used this in the last day. This scouting raft just broke loose in the storm and worked its way here. Let's use it to take the lead. If we spot any Hun stragglers, we can field warriors more quickly."

Two men from the back raft were assigned to join the two already in the scout raft. The two dropped over the sides of their raft into the cold river water. They yelped and grunted, cursing loudly. The two aboard the scout raft watched them as they entered the water, pointed, and began laughing at their pained expressions. Amused, Traveler quietly opined, "Misery definitely loves company."

Continuing, he said, "I believe curses are a form of verbal art among these warriors, it's one of their forms of poetry. I bet they have drinking contests to vote for the best curses. We Americans have a limited number of curses, and most start with the letter 'F'…we exert no imagination or effort to excel at our cursing."

Glenda had ignored the language but now started to laugh, "Yeah, swearing is a dying art. We Norwegians still use some popular Viking curses. While quite crude they are now considered acceptable verbal history and are studied by linguists to help understand our past. I'm sure berserkers would laugh at the academic ponderings."

The two watched as the three rafts were preparing to move out. They saw several long poles were passed to the scouting raft crew. The long poles were quickly pushed into the riverbed as the scouting raft took the lead. The raft caravan headed up the center of the river. They were a small but mighty armada.

Chapter 65

Above the Falls

Once the three rafts were out of sight, Traveler sighed. "I guess we need to get going. Boy, I was sure looking forward to drifting on the river. I had a whole day planned for relaxing and doing nothing."

"Me too, but sadly here we are. We'll just hike through the forest as best we can. I assume you'll continue as our lead scout?"

"Yeah, I'll lead. Maybe it'll snap me out of my lost river-cruising funk. Anyway, it's time for me to remember why we're here and stop whining. There's stuff coming that'll give me something serious to whine about." With his hiking stick in hand, he moved forward.

As the day progressed, it was notably cooler than the day before, and their hiking was easier. They stopped every few hours to rest and drink from the water bags. When the sun was high Glenda said, "I think we deserve a rest-and-eat stop. I see a nice, open spot up there on the right."

With Glenda leading they shortly reached a glen high above the river. Looking down at the distance to the river, Glenda commented, "We've been walking uphill. The grade was gradual, but I felt it."

"You're right. I've got some soreness in my thighs, but just assumed it was from the last couple of days' hikes." Traveler then lifted his walking stick and pointed. "If you look in the distance what do you see?"

"Snow on a chain of mountaintops. I do believe we're moving toward the serious part of the Carpathians. I never noticed the peaks before since we've been moving through a forest."

Once lunch was over, they fell back on the heavy, mossy ground. "Soft! Perfect for a little nap," said Glenda. "Wake me when you're ready. I'll just grab a few winks."

The long catnap refreshed the two travelers. Glenda opened her eyes first, and slowly removed her head cover. Placing a hand gently on Traveler's shoulder she gave a soft shake. The predictable grumble came from under his blanket, then he was awake and in good spirits. "An excellent nap. Refreshing, but not too long. I'm ready to move out."

With their blankets and packs in hiking position, they moved from the glen back to the trail. "You'll note this trail is running parallel to the river. We are gaining elevation from the river but at an acceptable scouting distance. I like our vantage point of looking down," said Traveler. "Those raft warriors may decide to stop early, we can watch whatever they do."

While Traveler was talking Glenda suddenly stopped. Placing a restraining hand on Traveler's arm she motioned for him to be still. "There is something in the air," said Glenda. "Do you sense anything?"

Traveler had learned a long time ago to trust Glenda's instincts. His first awareness of her advanced warning system came in the Chicago museum. She had not only deciphered the hieroglyphics on the portal but had felt a vibration coming from it. She seemed prescient in her ability to detect danger.

The two stood totally stationary, focused on the distant tremors. They recognized that these were the signature vibrations emitted from jinn. Forewarned, they applied their stealth training to further mask their own vibrations.

With stealth protection around their own vibrations, they cautiously moved along the narrow path. Their senses were on high alert. Both sets of eyes and ears searched for any warning signals coming from the trail ahead. In hindsight the trail was not a place of danger. Life-threatening danger was down by the river. The Gepid armada was oblivious to what was lurking along the shores.

The first warning for the armada came from the pilot raft. The scout was well ahead of the two trailing rafts when it sent a shout back. The shout was well known to all who have traveled unexplored rivers. "Falls ahead! Falls ahead! Slow and steer toward the bank."

The warriors with the guiding poles were quick to respond. Those on the right side immediately pushed down to steer toward the closer left shore. Thick arm muscles and powerful legs bent down and challenged the river's drift. The raft slowed and began a course change.

The sounds of crashing water announced the falls' presence as disappearing water smashed below on large rocks. Visual confirmation presented itself as thick plumes of dense vapors rose upward to swirl around the falls' edge. Both plumes and sounds increased as the rafts advanced.

The lead raft was aware of the oncoming disaster. Energized arms and legs struggled with poles against the power of the approaching falls.

Glenda and Traveler were positioned on the front part of a rocky ridge that rose high above the forest and river below. The ridge appeared like a long finger pointing outward, seemingly to warn river-goers of coming dangers.

Resting on their bellies, they had an expansive view. They saw how the river had made a final curve then narrowed as it traveled through the dense forest. As the river narrowed it increased its speed.

Small, frothy waves appeared on the surface as the river raced toward a majestic waterfall. Beauty is often in the eye of the beholder. The falls were a majestic sight to safe, land-based observers. It was a nightmare sight to the approaching raft riders.

It was clear to all observers that the height of the falls, and the waiting rocks below, would produce a deadly result for anything that passed over the rocky lips at the top. Expressing its sympathy, the lips would give a final goodbye kiss to any object moving across it.

Shaking himself from staring at the captivating scene, Traveler said, "It's a smaller version of Niagara Falls. It's magnificent in its own right."

Nodding, Glenda said, "It reminds me of my Norwegian favorite, Henfallet falls. If you hike the mountain trail to the falls and witness the northern lights coloring both the sky and the falling water, you can imagine our Norse gods showering under it."

Well ahead of the lip of the falls they saw the intended landing place for river transports. A large dock extended from the river's bank. Anchored in the center of the dock was a lifting crane. As they studied the dock and crane, they noticed twin hawser ropes crossing the river beside the dock and secured on the opposite shore. Each hawser was as thick as a large man's clenched fist. The engineer in Traveler focused on the hawser lines.

"Those are catch and hold lines. The lines operate like a catch wire on the deck of an aircraft carrier. They're a back-up system in the event you missed anchoring yourself to the dock. With the speed and turbulence of the river at this point, it would be easy to misjudge your approach."

Nodding at Traveler's assessment, Glenda said, "I think that big crane is used to unload the cargo rocks. After the rocks are unloaded, I bet it's used to lift the raft onto the dock. I think they cut the bindings and recycle the logs. Logs are returned by horseback to the upstream loading area where they get reassembled. Very efficient use of materials and labor, they practiced recycling even back now."

Their eyes shifted away from the stunning falls and loading dock to the approaching rafts. The falls were less than a football field away and dominated their attention; it dominated the rafters' as well.

When the forward raft crew's eyes left the approaching falls, they spied the safety of the loading dock. The two side pushers quickly went to the far side to push the raft toward the dock. Powerful arms bulged as their owners were in survival mode, exerting their maximum efforts.

The rudder man had instantly reacted to change the raft's course. The free warrior joined him in resisting the river's force. Together, the two worked the thick rudder. They braced together against the increasing water pressure. Their combined efforts, joined by those of the poling warriors, were succeeding. The scout raft would safely reach the dock, without the need for the catch ropes.

The two larger, trailing rafts were copying the tactics of the scout raft. The larger rafts were heavier and required more effort to change course; however, they had the advantage of an eight-man crew. Again, two men worked the rudder while the remaining six used poles to push off the river's bottom.

Watching from above, Glenda and Traveler saw that all three rafts would reach the dock. Observing their swift adjustments, Glenda said, "Impressive teamwork in the face of unexpected danger."

Traveler nodded, adding, "Tell the Huns about how that Gepid teamwork pays off in battle, they experienced it first-hand."

Glenda was thinking ahead about what would happen after the rafts landed. She smiled as she said, "I think we've lucked out. They will land and explore. They'll be our recon scouts. All we need to do is follow them and see what dangers they walk into."

Chapter 66

Another Ambush

Relaxed, the two teens sat in secluded safety and watched the three rafts move toward the safety of the dock. The Gepid scouting crew would serve as their advance hunting dogs. Shouting warriors would give them plenty of warning.

The forward raft crew saw the blocking hawser lines with a sense of relief. They angled the raft to settle against the dock and rest. They would be secured by anchoring posts and hawsers. They were safe. They shouted to the rafts behind them to fall in line. While focused on the docking maneuver, none saw the ambush coming.

Their first warning was the soft, thudding noise of heavy arrows falling into their raft. Like autumn cornstalks they quickly created a small field of vertical spikes. Then they saw the enemy. Hun archers had risen from the tall reeds that had shielded them from the rafters' view. Archers began a steady aerial attack. This time they had many quivers for a continual bombardment. A second flight of arrows began to arc downward onto the deck.

Surprisingly, no warrior was hit. Once alert to the danger, Gepid training took over. After the first flight struck the floor of the raft, the two pushers ran the short distance to the open bin to secure protective shields for themselves and the rudder men.

While the pushers only paused briefly in their efforts, the river did not pause at all. The moment the pushers stopped fighting the current, the scout raft was jerked back into the river. Hun arrows continued to thud against the raft's floor, discouraging the pole men from dropping their shields.

Decision hesitancy has doomed many. Earlier, the youngest Hun brother had hesitated to release the reserves. Now the polers' hesitancy to continue pushing doomed this crew.

Freed from the crew's pushing force, and not anchored to the dock, the lead raft quickly entered the center of the river. Jerking and swaying, it sped toward the hawser lines. The two-man rudder crew felt the thick steering board snap as the river's full force struck it.

Fearless land warriors stood paralyzed. They had no escape path. The crashing waters at the bottom of the falls brought a pounding crescendo of violent sounds to their ears. They saw their approaching fate reflected in the rising plumes of water. The raft's shaking predicted that it would soon snap the bindings that held logs together. The only good news was that the Huns no longer launched arrow volleys at them.

Looking down at the raft-fly caught in the spider web, Glenda felt the fear of the defenseless men. A rush of sympathy with their lost cause passed through her. She placed a hand on Traveler's forearm and squeezed.

Traveler was equally absorbed in the drama and plight of the crew. "It feels like Throbb being questioned by the mage. You don't want to watch, but you can't take your eyes away."

With the pilot raft in the grip of the catching ropes, the Huns' aerial attack shifted toward the two oncoming rafts. The warriors were caught in a dilemma. They could remain exposed to the deadly threat of Hun arrows and continue to push toward the opposite shore, or they could raise their shields. Decision time arrived too quickly.

With the suddenness of the ambush, there was no leader on either raft to direct a group response. Limited time, instincts, and falling arrows dictated their actions. They made individual decisions.

Several warriors on the right side considered trying to swim to shore. Their heavy armor and the falling arrows, however, discouraged the swimming option. A few warriors considered a hand over hand crossing using the approaching hawser lines but discarded it. They knew they would be slow-moving targets for Hun arrows.

Then Gepid courage asserted itself. One large warrior decided to sacrifice himself and continued to push. Inspired, his comrades dropped their shields and rose to join him. Arrows immediately struck his legs and he collapsed. Shields returned to desperate, shaking hands.

A veteran warrior on each raft held a shield over himself and attempted to control the foaming-mouthed, wild-eyed horses bucking against the container stalls. Hun archers are a great threat but a crazed horse beside you on a raft is a nightmare. Both warriors received paralyzing body kicks for their efforts and collapsed, only to receive further kicks.

On both rafts, all capable warriors instinctively held shields over their heads. The two-man rudder crew could feel that the rudder was ready to snap without the pushers' help. They had no option except to ease it partially away from the full force of the rushing river. Without the rudders' full deflection, the rafts quickly returned to the river's center.

Both rafts were immediately pulled into the main channel and began shaking from the increasing speed and turbulence of the river. Without steering control, the front raft nudged a large protruding rock and began a slow spin. The trailing raft swept forward and was hit by a turning corner.

The rafts twisted slowly together in a pas de deux. Their dance was far removed from an elegant waltz. It was a death tango. The locked rafts briefly separated, then embraced once more driven together by the pounding current. Their tango ended abruptly when they plowed into the scout raft.

Observing a pattern to the Hun arrows, Traveler said, "Those archers don't miss, particularly with slow-moving targets. I have a very bad feeling about this." Before Glenda could respond, Traveler's premonition took on shapes they knew too well. "Jinn!" he said, and both shuddered.

Three dense, reddish cloud shapes emerged from the forest to move along the top hawser rope. The shapes extended thick tentacles as the jinn reached the captured rafts. Each jinn moved onto a selected raft, then there was a slight pause as they studied the motionless prey.

A few warriors regained their fighting spirit. Long, metal-edged spears were pointed outward. A small shield wall formed. Even in the face of demons Gepid courage evidenced itself. Sadly, courage was no match for a demigod's power.

The spears and shield wall were of no consequence. The jinn flowed forward into the closest warrior. The slaughter began and ended in moments. Information was retrieved. The three jinn then flowed back across the thick hawser rope and disappeared into the forest.

The holding safety ropes were suddenly released. As they dropped down, they lost contact with the rafts. All three rafts were freed from the holding restraints. The rafts now caught the full impact of the rushing water. As a single unit they bolted up the river's playing field toward the edge of the falls.

Glenda and Traveler watched as the joined rafts reached the waiting lips. The three entwined log masses slowly tipped forward then the rear rose upright at an increasing angle. As they increased their angle of descent, they presented the bottom of the logs. Logs creaked in agony as bindings snapped. It was the *Titanic* moaning in its death throes.

Bound together, the three-raft brotherhood jerked forward from a final river push. It vanished in a second over the edge, making a swan dive into the rising plumes. The only sound was from two screaming horses as they ran their last charge. The warriors were far past making any sound.

Finding her composure, Glenda released her death grip on Traveler's arm. She found her voice. "We have found what we came for. The jinn are here and in numbers. They are as merciless as we have seen them to be. They swept through the raft men to gain whatever information was available then discarded them as wastepaper.

"The speed with which they absorbed the warriors shows they are masters at scanning our brains and leaving empty husks. I think they have had way too much practice."

Traveler was still adjusting to the mass executions he had witnessed. "Twenty warriors taken as easily as picking weeds. These jinn are absolute nightmare monsters. I worry about how many there are and where they are. I think Theo knows more than he has shared. He must know there is a jinn nest here. He may deliberately hide information from us in the event that we get mind-wiped."

"That's possible," said Glenda, accepting Traveler's conjectures. "But it's still our duty to press ahead. We must determine exactly what the jinn are planning, that's what Theo needs to know. He would not abandon us but he must survive…even if we are the price of survival."

Glenda suddenly shuddered as her body started to shake. Traveler immediately held her saying, "I feel terrible about them, too. It's not fair but it's what the jinn do."

Glenda softly whispered back, "It's not just about them. That would have been us if they hadn't shown up and taken our raft. I could see us trapped down there."

Traveler felt a long shiver pass through him as he accepted her thought. Giving another stronger hug, all he could say was, "Don't go there Glenda, that's the 'what if' black hole and you can never climb out of it. I choose to believe we have a good spirit watching over us. I'm keeping that thought for what's ahead." He saw her relax as calmness and strength entered her. The Valkyrie was back. He knew he had done well for both of them.

Chapter 67

A Night on Bald Mountain

Traveler knew he had to agree with Glenda's conclusion about observing the jinn. It was essential for their mission. Figuring out exactly how they could observe the jinn would be a daunting task. Unlike spying on the three Hun brothers, they had no way to listen in on jinn communications.

Trying to give Glenda his best game face he found himself saying, "Well, here we are again. This time instead of neutralizing a jinn, we need to observe and maybe find a plan for Theo to defeat a whole nest of them. I can hear M right now: 'Theo and I believe in you. We believe you will solve the challenges you find.'" While he fought to keep sarcasm out of his voice, he came up short.

Glenda heard the tone of voice more than the words. She understood he was struggling with their charge from Theo.

Looking him in the eyes she gave him her sweetest Valkyrie smile. "Yes, we do have our hands full. I really wish we had more hands. However, let's not get in a funk. You're the 'can do' guy. I need that guy to anchor me like you did when I had to get under the sunken grate. You anchored me again when I had to face the jinn after it had me cornered beside the alcove. I need your bravery."

Traveler felt a surge of embarrassment, energy, and confidence sweep away his hangdog blues. "Be of good cheer, my lady. Sir

Gawain your faithful, brave knight is back! I'm ready to charge forward in a two-person light brigade!" Pausing with a slight grin he added, "Could we possibly charge forward tomorrow morning?"

Glenda was relieved that her knight had returned. She kept her own smile while nodding in agreement. "I'm with you. I say we charge into dinner, then charge into a well-deserved sleep." Looking around the rocky ridge, then at the dense forest below, she asked, "You're the forward scout, any thoughts on where our dinner and sleeping quarters should be?"

"Not many options, I think right here works. The bad guys, jinn and Hun, are below us and nobody is coming way up here. These flat rocks are going to stress our backs, but we have our blankets to soften the pain."

He pointed down. "For tomorrow's scouting venture I spotted a long trail going around the base of the falls then up a steep incline. The trail is a reasonable hike down from up here. I'm guessing the trail emerges from the woods below and becomes an uphill mountain passage. I think the jinn are far ahead, somewhere up in the mountains."

Now in good spirits he closed with the familiar nursery rhyme, "Hi ho the derry oh, a jinning we will go." Glenda felt the tension leaving as she joined him in the childhood chant. Sir Gawain, the bravest of King Arthur's knights, was back and she was relieved.

Traveler's hand descended into his travel bag and began preparing his evening stay. "That's enough fun for right now, let the camping good times roll."

Glenda nodded. "We can't build a fire. Any fire up here would be a beacon below demanding to be investigated. Let's brace ourselves for a cold night on Bald Mountain."

Traveler had been so worked up with the deadly scene below and the following reflections that he was oblivious to their surroundings. The sun was rapidly setting and with it the warmth waned. Glenda's reflection on the "no fire tonight" and the ever-increasingly chilly night air had Traveler feeling just how right Glenda was. It would be a very long, very cold night.

A little end-of-day luck came their way as their elevated site permitted a bit more residual sunlight. Taking advantage of it they quickly set up their bedding and dinner. The two created their sleeping areas and placed their folded blankets close together. Neither acknowledged the proximity of the bedding. They knew shared heat was essential to surviving the challenges of the approaching night.

As she settled into her evening meal, Glenda quipped, "I loved Disney's *Fantasia*. Here we are, high atop Bald Mountain. The only difference in our situation is that the *Fantasia* devils are far below us. Let's hope they stay down there."

"Amen," mumbled Traveler through a mouthful of chicken and bread.

Dinner progressed rapidly with little conversation. Both wanted to escape to the warmth of their blankets before the evening's arctic cold arrived. Dinner over, they snuggled into the makeshift beds and pulled a shared heavy blanket up to their chins.

Lying on their backs they looked upwards. It was a cloudless night, and once again stars lit the heavens. The majesty of the visible universe humbled both. Each reflected on the events that had brought them to this place in time.

Traveler had a flashback to being a five-year-old in bed looking at the cover of the book his father had brought him from Boston. The cover's giant appeared to look at him and seemed to almost move.

Glenda was suddenly back in the dining room of the orphanage. She was laughing with her mates over a Christmas Eve dinner as they discussed Santa's approaching sleigh ride.

As she was drifting off, Glenda said, "Move yourself closer, big boy. No Rumford fireplace here, the only warmth we've got is each other. Now, pull that shared blanket higher, my chin has an icicle trying to form on it." Once under the cover, her final comment was, "It's going to be a long night."

Traveler needed no encouragement for a close encounter of the Glenda kind. Rolling onto his right side, his back settled against Glenda's. *We're a pair of popsicles stuck together, and the blanket is the wrapper* was his last thought.

Chapter 68

A Morning on Bald Mountain

Morning rays hit the top of their Bald Mountain retreat. Unobstructed sunbeams declared that a clear day was ahead. While the light was bright, the air resisted the warming rays.

As she peeked out from her side of the blanket Glenda saw the thin film of hoarfrost across their shared cover. Her eyes shifted to the nearby ground and she admired the surrounding bed of grass presenting itself as a sea of frozen green stalks.

Her eyes lifted upward from the glistening blades of grass to large eyes looking down at her. A horned head with a pointed beard was studying her. Her body jerked under the appraising stare. Had the Bald Mountain devil snuck up on them?

The horned head lowered itself to the ground and a soft crunching sound reached her ears. Smiling, she relaxed. *No Bald Mountain devil here. We are in the land of Transylvanian mountain goats.* She whispered, "Traveler, wake up! We're surrounded by horned demons! Bald Mountain has come to pay us a visit. Move slowly so they don't attack you."

Traveler was instantly awake and at DEFCON one. Following Glenda's instructions, he went into stealth mode before moving his blanket down to eye level. A horned head was now a few feet away and happily cropping the frozen grass.

With a sigh of relief, he laughed. "You definitely got me, princess! They're mountain goats called ibex! Saw them in a zoo. Trust me, this elephant will record this in the 'get even' book."

Glenda simply gave a sweet smile back. *Bring it on, Dumbo.*

Glenda was now sitting upright and was watching the small group grazing on the grassy patch. Two large male ibex were eating while kept alert eyes on the human invaders. Half a dozen nanny goats and several kids were enjoying their morning frühstück of frozen grass.

Sitting up, Traveler opened his bag and removed an apple. He took a bite, swallowed, then took a second bite. A nearby nanny heard his chewing and slowly approached. She was rewarded with the third bite and she stayed in place as she swallowed. Lifting her head to stare at him she let him know seconds were expected.

Now the small herd moved closer to the human food dispensers. They stood patiently, waiting for their reward. Glenda followed suit and now apple bites came from two directions. The large billies pushed forward to establish their alpha place in the eating order. Their aggression called for higher tosses to reach the nannies and kids.

"Typical guys, hogging the treats," joked Glenda.

"Well, they are the protectors, so they deserve a little consideration for their risk-taking," said a defending Traveler.

"Big risks here," retorted Glenda, throwing a large bite over the head of a nearby billy to reach a small kid.

They proceeded to distribute several more apples then they closed the freebie bar. "You're on your own," said Traveler, and clapped empty hands together. The herd apparently understood the dismissal and returned to the grass.

"Time for us to chow down," said Traveler as he took a piece of ham and a slice of cheese from his bag. He added a thick slice of black bread and proceeded to enjoy breakfast. Glenda was already ahead of him.

When breakfast was completed Glenda looked around, then said, "Where did our friends come from?"

Traveler lifted his hand and pointed toward a small opening in the surrounding brush. "From the trail I spotted yesterday. I think their presence here confirms our way down. It should be secure. It's a narrow goat path to reach this grazing plateau, no reason for the Huns to come up here.

"In any case, it's the only way down toward the mountain that I can see. The good news is it's going downhill, and that's a sweet way to start a day's hike. As we descend, we'll survey the lower lands. Maybe we'll figure out where the Huns are taking the rocks."

"Lead on, scout, but watch the ground. It's still got frozen dew on it so it's slippery. Goats are OK with that, but we humans don't want to slip, trip and roll down." Laughing she said, "Like the song says 'it's a long way to Tipperary' …and that's a very long way down."

With their sleeping gear packed over shoulders and cinched by their bags, they walked to the opening of the downward trail. Looking at the path, Traveler said, "I feel like a mule going down into the Grand Canyon. I've even got my backpack in place. Too bad I don't have a mule's surefootedness, slow is the word."

"I'm in no rush. Besides, what's waiting for us down there except a pack of jinn?"

As they began the slow descent Glenda glanced over her shoulder. The goats were watching them leave. She thought there was a touch of sadness in their eyes. *Are you sad to lose our company or sad about missing more food?*

As an afterthought she called back, "Stay up high and avoid those nasty Huns, they eat goat." *Did that big billy just nod his head? I think I need more oxygen.*

As they continued their descent, they found the path frequently curved to offer open views outward. Traveler stopped by a series of flat rocks that offered a sitting place for views. "Let's see what we can see. We're going to be in the tree line pretty soon and we'll lose these views."

Sitting beside him, Glenda removed her bag. Reaching inside, she removed two oranges. "A little pick-me-up is in order." The teens peeled the oranges and were pleased that the overnight frost had not ruined the fruit. Now it was sweet, juicy, and chilled. "Perfect," said Glenda, chewing on a large wedge.

Traveler nodded as he chewed, then opened his water pouch. He handed it to Glenda. "Ladies first. The juice of the orange reminded me that this elevation dehydrates us. We've got to stay hydrated, plus we need to breathe in more oxygen. We're going to need all our mental and physical faculties shortly."

Chapter 69

Goat Trails

Finished with the morning snack, the two studied the landscape far below. They noticed the river had turned and disappeared into a mountain pass. Pointing down, Glenda said, "I believe there is an actual road down there. I bet it's how the rocks are transported to their final destination."

"You're right. Notice how it separates from the docking area and the falls. It looks like it's going up that mountain ridge on the right side and curving around it. Can't see exactly where it's heading other than up."

"I question how far up the mountain it can go," said Glenda. "Look at the heavy snow covering the sides. That mountain chain looks like it's still part glacier."

Traveler focused on the joined mountains and the road as it disappeared into them. "I think you're right. That may be the remains of one big mother glacier. If we're going up there it's going to be a challenge to climb, particularly when we'll need to be off the road. I don't think the Huns can be taking rocks very far up that slippery glacier. Plus, it looks really cold up there."

Shrugging, Glenda said, "It's not going to get any easier looking at it. We might as well keep working our way down."

The two carefully worked their way down, staying on the narrow goat path. In places they had to pause to see where the path went. As Traveler stumbled, he said, "Apparently, goats can jump across these nasty little crevices." Glenda could only nod as she stayed focused on the path immediately in front of her.

After another hour of descending, they came to the beginning of the tree line. "Let's take a final look-see while we can. Once we're in the trees this curving path will disorient us pretty quickly."

"My scout leader is never disoriented," said Glenda, smiling. Looking far down, she added, "Do my eyes deceive me, or is that a cart on the road?"

"You have an eagle's eye. It is a cart, and it's got several large stone blocks in it. Let's see where it's going."

They continued down and watched the slow-moving cart. It advanced as the hitched pair of Hun ponies leaned into the grade, pulling the weight. A Hun walked beside the cart, both directing the horses and encouraging them. Occasionally he gave a nibble reward from a flat palm, and the ponies responded with greater efforts.

Glenda commented, "These Huns are bad guys toward people, but they do love their horses. It appears it's a two-way love affair. Look at how the horses respond to even a head pat, much less the treat."

Traveler had observed the same pony-Hun love-in but wasn't going to cut the Hun any slack. "Let's leave it at, 'they are bad guys.'"

The cart was now to the point where it was disappearing around the curve into the mountain. "How far up does that cart need to go?" wondered Glenda. "Let's get further down and find a viewshed that might show us where the destination is."

"Agreed. I bet that wherever the stone is finally unloaded is where the jinn will be clustered. Possibly their grand scheme will be obvious. I hope so after all this."

As they continued down, they found the walking became easier as the air thickened. Oxygen was present in increasing amounts and breaths became more refreshing; at the same time the forest temperature rose. Traveler paused and then sat down. "This billy goat needs water and a little leg rest."

"Gives you a whole new level of respect for mountain goats, doesn't it?" Glenda responded as she wiped the perspiration from her face. "That's a rhetorical observation, not a question. I really liked those goats. I wonder if M would permit us to have one in the sanctuary as a pet."

"I'd go slow with that. Theo may be a god but he's also one big tiger cat, tigers eat goats. Even if he didn't eat it, I think the poor goat would have nothing but nightmares twenty-four-seven."

Glenda was not backing down. She had a positive focus that took her mind off the approaching dangers. "Not necessarily. Lots of natural predators and prey get along quite well if they are raised together. Give me a baby goat that can snuggle against a purring Theo's soft coat and I'll show you a happy goat."

Traveler decided not to argue about what he thought was a silly idea. He realized this was not about the reality of a pet goat but about Glenda seeking some image of a normal life back in the sanctuary. "I guess that could work. Yeah, I liked those goats a lot, and they helped us get down here. Maybe we owe them one."

Glenda responded with an appreciative sweet smile. *He can be flexible and understanding when he listens. That's a nice side to him, I think I'm rubbing off on him.*

Standing up, Traveler offered Glenda a hand. "Time to rock and roll. Roll around rocks of course." Glenda cringed at his pun. Unfazed, Traveler continued. "It's noon or later, and I want to see what's around that curve. The curve is hiding something. It's like the screen in *The Wizard of Oz*, I want to see behind it."

"Be careful what you wish for. I think that behind the screen there's no sweet wizard just true monsters."

"Yeah, I know, and curiosity killed the cat."

Motioning to the right, Traveler said, "We need to go in that direction. Once we get out of these trees, I think we're going to be close and should be able to see where it's going."

"Lead on, your sense of direction is better than mine. I would need to climb a tree to figure out where we are."

Rested, hydrated, and with a direction in mind, the two moved forward. As they walked, they felt secure in their passage. Overhead birds were busy carrying out bird activity. There was a constant chorus of calls and chirps that indicated a lack of dangers. Smiling, Traveler said, "Birds as a security system, don't travel without them. Ask any coalminer about bird warnings."

Glenda nodded back. "They remind me of Dracula's comment in the old Bela Lugosi movie. 'Children of the night. What music they make.'" Laughing, she added, "Of course he was talking about wolf howls, not bird chirps, but kind of the same forest music idea, and we are in Transylvania."

They stopped talking and set their pace as brisk as possible. Time passed, sweat flowed, legs again began to protest. Then Traveler raised his right hand in the universal signal to halt. Then he suddenly signaled to go to the ground.

Both dropped and pressed against the soft soil. Shortly after, they heard the rumble of large wheels moving on a hard surface. Barking voices were calling to the pulling teams and to each other.

Traveler motioned for Glenda to remain in place while he began to salamander-crawl forward. He moved in small increments. After less than ten minutes he arrived at a large tree that fronted an open road. Lying there, he saw a huge wheel pass by, twenty feet from his position. After the cart had passed, he rose while remaining pressed against the trunk.

Looking back, he saw that Glenda had moved forward and was joining him. *Taking orders is not her thing, I guess I have the same problem. Maybe that's why we're a good team. If we survive, I'll push M for her pet goat.*

Before he could motion Glenda to come closer, she was beside him, pressed against the trunk. "Hi, Traveler. This looks like a good seat for watching the parade." Traveler gave an accepting wink back. Leaning against him, she whispered in his ear. "Should we elevate and get an even better seat?"

Traveler nodded, pointed to a large limb over their head, and went vertical. Once secure he motioned for Glenda to join him. They proceeded to monkey-climb the tree, staying close to the massive trunk for covering. As they proceeded upwards, they found the limbs were gradually thinning. Finally, Traveler stopped, and Glenda climbed beside him.

"I think this is high enough. Our cover is thinning out, no reason to give searching eyes anything to focus on. Let's circle around and check the view." Glenda nodded and Traveler began the slow move around the trunk.

Glenda waited until he had disappeared, then she began her own circling movement. After a minute she saw a hand reaching around to welcome her. Moving another step, she was standing beside a pointing Traveler. Her eyes followed his arm. For the first time they had a clear view. The mountain chain presented a steep V between adjacent ridges. Disappearing into the V was the transport road.

Both sides of the flanking ridges were covered with snow that was thick enough to survive the sun's heat. How thick it was could not be visually determined, however, it appeared more than adequate for serving as a downhill ski slope. Without thinking, Glenda's feet shifted into a slight lean that was instinctive from growing up on skis.

Regardless of depth, snow always suggests fun for all ages. For a moment, both teens thought of past snowmen and snow forts. Glenda recalled making snow angels while Traveler naturally recalled snowball fights. Both had sweet smiles across their faces. These were good, pure childhood memories without any disturbing monsters.

As they studied the mountain passage their eyes scanned the surrounding terrain. They noted the roadbed was firm due to a thick layer of gravel. The gravel had to be constantly replenished as heavy wagon wheels forced it into the ground. This was a maintained road that a Roman engineer would have approved of.

They saw that the road terminated some distance ahead. The road did not appear to offer passage through the mountain ranges. It had a specific purpose, which became clear as they studied the dominating structure and the Hun workers.

Chapter 70

Jinn Constructs

They watched two rock-filled wagons arrive at the unloading station. A team of Huns immediately began unloading the stone from the cart and placing them onto skids. Skids were organized into groups based on their stones' size and shape. Walkways between them provided easy access for a pony to bring a desired skid to the rising structure.

The structure stunned both staring teens. "Now we know the jinn's intent," Glenda finally whispered. Traveler could only nod back. This was a structure built with very bad intent.

They recognized the rising portal from the museum. This structure, however, dwarfed the museum's portal. It was larger than the entire front of the museum. It was a portal whose base was anchored in leveled, solid rock using the mountain as its foundation. Huge columns flanked both ends of the base and were actively under construction. They knew that when the columns were finished, an arch would be placed to bridge them.

From the estimated width and height of the arch, the portal's opening would be enormous. It could accommodate a herd of charging bull elephants joined on each side by galloping giraffes and head-tossing rhinos. High above the imagined stampeding animals, a flight of honking geese would have plenty of room to soar in any direction. Glenda studied the constructs and whispered, "This is the portal for the full host to enter our world. When it's completed it will give the jinn the massed power to confront and absorb Theo."

Traveler had reached the same conclusion. "I hate to pile grief onto grief but look there." He pointed down the road.

Glenda's eyes focused, widened, then narrowed. "Oh no!" The road had been widened and leveled to provide a cut-out parking lot. This was no parking lot for cars but a parking place for a sinister structure. Resting in the center of the lot was a portal similar in size to the one in the Chicago museum.

The overhead arch and supporting columns were inlaid with the same glyphs that Glenda had read. Both teens knew this portal did not come from the mountains of Syria; it was recently constructed on site. Staring at the now glimmering, shifting glyphs confirmed their fear. this was an active functioning portal.

Glenda shook her head. "We failed to neutralize our single jinn. We gave him a setback, that's all. Once he escaped, he came here and created a private construction crew using the Huns as labor. He knew that a supply of the magnetic stone necessary for the portal was available by the upstream quarry. He went about getting this portal constructed using the Huns as manpower and the river as transportation. Smart jinn."

Traveler nodded. "Yeah, he was a busy little jinn. Now there are lots more of his buddies helping to build this main portal."

Studying the large structure, Glenda said, "I'm scared. I think that the base appears done. The support columns are underway. Once the support columns are finished, and they set the arch, the welcome mat for the host is in place. We need to try and slow that construction down before we report back to Theo."

Studying the arch's construction, Traveler said, "Yeah, you're right. The question is 'How?' That base and those rising columns are beyond solid, they're like a stone mountain themselves. Big time construction dozers would have their hands full."

Scrambling for a solution, Glenda suggested, "What if we could convince Ardaric to bring an army here and tear the construction apart, stone by stone?"

"The 'we' in this case is definitely you, I only matter to him as your tagalong slow brother. Even if you could convince him to come, all that would happen is the jinn would eat his army for lunch and add to their manpower pool. There must be at least half a dozen jinn down there, maybe more."

Glenda immediately accepted the analysis, *Traveler is right, bringing Ardaric here would just make the situation worse.*

While staring at the Hun worker ants, Traveler suddenly had an unfocused look. A "lost in thought" expression blanked his face. Recognizing the look, Glenda perked up. "You're seeing something, please share it."

Snapping back into the present, Traveler gave Glenda a sly "I may have a plan" look. "This is a wild idea but look at that snow on the mountain. It could be deep, I'm thinking really deep. It has possibly been resting there since the Ice Age. Maybe it wants to move after sitting for so long. I'm thinking avalanche."

Staring at the mountainside, Glenda reexamined the snow as potentially offering far more than a ski slope. Her face broke into a wide smile. "Brilliant idea, Traveler! It's absolutely worth a shot. How could we make it happen?"

"Not sure. Dynamite would do the trick, but dynamite wasn't invented until the 1860s, we're a little early for that option. You know, of course, it was one of your Scandinavian neighbors, a Swedish scientist, that invented it. It was good old Albert Nobel, of Nobel Prize fame, who made the big bang happen."

"Of course I know that. The good news is our Swedish neighbor did a lot of his experimenting and testing in Paris so we Norwegians were spared his annoying explosions."

Traveler was now racing ahead in full problem-solving mode. A big grin passed over his face as he said, "Loud noises always start avalanches, at least in movies. I think if we had something to bang loud enough that could work. Any ideas?"

Her own face was now lit up as she responded, "Yeah! Well, a qualified maybe. We made really loud noises in the orphanage every May 17th, celebrating our National Day. It's like your Fourth of July. That's the date when we declared our independence with our own constitution in 1814 after four hundred years of a union with Denmark. We went crazy at the orphanage banging pots and pans with big spoons. The gods had to shudder at our bedlam.

"Anyway, we probably made as much noise as your biggest firecrackers, maybe more. We were so loud the teachers put cotton in their ears." Grinning, she added, "And I definitely remember how to beat the pots so prepare your earplugs!"

Traveler was instantly on board with the idea. "Cool idea! That could really work! I think I know where to look for our drums. We'll find our noisemakers in the Huns' kitchen. They cook in massive amounts and must have enormous pots; we'll take the biggest pots and the best drumming spoons. No wooden spoons, just the longest, thickest metal ones. Metal pot meet iron spoon!"

Glenda was excitedly nodding her head, waves of reddish blonde hair danced in the sunlight, she could see the possibilities. Having fun and releasing pent-up stress while creating an avalanche, this was a big twofer. "Pots to the rescue! I see where the kitchen is. There's a path right to it after we cross the road. We'll come at the cooking shed through the woods. We'll be well away from the construction site."

With the approach strategy laid out, the two returned to the green forest floor. Glenda found herself drifting off in the warm sun. "I think an afternoon nap is deserved, let's stay right here and wait for nighttime. I think a snooze is in order."

The warm forest embraced them both. The two sleepers finally awoke when stars appeared overhead, and night owl predators began hooting to each other.

Chapter 71

Lofty Music

Their brains had used every minute of sleep to recharge bodies and spirits. Glenda slowly lifted her head and saw that Traveler's eyes were open. He was alert and considering the noisemaking set-up. "Are we ready to do this thing?" she asked.

"Can't think of a better time. It's way past the end of the workday, look at the moon. The cooks have to be in a deep sleep by now."

Standing up, they first bent and stretched. Both took deep breaths to fill sleepy lungs then they proceeded to study the nearby crossing road. The road was lit by a three-quarter moon. They easily spotted the small path leading toward the kitchen's large cooking shelter.

To minimize time in the moon's shimmering light, the teens had to cross the open road quickly. Once their blankets and robes were secured by the bags, they stepped in front of their tree. Before moving they studied all sights and sounds. The forest murmured with normal nighttime activity. No danger seemed to be afoot.

Nodding to each other, they took two steps out to the open road then did their Olympic broad jumps. One jump and they were safely hidden inside the opposite tree line. As they landed, they immediately went into ground-hugging mode and listened. No warning shouts came, their passage went unnoticed.

They began a slow advance toward the deserted kitchen area. They moved like dark clouds of fog passing between trees until they spotted the cooks' sleeping area. A heavy hide awning was supported up by thick posts that secured it overhead. The awning sides came down to within four feet of the ground.

In the center of the sleeping enclosure, a firepit exuded heat in all directions. The tent's vertical sides contained the heat while offering a flow of air to the pit. Cooks slept comfortably inside their hide shelter. Exhausted from daily stress and work, the cooks had no awareness of the thieves entering their kitchen domain.

Once inside the cooking shed the two would-be noisemakers found the stacked kettles, pots, and pans of all sizes. Beside the various cooking containers were racks with long-handled utensils for stirring and ladling. These were obviously their drumsticks and each removed a pair of the iron stirring spoons. Next they studied the various sized cooking containers for potential drums. "Bigger is better," whispered Glenda, and Traveler nodded.

They each selected the largest metal pot they could find. Glenda had enjoyed banging hard on the makeshift kettledrum at the orphanage and saw that these pots were far larger, they would offer much more merrymaking. She was excited to test them out.

Traveler saw himself as a cool Gene Krupa blasting out a loud 1940s swing song for energized dancers. He heard Krupa's famous song "Sing, Sing, Sing" blast in his head. The teens were suddenly young grade school kids eager to start drum pounding.

With their selections made, they pressed the huge pots to their chests and lowered themselves as close to the ground as possible. To keep the lowest profile, they duck-walked back to the road.

At all times they were careful to keep the large pot-drum and long metal drumsticks well away from each other. At the road's edge they paused to listen. Assured that their theft was unnoticed, they made a return leap.

Once back in the surrounding forest, Traveler said, "Let's keep going and head up the mountain while it's dark." Glenda was already committed to the long climb and had tucked the long, heavy metal spoons into her cinching belt. *Good idea* thought Traveler. *Last thing we need is an unintentional bang announcing us.*

Both continued to press the large pots to their chests. They accepted that they would be arm-weary from the sustained holding effort, this was the cost of making the big bangs. Gritting their teeth, they moved forward.

Their route was a long, circuitous one. They wove between tall thickets that surrounded the encampment and ducked from tree to tree. Their movement was helped by the packed ground that had resulted from the many carts' wheels and horses' hooves.

Finally, they reached the spot where the road ended. Noting the abrupt end to civilization, Glenda quipped, "They need to put an 'End of Road Maintenance' sign right here."

Traveler's father, Daniel, had experienced the same thought when he had stumbled onto an out-of-the-way cluster of small Boston shops. The shops had appeared off a long-deserted road he had followed from his hotel.

Unknown to Daniel that dead-end road changed his family's life. The road had led him to M's hidden antique shop. Inside Daniel had unknowingly selected the first sentient book for Eddie, his four-year-old son.

Although the maintained mountain road was gone, there remained an upward path. The ascending trail seemed to be a way for shepherds to move herds to an upper pasture. The access path was inside a steep uphill gully. Both the gully sides and the surrounding slopes were covered with thick snow.

Observing the snow's thickness, Traveler said, "I think we have the potential for an avalanche of epic size. If we can make it happen it will be a game-changer for the construction crews down there."

Glenda studied the gully path. "Let's pray no more snow or rain is coming for a few hours until we're there. The footing is uphill and slippery, with our pots we could end up being a mini-avalanche ourselves."

The curving gully turned out to be a rewarding path. It provided upward ascent while blocking views for any searching eyes below. As they walked, they felt an increasing strain on thigh muscles. "Lean forward into the grade," said Traveler over his shoulder between deepening breaths.

Glancing back, he saw his advice was unnecessary. Between the two, Glenda was clearly the more skilled uphill climber. She gave him a smile for his advice as she focused on her steady breathing. *I learned how to do this climbing up Norwegian mountains to ski when I was four while big boy was riding his training wheel bike on a paved road.*

The moon was a shining globe. Its nighttime radiance hit the snowbanks on each side, lighting the path upwards. The enhanced visibility permitted them to maintain their steady pace. They were climbing machines, determined to get far above the encampment before daybreak. They knew they needed to be high enough up the mountain to be clear of any avalanche they created.

Finally, their exhausted legs found relief when they arrived at a small level plateau. The plateau suggested they had gotten close to the top of the surrounding mountains. Their elevation promised they would be safe from the avalanche they intended to send downhill.

"Where is Thor, the god of thunder, when we need him to make his big noise?" quipped Traveler, as he regained his normal breathing.

"Resting in Valhalla chatting up Valkyries over wine is my guess," answered Glenda. "Right, now I need to rest and gather myself." She proceeded to place her folded heavy blanket on the ground and sat down.

Traveler dropped his blanket beside her but remained standing. He had a look on his face that suggested he was up to something. "I'm going to give this drum a short workout. After carrying it all the way up here I want to test its mettle." Grinning down at Glenda, he said, "Get the pun? Test its metal?"

A slight smile and groan followed. "Sure," was her answer. *Humor boy is still with us*, Glenda thought. *Won't admit it to him but I rather like it…actually need it right now.*

Before testing his drum inside the ravine, he checked to confirm that the ravine's sides would not collapse on them. Scraping the nearest side clear of snow, he found it was rock-solid ice.

Studying the now-cleared side, he saw it was indeed very old ice. Once exposed it was a window into an ancient glacier. Staring into it he could see the immediate interior was a mix of dirt, small rocks, frozen tree debris, and brown fur, likely from a trapped slow animal. Fortunately, no mastodon or Neanderthal eyes were staring out.

Bringing the drum to his side, he kicked the soil around to create a level platform for his instrument. With the holding platform ready he sank the big iron kettle, open end down, into the plateau's surface. Before he started a Gene Krupa riff, he said, "These snow walls will muffle the effect, so no alerting those below. When we're ready to give the gang below our serious serenade we'll do it out of this ravine."

"Drum away, big boy, but don't be offended if I plug my ears. I think this will sound like being trapped inside a phonebooth with an alley cat whose tail is caught in the door."

Traveler was now a happy young boy focused on a very big drum. It was an excellent Fourth of July noisemaker for a boy too young for firecrackers. Glenda watched with amusement as she saw a six-year-old Traveler in action.

Holding his battering-ram drumsticks up high, he gave them a drummer's big twirl. Then they descended with a vengeance. Fortunately, she had her fingers in her ears. Her phone booth prophesy was spot on.

Traveler felt the ravine-trapped noise hit his own eardrums and quickly realized it was damage control time. He had ringing ears. Two more quick beats and the six-year-old morphed back to a teen. With a sheepish smile, he said, "How do I drum with fingers in my ears?"

The two began to laugh so hard that if they were above the ravine their laughter could have almost triggered an avalanche. Finally, they wiped tears from cold faces, looked at each other, and began a second round of laughing. Laughter worked wonders on chasing away their pent-up stress.

Chapter 72

An Old Friend

Their laughter froze in the air when the glacial snow-covered ice bank beside them began to open. An enormous head emerged from the opening. Traveler's legs went limp as he remained seated beside his drum.

Glenda remained standing, frozen in place. For a brief moment she recalled being trapped by a huge bear on their picnic knoll. This head was as large as the bear's and had more hair. *There really are abominable snowmen*, flashed through her mind. *He's Bigfoot's father.*

Following the head came a supporting set of shoulders, over five feet wide. Arms like tree trunks terminated in hands larger than a catcher's mitt. As the full body emerged it straightened. The height was well over eight feet, maybe more than nine, depending on how the giant's spine was straightened. Blazing blue eyes became visible on a Mount Rushmore head as the catcher's mitt hand wiped long, thick dark blond hair from the face.

Then the face broke into an enormous smile. Brilliant white teeth flashed, and a booming voice said, "Who dares to wake me? Princess Glenda! Warrior Traveler! They dare!" The two youths were lifted off the ground in an encompassing bearhug. This bear dwarfed any grizzly.

"Olaff!" Glenda and Traveler exclaimed in unison.

The giant set the two down, pointed to the entrance, stepped inside, and beckoned them to follow. Once inside the cavernous domed room they stood entranced. They were in a glittering house of ice mirrors.

Wall torches lit the central space and identified various alcoves. Torchlight bounced off hanging stalactites creating a ceiling-based sparkler effect. The overhead displays were a sea of stars so close they could almost be touched.

Their breath caused small clouds of foggy mist to hover in front of their faces. For brief moments their breath-clouds glowed as they captured the bouncing light rays. Traveler touched a wall, and then quickly pulled his hand away, exclaiming, "It's ice!"

"It's a winter wonderland!" Glenda gushed with awe in her voice. "It's like we're inside one of the glass Christmas balls you shake and watch the snow drift down on a village scene. Is this where Santa lives when he's off duty?"

Olaff smiled at their reactions. "Well, it's a true ice cave. We're inside the remains of a great glacier. The mountain you climbed is mostly glacier. Our ice mountain's size is such that it has survived for a very long time."

Traveler was fascinated as he first explored the large central space then a few of the recessed alcoves and then finally he studied the ceiling once more. *This is a magical place, M and Theo would be right at home.* "How did you find this place? We never thought anything was here except solid rock and ice."

Olaff responded by pointing to a branching tunnel. "Join me for a meal and I will tell how we found our ice sanctuary. It is a good tale." With a broad smile, he added, "You are welcome to stay as guests until the glacier melts."

They followed the giant into a short tunnel which opened into a second open cavern. Centered in the cavern were seats and a table, all carved from ice. "Be seated and be comfortable, there are thick furs on top of the ice." Laughing, he added, "Your bottoms will not freeze on you. No butt-frost for my dear friends."

From a shelf he removed drinking horns and filled them from a wooden keg. Next came heavy bronze bowls with ornate carvings on the sides. The carvings displayed mystical ice age beings of woolly mammoths and saber-toothed tigers. The beings became animated if the bowls were quickly spun around. Mammoth tusks and trunk raised and lowered while a tiger opened a mouth to display teeth like swords.

Placing large chunks of black bread in front of each of them, Olaff then ladled steaming stew from an enormous covered kettle. "Enjoy! The bread is fresh and the stew is hot. We have a working kitchen with firepits for baking bread and cooking stews. It is all quite civilized."

Traveler and Glenda needed no further encouragement. Hands reached for bread and spoons. Mouths accepted the inviting offerings, and silence filled the space.

Olaff's portions were enough for a small army. He studied the bread and stew as he consumed each. His spoon was a large ladle that never lost a piece of the stew. Somehow, he never soiled his thick beard. Watching him at work was watching a master gourmet partaking of his fare with efficiency and obvious delight.

Traveler was done with two rounds when Glenda was still finishing her first helping. "There is so much to catch up on, Olaff! Can we start with how you have come to be here in this hidden ice-fortress?"

Olaff lifted his ale-filled stein, drank deeply, and began. "We are here because we needed to escape the red demon, the jinn as you called it. After you left Dall and me in the fortress, we mourned your absence. Dall knows he owes you his life and will repay that debt when he can. He also became attached to each of you, and that is more than rare for him. I am the social one and he the quieter one.

"I told Dall more of your tale and he accepted the truthfulness of it. He understood you came from a future time which has its own manmade magic, called science. Dall is a great guardian. He was particularly interested in how your magic protected people of your time. Sadly, I could answer only a few of his questions, I had many of the same questions.

"Following our conquest, or rather containment, of the red creature, Dall and I began to rebuild confidence among warriors and farmers. We assured them the evil mage was vanquished and the fortress again offered protection.

"I did not know that the fortress had been named 'The Blighted Fortress.' That name is unfair as it declares the fortress to be an evil place. It was not. It was a protective structure. Any evil within was due to the presence of the mage who had a demon residing inside his body.

"It was difficult, at first, to assure the neighboring people that Dall and I were indeed back and in control. All wanted to believe the mage was gone, but it took time for them to accept this truth. Gradually people returned to live and work in the fortress. For a long time, however, all inside or close by the fortress would look over their shoulders.

"Gradually, as the years passed, the mage was slowly forgotten. As the memory faded more people accepted the protecting fortress. Merchants returned from distant places to ply their wares in security. Travelers sought its lodging as they traveled through our dense and dangerous forests. Like the people, Dall and I grew lax.

"The blight returned nearly twenty years later when the demon red cloud reappeared. It descended the staircase and entered the kitchen. Cooks and warriors were absorbed and fell. They were dead before striking the ground. Shrieks of terror and warnings filled the space. Nearby stable workers were put on alert but could only free less than half of the warhorses.

"All those who could fled the fortress, by foot or on horse. Many horses remained trapped in their stalls. The number of people and animals who died was never determined. All who escaped fled in many directions and sought safety as far from the fortress as possible.

"Fortunately for us, Dall and I were not in the fortress. When news of the terror reached us, we immediately knew the red beast had escaped. We knew we could not contest it. We are fierce warriors but know our limitations. This was not the time to do battle.

"We knew we needed to survive long enough to be joined by others who bring strengths to add to ours." Looking at Traveler and Glenda, Olaff beamed. "Now you are here, and our spirits are lifted, we are far stronger together.

"As to how Dall and I came to this hidden place, that is an interesting tale. We first hid in the thick forest to survive. Once we felt safe, we began tracking the movement of the jinn. Its activity was easy to follow as it openly subdued warriors then directed them to perform many tasks. It had no fear and made no attempt at subtle efforts. It was in a rush to construct the first portal and acted accordingly.

"The jinn has great power but also great luck. It received a fortunate roll of the dice when a small army of Hun entered this region. They were fleeing from an attacking Germanic tribe called the Gepids. These fleeing Huns became the jinn's workers.

"The Gepids reputedly have a formidable warlord named Ardaric. This Ardaric has given the Huns a series of small defeats after their leader, Attila, passed. The Huns are now massing their army to defeat this Ardaric." Looking at the two and their reactions, Olaff paused. "I sense you may have heard of him."

Both youths immediately nodded their heads. "He is a good guy, Olaff, we like him," said Traveler. "He just defeated the massed Hun force several days ago. The bad news is that the jinn will now capture even more escaping Huns for their workforce."

Olaff accepted this as indeed bad news. "We watched as the jinn quickly took control of the leaders of the captured Hun warbands. Once it controlled the leaders it began a construction project. You have seen the results. The first construct, once it was completed, permitted others of its kind to join it.

"As the jinn grew in numbers, Dall and I knew we risked being found. We needed a place to hide but where we could also continue to observe. How we arrived here is an interesting twist of fate.

"Dall had a nighttime epiphany, he said it was a dream. He said he had a distant memory of being in this mountainous region in the past. He said we should let the dream memory lead us. I reluctantly agreed. I did not believe a dream memory was our answer for hiding, but I had to support my brother.

"There is a time to argue and a time to let events provide the answer. I believed he would finally admit this was not our destination if I just went along with him. We began the long climb up the narrow gorge. I followed behind Dall to let him go as high as he wanted before his dream left him.

"Like you, we were exhausted when we finally reached the small landing area. We immediately sat down and quickly drifted off to sleep. Dall was the first to awaken. He stood up with a puzzled look on his face. He said his dream had returned. I smiled encouragingly at him as I said, without a trace of a reprimand in my voice, 'Brother, it is alright if this is not our path. I believe in dreams, but not all should be followed.'

"Dall listened to me, then shook his head. There was no expression of anger or self-doubt. Out of nowhere he suddenly followed his dream. He plunged his hand and arm into the thick snowbank. With his arm buried to his shoulder, he began to exert his full energy to push further through the heavy snow and ice.

"Dall has great power when motivated, nothing withstands his force. To my amazement, and frankly, to his own surprise, his hand found purchase. A huge snow-covered rock slowly slid forward to reveal an opening. His hand was the key that opened the rock-door.

"Stunned, we stood staring into the darkness. Then Dall said in a matter-of-fact way, 'Inside is our safety.' He lit a torch and entered. Once inside, we found all you see. Dall's dream had reminded him of this sanctuary. Some great power had led us back. We suddenly felt that we were not alone."

Glenda and Traveler sat mesmerized by the tale. What power could have led the giants to discover this place? How could Dall's hand become a key to open an impregnable door? The answer came to both at the same time. *Theo!*

Glenda continued to digest the story and all it contained. Shaking her head, she asked, "Olaff, where is the duke? I mean, your brother, Dall."

"Best guess is that he is sleeping. We sleep in shifts to maintain awareness of all below. I think it's best we let him recover his energy. Besides, who knows what other rewarding dreams may come to him."

Traveler was now walking back toward the entrance. "Enough hiding. Let's see if we can break the back of the jinn below and their constructs."

Olaff looked deeply at Traveler for a considering moment. A question was beginning then was retracted. "I have learned to trust your ideas. While my brother dreams, you think. I trust your thinking, it let us contain the mage jinn for many years. What are your current ideas, my young warrior?"

"Well, it's a shared idea, Glenda and I had it at the same time. We think we can roll this mountain down on top of the work below."

Olaff started to laugh. "If only we could! My brother and I each have great power, but not even our combined strength will move this mountain. How exactly will you two do that?"

"Follow me and we'll show you." When they reached the blocking-rock Olaff pulled it inside. Out of curiosity, Traveler touched it in passing and felt a jolt of power. *Theo!* Traveler instinctively knew that he and Glenda together could never move the blocking-rock. The rock was a sealing guard set there from a distant past to provide shelter for the two giants.

When the door opened the bright sun struck their faces. All three stopped to squint hard before going out. Once outside, Traveler pointed to the two large metal cooking pots. "There are our avalanche makers. We need to get out of this ravine and then beat the drums on the open slope. If we beat hard enough and in rhythm, the synchronized soundwaves will create a common vibration. The vibration, in turn, will start a slow slide of the snow. As the snow slides downward it will grow into an avalanche...we hope. Anyway, that's how modern science says it can work."

Olaff listened, nodded, then said, "Noise can disrupt many things; however, I don't believe your drums can produce the level of disruption necessary to wake the mountain."

"Possibly, but as the saying goes, 'nothing ventured, nothing gained,'" replied Glenda. "Let's give it the old college try."

Olaff frowned at the strange words. "What is a college try?" he asked.

"It means to give something your best effort, that's all." Looking overhead, she said, "To give it the college try we need to be up there. How do we do that?"

"I have a college try in me," said Olaff. "Please stand back."

With that he began to carve steps into the ice and stone cliffside. His iron-gloved hands acted as pickaxes, and indented ice steps appeared. With his height and power, he built their access ladder in minutes.

"You two climb up and see if that's where you want to be. If it is, I'll hand these pots up and join you."

"I'll try our ladder first," said Traveler, beginning the ascent. He inserted his feet as far into the indented steps as possible while using his hands to grip the step above his shoulder. *He's a squirrel climbing up an ice tree*, thought an amused Glenda.

Traveler quickly reached the top, then called down. "We have arrived at the rock band's performance platform. This is a perfect place, join me."

Glenda was a second squirrel and was beside Traveler in less time. The two caught their breath and looked down. They were on top of another Bald Mountain. The tree line was far below. As they adjusted their eyes, they tried to focus on the distant Hun worker ants far below. All they could see was a dark shape of the ants moving like a carpet hanging on a clothesline, rippling in the wind.

"I believe this is the place to bang our hearts out," said Glenda.

As Traveler was agreeing, he inverted the large cooking pot and placed it in front of himself. Immediately beside him Glenda was securing her own drum in the packed snow. "Earplugs definitely advised. I suggest we use wool," said Glenda. The two quickly rolled soft wool threads into compact plugs.

Traveler grinned at Glenda as he then moistened his plugs with his mouth's natural lubricant. "Wet them and get a better seal." Glenda paused a moment then followed suit thinking, *Must be what he learned in grade school to make better missiles. Wonder who he fired them at?*

With ears well-sealed, they were set to make big noise and hopefully big trouble for the bottom level workers. Their show was ready to open.

While holding his heavy iron spoons in front of him Traveler first tapped the sticks together with a satisfyingly loud click. He nodded to Glenda and performed a drummer's twirl. He flipped the long-handled spoons into the air at the same time. Catching them, he clicked them together again. With a self-congratulating look, he gave them another toss and twirl. Grinning he said to his audience, "Just warming up the old hands, flexibility is key."

With the warmup act over, he lowered each drumstick and gently tapped the drumhead. Looking at his noisemaking partner he said, "Hold back a little to start, we need to find our shared rhythm before we go crazy. Now, are you ready to rock that world down there?"

"Absolutely," said Glenda as she gently tapped her metal drumhead. "You can be Gene Krupa but I'm Cindy Blackman, best female drummer ever. Just ask Lenny Kravitz."

With her earplugs inserted Glenda gave a returning grin and nod at Traveler. The two sets of heavy spoons descended, and bedlam broke out. Olaff jammed fingers into his ears. A resting eagle was no longer resting. If there were any pterodactyls, even frozen in the ice, they would have scrambled free to escape the cacophony.

The two started slow, found their shared rhythm, then picked up the beating tempo. They were soon putting their hearts, souls, and best licks into their vibrating instruments. Percussion was being redefined by their efforts, they never looked up. They establish a coordinated beat that blasted against their protected eardrums. Their bodies were tuned to the frenzied beat. They increased the tempo and force of their flying sticks. Olaff quickly wet his own fingers for a tighter seal while staring at the flying sticks.

Finally, body energy lessened. Tiring arms and hands had to settle down. Sadly, the thick snow seemed to be deaf. The only movement came from their now slowly beating drumsticks and escaping birds. A white fox poked its nose out of a snowbank then burrowed deeper. *Rats, we never got liftoff* flashed through both minds.

Chapter 73

A Brother Arrives

Sitting in their dark funks a large shadow crossed over both drummers; the sun appeared to dim. Looking up they saw a second giant had arrived. Dall had joined them. "My two best friends, and my saviors! I'm stunned to see you again. You are each unchanged. The years have not appeared on your faces."

Glenda accepted the compliment with a gracious smile. "Thank you, Dall, I would return the same observation. You and Olaff are also unchanged, and you are both a welcome sight! You are both just as I remember, this is a joyous reunion.

"Now tell me, how did you know we were all out here? Olaff said you were sleeping in your bedroom, and that's buried inside this mountain."

Dall beamed at the compliments as well as at the question. "I have been blessed, some would argue cursed, with hearing skills that forest owls would envy. I have always been sensitive to sounds or vibrations coming from great distances. Sitting here I can understand the conversations below as easily as if I was down there among the Huns. Of course, I easily heard your drumming sounds, so here I am."

"But you were inside a mountain, how could you hear us?" asked Traveler.

"My mind detects those sounds that I need to hear and understand. The surrounding mountain does not interfere. It's weird I know, but I was born this way.

"Now please explain, why are you making the loud noises? You must be aware that the sound will carry to the camp below. Drawing Hun and demon attention to us is a very bad idea. Huns are of little concern, but the red demons are a most serious danger…as you too well know."

Traveler nodded. "We are studying what to do about the large portal that's under construction. We saw the completed smaller portal and the demons that have already arrived through it. That's a big threat by itself. A much greater threat will come through the second portal once it's completed. The full jinn host will arrive in our world, that's a disaster that cannot be permitted to happen. We tried to slow the construction with an avalanche, but we failed. Still it was our best shot and we needed to try."

Dall accepted this with a sad look. "Even without the giant second portal completed the demons below are beyond our power to contest. It took only one to immobilize me, and I am not easily controlled."

Olaff had been listening to his brother's concerns regarding the drumming. They were veiled criticisms that ignored any consideration of their purpose. His brother needed to better understand the intent. He proceeded to explain and defend the drumming.

"Brother, they have a plan which I agreed to. They are creating a vibration pattern that could cause the snow to break loose of the glacier. Once loosened it will flow downhill. As it speeds up, it will gather ever-greater mass that will become a destructive force to those below."

Olaff saw his brother was still unconvinced of the merit of the banging and continued. "It was an excellent plan despite not working. Actually, it was our best and only plan. This snow has been frozen to the glacier for a very long time. The snow's base must be so attached that nothing will disrupt its restful sleep. Even the sun's heat is not enough to penetrate the thick cover sufficiently to warm the base."

Dall listened and slowly shook his head. "I believe I better understand the intent of your efforts and reasoning. Your efforts are not without consequences, however. If you look down the long slope you will see that while the snow is not moving, the Huns definitely are. You have gained the attention of the demons and they are sending a mass of worker warriors to meet us."

Glenda and Traveler stared down the mountain and saw nothing. "Excuse me, Dall," said Glenda, "but there is nothing that I can see heading up here."

Dall gave an understanding nod. "Like my hearing, my eyes see much at a great distance. I can count the arm rings on each warrior who is coming up. I can count the beats of a hummingbird's wings by sound and by sight.

"I must live my life permitting all this information to come to me. My mind's challenge is to sort out what represents a risk while ignoring the acceptable. As I say, it is both a gift and a curse."

Looking again at the base of the mountain, Glenda squinted. "I do believe I can start to see movement down there. I can't separate out individuals yet, but it appears to be a significant number. It reminds me of a moving ant colony."

Olaff listened, then suggested, "I think while we have time, we should lay a false trail away from this spot, then retreat into our ice sanctuary."

Dall had a look of deepening concentration as he said, "I believe there is another approach, brother. Permit me to go back to my sleeping quarters and retrieve something. You, however, can certainly sweep away signs of our presence."

Olaff nodded. "As you wish brother. Please keep our entry open for our fast retreat."

Chapter 74

Gjallarhorn Sings

The remaining three stood in the snow, watching the ant colony begin to separate into individual ants. As the minutes passed the ants began to grow in size. "Warriors," said Glenda with a tremor in her voice. "And a lot of them."

As individual Hun climbers became clear, Traveler said, "I think we need to assume that whatever Dall has in mind will not save the day. Olaff, you and I need to start sweeping our presence up here away. Glenda, you can erase the ice steps. Use the drumsticks to break them up. Once the evidence is gone, we'll take our drumming gear, get inside and wait them out. Let them try and figure out what made the noise. They'll go nuts."

"I'm on it!" said Glenda as she scampered down the ice steps.

Alone with Olaff as they swept their presence away, Traveler observed, "The good news is it's really cold up here. They'll have limited time to explore. I think that the jinn are sending the Huns just to see what was going on more out of curiosity. I can't imagine the jinn see any threat up here."

As Olaff was agreeing with Traveler, Dall suddenly reappeared and placed Glenda down on the swept snow.

He's only been gone a minute, how does a guy that big move that fast? flashed through Traveler's mind, followed by *Why does he have Glenda?*

As a breathless passenger Glenda had found herself on a fast-moving Dall ski lift to quickly rejoin her comrades. She had seen Dall enter the cave, emerge after a moment, remove the ice steps with one blow, and then bring her to the site. *He makes impossible things happen really fast*, was her only thought.

While Traveler was still focused on Dall and Glenda's return, Glenda was focused on the curving golden horn that hung from a heavy gold chain around Dall's neck. Her eyes were drawn to the elaborate glyphs carved into the sides of the horn. The glyphs began to explain something to her as she focused on them. As she studied them more closely a headache started. She left the glyphs and began to study the body of the horn.

The horn reminded her of a complex French horn; however, it twisted in strange directions. When she tried to follow the construct of a specific curve it seemed to subtly change shape. A curve here and an opening there morphed into adjoining parts. *Highly frustrating*, she thought. *Nothing stays still when I follow it around. How can air even get out? Where is the opening to breathe into it?*

Traveler was now also studying the horn. The shape and curves reminded him of a drawing of a Klein bottle he had seen in math class. The Klein bottle was a four-dimensional shape from topology represented in an artist's three-dimensional drawing. The bottle's surface curved into itself much as a two-dimensional Mobius strip curves back on itself.

Both teens found that as they tried to follow the horn's structure their minds got confused and they had to start over. Their increased focus only resulted in starting strong headaches. They abandoned further study out of brain preservation.

Dall stood between the three, facing down the mountainside. His eyes took on a glazed look as he brought the large horn to his lips. He was no longer with them on a high mountain. Where he was now, even he did not know. Roles had reversed, the horn was now the master while Dall the instrument.

Watching closely Glenda saw the elusive air opening suddenly appear. Dall's lips immediately created a tight seal, ensuring the opening could not move. His chest expanded like an enormous bellows, and his exhale into the horn began.

The result was not what was expected. Unlike the long Swiss mountain horns, there was no earsplitting call. The call was a vibration not detectable to human ears or brains. No earplugs were needed. It was a dimensional call reverberating somewhere in space, time, and elsewhere. Its message depended on the listener.

The call was felt by the two teens as a warm, gentle, nudging whisper. The teens sensed there was a promise spoken within the whisper. The whisper calmed them.

The call was a welcoming song in Olaff's mind. It spoke of his great power and great responsibilities. It reminded Olaff of a time far in his forgotten past.

Olaff stood staring at his brother with a perplexed look. Dall did not return the look. He had a distant look on his face that said he was also hearing a call reminding him of his own distant past and much more.

The call's power strengthened as Dall exhaled into the opening with an endless amount of air. Dall never seemed to inhale but maintained a constant exhale. *How?* Both teens and Olaff wondered.

As Dall exhaled, the horn's structure continued to make subtle twists that never ended in a fixed position. It was like watching a stage magician's balloon as it expanded into ever-changing shapes of first a dog followed by a rabbit followed by a giraffe. The teens could only catch brief glimpses, they were unable to hold a shape long enough to identify it.

The first sign of the horn's purpose was a slight shifting of the ground under their feet. Glenda and Traveler were flanking Olaff, and both grasped onto one of his arms to steady themselves. "That felt like a definite tremor," said a grinning Traveler. "I think the *Star War*'s Force is trying to be with us. Where's Yoda when we need him?"

In a blink, his wit and grin were replaced by something approaching awe, then fear. He was back on Disney's Bald

Mountain, and scared. "Oh, oh, something is happening and it's a lot more than a tremor. Sorry I was trying to be funny. We all need to sit down… right now."

Dall, now holding the horn by his side, nodded in agreement with Traveler and sat down. Once the four were seated they realized that Traveler was prescient. The initial tremor was a yawn. The real action was just beginning.

The tremor's mild shiver was replaced by a shaking that drove the Richter needle off its scale. The mother of earthquakes was just beginning. Mother was angry.

The Huns, who were now a football field away, had all stopped climbing. A number of them flailed their arms about for balance before falling to the ground. Others remained swaying upright while staring up the vibrating mountain.

The mountain was awake. After eons of restful sleep, it had been roused. Awake, it sought movement. The snowbank in front of the four sitters began a gentle slide forward. As it advanced down the steep grade, it quickly became a rising wave.

The wave's mass increased at a geometric rate, then an exponential rate. The greater the rushing mass became, the larger the all-enveloping wave became. One fed on the other. It was now a roaring tsunami, the likes of which was last seen when glaciers were alive and moving. The wave was feeding off the entire mountainside.

When it hit the first of the Hun climbers it was already forty feet over their heads. None of them would ever live to become snowboarding surfers. They all disappeared in a blink and a squish under the wave.

The wave's growing power shook the mountain with its descending force. Accompanying the mounting vibration was a thunderous moan as the wave struck giant trees and rocks. Everything was swept into its ravenous maw. The wave generated the dooming cry of an apocalypse. It was death on a white horse descending into the world of humans and jinn.

No longer a wave, it was a transcendental force of unstoppable power. Nothing stood in its path. Unlike the slow destructive advance of a glacier over eons, this destruction happened in brief minutes.

As it reached the lower base it swept away all constructs for both portals. The massive resting base that secured the columns was ripped away and hurtled outward like a spear. This could be Gungnir the spear of Odin. There were cries of helplessness coming from the small portal as jinn were caught entering, exiting, or ducking away from Gungnir.

Trees and Huns wailed as they were torn apart. When the mountain's roar and anger finally subsided, a deep quiet settled over the remains of the avalanche. The mountain had calmed. Mother was at peace.

All the jinn's careful planning and efforts were unraveled in a single stroke. Gjallarhorn's song was a new vibration that brought great power. This was a force that the jinn, in all their long history, had never encountered. The dark gods were displaying their powers.

The completeness of the destruction would only become apparent to the jinn once they slowly emerged from the deep, burying snow. While buried, the jinn soon discovered that snow is a form of water, and the trapped jinn felt the unpleasant effects of suffocation.

For one trapped jinn, its snow containment had it recall the feeling of its imprisonment in the lead coffin. It vibrated with the disturbing memory. It was a greatly humbled demigod.

Glenda and Traveler sat, spellbound. Even Olaff remained seated before slowly rising. He embraced his brother, both had strange looks on their faces. Old memories were coming back after millennia of being buried.

Finally, Traveler said, "If I was a student of the Bible, I would say that Dall is Gabriel blowing his horn." With a widening smile, he added, "The jinn seem to avoid water if possible. Wonder how they like being submerged in an ocean of frozen water."

Glenda joined him. "May they know a great deal of unpleasantness for a long time. They have earned every bit of their comeuppance and much more! Suffer, you demons, in your frozen water container! Suffer for your lost portals! Suffer knowing that the host won't be arriving anytime soon. You're trapped and alone."

Dall smiled at the comments. "The avalanche show is over, and a great show it was! I suspect the demons will reappear but for now a victory celebration is in order." Three heads rapidly nodded in agreement as they entered their ice palace sanctuary.

Chapter 75

Quiet Time

Inside the ice palace the four sat at a large carved table. The thick fur cushions did their job, and bottoms were comfortable retaining body heat while being cushioned by soft fur. Olaff presented offerings for the table and the celebration began.

Large ale horns were filled for the two giants while Glenda and Traveler enjoyed mugs of a watered-down hard cider. The cider gave a small kick but was far softer than Olaff's angry mule-kick ale.

Toasts began by recognizing what Dall had just accomplished. He had swept away the Hun threat, and more importantly, swept away both portals. He was naturally bombarded with questions about the horn and found he had few answers.

"I never knew its purpose, or if I ever did, I forgot. Even going in to get it I didn't know why. I felt another force was in charge of directing me. It was as strange an outcome to me as to you. The closest I can say about it was that I felt like I did in my dream when I was led to discover this sanctuary." *Theo* flashed through both teens' minds.

There were further toasts to both Glenda and Traveler as their recent challenges were recounted. Traveler's time in the arena, surrounded by the wolf pack, and Glenda's quick thinking for their escape, made both giants shake their heads with appreciation.

"You two act as a team in the face of extreme danger, each shares the risk the other faces. That is the sign of true brotherhood warriors," said Olaff.

For a moment Glenda considered redefining the word "brotherhood" but she understood the meaning. The meaning spoke to courage, not gender, she wisely remained silent.

No storytelling would be complete without Traveler poking fun at Glenda. He described how she had immediately caught the eye of Ardaric, the Gepid leader. He described in embarrassing detail how she had charmed the warriors in the arena. "She always has a guy waiting to crown her," he concluded with a big wink at the redhead.

Her face was now approaching the color of her hair, as she said, "I am ready to crown somebody else. Let's change the subject!" Both giants were highly amused and broad smiles added to her continued embarrassment.

As the feasting wound down, the ale drinking continued at an even faster rate. *Is there any limit to what these guys can drink?* wondered Glenda as she watched horns being refilled. *I hope they don't pass out before I can ask a few questions.* Little did she know they were far from any danger-point of excess imbibing.

Her first question came when she was once more studying the horn and its carving. "Was it my imagination, or did the horn's shape change when you blew into it?"

Dall shook his head. "Really don't know. My full concentration was in the effort. Mine was simply the body that operated it; it felt like somebody else was playing it."

Traveler waited his turn, then asked, "Is the horn a family heirloom? I bet it has a name."

Dall perked up. "An astute question. I now remember that it was given to me by my father, and yes, it has a name." He paused a moment, and said, "It is called Gjallarhorn." Looking at the puzzled expressions, he added, "It means 'The horn resounding.'"

Traveler nodded, "'Resounding' is a big understatement. After today I say it should be named the 'Horn Astounding.'"

Dall looked at him with an appreciative expression. "An excellent name also."

A quiet peace fell over the table that was followed by Olaff rising. "Please excuse us, young warriors. My brother and I are much older and need our rest. We expend a great deal of energy when awake." Dall nodded, rose, and took his leave with a smile and massive hand wave. His wave resembled a flag fluttering in a brisk wind.

Hesitating, Olaff came to each youth. He lifted them in a giant's bearhug and whispered, "I know your ways and know you will depart now. We will meet again."

Alone in the palace, Glenda looked at Traveler. "I believe our mission is more than accomplished. Theo will not only know what the jinn intended but will be pleased with the added grace time we have given him. Now get over here and give your girl a nice slow dance."

Traveler found his face reddening as he stepped into the outstretched arms. As heads passed, lips briefly brushed against lips and paused. Eyes looked into eyes. Both found themselves lingering before slowly moving to nearby cheeks.

As they held each other in the final departure position, both hesitated before touching bracelets. The hesitation brought increased color to both sets of cheeks, then the Tilt-A-Whirl departure motion took over.

Chapter 76

No Place Like Home

The two arrived in their Chicago sanctuary clutching each other tightly. A smiling M said, "You can let go now. There will be a feast in your honor and it's difficult to eat without hands."

Redness appeared on necks and faces, wiping away the paleness created by the travel experience. Both quickly stepped out of the circle and avoided looking at the other. The bonding moment was replaced by the awareness of beckoning odors coming from the kitchen.

Continuing with his welcoming smile, M said, "There is plenty of time for a soothing water treatment, either by a tub soak or shower, you choose. All is ready and will stay perfectly warm until we begin. Naturally, I want all the details."

Looking toward the fireplace, Glenda said, "Where is Theo? He is way too big to be here unnoticed. I don't hear his welcoming purr."

M answered with a casual hand wave. "All is well with him, and that's an understatement. He and I are both much better than 'well.' He knew of your victory when he heard Gjallarhorn's call.

"That call was a sound of triumph, but also a train conductor's call for Theo to be 'All aboard.' He needed to depart, something about visiting his children. Believe me, you have given him great encouragement for the coming challenges."

Glenda and Traveler stood openmouthed. Glenda said, "He heard the horn? How can that be? Dall blew it half a world away and a thousand years in the past."

M smiled at the question. "How indeed. I cannot explain the 'how' in any terms of science. After five thousand years I simply accept he is the absolute master of space and time, as well as other dimensions. There is so much more to Theo then we have seen, and trust me, I have seen a lot in my years with him. He is Theo. His is a story that continues to unfold for we mortals fortunate enough to see it."

Accepting M's answer meant accepting there are ghosts and other supernatural beings. Most people cannot do that in the modern age of science, they feel too enlightened. However, Glenda and Traveler had experiences that permitted them to accept the unacceptable.

With head nods, they moved quickly to their personal retreats. Clothes flew off into waiting hampers. Both considered a long soak, then realized they would likely fall asleep. Showers delivered the needed cleansing and relaxation.

When they emerged from steamy bathrooms, they came to their beds to find the selected dinner wear laid out. Traveler was initially hoping for jeans and a turtleneck but realized he actually, and surprisingly, wanted to dress up. The presented clothing fit the self-image he had in mind for the evening. He wanted to look sharp and grown-up. The offering assured him he would.

Once dressed, he stood in front of the full-length mirror. The tux was as modern as today, yet still captured the elegance of an earlier time. The buttons were authentic black onyx. The cuff links were heavy gold, shaped like lightning bolts. As he admired the bolts, he noticed they seemed to shimmer with the overhead lighting. *Zeus and Thor would be proud to wear these*, went through his mind.

Excited, he was first out to the dining table. As he sat back, he looked up and admired the softly glowing overhead candles as they emitted a flickering light. *Those look like real candles. I believe I can smell a little incense coming off them, how cool.*

391

M appeared with a covered tureen and placed it down. "Would you like a little conversation while we wait for the goddess to grace us with her presence?" asked a smiling M.

"Please! Catch me up on Bears' football, the season is heading for the playoffs. What have I missed?"

M began describing the likely outcomes for the season. He noted the new players on both offense and defense, as well as new coaches. "Of course, they lack a Joe Montana or Tom Brady quarterback, but so do most teams."

M continued as he observed, "The game you and Glenda have signed up for is far more brutal and the outcomes far more important. Either of you would each make a superhero quarterback. How you have faced attacking jinn linemen is truly amazing.

"Watching the two of you is like watching a young Joe Namath beat the great Baltimore Colts. Frankly, Theo is amazed at your progress. So am I, but Theo is the coach and the ultimate judge of your growth as allies."

Just as Traveler was ready to discuss the best running backs the conversation stopped. Glenda made her grand entrance in her holiday dress and sparkling jade shoes. She did a series of slow pirouettes for her captive audience. The dress floated around her. For a moment she looked like her namesake Glinda, the white witch in the *Wizard of Oz*.

"If I didn't know better, I would think this is a sports discussion." Both seated men couldn't help but nod. Sitting down, she said, "Well, let's continue. Let's talk about the strongest men, either on TV today or in legends of the past. Or we can argue about the best all-time fighters. Can you two handle that?"

M began laughing. "I do have an advantage over you two. I have seen the real deals in action. I can describe Tunney's long count win over Dempsey. I watched Jim Brown in his heyday, and every one of his games was a heyday."

"What about Walter Payton?" challenged Glenda.

"What about Bronko Nagurski?" came Traveler's fast retort.

With those opening comments, the three began heated debates on games and players. The conversation was fun and engaging. As each course was served a new sport's topic came up. M's serious analysis joined with stories from personal observations created a feast of sports lore.

Finally, the meal was at an end. Traveler leaned back. "I'm one stuffed guy."

Glenda reached down and playfully snapped his suspenders. "Stuffed is the correct word. It's time to get some outside air! Dare I say it, big boy, it's mache schnell time."

Accepting the rightness of an after-dinner walk, Traveler stood. Donning a long, thick black dress coat, he was joined by a decked-out Glenda. She was wearing her high Christmas boots with bells along the top. Her bright green cap had additional bells on the top and she jingled with each step and head shake.

Heading to the door, they waved at M, then entered their alley. Moving up the alley they reached the entry point onto the normal sidewalk. After checking both directions, they stepped out. "Don't want to scare the shoppers with a couple of Dicken's Christmas ghosts coming out of a brick wall," laughed Traveler. Glenda grinned back nodding in agreement as the bells on her hat joined in.

As they got to the end of their street, they felt the blast of cold wind coming off Lake Michigan. Glenda said, "Wow! I feel we're back on Bald Mountain. What's colder, Lake Michigan, or a Carpathian mountaintop? Freezing either way."

Looking at Glenda's warm hat, Traveler suddenly reached into a deep pocket and removed earmuffs. Without hesitancy he put them on.

"One good thing," said a happy-eared Traveler, "we'll never get separated, regardless of the snowfall. With your bells I can hear you wherever you are, don't need Dall's super-hearing." Glenda responded with a full body and head shake and street passers gave her appreciative smiles of Christmas cheer.

Rather than walking on Michigan Avenue, they chose to stay on the less-traveled side streets. Moving along the decorated streets with tall lampposts lighting the sidewalk snow, Glenda began humming a Norwegian Christmas carol. The melody was captivating.

Traveler found that the song reminded him of his early caroling walks in Charlottesville with his parents. When Glenda finished, but before she could switch over to the seasonal favorite "Silent Night", Traveler said, "I really liked that last tune, what is it?"

"It's a top Christmas song in Norway, and fairly new. We call it 'En Stjerne Skinner I Natt.' Watching Traveler working on the translation, she added, "It means, 'A star shines tonight.' It can be sung alone or by a choir. The children at my orphanage would sing it as we caroled to the sick or those living alone."

With that she became a sweet Lorelei of Christmas singing "Silent Night." Traveler found himself joining in...but softly. Passersby nodded and many quietly found themselves humming the tune.

The magic of the winter walk caused time to freeze without Theo's help. As they passed lit store windows and watched shoppers searching for perfect presents, they eased into the comfort of a normal time and place.

Finally, just as their bodies suggested it was time to turn around, they heard caroling coming from large, open cathedral doors. Looking at each other, they nodded in agreement and walked up the inviting steps to listen more closely from inside.

The inside was an inspiring space that reminded them of the recent ice palace. Candles from a multitude of candelabras and wall mounts lit the interior. Candlelight flashed off stained glass windows and ceiling frescos. A choir decked in festive clothing was holding a large audience transfixed in the pews and aisles.

Standing at the rear, they glanced around at the other late arrivals. Their eyes landed on the back of a head that they recognized from their back-seat perspective. It was their cabbie. Suddenly the cabbie felt a chill go down his back that broke the mood of his listening and meditating. Turning around, he found himself staring into the faces he had seen disappear from the street.

His body gave a small shiver and shake. *Are they angels coming for me? Is this my last night to be here? Thank heavens I'm in a holy place.*

Traveler and Glenda knew from the look on his face what his thoughts were. Since they were the last to come in, they were standing alone. They simply leaned against a large column, smiled at the cabbie, and blinked out. Before disappearing, both gave the cabbie a joyous thumbs-up.

Watching him, they saw that his face was lit with a glow of relief followed by true belief. He had experienced an encounter of the angelic kind and had been found worthy.

"I believe we have given a true Christmas present," whispered Glenda to Traveler.

She noticed that Traveler had a similar glow as he watched the cabbie move to join the communion line. With the cabbie's back to them, they quickly slipped outside and began their return walk.

The next morning, the cabbie's tale was told over breakfast to his family. Adding to his own tale he described the experience of his limo driver friend. As he described the events, both of his teen children put down their smartphones and were drawn into their father's story. His wife paused with her fork in mid-air and placed it quietly back on her plate. The cabbie held them as spellbound as he himself had been the night before.

He told the story with such sincerity and in such vivid detail that his son, daughter, and wife all sat transfixed by the tale. As they listened, each found themselves reacquiring a belief that each had abandoned in early grade school. The family became recovered believers in the magic of a spirit world. Christmastime magic and the existence of angels brought great joy to their lives in the many holidays and years to come.

FINIS

Epilogue

The battle of the Nedao River decisively ended Hun dominance in Europe. Not all the Huns were killed that day. Dengizich and the reserves managed to escape. Dengizich made a final attempt, ten years later, to reassert Hun dominance in the region. He was not his father. He was soundly defeated.

Ardaric built on his battlefield success. He unified many Germanic tribes and created a large region aptly known as the Kingdom of the Gepids. Look to old maps to see his legacy.

About the Author

Dave lives with his wife Nancy and a free-range, house-roaming tortoise named Braxton in rural Virginia. They are surrounded by nature including large oak trees having many growth rings.

Dave likens his life's experiences to that of the tree rings. Important early rings include being an Eagle Scout and class president.

Following graduate business school he became an actuary and a consulting mathematician. As he advanced over his working years his career led to CEO and COO responsibilities with a national consulting firm.

Following an early retirement he taught pre-algebra and algebra to middle schoolers. It was a most satisfying experience for him as he helped many math-averse students discover that math mastery was well within their skill set.

His ongoing growth rings are as a storyteller and writer.

***

Readers can contact Dave by email
at TheAlliesofTheo@gmail.com

Visit his web site at DavidEDresner.com
for updates to *The Allies of Theo*.

www.ingramcontent.com/pod-product-compliance
Lightning Source LLC
Chambersburg PA
CBHW030628020726
47493CB00006B/1611